Epochal
Dream

Epochal Dream

Caleb Batey

iUniverse, Inc.
Bloomington

EPOCHAL DREAM

iUniverse books may be ordered through booksellers or by contacting:

iUniverse
1663 Liberty Drive
Bloomington, IN 47403
www.iuniverse.com
1-800-Authors (1-800-288-4677)

Book cover illustration by Susi Galloway, SusiGalloway.com
Book cover graphic design by Travis Miles, ProBookCovers.com

ISBN: 978-1-4759-8787-4 (sc)
ISBN: 978-1-4759-8789-8 (hc)
ISBN: 978-1-4759-8788-1 (e)

Library of Congress Control Number: 2013907344

Printed in the United States of America.

iUniverse rev. date: 5/24/2013

And we pried into the secrets of heaven; but we found it filled with stern guards and flaming fires.

—Qur'an, Al-Jinn 72.8 (Yusufali)

Section 1: Zoagenesis

CHAPTER 1

Forever in a moment, and I see her clearly. Her silvery, white hair floats in the photonic sea of heavenmist, a breeze of stellar winds carrying information over vast distances from many eons ago. Hovering between the solar nebula in front of her and the starship *Intrepidium* behind her, she anticipates advocating for life. She resists the pull of the forming solar system without much effort, moving her arms and legs in constant but gentle strokes to sustain her position. The hem and the cuffs of her white robe leave behind a misty trail, information spilled over from joy in spirit to the passing of time. A gold sash wraps around her waist. She tilts her head slightly to the left, her smile never faltering. She inhales the cool hydrogen gas, and it refreshes her soul. A tiny yet intense gold string of energy flows from right to left across both the mirrored orbs of her eyes. Within, she sees clearly. There is truth from the light, the truth of reality that light carries with it wherever it goes. She sees the measurements, the calculations, the pinpoint precision needed to influence the solar nebula's accretion ever so slightly. She sees equations and numbers projected in her periphery as she scans a region of the solar nebula. A particular set of dust rings has only just recently split from one into two. She chooses a location between them to counterbalance the current configuration, which, if not altered, will produce two planets. She then calculates the power necessary to sustain a brief but intense conveyance of positronic energy, just enough to heat the area between them. This will induce enough gravity to pull the accretion inward, to recombine the two future dead worlds into one viable for life.

Addia-Sahl, Guardian of Life, raises her right hand in front of her eyes. She gestures as if gently caressing the rings of dust that will produce the new world. "I love you," she says, pausing to consult a list within her peripheral vision. From the list of bright-red lettering, she chooses a name and returns her focus to the place of her favor. "Endhera." She puts her hand to her mouth and then blows a kiss to her new love. Another string of energy flashes across her eyes. "Soleran, I am ready."

"Let us proceed." The thunderous, booming, masculine voice seemingly sounds from everywhere. "Opening port to calabi-yau corridor. Initiating conveyance of information."

And then

> *there is light and the light is good; always*
> *contingency in continuity—*
> *For we are Guardians Celestial*
> *And thus we bear the mind acuminous,*
> *Never resting, theretofore Life ensues*
> *within the spatial temporality;*
> *humanness is the typicality*
> *whose explorer spirit henceforth pursues*
> *the stellar light, exhorted luminous*
> *to bear the soul, to wit the natural*
> *the agency of perpetuity—*
> *truth and justice exalted in high praise*

I observe carefully, seeking truth always. And thus I see her clearly. Addia-Sahl's shielding expands and erupts with an intense beam of light. The circumboundary of the positronic energy interacts with the surrounding matter, the dust and gases, antimatter annihilating matter, so much so that its radiative noise roars and crackles in the vacuum. The energy plummets in a straight beam toward the solar nebula. Time passes, an eternity contained in a moment. The light reaches the location of her desire and collides with the dust. Moments later, Addia-Sahl closes the calabi-yau ports to diminish the conveyance. It takes more time for the conveyance to terminate completely. She scans the region and observes that the new temperature variation has properly altered the accretion. She smiles and turns to face the *Intrepidium*. In a flash of light, Addia-Sahl teleshifts back onto the bridge of the Guardian vessel.

The seemingly boundless room teems with thousands of Guardians, all dressed like Addia-Sahl. Whatever color is present derives from the variations in the shades and tones of their skin and hair, as well as from their sashes of gold and silver, red and purple, blue and green. Otherwise, everyone wears white, shimmering robes. I take a moment to look around the room. It's empty but lit brightly. There are no consoles, no seats, no windows or even doors. I can't see the walls, as the room is huge. The ceiling seems high, and both the ceiling and floor are solid—and glimmering, bright white.

Addia-Sahl approaches a group of Guardians standing in a circle, and they step aside to provide her a place amongst them. I approach and stand at a distance, peeking in between them to look at the holographic display in their center. The three-dimensional image is of the solar nebula, its center aglow from the two protostars.

The Guardian named Soleran steps forward. His skin tone is dark olive, but it shines with a metallic luster, and his hair is light brown with a gold tint. It hangs long and straight down to his shoulders and is parted down the middle. He sports a brown beard with golden highlights. Soleran motions to the holographic image with his right hand.

"In review, the initial configuration would have produced the following planetary systems," Soleran says. He gestures, and the time lapse of the holographic image speeds up, until one of the protostars ignites. The second follows shortly afterward. He gestures again with his right hand, and the image shows two planets rising from the solar schematic. "Both of these worlds are rocky and similar in size, but they consist of two contrary environments. The one closer to the primary sun contains a hot, acidic atmosphere. It is too hot for water to liquefy." Soleran motions with his hand, and the first planet shrinks in size, and the other planet enlarges. "The planet farther from the primary sun has a thin, sparse atmosphere. It will be unable to retain its inner heat. The core will cool and condense and then solidify, leaving behind a dead, rocky hull of a planet. Solidified, the core won't be able to generate a magnetic field to protect it from solar radiation. The binary suns will both strip this planet of its atmosphere, preventing water from accumulating on the surface. There will therefore be no catalyst for life to emerge and sustain itself." Soleran gestures again with his right hand, and both planets fall back into the solar schematic. "Addia-Sahl?" Soleran returns to his spot.

Addia-Sahl steps forward to stand over the schematic. She motions with her right hand, and a single planet emerges. "With my alterations, a new world will form in place of the original two. It will occupy the habitable zone, allowing water to liquefy and accumulate. The core will remain molten to generate a magnetic field, which will protect the atmosphere from solar radiation."

I hear her clearly. She explains every detail, from the rate of accretion, to accumulated mass, to its projected radius, to the degree of the axis, to the number of moons—there will be four tiny moons—to the number of oceans and landmasses. She pinpoints moments in time when further adjustment to the planetary system will be required. She mentions a projected protoplanet that will need to be obliterated, since it lies on a collision course at a critical juncture. There will be a total of six planetary systems and two asteroidal rings, one of which was caused by a collision of protoplanets early in the solar system's formation. Five of the planetary systems will be gas giants. The hologram in the center relays all of this information visually. Every detail is revealed, even down to the most minute fraction. Addia-Sahl concludes the discussion on the solar scheme. The holographic image resets, and the solar nebula appears in its current state.

"Let us begin," Soleran says. Hundreds of Guardians phase in and out, and some take more strategic positions in the room. Holographic interfaces activate throughout. One particular holographic image is a set of zeros placed above the solar schematic.

I don't know exactly what's going on. Someone must have sensed that, because a hand is placed gently on my shoulder. As I turn, the Guardian named Evalene is there looking down at me. Her hair is shoulder-length and black as night. Her skin is a slightly dark tan, smooth and silky to touch. A purple sash holds her shimmering, white robe in check.

She says to me, smiling, "You'll enjoy this."

"What's gonna happen?" I ask.

"We will spin," Evalene answers. The Guardian tilts her head and raises her eyebrows. "Very fast," she adds. "The ship will slightly outspin our perspective, so it will look very weird."

"Let us initiate the time shift," Soleran says.

Evalene squeezes my shoulder, and the room explodes with a bright light. I stare at Evalene as her appearance becomes strange—almost blurred and ghostlike. Above the solar schematic, the zeros begin to change, with the first few blurred beyond recognition. Soon the fourth zero blurs—then the fifth and then the sixth.

"The number you see is the number of solar revolutions—you see is the number of solar revolutions referred to as years," she says. Her voice possesses some kind of strange echo. "—solar revolutions referred to as years. We are moving to the next incremental—years. We are moving to the next incremental phase of the system's evolution."

Suddenly, the room bursts with more light, and everything returns to normal. Guardians phase in and out on the bridge.

"Something's wrong," Evalene says. Her eyes are wide, and her lips are pursed tightly.

A digitized cry sounds out and reverberates throughout the area. Soleran turns to face another Guardian, whose skin is dark black. His hair is black and curly and cut short. His face is slender, but his jaw is firm and square.

"Natharon?" Soleran asks.

"I interrupted the spin because the Omnitron picked up a perturbation on the continuum," Natharon says, his voice deep and strong. The cry sounds out again. I then notice a holographic image appear next to Natharon—a green wavy line. The wave appears to be the frequency of the disturbance. "We are listening to a prayer of distress," Natharon says. He analyzes the information through his holographic interface. "It is of the Segerid species." The cry intensifies in number, and more green wavy lines appear. Soon there are thousands.

"Let's investigate," Soleran says. "Get us there, please." He sighs and shakes his head slightly from side to side. I follow his gaze from frequency to frequency. There are so many.

Natharon immediately opens another holographic window containing a series of commands. As he touches a command, it highlights and sounds a light tone. It's almost musical to the ears. The *Intrepidium*'s outer ring begins to rotate, and the vessel ordained as the *Order of the Intrepidium* lunges

forward toward tomorrow
to answer the universe
and trumpet strident the cause
gauging sagely per diem
the stellar voluminous
harboring the numinous
piercing fierce the medium
governed by natural laws
discerning a final purpose:
anoint the morning hallow.

The Huvril slave ship, the *Armenkkerik*, passes the last moon orbiting Segeri II. The vessel is hulking and purple-brown, its hull consisting of an alloy contaminated with impurities. Its shape is irregular and elongated, with massive compartments protruding like appendages from the primary body. The name of the vessel derives from an ancient Huvril deity, honored only in traditional lore and sustained in ritualistic emulation of a dark religion. Its precepts simplify its cause. War complements honor and valor. Plunder pays the wages.

Its insides are projected holographically into the *Intrepidium*'s bridge. It's as if I'm there on the Huvril ship, but I know I'm still on the *Intrepidium*. The sensation is a little disorienting. Throughout the *Armenkkerik* the sounds of heavy machinery reverberate. Cries of distress barely overcome the deafening roars and constant clanging of metal on metal. The corridors are dimly lit, so that every nook is encased in darkness. Grilled floors and walls expose the mechanical guts of the vessel. Condensation forms around the cooling conduits, rusting the outer coating of metal and souring the air.

At the deep center of the vessel's bowels are the slave pens. Rusty, filthy runoff water collects at a central pool within the pens. One particular slave, Shashamar, was just recently a mighty warrior and clan chief. At the moment, however, he is neither of those things. His frame consists of a red-hided torso on a thoracic, six-legged body. Brown blood trickles down his face from a gash across his forehead. He whimpers, the pain racking his entire body. He tries to lift himself from the misery of sitting in wastewater. He sloshes toward a gate and grabs the bars to pull himself up. He presses his face between two bars and convulses, laboring to capture a breath—one breath, a breath free of heavy pollution. His gaze falls upon a group of Huvril soldiers in thin, light brown uniforms sitting at a small, enclosed station above the central pen.

The hide of the Huvril is dark green-gray but smooth and glistening with a secretion of putrid sweat. The centauric frame of the Huvril consists of a stubby body with four long, spindly legs and a slender torso with two spindly arms. The face is childlike, having no aged features. The nose and mouth are small, but the binocular eyes are large, bulbous, and dark.

The station has a single air conduit poised above them, which gives this small area a more comfortable environment. The soldiers are seated on curved benches, engaged in various activities. One soldier munches on a snack—small slabs of meat dipped in a white sauce. Two other soldiers play a board game; one arranges his pieces in a certain configuration and then declares victory. The other slams his fist on the table and utters an obscenity. Another soldier is speaking to a few others, and the whole group bursts into laughter.

Shashamar cries and whimpers, tears flowing down his face. I empathize with him, and it is more than just feeling the same feelings as he. I can actually see what he sees and feel what he feels. His memory unfolds before me. Again, it's a little disorienting, but I concentrate, and I perceive his thoughts. Staring at his captors, Shashamar remembers that he had tried to stop them. He had tried to save his people.

He and Rhansir are resting near a lagoon. Massive trees offer shade from the scorching Segerid sun, their leafy branches hanging down as if weeping. The sound of water breaking on the sandy shore fills the air. Rhansir is startled. She shakes her love awake. He opens his eyes and sees the demons approach. The beasts, obviously from the hellish bowels of the Earth, carry strange-looking staves.

"Arrr," Shashamar roars, jumping to his feet. He stands tall and muscular. There are ten of them, but he has the faith of his elders. He can cast away demons and apparitions. But something happens, something strange. One of them laughs and raises his staff. With a flash, Shashamar feels his body twist uncontrollably. He falls to the ground. Rhansir screams and runs to his side. Shashamar lifts his head and watches helplessly as two of the demons approach from behind her. One of them raises a rod to her head. With a flash of light, she drops down beside Shashamar. He lays his head down and stares into the empty eyes of his lover. A demon comes to stand over him.

"Rhan ... sir," Shashamar says. "Noooo!" He begins to cry. The creature lifts up a staff and brings it down on the temple of the chieftain. All goes black.

The pain in his temple still hurts. He massages it and returns his gaze to the guards. A breath of pollution forces him to convulse.

"Please!" Shashamar says. "Please, somebody help!"

A flash of light directly in front of the gate startles him, and he gasps and jumps back. The entire area is now awash in blue-tinted light, and three figures emerge.

Soleran, Natharon, and Addia-Sahl stand at the gate. A gold string of light flashes simultaneously across both of Soleran's eyes. He scans the pens and locks onto the positions of each Segerid prisoner. Immediately, he raises his right hand and moves his fingers. Externally, he is merely gesturing. But he is actually pressing holographic commands. One by one, in a quick flash of light, the Segerid prisoners are teleported from the pens.

Soleran's shield is activated as the Huvril soldiers open fire. There are static, hissing sounds as the lit projectiles collide with the shielding. All three of the Guardians turn to face the Huvril soldiers.

Natharon steps forward, and a string of energy flashes across his eyes as he gestures with his right hand. Reality responds, so that a string of blue energy flashes across each of the Huvril's weapons. One by one, each soldier yelps in pain and drops his weapon. As the weapons fall to the floor, they begin to melt. One soldier reaches down to pick up his weapon, but within an arm's length of it, his hand is scorched by the heated air. He jerks back, hopping up and down while screaming and holding his wounded hand close to his chest.

The three Guardians extend their arms from their sides. They phase out as they lift off the floor toward the ceiling, all rotating in place as they rise. Several floors above, they phase into a large storage area. Thousands of towering glass tubes sit atop mechanical platforms, filling the entire area. Within each tube is a Segerid corpse sustained in fluid. Solid metal spans the floor, and light fixtures hang overhead. Several unarmed Huvril scientists cry out, collide with each other in panic, and finally run toward a side door.

Addia-Sahl steps forward. A string of light flashes simultaneously across her eyes, and she scans and locks onto each of the corpses. As she gestures with her right hand, the corpses are teleported from the tubes.

A group of five Huvril soldiers run into the central corridor. Each one brings with him a leashed, six-legged beast with razor talons and maws of jagged teeth. At the far end of the laboratory, the soldiers unleash the beasts. With feral roars, the beasts lunge toward the three Guardians. One by one, the beasts collide with the shielding and fall to the side, stunned. None of the three Guardians flinch. Soleran watches as one of the beasts lies on its side, writhing. He looks back up at the soldiers and sighs, shaking his head from side to side.

As Addia-Sahl turns to step back, Natharon steps forward. Simultaneously, his eyes flash with the string of light, and he gestures with his right hand. He scans and locks onto the tubes, which burst one by one, sending their contents to the floor. Just as the flow of the liquid chemicals approaches Soleran, Addia-Sahl, and Natharon, the three raise their arms, lift up off the floor, and phase out. The soldiers and beasts scream as they are carried down the laboratory by the flood.

The three Guardians rise through the remaining floors to the very top, emerging onto the vessel's bridge. As they phase in, the captain of the vessel runs over to one of his officers at a control station.

"Activate the dampening field," the captain commands. He's large and towers over the smaller officer.

The officer nods and frantically presses commands on his screen.

Soleran walks up to a navigator who is sitting at his station and panics, running for cover. Soleran extends his hand, and his shielding activates. A tiny arc of static electricity erupts from the shielding in front of his hand, impacting the navigator's console and sending up sparks and smoke.

"Argh!" the captain growls, as he beats on the back of the officer. "Do it now! Do it now!"

Finally, the officer hits the last command, and a dampening field erupts around the *Armenkkerik*.

Soleran's shielding deactivates.

"Shoot them!" the captain says. "Shoot them now!"

The soldiers on the bridge open fire, and the lit projectiles collide with the skin of the three Guardians, ripping it away to expose bright, golden light swirling underneath. Calmly, Soleran turns and walks back to the two others and then turns to face the captain and his guards. Soleran's eyes erupt, as if on fire, and his shielding returns. He then extends his right hand. The portion of the shielding at the end of his hand erupts with the conveyance of positronic information. The intense beam cuts through the bridge's flooring and then through the floors below. A brief moment later, the beam bursts through the bottom of the vessel and continues through space. Addia-Sahl, standing on Soleran's left, raises her left hand to the side, and a beam bursts from her shielding to the left wall. The beam continues through the Huvril vessel. An unfortunate Huvril is standing in its path. His upper torso disintegrates, his lower body dropping to the floor, lifeless. The beam bursts from the *Armenkkerik*'s side and continues into space. Natharon, on Soleran's right, does the same, extending his right hand at an angle, sending a beam through the right wall. The force throws the Huvrils present on the bridge to the far walls, and the ship begins to shake from the explosions, tossing everyone around. The captain struggles to stand while holding a hand over his eyes to block the intense light. The three Guardians continue slowly cutting and slicing the hull of the *Armenkkerik*, the antimatter crackling as it collides with matter.

"Turn it off!" the captain yells to the officer. "Turn it off! Turn it off!"

The officer labors to pull himself up to his console, but he flops around, unable to press the commands. The captain makes his way to the officer's side and places both hands on the officer. With all his strength, the captain throws the officer to the ground. Then the captain presses through the commands to turn the dampening field off. Within seconds, the dampening field dissipates.

Sensing reconnection to the *Intrepidium*, the three Guardians stop their conveyance. The ship convulses with an occasional rumble but otherwise calms enough that the Huvrils are able to stand up. The captain begins breathing hard through his gritted teeth, his eyebrows straining and cast down.

"Now you will return to your leaders and inform them of your failure," says Soleran. After a pause, he finishes the thought. "Again."

"Well," the captain responds. He raises his right arm to look at a gash on his elbow and dabs up some of the blood. "You can go now."

Soleran purses his lips in a frown but nods. He turns and walks to the other two. Addia-Sahl shakes her head in dismay, and Natharon gives Soleran a half smile and a raised eyebrow. All three teleshift back to the *Intrepidium*.

"They're getting more brazen each time," Addia-Sahl says.

"Let's cripple their ship," Natharon says. "That should give them some time during their return home to think about the consequences." He activates a holographic display. A few commands later, the outer ring of the *Intrepidium* begins to rotate. A portion of its shielding activates, and a small burst of photonic energy emits toward the *Armenkkerik*. It collides with the engines of the Huvril vessel, and the *Armenkkerik* once again shakes from the explosions, tossing around its inhabitants.

"Damn you!" the captain yells, his fist raised and clenched, sparks and fire flaring up around him. "Damn you all!"

I observe as Soleran teleshifts to a lower area of the *Intrepidium*. Like the bridge, it too is bathed in full light—the floors, the walls, the ceiling. Thousands of Segerids are grouped in circles, and Soleran walks amongst them. It is apparent to him, as it is to me, that the corpses are the females. Each male holds a female corpse and weeps. Some cringe as Soleran walks by them. Eventually Soleran approaches another Guardian. He is Leostrom. His skin is black, and he sports long, curly, black hair and a thin beard. His frame is tall and muscular. Several times strings of light flash across his eyes.

Both Leostrom and Soleran walk over to Shashamar. His mate Rhansir has decomposed progressively. The chemicals in which she was placed had dissolved her soft tissues, her tongue and eyes. Now her eye sockets and mouth are wide open and empty. The skin has shriveled taut upon her skeleton and has turned to a sickly, pale-green color. Her corpse lies in his arms, an empty husk.

"I scanned the Huvril's database to learn of their intentions," Leostrom says. He gestures with his right hand, and a partially transparent holographic image of a Segerid female illuminates before both of them. "The Segerid female's anatomy contains a thermal genus gland in the womb that regulates the temperature of menstruation as well as embryonic development." The image zooms in to the gland, which is oval-shaped. "The Huvrils are harvesting the hormonal fluid secreted from this gland." Leostrom diminishes the image and folds his hands behind his back. "It would appear that the Huvrils are primarily using this fluid, amongst other purposes, as an ingredient in one of their food products. Unfortunately, they are unaware that the processing of that particular food destroys the molecular structure of the fluid. They are not reaping any benefit whatsoever. They are killing the females in vain."

Both Guardians turn to face Shashamar and Rhansir. The former chieftain cries and rocks back and forth, clutching his love tightly. They pause briefly, studying the emotions of the chieftain.

"Let's reinstate," Soleran says.

"Scanning for template," Leostrom says. Strings of light flash across his eyes as he gestures. From Leostrom's perspective, holographic images of the Segerid female emerge, along with equations and calculations. A blue string of light flashes down the corpse, and Shashamar lays her down and quickly moves back, his eyes wide and his jaw dropped.

"Template scan completed," Leostrom says. "Repairing cellular necrosis."

The blue light flashes down the corpse. Shashamar watches attentively as the body of his mate is physically restored from putrid green to dark red. He turns to face Leostrom and Soleran. The chieftain's gaze follows Leostrom's right-handed gesturing.

"Mapping neural net," Leostrom says. Another flash. "Initiating neuronal signal oscillation." Another flash.

Shashamar's mate opens her eyes and stands upon her six spidery legs. Shashamar turns and sees her but screams and falls back. She does the same.

"Rhansir?" Shashamar says.

"Shashamar?" Rhansir responds.

"Rhansir!" Shashamar says, reaching for her. They embrace each other, hugging tightly. Shashamar pulls her away from him slightly. He looks her up and down, his eyes wide with joy and terror. His bottom lip trembles, and tears rush from his eyes. Then he turns to face Leostrom.

"Thank you," he manages to say amidst his tears, his voice cracking slightly.

Leostrom smiles and nods. He steps back from Shashamar and Rhansir and slowly rotates to scan the other corpses. Many of the Segerid males nearby are standing and observing. Light flashes across Leostrom's eyes as he gestures. In a brief moment, the females rise, alive and well. There are gasps and cries of wonder. Afterward, gentle sobbing rises amidst reunion.

Leostrom faces Soleran, who nods approvingly. Another hand gesture. More flashes of blue. The Segerids slowly lie down and fall gently asleep.

"I will apply subroutines to their neural nets to ease the trauma," Leostrom says. "This will be to them a forgotten dream."

Soleran walks over to Shashamar and kneels down. He gently caresses the cheek of the chieftain. "Let him remember."

"You are proud of him," Leostrom says with a smile.

Soleran looks up at his fellow Guardian. "He knows love. He knows it well."

"What do you have in mind?" Leostrom asks.

"Write one extra routine for this soul," Soleran says. He caresses the chieftain's shoulder and then stands.

Leostrom scans Soleran's optics and smiles widely. "Light. He will be captivated by light and will want to investigate its source."

"That should enhance the maturation rate by 7 percent," Soleran says

As the *Intrepidium* orbits the Segerid home world, Leostrom scans the populace on the surface. He traces the released captives' DNA to one region, obscure and remote, which the Huvrils thought to exploit. Two at a time, Segerid couples are teleported, still sleeping, to the surface and laid in soft brush, spread far apart from each other. They will awake with some confusion but otherwise unharmed.

Shashamar will write his dream down on a scroll. Others will perceive it as divine prophecy. He will recall the events of his dream with blurred detail. He will make a few errant assumptions and write them down too, the unfortunate consequence of free will, one that is progressive and learning. But he will add the following thought:

The Great Spirit is made of light. He carries light in his hands. With a motion, he sends the light wherever he desires, and everywhere he sends the light, darkness flees. He took me to his house, which was like being in the heart of the greater sun, not the lesser one. Light was everywhere, so there was no shadow or darkness anywhere. Love was found there. Peace also. And joy. It was a temple in heaven, a temple of light. I don't know whether I was there in spirit or body; only the Great Spirit knows. Half of us were dead, and half of us were alive. With a mere wave of his hand, the dead were raised. They came back to life. They stood up. They were made completely whole.

Then I heard his thunderous voice ask me this question, saying: "From whenceforth comes light and whereto does it go?" And I responded, saying, "I don't know, Lord. Surely you know!" And he answered, saying, "The light of which I speak—true light—comes from the heart of stars, of which you call the Host of Heaven."

And then I was under the night sky, and I looked up and saw the specks of light, the Host of Heaven, the spirits poised in heaven to watch us from above. And the Great Spirit continued, saying, "And light is given to man, that he should see life clearly and without which he would not see life at all." I asked for more, saying, "How will I know what I see is true?" And the Great Spirit answered, saying, "The heavens give truth always, because the heavens exist on truth. Any untruth uttered by the heavens would cause the heavens to fold up like a scroll and henceforth cease to exist."

And there was pause, but then the Great Spirit continued, saying,

"You will know it is the truth, if, after hearing the truth, you have a desire to know more, for truth spawns the desire to know more." And I knew that was true, because I wanted to know more of what the Great Spirit was saying. And so I asked, saying, "Please tell me more." And the Great Spirit did so, saying, "Any notion that supposedly concludes a matter, commanding, 'That is that and there is no more to know,' is not the full truth of a matter. For the full truth of a matter is found in a lengthy journey pursuing the truth, which is discovered in small steps, here a little, there a little. Truth is one precept leading to another, and a discovery of one truthful precept ensures that another need be discovered, so that the full truth of a matter is never full but leads to further truth. Because of that, the truth of a matter is knowable only after many generations."

I asked, "How many generations would it take to learn the full truth of a matter?" And the Great Spirit asked of me, saying, "How many men standing one on top of another would begin at the bottom of the ocean and reach the surface?" And I responded, saying, "I don't know, Lord. Surely you know!" And he answered, saying, "Well over a thousand. That is how many generations it would take for your people to discover the full truth of a matter. Many generations have already passed, and there are many more to go. And the full truth of a matter remains hidden, knowable only to the last generation, who will lovingly share that truth with the other generations." And the desire to know more burned in me, setting my heart on fire.

I asked for more, saying, "Lord, how can that be, seeing that the first generation and even many after have already long died and passed?" And the Great Spirit answered, saying, "Every generation shall rise in the last day and shall face a judgment. Some will rise to eternal life. Others will be eternally forgotten, left to the darkness of nothing as their information is destroyed by the fires that rage at the end of time. Know that the last generation shall be first to rise and the first shall be last."

And I asked for more, saying, "How will I be judged?" And the Great Spirit asked of me, saying, "Which do you desire, to have eternal life or be forever forgotten?" And I, of course, responded as my heart desired, saying, "Eternal life, Lord! This you know!" And the Great Spirit advised, saying, "Very well, then. Pursue light, for the truth is in the light."

Shashamar will conclude his scroll with his own thoughts and ideas, proverbs and wisdom, especially regarding the nature of light. His ideas will be primitive and crude, but in comparison with the rest of the Segerid population, they will be profound and progressive. It will be a positive step in the progression of Segerid humanity. I am observing and contemplating all of this, having stepped closer to Soleran and the others, though Soleran's back is toward me. He senses my presence and looks over his shoulder at me. Then he turns to face me. He smiles.

"Observant One, come and stand with us," Soleran says. "We have much to share, as always."

I approach to take a place in the circle of Guardians, who stand around the image of Segeris. I look up at Soleran and admire his beauty. He is tall. I stand just above his waist. His hair shines in the light. It's a strange feature, since I am hairless, having first seen hair when I was invited to come with the Guardians. His eyes are like stars. Simply put, he is beautiful. They all are beautiful, and they are embodiments of truth. I look upon my thin fingers, my small hands, my pale-gray, rough skin. I so much want to be as beautiful as they are, and I know that I need to embody truth as they do. To do so, I must observe them, but also more than that. I must see reality through their eyes. I must see what they see and hear what they hear. This is how I'll come to know what they know.

This I willingly do.

Always.

CHAPTER 2

We had heard your prayers, Observant One. You had prayed long and often. We heard from afar, and we came right away. When we first noticed your prayer, a light perturbation upon the continuum, I asked Leostrom to tell me who this was that was praying so long and often. He informed me that it was one named Brinn. I further inquired, and Leostrom reminded me that your world had long since fallen to the warmongering Huvrils, whose cruelty and inhumanity are unmatched throughout the heavens. If we had been present, we would have certainly interfered with their destruction and frustrated their schemes. But our adversary, Maximeron, Son of the Majestic Star, detained us with his own scheme. It was especially heinous, prompting us to focus our attention on him. Had we known of his full scheme, to distract us so that the Huvrils could launch their massive galactic raids, we would have proceeded differently. Under his directive, they were to exterminate everyone, using a weapon he had devised for use against Ibalexa—a thermonuclear cascade. After defeating Maximeron, having done so a million times over, we immediately proceeded to put a stop to the Huvrils' campaign of destruction. We are saddened that we only came to know of this campaign upon hearing the outcries of your people, the Ibalexans. Although we made haste, knowing the situation was urgent, we were not able to prevent the Huvrils from destroying Ibalexa. But upon our arrival, the Huvrils were dispatched quickly, and their weapon was removed forever from their use, preventing them from carrying their destructive campaign to the next world. That didn't, however, alleviate our grief that the beautiful world of Ibalexa had been laid to waste and its beautiful people slain.

Your prayer surprised us, Brinn. You escaped our notice after Ibalexa's massacre. We had already determined that the Ibalexans were rendered extinct. Having scanned Ibalexa for any life, we found none. A photometric analysis revealed how you survived. From that analysis, we learned that you had stowed away on a Huvril drop ship and had remained hidden for days. Upon discovery, you were detained. Objectified, you were perceived as a valuable commodity, since you were the last remaining Ibalexan in existence. The value placed upon you was so high, only the Huvril emperor was worthy of possessing you, and so he made you his personal servant. Further photometric analysis revealed to us the extent of your suffering under the hands of the Huvril emperor. He trained you, but Huvril training means breaking the spirit and the will of the trainee.

Even so, under this especially heinous and cruel treatment, you held out hope. While you submitted to their rule in person, you hoped for hope in spirit, and that hope blossomed in your soul, so much so that you devoted hours to praying. You asked for anyone to help you, anyone who could hear. Brinn, we heard. From the other side of the galaxy, we heard you. We listened to these prayers and knew right away, with no doubt whatsoever, that we would visit Huvra to deliver you. We came from afar, just for you. We had plans to deliver the Huvrils from themselves. We hold out from overly engaging them for this reason. We monitor them from afar, and when necessary, we intervene just enough to undo what harm they are doing. We continue to implement our plan of action for this section of the universe, in furtherance of the Principal Cause. Upon completion of one task, we move to the next. The deliverance of the Huvrils is on that list, even though they have sold themselves to the rule of our adversary, Maximeron.

As for you, Brinn, your deliverance was very important to us.

We had retrieved all data that could be retrieved from Ibalexa. We engaged every scientific principle known. We performed every scan, every analysis, every particle was weighed, every light vector measured and traced, every permutation of every spatiality, even down to the neutrino background and the gravitonic stream. Even with our arsenal of science, the full spectrum of information regarding Ibalexa could not be fully and properly ascertained. We gathered much but not all. We grieved that to reinstate the Ibalexan race was not feasible. We had already removed the name Ibalexa from our data banks and consigned all related data to the archives. That information would be lost upon our transiting to the next epochal cycle of the universe. In the archives are the names of races and even individuals who cannot or will not be reinstated. Their information remains locked away as data in the coronal memory on our star world called Epsilon Truthe. But then we heard your prayers, Brinn, and inside each of us ignited joy. For within you is the key to reinstating the entire Ibalexan race. Your DNA, your memories, your thoughts, your dreams, your mind, heart, and soul, retain all the information we need to restore the full spectrum of Ibalexan information back to our databases. The name Ibalexa is now rewritten into our records, and the task of reinstating the Ibalexan race is so important to us, we have moved it far ahead of other pressing tasks. We thought it most appropriate to place that task just in front of the one to deliver the Huvrils from the adversary's rule. When that time comes, you will be in the forefront and will witness this all, and you will be celebrated amongst your own people as their savior. Therefore, let your soul be healed. Let no worries or fears or thoughts of future loneliness impose themselves upon you. To further your healing, we will share with you the story of your deliverance from the Huvrils.

Upon entering into Huvra's intermediate territory, just inside their solar system, their vessels began an assault, but since their technology was weak compared to ours, their weapons weren't able to penetrate our shielding. We didn't retaliate, since they offered no threat. After entering into high orbit around Huvra, Addia-Sahl, Leostrom, and I were poised to teleshift to the surface. I cast my gaze through the floor of the *Intrepidium*, locked in on the throne room of the Huvril emperor, Samadas the Great, as he likes to call himself. Then we together teleshifted through Huvra's atmosphere, and within less than a second, we stood at the entrance to the throne room. This was the first visit to Samadas after he had constructed his imperial hall. The throne room was huge and elaborate, as you know, having labored there during your captivity. A huge dais sat in the center with steps all around except behind it. That portion contained a walkway toward the back of the throne room, ending at a balcony overlooking a plaza that lay several stories below it. The entire inside was emblazoned with gold. Various giant gold statues of ancient Huvril deities stood, reaching to the ceiling, leading down the walkway toward the dais. Upon our entry at the front of the walkway, the First Platoon of the Imperial Guard, Samadas's own personal bodyguards, sprang onto the walkway so as to impede our approach.

Coming down the walkway, moving through the soldiers, was Samadas's own high counselor, Hesla the Lawyer. He was crouched over slightly. He wore a white silk cowl with a slightly red hue. His hooves were cracked from many travels by foot. His skin was darkened by the sun and wrinkled by the weathering of age. We waited for Hesla to reach us.

"I know who you are, Sons of the Morning Rise," Hesla said. "You are enemies to our Lord, Necronus, the Most High God." He approached closer but stopped short. Wisdom reminded him of our authority over nature. "What have you to do with us?" he asked.

We didn't answer. We merely teleshifted through the ranks of the soldiers and stood up at the top of the dais, along with the emperor. His throne was made of gold and was heavily decorated, with serpents wrapped around every extremity. The curved bench structure accommodated the Huvril's centaurlike body. On the throne, if you remember that day, Samadas sat straight with no crouching, dressed elaborately. The size of the train was absurdly large. Samadas employed five other smaller Huvril boys, whose sole job was to follow him around and maintain the proper shape of the train. Links attached the train to each Huvril boy's chest plate. Four bodyguards, the largest of the Huvrils, stepped out, away from the throne, so as to block us.

When the soldiers below the dais ran up the steps, Samadas barked at them. "You will hold your positions!" The soldiers froze. Samadas haughtily looked at each of us. He then stood up from his throne and walked toward us, followed by his entourage. "We are to pay our respects to these, our Elders of the Great Epoch, Sons of the Morning Rise, Guardians of Eternal Life!" Samadas knelt and lowered his head. A quick scan of his neural net revealed his presumption, and I was unable to contain a sigh. The three of us stood there silently and offered no response. "Have you come to pay me a visit?" Samadas began, turning and walking back behind the throne. He jerked back toward us to his left, and his entourage leaped in the same rotation to accommodate the train.

None of us answered him.

"Have you come to see me in all my splendor?" Samadas asked. He stepped forward toward us and stopped a meter away. He stood and examined the robes we were wearing, along with our sashes. He then looked into my eyes and studied me, looking for some kind of familiar response.

I gave none.

"You see me in my glory," Samadas said, turning to walk away. He strolled down the walkway behind his throne, heading toward the balcony. Stopping, he turned to face us. "Come! I want to show you something."

We didn't obey.

"Very well, then," he answered. "I'm sure that you could hear me perfectly from the other side of Huvra." Amused by his comment, he laughed. Samadas walked to the balcony and stood overlooking his kingdom, from the plaza to the horizon. "I own all of this. All of this is mine." Samadas kept his entourage busy. He jerked around, and they wasted no time in keeping up with him. "It was all given to me by my Lord, Necronus, Prince of Life and Death, whom you call Maximeron, Son of the Majestic Star." One amongst his entourage, the first to his right, stumbled slightly. Samadas stopped and glared at him, looking as if he had to fight every part of himself not to pounce on the servant. The frightened young boy stood before the emperor, trembling.

I just shook my head at the scene. I recall my thoughts at the time, that we, the Guardians of Life, would deliver the oppressed throughout all of Huvra. As that thought crossed my mind, I became content. First things first. We were to deliver you, Brinn, so that you would be safe from all risk.

"You recall my master, don't you?" Samadas continued with his interrogation of us. He pointed to the last statue, a reddish-gold monstrosity depicting every kind of weapon known to any reptilian beast: talons, jagged teeth, spiked tail, horns, armored spine with spikes. The idol was a red dragon. The eyes were fashioned to show rage, cruelty, and hate. We returned our gaze back to Samadas, who fell into an odd trance as he stared at his god.

Hesla made his way up the steps to the top. He circled around us and walked toward the throne. His body was stressed, and he clutched his chest while breathing hard. He looked up at me and met my gaze. Intimidated, he let his gaze fall to the floor.

"Long ago," Samadas continued, "my people were raised up from fields of fire set ablaze by the breath of life from our great God Necronus, the Prince of Life and Death. He lifted us up from the bowels of the Earth, calling our forefathers, one by one, each by their god-appointed name." Samadas began to scream out the names. "Armenkkerik! Morghonox! Devisgar! And the Others to whom we pay homage in this, our great Imperial Hall, in our great city, Samadasanae, on our great world, Huvra!"

At that, the four bodyguards and the soldiers bellowed in sync, "Honor to the gods! Honor to the lands! Honor to the emperor!"

I marveled at the spectacle, amazed at how much the proud love theatrics. Samadas continued his speech. "Armenkkerik the Terrible subdued the world, having received the promise of the Most High God, Necronus, who said to him, 'I will give you all the kingdoms of this world if you worship me as your god,' and Armenkkerik did kneel before the Most High and said, 'My life is yours, O Lord. Make me your right arm of justice.' And Armenkkerik went before the people of Huvra and slew the pagans and their prophets."

I turned to gauge Leostrom's and Addia-Sahl's reactions. Leostrom smirked and shook his head. Addia-Sahl just rolled her eyes.

"Morghonox, twenty-four generations from Armenkkerik, arose a mighty emperor," Samadas continued. "A weakling heretic ruled before him—an uncle and usurper of the throne. Necronus was most displeased with this fool. Damage to Huvra had been great under the heretic's rule. But Morghonox wrested control from the heretic's hands and reestablished Huvra's might and power."

Samadas seemed oblivious to our lack of interest in his droning on about the feats of his ancestors. I considered feigning a yawn but realized he wouldn't notice. His eyes were still locked on the idol of his adoration.

"Devisgar was thirty-two generations from Morghonox," Samadas rambled on. "He colonized the various planets in the solar system and beyond. Worlds have submitted to our rule, worlds that thought beforehand they were mighty and strong, only to learn the truth after resisting. Thus has Huvra become a powerful empire that spans the stars in the heavens."

I sighed and shook my head. Little did Samadas know that his empire was but a tiny speck in an ocean.

"And then there is me!" Samadas said, following with a laugh. "I will be the next canonized emperor to achieve godhood. I have subdued all religious movements. I have constructed new temples in honor of the gods, especially the Most High God, Necronus. I have tripled the size of the imperial fleet. I have conquered neighboring stars and enlarged the empire. My name will be written into the Pantheon: Armenkkerik the Terrible, Morghonox the Mighty, Devisgar the Wise, and Samadas the Great. Honor to the gods! Honor to Necronus, Prince of Life and Death!"

The soldiers erupted, "Honor to the gods! Honor to the lands! Honor to the emperor!"

"Most Holy Father," the elder Hesla said to the young Samadas.

"Everything you have stated is true." The lawyer still seemed to be struggling with his breath.

"Of course it is!" Samadas said. The emperor, along with his entourage, returned to the throne. With a display of grace, he slipped over the side and rested his centauric body on the cushioned bench. "Tell me, counselor. What is next on my agenda?"

"Holy Father," Hesla continued, walking to the other side of the throne, "it is time for you to partake of the blessed fountain of truth. The cupbearer stands at the bottom of the dais."

"Yes!" Samadas said, snapping his fingers. "It is time. Bring forth my holy vessel!" Samadas then raised his chin up high and glared at me through slightly parted eyes. "Are you impressed by all of this?"

None of us answered.

"Blah!" Samadas said. "You have nothing to say? Do you not know that I, Samadas the Great, am forty-eight generations from Devisgar?" He paused slightly to allow us to respond. Then he continued. "In forty-eight generations, no Huvril has risen up to establish himself. No Huvril has been found worthy enough to be granted godhood by the Prince of Life and Death." The emperor jumped up from the bench, startling his entourage. They yelped in surprise and leaped forward to keep up with him. "But I," Samadas continued, waggling his finger at me, "I will be the first since Devisgar to earn this right! My Lord, Necronus, will see everything I have done. He will reward me for my diligence."

"Perhaps," I answered.

"You speak!" Samadas asked, leaping back in surprise.

"Yes," I answered. "We are here to free a certain person from Huvril captivity."

"Oh?" Samadas said. "And who would that be?"

"Your cupbearer," I answered. At that point, Brinn, I looked over at you as you reached the top of the dais. In that moment, we teleported you to the *Intrepidium*. The tray and cup instantly fell to the floor of the dais, and wine spilled everywhere. You had entered the throne room from the side, and we watched as you mounted the stairs, careful to carry on a gold platter the emperor's so-called holy vessel, a gold chalice embedded with diamonds. We watched you climb the steps, slowly, carefully. You made it to the top without spilling one drop of the wine onto the tray. We know that in the past, you were mistreated if you failed to do this. And as you stood there, holding a tray with a cup filled with wine, forced to partake in an overly dramatic ceremony, my soul ached. We would have spared you the trouble of climbing the stairs, except that it was important that you come to stand upon the top of the dais. It was important that the emperor see you removed from his grasp.

"Arrrrgh!" Samadas said.

"No! The holy vessel!" Hesla said. "Pick it up! Quick, pick it up!"

"That Ibalexan is mine!" Samadas said. He jumped toward one of his guards in such haste that his entourage failed to respond quickly enough. Two tore away, and the others fell on the train. It tore from his shoulders and sprawled on the floor.

"Bumbling fools! Pick it up!" Hesla said to the group lying on the train.

Samadas snatched from a guard an ornamental crossbow-shaped weapon. "Give me back my cupbearer!" Samadas commanded. He slowly walked up to me with the weapon poised and ready to fire.

When he was within a few meters of me, I activated my shielding to let a glimmer of light shine down the front. I wanted him to know his efforts would be in vain. It worked, and he stopped and growled.

At that point, the guard who had picked up the cup dropped it by accident, and it bounced down the steps. Several of the diamonds broke out of their encasements and flew in different directions.

Samadas screamed in rage and aimed the crossbow at the guard. He opened fire, and a burst of energy slammed the guard in the chest, throwing him from the top of the dais. The soldier rolled down several steps and then lay sprawled, groaning and writhing in pain. Samadas turned around and opened fire on the entourage. They fell to the floor, wounded and crying. The other bodyguards at the top fled. The old lawyer fell to his knees as the emperor approached him. Samadas placed the crossbow to the head of the lawyer and stood there panting through gritted teeth. The emperor's face was contorted in rage.

"Please," Hesla began, "please have mercy on me, an old fool." The lawyer trembled.

"Ahh!" Samadas answered, swinging the butt of the crossbow against the side of the lawyer's head. "You worthless, overpaid leech!"

The old Huvril yelped in pain and fell to the side. He covered his head to block any further blows.

"I made you my highest advisor!" the young emperor said. "You should have known they were going to steal my cupbearer. You should have known!" Samadas then turned and tossed the crossbow at me. It collided with my shielding and fell to the floor. He stood and glared at me. Finally, he threw his arms up in the air. "Bahh!" As Samadas walked back to this throne, taking a moment to kick an injured Huvril boy, he uttered, "You got what you want. Why are you still here?" He sank down on his bench.

"We wanted to give you something in return for your cupbearer," I answered.

The emperor looked at me, dejected. "You don't have enough wealth to repay me for this wrong!" He pumped his fists a few times. "Well? What is it?"

"A token of our newly made promise," I answered.

"God!" Samadas screamed. "What are you babbling on about?"

I looked at Hesla, who had managed to raise himself up on one knee. I initiated the holographic commands in my optics, and as light flashed over my eyes, I scanned Hesla's neural net and chose the neural points from which I would insert several prewritten subroutines. As the subroutines activated, light flashed before Hesla's eyes. He screamed and fell back but then became captivated by the visions unfolding in his optics.

"What are you doing to my high counselor?" Samadas asked, jumping to his feet and walking over to the lawyer. "Are you thinking to steal him away from me too?"

"Hesla," I said. "Inform your emperor of what you have seen."

The old counselor struggled to lift himself to his feet. "Samadas the Great," Hesla said, "I saw the Guardian vessel hovering in orbit around Huvra. I saw seven lights emerge from the vessel and make their way down to Huvra. Each of these lights was a Guardian." The emperor approached the counselor with a scowl on his face. "These are seven who have been appointed throughout Huvra, then throughout the solar system, then throughout the rest of the empire, all for the preparation." Hesla looked up at his emperor and grew quiet. "I mean ... I ... I mean ..."

"Preparation for what!" Samadas finally asked.

"For our return," I said, stepping forward and approaching the emperor. "The next time we visit Huvra, it will be to oppose the agency of darkness. We will deliver the oppressed and those who suffer under the weight of imperial rule."

"You can't do that!" Samadas said. "We belong to Necronus!"

"You don't say?" I asked.

"It is the law of the Guardians!" Samadas said. "You are breaking your own law!"

"We do as we deem lawful," I answered. "We deem it lawful to intervene."

Samadas widened his eyes and hung his mouth open, panting heavily. He looked around at the debacle that lay before him, the spilled wine, the ripped train, the wounded entourage. "You choose to intervene at a time when I am set to rise in my prime," Samadas said. He composed himself, straightened up his blouse, and strutted back to his throne. He eased himself onto the bench and shifted slightly to find that one comfortable position. Then he glared at me. "Very well, then. I shall take the opportunity to defeat your schemes. My master Necronus will find the occasion to canonize me and place me in his pantheon."

"You can certainly hope," I said.

"I will crush all resistance!" Samadas said, jumping to his feet. He slowly walked toward me. "I will slay all of your prophets as traitors and rebels. As soon as they emerge from their hellhole, I will hunt them down and silence them without delay." He stopped short of my shielding. "Necronus will not allow you to commit this crime."

"Your lord will suffer our intervention, seeing that he has not the means to stop it," I answered. "And until the appointed time, you will suffer the intervention of this Guardian."

One of the seven appointed, a trusted friend named Sun-Li, teleshifted next to me. He had long, straight, black hair parted down the middle. His skin was pale white. His face was round and clean-shaven, and his eyes were narrow and sharp. A single dark blue sash wrapped around his waist and over his right shoulder.

"At your withdrawal," Sun-Li said to me, "I will assume my post."

I smiled and nodded in confirmation.

"The Imperial Pantheon will stop you!" Samadas said. "You will not corrupt Huvra with your heresy!" The young emperor pumped his fists at me. "We will be victorious! Our Great God Necronus has promised!"

I said nothing further, and Samadas returned to his throne. I turned to Leostrom and Addia-Sahl who stood with me. We teleshifted back to the *Intrepidium*. Sun-Li remained behind, along with the other six Guardians, whose roles were to be our emissaries in our absence, to implement the plan of salvation for the Huvril race and prepare for our return.

CHAPTER 3

I, Brinn the Ibalexan, the last of my kind, have been invited to remain with the Guardians as they facilitate the maturation of life on the future world of Endhera. Right now, it's still a dust ring, and the protostar binary system has not ignited nuclear fusion yet. After the Guardians delivered the Segerids from Huvril captivity, the *Intrepidium* quickly covered the distance from the Segeris System, which lies on the outskirts of the Huvril Empire, to the newly forming Endheran System, which sits in a neighboring galactic tidal arm. I watched as the *Intrepidium* traversed the medium between the tidal arms. I say that I watched, because the *Intrepidium* has no hull. It has a skeletal frame consisting of a material unfamiliar to me; the vessel is encased in an envelope of energy, which produces the visual effect of walls, ceilings, and floorings that shine brighter than a sun. With a mere gesture, any Guardian can expose the internal area to the external light, which is like seeing the walls or ceiling, or even the flooring, become invisible. The *Intrepidium* is huge, like a city. Guardians teleshift throughout the vessel, flashing in and out, from area to area, level to level.

The outer ring, however, is solid, made of the same material as the vessel's skeleton. The outer ring is held in place within some kind of energy field. The ring, I was told, is inlaid with thousands of warp cores using the superfluid neutronium. The cores are activated impulsively, which pulls the central disk along the space-time continuum. The science of it all is beyond my understanding, but what I've learned so far is fascinating, mainly because of the gentle grace and patience of Evalene, who accompanies me as I stroll about observing the Guardians in their various activities.

"Evalene?" I ask.

"Yes?" she answers.

"I heard mentioned the name Epsilon Truthe. What is that?" I ask.

"The Guardian star world?" she says, her smile widening. "It's a white dwarf, the remaining core of a collapsed, primary sequential yellow star. The name derives from a principle of science, which for us defines the truth of reality."

"A principle of science?" I ask.

"We observe by way of tensorial analysis the permutative relationship between a nonexistent static background and the real spatial fluid forefront," Evalene continues. "This externalizes our perspective, since the truth of reality is properly observable from a neutral point of view. The closer one approaches neutrality, the same as approaching infinity, the closer one approaches a clearer understanding of reality."

"I would very much like to see Epsilon Truthe," I say.

"You shall, Brinn." Evalene pauses for a moment and looks around her. "We are preparing to continue the maturation of Endhera. Shall we return to the bridge?"

I smile and nod. There's a bright flash of light and then we are instantly in the presence of Soleran, Natharon, Leostrom, and Addia-Sahl.

Evalene continues to talk to me about the process. "There will be a significant temporal disparity between the Huvril Empire and the Endheran System, partly because of the effect of frame-dragging between the galaxy's tidal arms, but mostly due to the spinorial consequence induced by *Intrepidium*'s temporal incrementation." She smiles, knowing I need further explanation. "Such an effect is localized. Time is governed by the motion of objects within a localized space. By inducing spinorial frame-dragging, time is sped up in incremental phases but only relatively speaking, as observed externally. Per the internal perspective, everything looks normal."

"Wow!" I say. "You can do that?"

"You mean to speed up the passage of time relative to our perspective?" Her smile widens. "There is not much that we cannot do. Our current limitations regard chaotic permutations caused by entanglement of light vectors, such as the ones that initially prevented us from reinstating Ibalexa to its native condition."

"Prevented?" I ask.

"Well," Evalene says, "we could have reinstated a modified form of Ibalexa and its people, based on our best guess as to the native form, even to 98 percent accuracy, but that isn't conducive to our philosophy. To us, it just wouldn't be the same."

Soleran activates the holographic imagery of the Endheran System. It seems to have improved somewhat in our absence, especially since the initial effect of the *Intrepidium*'s spin remained. The circumstellar rings are very distinct, with conspicuous large clumps of matter. My mind is slowly but surely grasping the science of it all. Still, I have much to learn.

"You will get to see the process that we call zoagenesis," Evalene says. "It is the natural consequence of stellar evolution. The meaning of life for us is to stabilize the universe."

The *Intrepidium*'s outer ring jerks into motion with a thunderous boom, and the room begins to move strangely. It's as if the background is moving faster than the forefront, so that everything in my sight is choppy. I notice the red digits above the holographic image of the Endheran solar nebula evolving.

"To stabilize the universe," Evalene's echo says.

To stabilize the cosmic fluid
of universal consciousness
per the intuitive providentiality
of sovereign humanness
A Principal Cause known to us that
a star contains life's endeavor,

and Life, a creation of Life,
creates Life, and Life lives forever

The larger protostar ignites first, since it is the more compacted and hotter. I see it, clearly, its solar eruption blasting away the envelope of dust and debris to the outer regions of the newly born system. In the wake of the solar storm are seven worlds, each with its own rings of dust encircled around it. The chaotic swirl of matter captured in gravity reminds me of the stormy seas on Ibalexa. It seems that only seconds pass before the second protostar, smaller than the first, ignites.

The second planet is the one referred to as Endhera Earth, an honorary designation for a former Guardian chancellor named Endheron. Its surface glows red due to its seas of molten rock. An image of a planetesimal forms between Endhera and a gas giant. Addia-Sahl had mentioned that this forming planet would need to be obliterated early in its evolution to prevent a future catastrophe, long after life had formed on Endhera's surface.

The *Intrepidium* ceases its spin, and the room bursts with an intense flash of light. I observe everything return to normal sight and sound. Natharon activates his holographic commands. In compliance, the outer ring of the *Intrepidium* booms into rotation, and several massive bursts of photonic energy emanate from its shielding toward the projected path of the killer world. We wait, and the planetesimal revolves around to the projected focal point of the bursts of energy. The collision is violent, and it spills the planetesimal's molten-iron contents back into the circumstellar disk. It also redistributes the ring's mass farther out, so that it is captured in the gravitonic current of the gas giant. The future of Endhera is safe.

Addia-Sahl, having been designated as the project manager of Endhera, continues with her configurations. I watch as multiple images of various creatures and plant life display holographically before the thousands of Guardians present.

"These, Brinn, are mere projections," Evalene says to me. "We predict by way of mathematical probability that these are the most likely life forms to arise under the dynamic conditions of Endhera's environment." She remains by my side as we both walk amongst the others, busy with their analyses.

"Will people emerge? Human beings?" I ask.

"It is our ultimate goal," she answers. "Even so, that process is complex." She stops to view one particular image. "The conditions have to be just right." The image is of a slender, reptilian creature with a muzzle. It is standing upright. "As you probably know by now, Brinn," Evalene says to me, "we define self-other awareness as the foundation of intelligence. This is the hallmark sign of humanity."

"Not only that," says Dyllon, the Guardian studying the standing reptile image, "but intelligence requires maturation through evolution." Dyllon's skin is pale in comparison to that of others, and his hair is long, straight, and as white as his robe. His face is clean-shaven. Thick, white brows sit atop heavy-lidded eyes. He manipulates the image so that it progresses through its evolution, eventually stopping the image at a late stage. The image shows a bipedal humanoid, with grayish skin and silky, off-white strands of hair.

CHAPTER 4

"In the beginning we envisioned and actualized the local heavens and the habitable Earth and established through scientific principles their origins. Although it is not necessary for the synthesis of life, which is autonomous, we modified and manipulated the variables underlying life's development. And now our face is upon the Earth, our eyes cast forth with light to see the Earth as it is, misshapen and vacuous, blanketed with darkness, with toxic, hot, vaporous, dust-ridden clouds racing through the sparse atmosphere. Sudden condensation induces rifts of cooler air colliding with torrents of hot winds. The result is tornadic, and funnels of fire arise with a roar to deliver dirt and ash into the atmosphere. Geysers of lava spray the Earth, adding to the hostility. As you can see, Brinn, this is no place for life. Not yet, at least. Thus, we would like for you to experience the very essence of our being, the reason for our existence. Witness and share our joy at the birthing of a world. In this manner, you will come to appreciate the reinstatement of Ibalexa.

"Do not be alarmed by the tumult. It is a natural process and one that we can observe with little intervention. The ocean of lava that covers the entire surface is churned up by the planet's rotation, as well as the planetesimal bombardment. Look up into the midst of the gaseous fog that blocks the starlight, and behold the fiery orb that now breaches the atmosphere. Hear its thunderous roar. Feel its heavy might press against the air. It is as a mountain on fire, and it carries in its iron-laden core veins of precious metals. In the distance is another, its roar and might lessened by perspective of distance only. Its core brings with it heavy metals. And yet, on the other side, a glimpse of a fiery orb reveals its bringing of certain gases thus far lacking. These, Brinn, are the building materials from which life shall spring up as a flower in a desert, a blade of grass in the middle of a wasteland. These elements were formed in the core of a star having long since died and exploded, enriching the local heavens.

"You may, if you so desire, reach down and grasp in your hands the molten rock. Fear not. You are protected. Examine it, and contemplate its nature. Consider the form it will take in the future. It generates much heat, but with every passing moment, it loses more heat than it creates. The more heat lost, the more the loss hastens. Its nature is changing, always. As we walk above the ocean, watching the waves of lava crash against our shielding, we are reminded that change appears chaotic. Even so, we have already calculated every scalar field, every permutation, every fluid metric. Long ago we had determined that even chaos is bound by order. To this moment, we can adjust any variable to induce long-lasting consequences. Should we desire to change the shape of the continents, all it requires is a field induction at a particular pinpoint within the vast ocean. Should we think it appropriate to mold a sea, the exact pinpoint is known to us. You yourself have just done so by picking up and dropping the viscous material, at which a particular rock will form and be called Absolute.

"The Earth's magnetic field is capturing the various gases, many of which would be toxic to most life forms. Aerodynamic compression induced by wind and gravity will drive the toxic gases under the Earth's surface. We make use of this principle to engage the winds and fine-tune the future atmosphere. The external winds, or solar winds from both the primary and secondary suns, will clear up the nighttime skies. As the hot, gaseous fog dissipates and condenses, the suns are revealed. And for the first time, the surface of Endhera sees day and night. With the secondary sun, Endhera has more daylight than darkness. Now we can measure Endhera's time relative to its revolution around the suns, although tidal drag will continue to slow it down for the rest of its existence. Its tilt gives it seasons to govern the cycles of life and death, and its moons caress the Earth and its oceans.

"As the Earth cools, its crust solidifies. Mountainous regions and deep chasms take shape. The Earth is assuming its form. The work isn't done yet, however. Long ago, having calculated with perfect precision the exact location of this star system, we engaged a heavenly body, a comet, to traverse the heavens and make its way to Endhera. During its long and arduous journey, it has accumulated vast amounts of water. As you can see, having looked up into the sky with anticipation, the comet approaches. It passes through the atmosphere and collides with the Earth. We can feel the compression forces collide with our shielding, but the *Intrepidium* compensates, and the shielding maintains its integrity. At first, there is fire, as the atmosphere ignites. The comet's water vaporizes and coalesces as clouds in the sky—dark, brooding clouds. The fire in the atmosphere is extinguished, and now the millennial rains will pour upon the Earth and fill up its trenches and chasms to make oceans and seas, lakes and rivers, ponds and streams. These pools of water are for the moment dingy, toxic, and putrid. Even so, the water contained therein is the catalyst for life. And what shall we say is the seed of life, Brinn? Behold, a smaller comet of dust and ice encroaches upon the Earth's atmosphere. Of all that we have prepared beforehand, this courier is the most special. For it contains frozen in its core organic molecules of glycolaldehyde. And now it has collided and delivered its contents to the hot Earth and its pools of hot, acidic water.

"Are you curious, Brinn, as to how life can sprout from such a simple molecule, a seed, if you will? Well, in its current state, it is just a physical property of the Earth, one more natural, geological process. Observe in the distance a storm approaching. This is an electrical storm, an induction of current via the collision of water vapors carrying a charge. And sure enough, the storm has produced an arc of lightning. See where the lightning has struck? It has struck the pool of water that lies before us, the same pool of water that contains all of the right ingredients for life. The radiative stimulus has transmuted the mixture, combining molecules and proteins and carbonates and sulfides and minerals. The pool now contains the building blocks of life. But the process has only just begun. The storm's winds have driven across the surface of the pool, and its waters are spilled into a steady flow toward the ocean. Hydrologic dynamics demonstrate that the truth of reality does not lie still but moves toward a singular purpose, always. Eventually, the flow reaches the ocean, and its precious contents are carried out into the deep blue. The tidal forces of the ocean, the thrashing back and forth, the sloshing to and fro, will initiate the evolutionary processes. The fight for survival has begun. Life will adapt. It has been designed to do so. Evolution of life is a natural consequence of the universe's stabilization per hydrologic dynamics. This principle underwrites the doctrine of the Principal Cause, according to which Life, a creation of Life, creates Life, and Life lives forever.

"Each tiny, single-celled organism maintains an electric charge, which initiates the cell's consumption of proteins to engage motility. This consumption produces oxygen as a waste product, which is expelled from the organism into the atmosphere. These organisms, which we call prokaryotes, will fill up the atmosphere with oxygen and will serve as the front for a symbiotic relationship between the future life forms, a balanced ecology, or, as we like to say, the womb for progressive humanity. The prokaryotes are seedlings for other life forms. As they evolve into eukaryotes, which are more advanced in their cellular structure, they will branch in two different directions. Those organisms close to the ocean's surface will adapt to absorb sunlight and initiate photosynthesis. Others will adapt to the lower depths and form into migrant life forms. Currently, the atmosphere is still too hostile to support life, so the ocean becomes in the beginning life's sanctuary. As atmospheric conditions stabilize and change toward supporting life, both branches will leave the ocean and emerge upon dry land. It is here, Brinn, that the fight for survival dramatically increases. Mutations result from drastic evolutionary changes. Symbiosis branches into predation. Asexuality branches into sexuality. Population controls initiate, which steadies the population growth in relation to the environment.

"Correlating to hydrologic dynamics, we have engaged a time-expansion spinorial effect for the solar region. By implementing a time-dilation bubble within our shielding, we can watch the world take form. The sky is perpetually dim because the bubble averages the light vectors for each cycle of day and night, calculable as the light vectors penetrate the bubble. While we walk upon the surface, you will see the ocean rise above all land. You will see it then recede, exposing a continent, which spans a third of the Earth. You will see that the land is shaped by natural forces, wind and water erosion, volcanic eruptions, earthquakes, meteorites. It fractures into multiple continents, and the pieces shift around, instigated by the rotation of the Earth's molten core. The Earth's crust is fractured into plates, and these plates reshape as they jostle one another. As the continents move, some collide, pushing up the Earth and forming mountain ranges. Others drift to the other side of the globe, widening the oceans.

"The breathable air consists of chemical compounds derived from elements that can only be produced in the heart of dying stars. When the star is in its last throes of nucleosynthesis, the force of gravity increases its pressure upon the core, fusing matter into heavier elements. So by living and breathing, a life form is consuming the very essence of being that propagates the universal fluid. All life is sustained and connected by that essence. That principle suffices as the universal cost of living and the consequent obligation to give back what has been consumed. Each individual creature's body, as bound into a biological construct, processes air differently. During that process, the body transforms the chemical compound, so as to consume some portion. Every individual is unique in that regard, so much so that every breath relays the signature of the individual. The meaning of life is to integrate oneself into the natural order of the universe, to contribute to the creation and sustenance of life. While life is a natural consequence of the universe's stabilization, eternal life is the reward of contributing to that stabilization, since, to accomplish such a feat, one must have already emerged from darkness to light, from brevity to eternity, from nothingness to infinity. That is our dream. As winds flow to and fro, dreams fade in and out. Even so, we approach all truth with steps and strides, carefully, thoughtfully. There is so much to discuss that time becomes irrelevant. Why falter in haste? Principle is at stake. The truth of reality is easily convoluted, requiring much patience and prudence in the pursuit thereof. So I beseech you, Observant One, to take great care in your steps and strides. Pause and consider. Always. As you breathe in, you have taken from the Universe. Breathe out to give back, for you are connected to the essence of being. You have so much to offer, and we receive every contribution. Life is precious, requiring that every moment be filled with effort, even if all you do is stand still and bathe in the warmth of the starlight. Your wonderment is not in vain. The stars have the truth, and the answers lie behind the dark clouds in the nighttime sky. You know the stars are there. That is true faith, which is having comfort in the knowledge of the fact.

"Dreams, Observant One, are the bridge between the real and the ideal. We know what is the best approach. We have always known. We pursue all truth steadfastly, never wavering from our objective. We share our dream, into which we were born from the first epochal, and we have transited from there to here, always mindful of the Principal Cause. To share our essence is our labor, to promote hope and faith in love and peace. Our offer is open to anyone who desires it, since such a desire is induced by progressive humanism. It transcends boundaries of islands, continents, planets, and galaxies. It transcends the scientific order of species and genera from anywhere in the universe. It transcends the biological constructs designed by the naturality of evolutionary processes. Skin, hair, sensory organs, limbs for mobility, these pertain to the most appropriate means for the biological construct to survive in a conditional environment. Humanism, on the other hand, is the supremacy of the intellect over the emotive state of the biological construct. Memory and dream dominate behavior, in contrast to ego and self-preservation. You see these things, Brinn. You have seen them, and you will see more of them. As you observe, think on these things, and consider their import to the natural order. Not only will you discover the meaning of life, you will come to realize that you have the ability to add meaning to life. If you find that the Principal Cause has some validity, then you'll learn and know the most appropriate means to accomplish such an endeavor."

CHAPTER 5

The Guardians willingly and lovingly share their thoughts with me. I hear them, one at a time, all at once, whatever I choose. It's a gentle wave of information, caressing my very soul. Truth. The truth of reality—I see it clearly. Light carries information, and every photon of light is traceable. The tiny particle of energy passes through the neutrino background. It bears a magnetic resonance, enough to wobble the neutrinos, leaving a brief tensorial displacement. When one sees light in its glory, the information it gives is truthful, and whatever is truthful is good. If the light is dark with inaccurate information, all one can see is distortion of reality. Photometry reveals from where an object had come and to where an object will go.

Soleran steps from the circle and approaches the holographic image of Endhera. "Which of the Endheran humans bears the greatest candidacy for our intervention?"

"I have traced lineage routes to nine potential candidates," Dyllon says, being the project manager over the development of life on Endhera. From the holograph arise nine images of Endheran people. "The most appropriate candidate from amongst these is one named Antraxid." One of the nine Endheran images enlarges to stand out.

Soleran approaches the image, which is half his size but hovers in the air at eye level. "What does your observation reveal?" Soleran asks Dyllon, turning to face his companion.

Dyllon folds his arms behind his back and speaks. "Antraxid is curious about his environment. He sees the world slightly differently from his fellow Endherans. But within, he struggles with dissonance induced by the conflict between what he feels is truth and what his forefathers have told him is truth." Dyllon gestures with his right hand, activating holographic commands, and more information displays emerge from Antraxid's image.

One display is a neural-nodal model of his autonomous nervous system, including his brain. The other is a marquee flash-through of various bodily functions, such as hairs standing up, pupils dilating, rate of breathing, and so forth.

I observe all of this and wonder in amazement. This analysis is speculative, but the accuracy seems uncanny. Every detail can be scrutinized, so that every tiny bit of information can be extracted. On Ibalexa, there were these two opposing doctrines, predestination and free will. As I think on these things, I realize that one doesn't negate the other. Both are true and perhaps even contingent on each other. There are so many factors that contribute to a person's development and well-being. Behavior is predictable, so a person's choice can be foreseen from afar. Within that person's perspective, there is freedom of choice. From without, however, choices are predeterminable.

I return my gaze to the holographic images. They flash quickly as the *Intrepidium* records each projected outcome of every point of space and time on Endhera. I learn what I can. I contemplate what I learn. I hear … no, feel, the thoughts of the Guardians.

O precious Earth, how you bear the love and hope of Eternity. You yet do not know that you are favored by the Morning Rise. The Hosts of Heaven listen for the cry of that newborn marked for the destiny of saving grace, at which their souls will rejoice with the purest joy. When news of success reaches the depths of Epsilon Truthe, all Guardians everywhere will cease their activities for a moment to reflect on the purpose of our existence: to promote life, living and aliveness, the awakening of consciousness, the mind's connection to the essence of the universe. The mind speaks out, and all the universe hears, "I am." The heavens will resonate with the song of joy.

I've heard that song before. How can I describe it? It's like bathing in an ocean and feeling the waters slowly pick you up and carry you to another location. It's like a mother gently rocking her infant and then laying the child down in soft bedding. It's like sunlight and a cool breeze laboring together to comfort the skin, taking turns in a swirling caress.

Through much of Endhera's evolution, I am silent and contemplative. I am allowed to activate a real-time holograph image of a region and observe nature give it form. At times, I accompany Guardians to the surface to see Endhera, face-to-face. I walk upon the clouds and cast my gaze down below. I step through torrential storms and on occasion allow winds to caress my cheeks. I feel the earth tremble below my feet and can hear the swish of its molten-iron core churn deep within. I do not feel the effects of time except within my soul. The conflict is threefold. When time passes, I mourn. When something new is set to arrive, I am anxious. I labor to find contentment in the moment.

After the passing of much of Endhera's time, which is to me nothing more than the passing of a light breeze, I watch as the Earth endures the changes of its ecology. A blanket of white flows across the central landmass from the north to the equator, where it eventually fades into a variety of colors—blues, greens, browns, and reds, but mostly green. So much of Endhera reminds me of Ibalexa. It's a beautiful world teeming with life. Using the holographics of the *Intrepidium*, I can pan anywhere on Endhera, zooming in and out, lifting geological layers, even experimenting with simulations. For example, what would happen if this particular river dried up, or what would happen if this particular volcano erupted, things like that. A few humanoid populations evolve. One species resembles Dyllon's candidate. The creature has a feature resembling a mix of feathers and fur, although it still looks reptilian. Another species appears to be losing its reptilian features and evolving more toward mammalian. A third species seems to be retaining only reptilian features, yellow bulbous eyes with dark-green scales and brown plates and with combs and horns instead of hair.

The landscape changes, as people migrate across the surface of the Earth. At night, specks of light shine up as communities grow larger and larger. The night is peaceful and quiet with the occasional celebratory noises of songs and cheers. The day, however, is mostly filled with the noise of war. Hordes of Endheran warriors march across the surface, clashing, fighting, killing. This saddens me at times.

"Soleran?" I ask.

As he turns to look at me, the sun reflects off his hair, and a gold tint flows down the locks. A cocked eyebrow prompts me to continue.

"War and violence aren't just phenomena of Ibalexa," I say. "Are they common throughout the universe?"

He sighs and looks off into the distance. He appears to be thinking of a good answer before responding.

"Each entity born and living in the universe, Brinn, bears a biological construct correlating to its environment," Soleran says. "Contingent on the hostility of one's environment, one develops the propensity for war. It's a self-preservative inclination. The people below us are fighting over territory, which is to say, they're fighting to control the natural resources—lumber, food, water, and so forth."

I understand Soleran's answer, but it doesn't alleviate my sadness. From my vantage point, it appears that there are enough resources for everyone. No one has to go hungry. No one has to thirst. No one has to suffer. But the Endherans not only don't know that, they can't know it. They just don't have the capacity to see such a truth. And if they did, would it make a difference?

Soleran rests his hand on my shoulder.

"Don't worry, Brinn," Soleran says. "They will come to see the truth of reality. That is why we are here, to assist them. We only await the birth of one named Antraxid. Then we'll have a precise entry point into Endheran progression. We'll have an opportunity to share a universal truth."

I am comforted by the thought, and I smile.

CHAPTER 6

The infant opens his yellowish, slit-shaped eyes and sees a grown, reptilian man looming over him. A reddish-brown comb dangles from his chin, and green scales cover his face. The man parts his lips slightly, revealing fanged teeth—yellowed, chipped, and slightly worn away. The two are inside a cave.

"Boy," the man says, following it with a hiss. The man looks around and then returns his gaze to the infant. "Oh, the gods will your mother to forgive me! I don't have a choice!" He lifts tightly braided cords connected to the basket in which the infant lies. He raises the fold of a cover upon the infant. He then lifts the basket off the floor and proceeds to the door.

Outside, the infant feels the sting of the chilled air seep in under the blanket. With a motion unintended, the infant manages to pull the blanket down a little. Tree branches hang overhead, with white powder stuck in patches. The basket shakes violently a couple of times as the man hurries along. The infant whimpers occasionally, to alert the man that he is uncomfortable.

"Hush now," the man says. "Don't betray us."

The man stops at a tree. He lays the basket on the snow-laden ground and leans against the tree. He's breathing hard, his misty breath captured in the cold air. Sweat flows down his face. He looks around frantically. Voices behind him prompt him to jerk around and stare in the direction from which he had just come. Quickly, he picks up the basket and starts running again. Soon, the voices are more distinguishable as shouts of "this way," "over here," "I think I see him."

At great length, the man falls to his knees and mumbles to himself over and over, "I can't … I can't …" His breathing is labored, and he is favoring his right side, which drips red. He softly caresses the infant's face. "I've done what I can. You're in the hands of the gods now! May they give you mercy." Finally, he covers the infant tightly with the blanket and pushes the basket into some brush. He then jumps to his feet and runs farther down the trodden path.

The infant boy still manages to pull the blanket down a little. He stares up at a fluttering leaf blowing in the wind. He jerks a little as a blurred image darts by him, then another, and then more. A moment later, everything settles. Quietly, sunlight flutters through the dancing branches onto the infant. As the light flows down the infant's face, he feels its warmth and begins to make a gurgling sound while playing with his fingers. Suddenly, the branches part, and a face appears. It is a strange creature, with long, flowing, silver hair and smooth, dark, tanned skin. She wears a glimmering, white robe. Light radiates from her, brighter even than the sunlight. She is smiling, and the infant makes a little noise, "Eh … eh … eh …"

"You can't stay here, little one," the stranger says. She carefully lifts the basket out of the brush. A flash of light, and she's standing at the door of a cabin. She looks different, smaller, younger, familiar, a pale-gray skin with a light blonde hair pulled back into a ponytail. She wears a heavy, dull-brown wool coat.

A moment later, the door opens. An elderly woman staggers into the doorway. "Yes?" She's short but heavyset and hunched over slightly. Her gray hair is thinning, showing scalp below.

"Hello, Tooxu," the stranger says. "You may not remember me. It's Addy. You gave me shelter and food last year."

"Oh, yes, child, I do remember," the old woman says. "I remember your voice. Come in, come in. Get outta that cold!" Tooxu steps aside and allows Addy to enter.

The infant gurgles a little, and the old woman startles slightly. "Do I hear a baby?"

"You do," Addy says. "A boy."

The old woman stares ahead and slowly stumbles toward the infant, her hand extended to feel her way. Addy grasps the old woman's hand and gently moves it toward the infant's face. The old woman's wrinkled hand touches the infant's skin and feels up and down his face. Tooxu lets a gasp escape her mouth.

"He can't be but a few months old," Tooxu says.

"I found him," Addy says. "His basket was hidden. I would have passed him, but I heard his playful noise."

"In the cold? All alone?" Tooxu says. "The heavens!" The old woman makes her way to a rocker near the fire. She sits forward and motions to Addy. "Bring the infant near. Hurry! Before the chill sets in. Oh, poor babe, left to the wind and beasts."

"I don't think it was abandonment," Addy says. She obeys the old woman and brings the child closer to the fire. Addy sits upon the stone hearth and gently rests the basket between her and Tooxu.

"Why do you say, child?" Tooxu asks.

"Eh … eh … ooo …" the infant coos, his gaze following his own hands hung in the air.

"There was an obvious disturbance in the snow," Addy says. "And blood. I think something has happened, something bad." Alarmingly, Addy reaches over and grasps the old woman's hand resting upon her knee.

"Heavens have mercy!" Tooxu adds.

"Mother Tooxu?" Addy says.

"Child?" Tooxu says.

"I can't stay," Addy answers, pulling her hand away. "I have urgent business in Shelquin Village."

There is silence. The old woman sighs and slowly starts to nod in understanding. "You mean to leave the babe with me?" Tooxu asks.

"I can't take him with me," Addy says, looking out the window. "My journey is long and hard. As you say, the wind and beasts."

There is more silence.

The old woman casts her blind eyes toward the fire, focusing on the crackling sound of the wood. "Is this your baby?" Tooxu asks softly.

"Oh no, Mother Tooxu," Addy says with a light chuckle. "I have yet to know a man in such a way." On her knees, Addy approaches the old woman. She takes the old woman's hand and places it upon her belly. "See, my womb hasn't carried a babe yet."

The old woman lets out a sigh of relief. "Very well, then," Tooxu says. "I will take care of the baby. But I must ask something of you." The old woman leans forward in the rocker and grasps about until her hand finds the side of the basket. She then gently pulls the basket closer to the rocker.

"Only ask, Mother Tooxu," Addy says. "Know that I love you and will do whatever you ask." Addy leans forward and rests her hand and chin on the old woman's knee.

Tooxu then softly strokes Addy's hair. "Visit me often, child! I'm an old woman and was content to leave this Earth during my sleep. But now ..." She sighs.

"Mother Tooxu," Addy says, taking Tooxu's hand and lightly kissing it, "I will do this."

"Very well, then," Tooxu says. "What should be the baby's name?" She leans over and feels for the infant. Her hand finds his belly, and she squeezes and shakes playfully. The infant giggles.

"What do you think?" Addy asks.

Tooxu chuckles.

"What?" Addy asks with a chuckle of her own.

"Long ago," Tooxu begins, "way, way, long ago, I had a child, who didn't survive the night."

"That's sad," Addy comments with a frown.

"It was a hard time for me," Tooxu says. She inhales deeply and releases a slow sigh. "The next day, we buried him, me and my husband. I gave him a name right then, not at his birth or during the night, but after he had died. I named him Sontrixid, which, in the old tongue, means 'the hurt in my life.'"

Addy takes her hand again and squeezes. The old woman pauses and pats the top of Addy's hand.

"What will you name this baby boy?" Addy asks.

"Perhaps the opposite word—Antraxid, which means 'the pleasure in my life.'"

"Oh, that's so nice," Addy says. "I like it!"

"So be it," Tooxu says. "Let this boy infant be called Antraxid from here onward."

"Antraxid," Addy says, reaching over and stroking the infant's cheek. "That's your name, little one."

An hour later, Addy steps outside the door. She takes a deep breath, inhaling the chilled air mixed with wood smoke. In a flash of light, she resumes her celestial form, putting away the Endheran disguise. Then she teleshifts away.

"Wow," I say, looking at Evalene. "You guys are good!"

She smiles. "We do have our moments."

Addia-Sahl appears on the bridge and walks over to Soleran, Dyllon, and Leostrom. Dyllon is analyzing more data on a holographic prompt.

"If we intervene at these points in his life," Dyllon says, "he will survive to find himself in the position to become leader of his people." He motions to the prompt, which depicts a timeline.

One moment shows a boy running along a path in the wilderness. The hair on his head consists of long, thin, black feathery down. He's a little on the thin side, but he is fast and strong, as if energy has built up in him and needs release. He wears cut-off pants that sit above his knees. Tufts of thin feathers grow from the sides of his knees and elbows. A small, reddish comb dangles from the boy's chin.

The image shifts slightly, moving from the boy and up into the trees a distance away from him. A predator hides on a limb and watches the boy approach. With its elongated body, it resembles some of the wild cats we had on Ibalexa, but it's huge, easily two meters in length. Its face is flattened, with pointed ears and long whiskers. A nine-year-old boy would normally be an easy meal. The beast yawns, lifts itself, and stretches. Antraxid sees it and comes to a quick stop, his foot digging into the dirt. For a moment, beast and boy stare at each other. Then the beast begins to growl. It bares fangs and leaps.

I can feel my heart pound heavily in my chest. As I watch through the holographic display, the scene slows to show a surreal image of hovering beast poised above a frightened boy holding his arms in front of his face. Addia-Sahl emerges from the shadows, partly transparent. Her eyes flash, and a blue light flashes down the backside of the beast. Just as quickly, she disappears, and the time dilation ceases.

The beast lands on its feet just a forearm's length from Antraxid. The boy turns and starts to run, but he stops himself. His breathing is hard, and his eyes are wide with terror, but he stands his ground. The beast sits but keeps its eyes locked onto the boy. Antraxid steps forward slowly, carefully. He leans in so that his face is directly in front of the beast's flattened muzzle. It sniffs him and then turns and walks away.

Antraxid watches as it disappears into the brush. He then peers up into a beam of sunlight that has penetrated the wood's canopy and spotlighted him. He squints his eyes and turns his face slightly. He exhales slowly, catching his breath, and then turns and darts down the path.

"Yeah!" the boy says, leaping into the air.

The bridge erupts in chuckles. I turn to look at the other Guardians, whose eyes are locked onto their own displays. Addia-Sahl has reemerged onto the bridge near my display.

"Whew!" I say.

Addia-Sahl smiles.

"What was that about?" I ask.

"It's a gift, one of many we plan to share, a moment of smallest courage that will blossom later in life when he needs it the most."

Dyllon maneuvers the timeline to the next point. Holographic lines end with conclusory data. An image phases in, an image that occupies the entire room. It's as if the planet's surface is taking form. Soon, the white of the room is replaced by the greens and browns of the Earth. The view pans around and sets upon Tooxu's cabin. The building remains unchanged, but the greenery around the cabin has grown.

Antraxid appears from the woods. He carries a basket filled with fruits and tubers. He's much older now, still not yet an adult, but close, perhaps a couple of years off. Antraxid rushes up to the porch. He barges through the front door, spending a brief moment to stand in the doorway as if expecting a welcome. He sighs and closes the door. Then he places the basket on the table and empties its contents, examining each piece of food. He then walks over to the bed. Tooxu lies there asleep, covered tightly in a worn, gray blanket. The old woman is thinner and most of her hair is gone. Antraxid sits on the edge and lays his hand gently on her shoulder. With a delicate touch, he shakes her shoulder.

"Mmmmm," Tooxu says. Her breathing hastens loudly. "Oh," she groans. Tooxu then slowly rolls over to face Antraxid. Her eyes aren't fixed on him perfectly, set just over his shoulder. He leans over to occupy the space.

"Child," she says, her voice low and weak, "have you prepared yourself?"

Antraxid smiles. He returns his hand to her shoulder and gently squeezes. "I'm prepared, Mother Tooxu." His smile fades, and he closes his eyes and lowers his head.

"Don't be sad, child," Tooxu says. "I have lived a very fruitful life." She fumbles around a little with her right hand until she finds Antraxid's hand. She pats it and then takes hold of it tightly, lifting it up and placing it on her chest. "You have been the delight of my heart all these years. You gave me reason to go on living. Long ago, I would have been satisfied to lie here and go to sleep for good. I remember …" Tooxu falls under a coughing spell.

"Easy, Mother Tooxu," Antraxid says, helping her restrain herself.

"Mmm, yes," she manages. "I remember—I remember on the day I buried Sontrixid—on that day I prayed to the gods that I would be given another chance to raise a child, just another chance." Tooxu pauses, as if resting. "Destiny brought you to me, Antraxid. Destiny.

Go now, and I'll fall asleep for one last time, having fulfilled my duty."

Antraxid rests his head on her shoulder. He cries.

The young man exits the cabin and heads in the direction of the city of Khatid.

The city walls jut from the earth, appearing from behind trees. Antraxid emerges into the outer grounds and passes various people, mostly vendors, some entertainers, and a few city guards. They eye him as he walks by, taking note of his humble clothing and lack of shoes, some scoffing, others snickering. A few even pinch their noses. Antraxid takes notice and lowers his head in shame. Suddenly, a wind blows hard. Many booths lose valuables in the wind, and the vendors run off in pursuit. Just as quickly as it started, the wind stops. Antraxid chuckles. He approaches the front gates and notices that the wind has blown through the city's blossoming trees. The road is eerily covered in broken branches, leaves, and flowers from the trees. An older gentleman dressed in an elaborate red-and-black long coat watches Antraxid walk down the street. The gentleman is mostly reptilian, with some feathers sprouting from his scalp. As Antraxid approaches, they lock eyes. The gentleman steps out into the street to intercept Antraxid.

"Come here, boy," says the man. He takes hold of Antraxid's arm and pulls him near, looking on the back of Antraxid's neck. "The gods!" The gentleman looks around frantically. His eyes fall upon a soldier, who is watching the two. The gentleman motions to the soldier, and the soldier immediately obeys. "I had a dream," the man says to Antraxid. "I saw a son of a king walking down this very street. There was celebration and cheering. Flowers and palms were cast down in front of him as he strolled." The soldier steps up but waits for the gentleman to finish. "Except, there was no one in sight. I then noticed that the sounds came from the above the trees, in the air. It was as if the messengers of the gods were the ones celebrating. It was as if they tread upon the treetops."

Antraxid looks up at the treetops in bewilderment. He then looks back at the man.

"Garakis is king now," the man says. "He was cousin to a former king named Derlach."

Antraxid remains silent.

"You don't know this, do you?"

Antraxid shrugs.

"The king's son is marked, having been marked from birth," says the man. "It's a tattoo etched in the scales on the boy's neck. It's a cross topped with a loop." The gentleman finishes and looks for Antraxid's reaction. Upon witnessing Antraxid's continued confusion, he chuckles. "You bear the mark." The man turns to the soldier. "Take this boy to the king. Inform His Majesty that I hurry to conclude my business and will return immediately."

"Yes, sir, Counselor Mheruse," the soldier responds.

The soldier leads Antraxid toward the palace. After several paces, Antraxid looks over his shoulder at the man one last time but returns to the soldier's direction. As boy and soldier walk down the street, Antraxid observes the palace towering over some buildings. Three balconies, a large central balcony, and two smaller ones on each side overlook an area hidden by buildings. From the left-side balcony hangs an orange banner, with some imagery that's hard to discern. From the right-side balcony hangs a purple banner, with different imagery etched in black that is harder still to discern.

"Stop here," says the soldier. He faces the balconies, standing at attention. Suddenly he salutes, bringing his left fist up to his chest. He holds it there and waits.

Antraxid sees a man emerge onto the central balcony. There is a cheer from the unseen area below the balcony hidden behind the buildings. The man raises his hands in the air. The cheering quiets. The man then speaks, but Antraxid and the soldier are too far away to hear. Finally, the man points to the orange banner. Two figures emerge onto the balcony left of the king. They release the orange banner. A commotion sounds from the unseen area, as if a battle has taken place. But it's over just as quickly.

"Victory," says the soldier. He drops his salute and then leads Antraxid to the palace.

A while later, Counselor Mheruse enters the king's hall and walks past the attendants. At the end of the hall is King Garakis, sitting on his throne. He is reptilian, with greenish-gray skin and a black-and-yellow stripe flowing between his eyes down the length of his muzzle. He wears a red coat with gold embroidery and hard, blackened leather boots. Under the parted coat, the king wears chain-mail armor. A gold crown rests upon his head. The throne is made of wood embedded with pieces of animal bones and leather straps.

Antraxid stands off to the side, quiet and contemplative.

"Greetings, Counselor," Garakis says as Mheruse bows.

The counselor straightens and takes a deep breath. "It is he, Your Majesty," Mheruse says at last.

"Are you positive?" asks the king, reaching over and lifting up a copper-colored goblet. He takes a drink and then locks his eyes onto the counselor.

"I am, Your Majesty," Mheruse responds.

"Are you sure?" the king asks.

"Yes, Your Majesty," Mheruse answers immediately.

The king leans forward. "Do you stake your life on it?"

The hesitation is brief. "Yes, I do," Mheruse says with some nervousness.

The king leans back. "Come forward, boy," he commands, setting the goblet down on the small table next to the throne.

Antraxid obeys immediately.

The king looks him up and down and releases a deep sigh. He studies the boy for several minutes. "Where you been all these years?"

"I was raised by an elderly lady in the woods," Antraxid says. He looks the king in the eyes only briefly, lowering his gaze to the floor after speaking.

"You're supposed to be dead. Do you know who you are?" Garakis asks.

"Yes, sire," Antraxid answers. "The former king Derlach was my father."

The king remains quiet.

Antraxid continues, "My godmother—Tooxu was her name—told me who I was a few days before she passed. It is by her counsel that I stand before the King of Khatid."

"I killed your father, who was my cousin," Garakis says. "He forced my hand. Nevertheless, I killed him and took the throne."

Antraxid nods.

"So," the king says, lifting up the goblet, "you here to reclaim your father's seat?" He lifts the cup and takes a drink.

Antraxid shakes his head in denial and lowers his gaze.

"Give me a reason why should I not fall upon the progeny of my worst enemy and slay him without mercy?" Garakis asks, turning his head to peer at the boy with one eye.

"Ahem," Mheruse coughs slightly.

The king's attention shifts to the counselor. "Speak your mind."

"Your Majesty," Mheruse begins, "the gods have laid this design before us in my dreams and have now brought it to full fruition, exactly as expected."

"The gods," Garakis utters unenthusiastically.

"Now, considering the queen's situation, Your Majesty," Mheruse says, "it may be part of the gods' design that the king adopt this son as his own. With the boy bearing Your Majesty's surname and also being of the line of kings, it seems very fitting."

"Do you believe in the gods, boy?" the king asks Antraxid.

The hesitation was brief but blatant. "I wrestle with my doubts, but I confess that I don't know."

The king laughs. "That's good enough for me." The king then leaps to his feet. "Hear me, Court of Khatid," Garakis begins, "due to the barren womb of my wife, the queen, I hereby adopt this boy as my son."

The guests in the throne room, numbering about forty, all erupt in applause.

Antraxid looks at Mheruse in amazement. The counselor responds with a wink and a smile.

"Now," Garakis continues, "would someone please take this ruffian and clean him up?" Servants quickly approach Antraxid and coax him to follow. "Give him a much-needed bath. Don him in royal garb. And someone summon the queen to this court so that I can tell her that my promise to her years ago has finally been fulfilled. I have given her a son." The king sits down and mumbles to himself, "Now maybe she'll get off my back."

The image of Khatid begins to fade, and the bridge of the *Intrepidium* takes its place.

"We calculated all of this, Brinn," Evalene says to me. She places her hand gently upon my back. "We saw this in our projections."

I'm wide-eyed in amazement.

"And thus we approach the final temporal node for intervention," Dyllon says. He touches the last node on the holographic timeline. "This is the most important entry."

Antraxid is sitting on his throne in the main hall, along with the usual attendants— guests, servants, counselors, and soldiers. His comb is more pronounced and longer. He wears the gold crown and a coat inlaid with many colors. Soleran, Leostrom, and Addia-Sahl teleshift near the main doors. The guests panic and rush to the walls. The king's guards, numbering twenty, immediately leap in between Soleran and Antraxid. They raise their spears and wait for Soleran's response. Soleran teleshifts past the guards and stands before Antraxid. The king panics and falls back onto his throne. He frantically grabs for safety, eventually pulling himself up on the throne. The guards turn and see Soleran behind them and rush to attack. As they thrust their spears, the heads of the spears collide with Soleran's shielding, producing static, hissing noises.

Antraxid watches as the guards labor in vain to defend him. He does this for a few minutes. Soleran stands as if waiting for Antraxid to do something.

"Stop!" Antraxid commands the guards.

All but one obey. The one guard continues to thrust his spear into Soleran's shielding. Antraxid leaps to his feet and looks at the guard threateningly. The guard notices Antraxid's look and stops. He backs away, his eyes to the ground.

Antraxid looks hard at Soleran, studying the stranger up and down. He then sits back down on his throne. The king sighs and gazes into Soleran's eyes. Soleran answers the gesture with a raised eyebrow. Antraxid takes a deep breath.

"Lords," Antraxid says, "who can oppose your authority?"

"Greetings," Soleran says. "We have much to discuss."

"How can I be of service to you, my lords?" Antraxid asks.

"We are paying you a visit, King Antraxid," Soleran says. "Forgive us our abrupt arrival."

Antraxid pauses, caressing his chin with his right hand. "Of course," Antraxid answers. "There is no offense, my lords. You are most welcome in my court."

"We are grateful, King Antraxid," Soleran says. "We come in peace."

"That much is obvious," Antraxid says. "But again, I ask, how can I be of service to you?"

"We observed that you have a dilemma," Soleran says.

"Dilemma?" Antraxid asks. The Endheran king sighs.

"This day, of all days, bears heavy upon you," Soleran says.

"You?" Antraxid starts to ask, standing. "You know of my dilemma?"

"Yes," Soleran says, "we are here to assist you in your decision."

The king walks down the steps toward Soleran.

"Who ..." The king starts to ask but waits until he is before Soleran. "Who are you?"

"We call ourselves Guardians," Soleran answers. "We heard your prayer for relief."

"You heard me pray?" Antraxid asks.

"Yes," Soleran answers, "we did." He smiles and takes in a deep breath.

"Then you already know of the burden that weighs upon my heart," Antraxid says.

"That is correct," Soleran responds.

The king walks past Soleran toward the balcony. He walks past the doorways out onto the balcony itself, which overlooks the plaza below. The plaza is full of people, arranged in particular patterns.

There are a hundred Khatid soldiers standing with swords poised at their right side. Kneeling beside each soldier is a Silithid prisoner. The prisoners are not distinguishable from the Khatid soldiers.

"We are aware of the significance of this day, King Antraxid," Soleran says, following the Endheran king onto the balcony. The other two Guardians remain in the throne room. "I hope to share my counsel with you, to help you resolve your dilemma."

The king turns from Soleran to overlook the people below him. "The former king, whom I called my father, taught me this tradition," Antraxid says. "He taught me that it was my duty to see to the slaughter of my enemies, in times of peace and war."

"This hurts you?" Soleran asks.

"It does," Antraxid says, his eyes riveted on the plaza.

"Is it possible your father erred?" Soleran asks.

The Endheran king turns to look at the Guardian. "Only you, sir, can know that answer."

Soleran reaches out and places his hand on the king's shoulder and squeezes gently. "Every generation bears its own errors, Antraxid," Soleran says. "Each generation answers to its own responsibility."

The Endheran king glances at the gesture and then looks into Soleran's eyes. Antraxid then closes his eyes and breathes deeply. "What am I to do? You probably already know of this tradition, held every fifth year for the last three hundred years."

"Hundreds of years ago," Soleran begins, "King Arkalonod repelled an invasion by the neighboring kingdom, Silithid. In response, he counterinvaded along the border, rounding up villagers as prisoners. Then he initiated a blood sacrifice to the Khatid god of war, Rhakidon. The tradition continues to this day."

"Then you know the nature of my dilemma," Antraxid says.

Soleran scans Antraxid's neural net to reconfirm his initial study. "Your dilemma is to find justification for the death of innocent people not associated with an invasion that occurred hundreds of years before their birth."

Antraxid remains silent as he looks at Soleran incredulously.

"The ritual of the blood debt," Soleran continues, "calls for two banners to be hung, each on one side of the royal balcony." Soleran steps to the right. "The orange banner of war commands the soldiers in the plaza below to slay the prisoners in their custody." Soleran then turns and takes a few steps to the left of Antraxid. "The purple banner commands the soldiers to stay their swords and release their grip upon the prisoners. Purple lets the prisoners go. It is a banner of peace, of mercy. The entire spectacle is to show the enemy that, although mercy is an option, it will never be given."

Each banner dangles from a small balcony populated by two soldiers, whose sole duty is to watch for the king's gesture and release the banner from the balcony. When the banner falls to the ground, the color tells the soldiers in the plaza whether to kill the prisoners or let them go.

Soleran turns from the purple banner to Antraxid. "Your dilemma," Soleran continues, "is whether innocent people should die."

"Tradition says so," Antraxid responds.

"What authority does tradition bear on the full spectrum of time?" Soleran asks.

"Tradition tells us what our fathers did," Antraxid answers. "We need it as a guide."

"And your fathers," Soleran continues, "were right in their decisions?"

"We have to think so," Antraxid says. "What else do we have to use as a guide, if not tradition?" The king huffs and bites on his lower lip. He looks away, shaking his head.

"Your conscience," Soleran says. "In the same manner you are doing right now."

The Endheran king sighs heavily and turns to face the soldiers in the plaza. "King Garakis counseled me to show no mercy to the Silithid," Antraxid says.

"Why?" Soleran asks.

"Because they showed no mercy to Khatid," Antraxid says. "Wound for wound, he told me."

"But you struggle with the concept?" Soleran asks.

"What is mercy?" Antraxid says. "Who deserves mercy?"

"Mercy is granted to those deemed undeserving," Soleran answers.

"Who," Antraxid begins again, whispering to himself as if no one else is present, "deserves mercy?"

"No one deserves mercy, King Antraxid," Soleran says. "For such an idea would mean that mercy could be earned. Unfortunately, mercy earned is no longer mercy but a mere compensation."

Antraxid turns to his counselors still in the throne room. One named Vhatik was listening and steps forward to join Antraxid and Soleran on the balcony. The counselor is dressed in brown robes of elaborate patterns and laces. His skin is wrinkled, and small clumps of matted gray hair protrude from under his bowl-shaped hat. Instead of the reptile's muzzle, he has a flatter face.

"Tell me," Antraxid says to Vhatik, "what is mercy?"

"Mercy," Vhatik answers, "is a folly."

The king scrunches his eyebrows.

"We have already discussed this, Your Majesty," Vhatik says.

"I'm not satisfied with the arguments," Antraxid answers. He bangs his fist on the railing of the balcony.

"Mercy is weakness," Vhatik says.

"Why?" Antraxid asks.

"An act of mercy to one's enemy tells the enemy that his actions have no consequences," Vhatik says.

Antraxid turns to Soleran. "What do you say?"

"Mercy overrules judgment," Soleran says. "Mercy requires one to overcome one's own desires for vengeance. The desire for vengeance is a natural, emotional response to a perceived wrong, administered without care to the consequences. An intellectual study of a perceived wrong provides the means to yield mercy."

The king turns and grabs the balcony railing, gazing out at the people below. "I don't know what to do!"

"Drop the orange banner, sire," Vhatik says. "Show no mercy to the Silithid. That is the law. That is the tradition of your fathers.

That is the way of Khatid." Vhatik casts a menacing look in Soleran's direction.

"On the contrary," Soleran says, looking from Vhatik to the king, "you already know what to do."

Antraxid stares at Soleran for several minutes. Casually, Antraxid raises his hand and points to the side of the purple banner. The two guards overlooking the purple banner panic. They jump to their feet and quickly release the ropes. The hundred soldiers below watch in amazement as the purple banner falls. The prisoners themselves cry out in both awe and joy. Vhatik growls in disgust.

Antraxid ignores him, studying the plaza below. A commotion to the lower right catches his gaze. A soldier disobeys the purple banner and slays his prisoner by stabbing him in the chest with a ritual sword. Several Khatid soldiers around him rebuke him for his hasty behavior.

Antraxid hangs over the balcony and yells, "Bring me that soldier! Bring him to me now!" It takes a moment for the soldiers below to interpret the king's desire, but eventually they fall upon the disobedient soldier and subdue him. They drag him toward the palace, along with the slain body of the prisoner.

Both the disobedient soldier and the corpse of the slain prisoner are brought into the throne room. King Antraxid quickly seats himself upon his throne. He bellows in anger at the soldier, "Why did you disobey?"

"I ..." the soldier begins with a tremble. "I was always ... was used to thrusting ... trained to thrust my sword into the ... I ... I was not ..."

"He was obeying tradition," Vhatik says, standing at the king's side.

The king jerks his head to face the counselor.

Vhatik strolls down from the throne dais to the arrested soldier. "He committed no crime, if we recognize the legality of the blood debt."

"I decided there would be no bloodletting this season," Antraxid yells. "He violated my wishes."

"True," Vhatik says, "but tradition is superior to a king's whims."

Antraxid begins to fume silently. He grits his teeth. "Your behavior is equal to the soldier's disobedience."

"No, sire," Vhatik argues. "I have the law on my side. I am sorry to inform your Highness that the king is errant in regards to the law."

The king leaps to his feet. He looks at each of his counselors. They lower their gaze, a small gesture that Antraxid interprets as agreement with Vhatik. Antraxid then looks to Soleran, who stands with Leostrom and Addia-Sahl near the balcony.

"Well?" Antraxid says to Soleran. "How do I answer the charge?"

Soleran raises an eyebrow.

"I have just been rebuked by my counselors as having broken the law," Antraxid says. "How do I answer them?" The king takes a few steps down from the throne toward Soleran. "I made my decision on your counsel."

Soleran nods. "You did." The Guardian takes a few steps forward, as if occupying a place of importance. "And my answer is simple. The tradition of the blood debt was appropriate only for the year that it was initiated, in response to the Silithid invasion, as nothing more than a deterrence to prevent a responsive invasion. It's been three hundred years since the tradition was initiated, long after the Silithid offender had died and left his kingdom to heirs who preferred peace to war."

"But it is tradition," Vhatik counters.

"Tradition is merely a guideline," Soleran answers, casting a disapproving look toward the counselor. "Tradition can be started and ended at the whim of the ruler."

"It is the law, sire," Vhatik continues. Spittle flies from the counselor's mouth. His forehead is tense. He squints his eyes at Soleran.

"Laws made by men," Soleran says, walking toward Vhatik, "can be unmade by men." Soleran and Vhatik lock eyes. The counselor appears undaunted by the Guardian's great height. Soleran continues. "It is the law of the heavens that all men obey without choice."

"Law of the heavens?" Antraxid asks. He steps in between the Guardian and the counselor and faces Soleran. "Can you explain what you mean?"

"Yes," Vhatik says. "Explain what you mean, because our laws are created by the signs of the heavens."

"You are in error," Soleran says to Vhatik. "The laws of men are interpretations of the heavens. Considering that you're missing much valuable information, your interpretation is errant and your laws are fallacious."

"How?" Antraxid says, stepping closer.

Soleran turns and walks back to the balcony, where both Addia-Sahl and Leostrom are standing. He turns and faces the room's occupants.

"The laws of men can be disobeyed. Is this statement true?" Soleran asks.

"Yes!" Antraxid says. "Our prisons testify to that fact!"

"But if a man was to throw himself off your balcony," Soleran asked, "could he disobey the laws of physics that command him to plummet to the Earth?"

"No," Antraxid says. "I suppose not."

"Could your counselors create a law," Soleran continues, "that commands the Earth to release its grip and allow men to softly glide to its surface like a leaf?"

The king turns to Vhatik. The counselor squints his face as if a foul odor had wafted by his nose. "Of course not!" the counselor says. "That's absurd."

"Counselor Vhatik," Soleran says, "the greater sun rises in the east and settles in the west, followed by the lesser sun and the moons."

"And?" Vhatik says.

"Day after day, year after year, generation after generation," Soleran says, pacing back and forth in front of the balcony, "the suns, the moons, and the stars never falter in their obedience to the laws of the heavens." A light breeze flows into the room, and Soleran's robe flutters gently. "Man is bound to the laws of the Earth." Soleran stops and looks to Vhatik. "Is this statement true?"

"Yes!" Vhatik says hastily, then sighs impatiently.

"But what if man learned how to disobey the laws of the Earth?" Soleran says. He lifts the palms of his hands upward and slowly levitates.

The counselors begin to murmur.

"Sorcery!" Vhatik says, pointing his finger at the Guardian. "I am not amused by your sorcery!" His stance is aggressive.

Soleran turns his palms to the floor, and he slowly lowers again. "On the contrary, if one was to understand the laws of nature—every aspect, from the Earth's pull to the ground all the way to the course of the heavenly bodies—and he was to learn how to make use of this knowledge so that he could liberate himself from the laws of the Earth, would you consider him a lawbreaker?"

Murmuring erupts.

"What is your point?" Vhatik asks.

"The laws of nature overrule the laws of men," Soleran says. "We, however, overrule the laws of nature." Soleran walks over to the corpse of the slain prisoner. Gold light flashes across his eyes, and a blue wave of light flows over the corpse. Immediately, the once-dead prisoner sits up and looks around, bewildered. The king, the guests, the counselors, and the guards all gasp and begin to look at each other in disbelief. The Silithid prisoner stands and looks at the stab wound on his chest. The shirt bears the ripped entry and even the bloodstain, but the skin below is completely healed.

King Antraxid walks up to the prisoner and looks him up and down. He then jerks around to face Soleran. The murmuring dies down and silence fills the room.

"With this power," Antraxid says, clenching his fist and shaking it in front him, "you can conquer worlds!"

"We do not conquer worlds," Soleran answers with a sigh. "We create them."

The king is silent, his eyes wide, his jaw dropped. He turns to Vhatik, whose expression mirrors his own. The king walks over to a statue in the corner. It is of an Endheranlike figure with four arms. Then Antraxid turns back to Soleran. "You? You are our ..." the king chokes, "the creators?" Then Antraxid turns to look at the statue.

"The statue that you look upon represents the imagination of men," Soleran says. "Misinterpretations of the signs of the heavens." He turns to look at Leostrom and Addia-Sahl. Both are smiling.

The king walks contemplatively to the throne. He turns slowly and alights gingerly upon the cushioned seat. "We have always thought that perhaps the heavens contained other worlds—worlds such as ours."

"It is the reason for our visit," Soleran says. "We have come to see how this creation, this world is faring." Soleran frowns again and sighs. "We are slightly disappointed."

The king breathes heavily and then runs to Soleran and falls prostrate before the Guardian. "Lord of Heaven!" The king begins to sob. "I am a wicked man! Forgive me! Forgive me my offenses!" The counselors and guards kneel; the restored Silithid prisoner hesitates but eventually mimics the others.

Soleran turns and sees Leostrom cock an eyebrow, smirking. Immediately, Soleran lifts his hand and gestures, gold light flashing across his eyes. The room shifts out of phase, and the occupants appear frozen. Soleran walks over to the other two.

"I suppose we knew we'd run into this issue," Leostrom says. He folds his arms across his chest.

"How do we proceed?" Soleran asks.

"Well," Addia-Sahl says, "we can't propagate the Angelian error." She crosses her left arm across her chest and rests her chin in her right hand. "We should remain aloof."

"The consequence of this moment is monumental," Leostrom says. "We'll have to adjust our approach after this encounter."

"Agreed," Soleran says. He shakes his head and sighs heavily with a frown. The three return to their original spots, and Soleran gestures. The room phases back into normal time.

The king continues to cry. "Forgive me, Lord! Forgive me!"

"Antraxid," Soleran says, "stand." Soleran bends over to assist him.

The king obeys without hesitation. He keeps his face downcast and composes himself a little.

"We are not here to rule over you," Soleran says. "We are here to offer you counsel." Soleran places his hand on the king's shoulder. "I know I said we were disappointed, but only in the fact that men continue to wage war against each other over trivial matters. There are many individuals, including yourself, of whom we are proud, because you strive to overcome humanity's vices and weaknesses. You know in your heart that there is more to living and breathing on the face of the Earth."

"I do, Lord!" Antraxid says. "I do."

"And you shall," Soleran says. "We intervene at this pivotal moment, in which you decide a course to take, one toward your conscience and the other toward your loyalty to the laws and traditions of men." Soleran takes hold of both of Antraxid's shoulders. "Our counsel is simple. Listen to your peace of mind."

Soleran slowly releases his hold on the king. The king looks to the side and then up to Soleran. The king, emotionally distraught, chokes but manages to swallow and take control of his breathing. Nodding, he steps past Soleran and approaches the soldier who had disobeyed him.

"You are … um … absolved," Antraxid says to him. "You are free to go."

The soldier bows and repeatedly thanks the king before taking several steps back.

The king then slowly turns to the Silithid prisoner. "You," Antraxid says to him, "are free to go."

The prisoner lowers his gaze, saddened.

"What is wrong?" Antraxid says.

"I have no place to go," the prisoner says.

"Go home!" Antraxid says.

Again, the prisoner lowers his gaze to the floor. "Please pardon me," the prisoner says. "My home is no more. It was destroyed in the last invasion."

Antraxid grits his teeth and sucks in some air. Before his anger gets the best of him, Antraxid looks over to Soleran. A thousand words of counsel are conveyed in Soleran's facial expression. Antraxid takes several deep breaths.

"I will repay you," Antraxid says, "for any wrongs you have endured at the hands of my father's invasion." The prisoner nods and backs up, as if afraid to lose what was just granted. Antraxid walks to Vhatik, who stands off to the side with a frown. "You, Counselor, are free to go."

"Pardon me, sire?" Vhatik asks. His eyes are sharp and piercing.

"You are relieved of your duties," Antraxid says.

The counselor's breathing becomes labored, and he presses his lips tightly. Without saying anything further, Vhatik turns and storms out of the room. The king returns to his throne. Calmly, he alights on the cushion, shifts to find the comfortable spot and returns his gaze to Soleran.

"What do I do now?" Antraxid asks.

"Your decisions here today will have long-lasting consequences," Soleran says. "And for the better, I might add. Even so, there is much more for you to do."

"I ... I need help," Antraxid says. He leans forward, rests his elbows on his knees, and stares at the floor.

Soleran turns to face the remaining counselors and guards. "Your king needs your help. You will, of course, have to decide if you'll help him or oppose him. But you should know that Antraxid is our chosen one to bring about our desired change for Khatid—and even all of Endhera. In the beginning, long before Khatid was a kingdom, we knew Antraxid would be our choice. Still, we don't stop looking for men such as he to carry out our plans for Endhera's well-being."

Mheruse steps forward. "What is it you want us to do?"

"Pursue justice and righteousness," Soleran says. "At least, do so for a little while. We know the thoughts of people, and many will follow a cause for a little while, until many generations have passed and softened their resolve. When the right time approaches, we will return and intervene in another just cause."

Antraxid leaps from his throne. "You will not stay?"

"No," Soleran says, again resting a hand on Antraxid's shoulder. "It is not our intent to rule over you, or to meddle in your civil affairs, or even to force change upon you. Explore your lives, seek your soul's desires, and learn how to prosper by the labors of your own hands. We will offer guidance, not manipulation or coercion."

"How …" Mheruse begins.

Soleran folds his hands behind his back and raises an eyebrow.

Mheruse sighs and looks down.

"You want to know," Soleran says, "how you can offer devotion to us, how to worship us?"

The counselor steps back and falls in line with the other counselors. He then meets Soleran's gaze. With a sigh, Mheruse nods, casting a brief gaze over at the idol in the corner. "We erred before. How do we not err again?"

"If you would, please, look at the people standing next to you," Soleran says.

The counselors and guards comply and quickly glance around at each other.

"Look, if you would, please, out the windows," Soleran again requests.

Everyone complies, even Antraxid.

"Whatever you do to others," Soleran continues, "from the greatest amongst you to the least, know that it is the same as doing to us." Soleran measures the success of his statement by the facial expressions of the group. The silence prompts him to explain further. "If you will offer love and devotion to each other, from the greatest to the least, it is the same as offering devotion and worship to us."

I listen as Soleran continues to offer counsel. Addia-Sahl and Leostrom join in, and the room is soon abuzz with conversation.

After Soleran finishes with a counselor's questions, Antraxid steps up to him.

"May I speak with you in private, my lord?" Antraxid asks.

"But of course," Soleran answers.

The two walk back to the balcony overlooking the plaza, which has mostly emptied, save a few groups standing here and there.

"I, um ..." Antraxid says. He inhales deeply and lowers his gaze.

"You want to know about your birth father?" Soleran asks.

Antraxid's eyes widen. He answers with a nod.

"Would you be saddened to learn that your birth father was a cruel and unjust man?" Soleran asks.

Antraxid doesn't answer. He makes no physical gestures either. Nothing but silence.

"Your uncle, the brother of your mother, on the other hand, was a just and compassionate man," Soleran continues. "He is the one who rescued you."

"My uncle?" Antraxid asks.

"It cost him his life," Soleran says. "You were delivered to the home of one elderly woman named Tooxu."

The king wipes his face. He stares off into the sky, watching the clouds race by.

"Your birth father became enraged with your mother," Soleran says. "He falsely accused her of adultery, which would have rendered you illegitimate. Fearing for your life, your uncle stole you away and fled the countryside. He traveled for weeks, stopping only for rest. But your birth father's assassins caught up with him. He hid you and fled the scene, only to be overcome by his pursuers down the path a little ways from your hiding spot. You ended up in the care of Tooxu. It was during this time that your father ordered the execution of your mother. Years later, your father's cousin killed him and took the throne."

Antraxid nods, sober and attentive. He waits silently for Soleran to continue.

"The assassins looked for you," Soleran continues. "It didn't take them long to stumble upon Tooxu's cabin." Soleran begins gesturing, and a holographic image unfolds before Antraxid.

There are three men standing outside a cabin. All three are tall and slender, with green scaled skin and yellow eyes with black slits. They wear brown hooded capes, and their clothing is plain, dark-brown.

"A crazy woman lives here," one says to the other two, the one in the middle.

"Oh?" the one on the left asks.

"Rumor has it that years ago, she gave birth to a child," the middle assassin continues. "The child disappeared, though. Folks swear up and down that she and her husband devoured the child." He finishes with a chuckle.

"The gods!" says the assassin on the right.

The cabin opens and the old lady steps out on the porch.

"Who's there?" Tooxu says. "I can hear you from inside, as if you were right at my front door." She wields a long, thick club.

The assassin on the left smirks at her. He approaches her steps to the porch. "Glory to the king," the assassin says.

"Indeed," she finishes. "What do you want, sir? Are you on official business?" Tooxu grips the club tightly.

"A child is lost in the woods," the assassin says. "The king's son was kidnapped by his scoundrel of a brother-in-law. We chased him to an opening in the woods nearby. But he disposed of it somewhere along the path. We can't find it."

"It?" Tooxu asks.

"Yes," the assassin says. "There is, of course, a reward for its ..."

"Look," Tooxu says, "I'm an old woman, long in years, lonely and hungry, having little to eat."

The assassin turns to look at the other two. They all chuckle.

"Fine," the assassin says. "Go back in and shut your door. Good day to you and glory to the king."

"As you say, sir," Tooxu responds. "Good fortunes in finding the child."

The three assassins walk away from the cabin. Tooxu grumbles slightly and returns to the cabin, closing and locking the door.

"If she finds the child," the middle assassin begins, "I wager that it ends up in her belly." Amused, he laughs.

"The child is dead," the assassin on the left says. "The old woman killed it. Let's return and tell King Derlach. I'm tired of wandering around in the cold."

The holographic image fades to nothing.

Antraxid stares at the spot where it imaged. He takes a deep breath and looks up into Soleran's eyes. "How did I survive?"

"We were there, Antraxid," Soleran says. "We weren't about to let anything happen to you." The Guardian places his hand on the king's shoulder and squeezes. "All they had to do was place an ear to Tooxu's door and listen for the sounds of an infant, and we would have cut them down on the spot. It's a little ironic. It was their arrogance that saved them that day."

"What about my uncle?" Antraxid asks. "Or my mother?" He pauses only slightly. Then he almost whispers, "Why didn't you save them?"

"That's harder to explain," Soleran says. "The fates of all involved, from then to today, would have been altered—and for the worse. Our intervention has to be at its minimum, or we risk dissolving the bonds of the natural occurrence. It's difficult to explain fully, but this I can promise: we will reinstate your mother and your uncle at the appointed time. Even so, it was important that the events unfold as they did, most especially for the moment of today."

Antraxid nods and breathes in deeply. He stares at the clouds in the sky. "Thank you," he says to Soleran. He walks back into the throne room.

After a while, the three bid farewell and teleshift back to the *Intrepidium*'s bridge, where Evalene and I are standing and watching the holographic display.

Natharon approaches and activates a holographic interface revealing calculations. "The survivability rating has increased drastically," he says. "It's at 9.7."

CHAPTER 7

Memorandum *Status Quo* re the Olegian Initiative, submitted by Leostrom, First Echelon Officer of the *Order of the Intrepidium*: having been designated by Soleran as the project manager overseeing the Olegian Initiative, I appointed Natharon and Dyllon as my second and third officers and discussed with them the project plan for the initiative. The primary objective was to continue to implement philosophical principles in the psychological development of the Endheran populace. Ensuing objectives would focus on alleviating prevailing philosophical variances. The Olegian Initiative is set for termination, and this memorandum will constitute our conclusions and findings. It will comprise an analysis of observations, including excerpts from the transcript of the subject Endheran named Oleg, herder son of the farmer named Armog. He was small and thin, a bit on the frail side. A scan of his neural net revealed he was both highly imaginative and highly intelligent. His clothing was always modest and made from common materials, like cotton and dull leather. On that day, he wore a light-tan blouse with dark-brown pants, leather strap sandals, and a herder's cloak.

The subject Oleg was a victim of a conspiracy. Photometric analysis had pinpointed the conspiracy as a viable entry point for Guardian intervention. By altering the philosophical development, we would increase the maturation rating from 9.7 to 9.8, the greatest increase compared with any other intervenient candidate at this stage of intervention. Not only that, but all secondary objectives could be fulfilled, which would calibrate time-current deviations and stabilize coefficient variances hindering philosophical maturation and development. We begin by analyzing the subject's transcript:

The Scroll of Oleg: I, Oleg, Son of Armog, upon the wise counsel from Azghak, Chief Counselor to King Sustek, Son of Verrek, deliver to the Asemuran people the Missive from the Divine One, the Most Absolute and Complete, that is, He who appoints Guardians to watch over us and defend us from evil. It was the year 1116, the second month of Arebides, the fourth day of the fifth week, and the twenty-seventh hour, an hour from midnight. It was of the City of Asemur, the city ruled at the time by King Verrek, a city walled and protected from the wild beasts of the vast realm of Kelidid. This was the night that the Absolute visited me.

In my moment of weakness, I called upon the gods of my forefathers, the gods whose names are Isgurud, Elestern, Modi-Vod, and the newest one, known for no more than the last 122 years, Prull the Mighty. In my moment of weakness, I fondled the small figurines depicting the images of these gods taught to us by our forefathers.

My father, Armog, was slain by an assassin and was buried. My mother, by law of her gender, could not inherit his estate, which only consisted of a house and three plots of land. This estate was meager, but I was supposed to inherit this estate, being his firstborn and only son. I, of course, would take care of my mother, so that she would not be in need of anything.

Unfortunately, someone else eyed my father's estate. One of the king's counselors, Vuhzrog, wanted the estate of land, even before my father's death. Vuhzrog had managed to gain ownership of the surrounding plots of land. He owned ninety-seven plots total. His rival, another counselor, Azghak, owned ninety-nine plots. The king owned the most, at 250 plots. But if Vuhzrog could gain my father's estate of a meager three plots, then Vuhzrog would gain the king's favor over the rival Azghak, because he would own a hundred plots. I came to learn of this in the aftermath.

I was horrified to learn that my father had been attacked. He was outside early in the morning. A poison dart was cast at his neck, striking it in the side. For four and a half hours, my father suffered severe convulsions so violent that he broke his own back and crushed his own chest, the latter causing him to suffocate to death within minutes. It was very cruel. My father's friends reasoned that it had to be Pinoxi poisoning. Of all the poisons an assassin could have chosen, he chose the Pinoxi root to kill my father. Such a choice was wicked.

Leostrom's memorandum to file: The pinoxi plant is a solanum class plant with two highly toxic compounds, a potassium-channel compound, decasintoxin, which induces a combined bronchospasmic and diaphragmic convulsion, and a sodium-channel compound, tetradotoxin, which causes muscular paralysis and suffocation by blocking specific receptors. In the case of Oleg's father, Armog, the violence of the convulsions was exacerbated by the body's natural defenses, in which the adrenaline is excreted to counter the muscles' convulsive contractions. With the neural paralysis and consequential lack of muscular support, however, this effect turned antagonistic. The more violent the convulsions, the more adrenaline excreted. The more adrenaline excreted, the more violent the convulsions.

But the worst was yet to come. I had no thought as to my father's estate. I was content to reside in the barn at Old Man Egdeg's place, where I tended his farm animals—a few ghads, a couple of flets, and several emeeshes—all for a humble wage. It was not hard work, as the animals were always easy to care for. I enjoyed it because I could watch over them while sitting under a tree, and I could spend my time writing poetry and daydreaming. I did receive many jeers for this activity, especially from the hunters, whose wages were high.

I was shocked and terrified when charges of murder were brought against me, with two witnesses coming forth claiming that they both overheard me daydreaming about taking over my father's estate. Then the worst of it came when it was discovered that a blow pipe was in my bag, and it was reasoned that my father was coming to see me that morning. The trial lasted for only a few hours, at which the king was so convinced of my guilt, he didn't even consult with his counselors in declaring his judgment and sentence: Exile. That meant death. More so than an execution. Serious crimes, such as theft and tax evasion, garner a quick execution. Gundzherek the Hunter was the king's executioner and lopped off the head quickly, without hesitation. Such death would be painless—I think. But exile is given to the worst crimes—treason and murder. It's a slow and agonizing torture as the criminal struggles to survive, usually no more than two days past the moment of being exiled. So my exile meant that the wild beasts of Kelidid would eventually find me and devour me for a meal. The thought itself terrified me and tortured my soul.

The vicious condrok, the largest reptile in all of Endhera, made Kelidid its home. The flying scavengers known as tethids, with their toothed beaks and their deathly, pale-colored feathers, could clean a corpse down to the bones within minutes. I knew I was going to die and probably before morning. And then I thought of my mother. She would become Vuhzrog's slave, no doubt. This hurt me more than my own plight. Vuhzrog was reputed to be extremely cruel to his slaves.

I was exiled in the time that I provided above, the twenty-seventh hour. I was escorted to the front gates and ushered through without mercy from the guards. The moisture I felt upon my back was their spittle. The hacking sound in their throats as they packed their spittle told me they hated me. So in my moment of weakness, I clutched the images of the gods of my forefathers. After walking aimlessly for a while, I fell upon my knees and leaned on a rock. I fondled each image, begging each one of the gods to rescue me, for I was innocent. Although Modi-Vod was a cruel god, I begged for his forgiveness. I begged Prull the Mighty to help me and defend me. I didn't get to cry for long, as immediately a condrok came around the far corner in the bend of the Kelidid Valley. The foul beast saw me, screamed its bloodcurdling scream, and charged for what would have been, or should have been an easy meal. All I could do was scream and fall back.

Leostrom's memorandum to the file: The Doctrine of Reason Absolute governs the interaction between intervener and intervenient. The doctrine permits the intervener to assume the characteristics of the prevailing deities en credo to sustain familiarity but calls for the intervener to refrain from actually assuming the identities, so as to prevent false-cause idolization. That carries a high risk of philosophical rejection and misdirection. The risk is measured to determine how the intervenient will perceive the intervention. Will the intervenient perceive us as competition with, or enemies of, his or her gods? Is the intervenient susceptible to philosophical redirection via cognitive dissonance, which promotes maturity? We were confident that, per our exhaustive study, the subject Oleg was the most promising candidate.

It was Addia-Sahl from the Intrepidium *who informed us of the approaching reptilian predator. She was perceptive of Oleg's environment and thought to look for any such contact units. According to her analysis, Oleg was releasing fear-induced pheromones into the air, and the wind was carrying the pheromones in the direction of the predator. The distance diluted the concentration, but the predator's olfactory sense was acute. The bipedal reptile picked up the scent and began to stalk its unseen prey.*

Natharon, Dyllon, and I reviewed the situation while observing Oleg in an out-of-phase state. I calculated the precise moment to intervene, which offered the greatest opportunity to separate Oleg from his idols. The three of us then materialized in Endheran form and stepped in phase to intervene.

As the condrok approached, the most miraculous thing happened. Three shining figures appeared before me. The condrok was distracted and attacked them, but in a flash of light, the beast lay on the ground alive yet stunned, one leg twitching in the air. The figure in the middle turned to me and spoke, saying, "We have heard your prayers, Oleg, and we have come to deliver you from the evil that has befallen your family." All three were the most handsome Endheran males I had ever laid eyes on. They were perfect in their every appearance, youthful and unblemished.

I asked the middle figure who spoke, "Which god are you? Isgurud? Elestern? Modi-Vod? Prull the Mighty?"

And the figure answered, "We are none that you just mentioned. We are Guardians of Eternal Life. Your gods are gods made of chiseled stone, gods fashioned by the hands of men. Those gods were born from your forefathers' imagination."

And I asked, "Are you from my imagination? How do I know you are real?" I asked because I was caught up in the fascination at the moment.

But the figure in the middle responded, "Has there ever been a time that your imagination has rescued you from an immediate threat?"

I answered, "No. This is the first time."

And the figure in the middle said, "This is because we are real, just as real as the condrok that attacked you, the very same beast that now lies here stunned and immobile." I saw the beast. It twitched its legs. I could hear it. I could smell it. It was real. And so were these figures.

And I asked, "What is your name? What do I call you?"

And He responded, "For now, I will keep my name a secret, so as to confound the agents of darkness that labor hard against humanity's progress. But if it is necessary to know who I am, then know that I am the Absolute One who brings justice, even to the poor and the humble, especially when agents of darkness rule from lofty places."

I asked, "What am I supposed to do?"

And the Absolute One stated, "Return to the gate and inform the guards there to allow you to speak to the king. We have a message for the king, and we want you to deliver it."

I said, "Oh no, my lord, I can't! The king will surely have me killed as I stand at the gate. He won't let me step one foot in all of Asemur."

And the Absolute One responded, "Do not be afraid of the king. We will not permit him to hurt so much as one hair on your head."

But I was too weak and begged further, "Please, my lord, choose another to deliver your message. Perhaps my former boss, Egdeg. He is a good man with a good heart, and he's pious and devout."

The Absolute One did not agree but stated, "We do not choose Egdeg. We choose you. What you have said, however, is true. He is pious and devout, but only to the gods of your forefathers, those same gods whose images now lie shattered at your feet."

I looked down and saw that the figurines were all broken into many pieces. I must have dropped them when the condrok attacked. They should not have broken, for they were chiseled from the hardest stone. Yet there they were, shattered, as the Absolute One had said.

I was still bound by my weakness when I said, "Oh, my lord, the king's counselor Vuhzrog aims to enslave my mother. If not for the mandatory law of mourning, he would most likely be forcing himself upon her as we speak."

The Absolute One answered, "We have dispatched a Guardian to watch over her. As we deliver you from the king's oppression, she too will be delivered, along with all of Asemur."

I turned to walk back to the gate, but weakness struck me one final time. I turned to the Absolute One and asked, "What is the message that you want me to deliver?"

And the Absolute One answered, "We will not abandon you as you go before the king but will remain with you through the whole ordeal. You therefore need not know the message until that time, for its contents would be unduly burdensome to you." The three then disappeared from sight, as if no one had been there, and I had imagined the whole thing. But I knew deep within me that I had not. The stunned condrok certainly proved that.

The condrok moved slightly and seemed to be coming to its senses. So I hurried away from the spot, which I called the Rock of the Absolute, for I was laid upon the rock when the Absolute One rescued me from the condrok. I made haste, though my heart pounded in me and beckoned me to turn and run. But as I looked around, I knew there was nowhere to run. I was in the wilds of Kelidid, and if the Absolute One and

His Guardians chose to do so, they could leave me to become food for the wild beasts.

It was still dark when I saw the gate up ahead. But I was exhausted, not having slept since my father's attack. The Absolute One knew this and knew my heart's desire, for he said, "Oleg, you may rest here until the morning. After the sun has been up for an hour, then we will proceed to confront the king."

Fear continued to harass me, and I startled at every noise. Although the Absolute One and His Guardians did not remain in my sight, I knew they were nearby. But no matter how hard I tried, fear would not let me sleep. And my stomach growled from hunger. I had not eaten since the morning of my father's attack. Fear and hunger are two of the three worst enemies of humankind. The third one is loneliness, but the Absolute One sent that enemy away, at least temporarily. Oh how I wished at the time I could ask for the remaining two to be sent away also.

Leostrom's memorandum to file: Having returned to an out-of-phase state, hovering a couple of meters above the scene, we continued our observations and calculations. I scanned Oleg's neural net and observed the corrupted ganglia offsetting his emotive equilibrium. We observed his thoughts via his neural processes and perceived his desires.

"He'll never get any rest under the strain of his anxiety," I said. "Yet, I don't want to alleviate the anxiety immediately, seeing that it will return just as quickly and three times as worse."

"His anxiety regards the reptiles," Natharon said, interpreting Oleg's scan. "Perhaps conditioning him to accept the reptiles' presence will ease the anxiety."

"I'll go retrieve for us a pack of the beasts," Dyllon said with a smile. Immediately he teleshifted away.

"It's easy to attach oneself to this little fellow," Natharon said, his eyes locked onto Oleg. "He's been through a lot so far."

"It's equally hard to stand back and watch it unfold without altering the reality of it all," I answered.

"True," Natharon said. "But hydrology precepts dictate."

At that moment, Dyllon appeared, his transparent aura leaving a misty trail behind him. "The brute beasts are on their way."

Continuing with Oleg's transcript:

Suddenly, I heard a noise. It was loud and obnoxious, and I knew it to be a condrok. I tried to remain still, with my eyes closed and my back to the beast, but my heart betrayed me. It beat so hard, I knew that the condrok would see me move up and down in the same rhythm. The beast approached me, and I begged the Absolute One to cast it away. A moment passed and then all was quiet. I breathed in relief and turned to see where it had gone.

The beast was but an arm's length from me, and it exhaled its breath. I began to cry, because it seemed that the Absolute One had left me after all. As I lay sobbing, expecting the condrok to fall upon me at any moment, the Absolute One spoke, "Oleg, we have the ability to close the mouth of any beast. This condrok will not attack you." To test me, the beast approached closer, even to the point that I felt its breath upon my face. Its breath was horrid, and it stank of death. I struggled to compose myself, but it was difficult. I reached up to pet the beast. It let me, although I startled two or three times before my hand came to rest on its muzzle. I had never heard of such a thing. It was as if the vicious condrok was as tame as the small, harmless emeesh.

Then the Absolute One spoke, "We wanted to help you rest, to put your mind at ease. So we brought forth the largest beast in the area. As you can see, it will not harm you. None of them will." Suddenly, other condroks came up the narrow valley and surrounded me, so that there were ten in all. And none attacked me. They each took turns sniffing me and wandering about, sniffing the ground.

This brought back memories of tending Egdeg's animals. The condroks were docile, and my heart was overjoyed. I was still timid, afraid that any sudden movement would provoke the beasts. But I petted each one, and none acted like they wanted to eat me. After a while, one by one the condroks left, even the last one, the largest. I named him Armogal, in honor of my father. I had always named animals, especially those of Egdeg that I tended. I'm not sure, but Armogal may have been the one that was going to attack me earlier when the Absolute One showed Himself.

I sat back under a tree, and my stomach growled so loud, I thought perhaps a condrok would hear it and mistake it for wounded prey. But at that moment, a tethid landed at my feet with a small branch in its mouth. The branch itself was loaded down with common blackberries. Yet I didn't make a move, for the tethid was mean-looking, despite its small size. Its little red beady eyes looked at me ominously. But then the tethid hopped up to me, dropped the branch on my lap and flew off. Needless to say that I feasted on the berries, which were very sweet and tasty. When I finished consuming them all, my stomach was satisfied.

I lay down and looked up at the stars in the heavens. I noticed that the noises around me were much more tolerable—peaceful, even. Nature sang. I used to listen to it from inside Asemur. But outside Asemur, Nature's singing was more beautiful. It was all around me up close, not some distant revelry of noise. I daydreamed that I could lift off the ground and soar up to the heavens and that I would go up and look at these stars and see what they were, perhaps even hold one in my hands. I don't remember much else. I may have fallen asleep at this point. My dream was interesting, so much so that I wrote it down—and other dreams too—in another book, *The Dreams of Oleg*.

I awoke as the sun was rising. The city wall ahead still blocked the sunlight, but enough lit the sky above. It was beautiful. I had enjoyed eating the berries and wouldn't have dared complain, but my mouth was extremely dry. I hadn't drunk any water for the longest time. I looked around and didn't see the Absolute One or any of His Guardians.

But He was near, for He spoke to me, though I could not see Him. He said, "Oleg, to your right, just up the rocky slope, is a small spring of water."

I didn't hesitate. Although in my mind the nagging thought came that no water existed outside of Asemur, since it was mostly desert and rocky terrain, I knew that if the Absolute One wanted, He could bring forth a mighty river down the heart of Kelidid. As I climbed up the steep slope, it seemed that my footing was secure. I couldn't help but feel safe and bold. As I approached closer, I could hear the small splash of water on a rock. Then I saw underneath a small ledge a single stream of water flowing down the rock face and then falling onto the ground below it. I drank my fill. It was cold and clean—the cleanest water I ever drank.

As a poet, I composed words to portray my experience thus far. My every need was being provided, and I felt refreshed and renewed. I spoke these words out loud. I repeated them several times, to memorize them. But I noticed that each time I did, I wanted to sing them. So I finally sang them from my heart. I offered this song of praise to the Absolute One.

Great is the Lord of the Hosts of Heaven!
Splendid is the name of the Absolute!
Compassion He has for the poor.
Justice He metes out for the oppressed.
To the soul that is wretched and fallen:
Cry out! Cry out to the Lord! Call Him!
Your prayers will not fall on deaf ears.
Swiftly will the Absolute come to help.
Hunger assailed my every thought!
Thirst scorched the inside of my throat!
Fear laid siege to the boundaries of my heart.
But the Absolute brought me to rest.
There was food and cool spring water.
The wild beasts stayed their cruelty.
Now shall I cast far away all doubt.
Justice shall follow me the rest of my life.

After I was fully refreshed and had regained all my strength and was not thirsty or hungry or exhausted or discomforted in any way, I focused on the task at hand. The Absolute One had commanded me to return to the gate, and I was going to obey. I did not know how the guards would react, but I knew that everything up to this point had not been in vain. I was supposed to see the king and deliver a message. That meant the guards would not be able to kill me. Thus, there was no reason to delay any further.

I approached the gate, and I beat upon it hard and loud. Finally, a guard named Dermegg opened the eye slot and stared at me from the other side. His face is as gaunt as mine, though he was slightly taller and had dark hair. "Get away, Oleg," he commanded. He then slammed the small slot door shut.

I called out to him. "Dermegg, we were friends once. I am innocent and did not murder my father."

He responded from the other side, "It doesn't matter. I cannot open the gate by royal decree. What do you want?"

I continued, "Dermegg, my friend, I ask that you go to the king and inform him that I survived the night and that I bring a message."

Dermegg responded, "Are you insane? I cannot leave my post! There is nothing I can do to help you. Go away!"

I could do nothing. So I found me a good rock to sit on, and I waited for further instructions from the Absolute One. Several guards appeared on the rampart above the gate door. At first they just stared. Then they began to toss rocks down at me.

Eventually they began to jeer. "The coward wants his mother," they said over and over. "The murderer wants to suckle on his mother's breast," or "The coward killed his father so he could take his mother as his lover." The jeers soon became even more obscene. I hollered back several times for them to shut up, but they wouldn't. This went on for hours, and I didn't think I could take any more.

I finally fell upon my knees and prayed to the Absolute One, "My lord, if you can close the mouths of beasts, can you not close the mouths of my enemies?" But still there was nothing. The Absolute One said nothing. There was nothing but silence. "Oh no," I said as I dropped my face into my hands.

At noon, I was moved to tears, because the insults were extremely cruel and harsh. The guards had taken to imitating my father's convulsions. They pointed at me and mocked me, stating that I had killed my father. But I loved my father. He was a good man. Visions of his suffering began to haunt me.

I finally cried, hollering, "My lord, do not leave me in here to suffer this! I would rather a condrok devour me as his meal. The wild beasts of Kelidid have more mercy than my enemies! I beg you! Do not let one more gross word from my enemies fall upon my ears. It is too much." The guards laughed at my agony.

A rock hit me in the back, and I fell over in pain. The guards burst into further laughter, pointing and laughing, mocking and accusing. How much more could an Endheran withstand? When I opened my eyes, I saw that I had rolled up next to the gate. Above me, two guards heaved a huge rock onto the rampart's railing. They then let it go. The huge rock fell toward me, and I closed my eyes and prepared myself to die. I cried out, knowing that I had failed and that the Absolute One had abandoned me.

I heard a loud crash and then a strange hissing noise. As I opened my eyes, the huge rock, bigger than my chest, had crumbled into pieces and fallen all around me, but not on me. I sat up, amazed that I was still alive. I suppose the guards were amazed as well. They all fell silent.

Then the Absolute One spoke to me, though He still remained hidden from sight, "Oleg, why have you laid down before your opponents? Why surrender to die by their hands? Have we not requested that you go before the king to deliver a message?"

I answered, "You have, my lord, but I did not hear from you. My enemies mocked me and insulted me and threw rocks at me."

The Absolute One asked, "Did we not close the mouths of the condroks so that they would not attack you? Did we not send a tethid to bring you food? Did we not open a dry rock to bring forth cold water for you to drink?"

I answered, "You did, my lord." I stood and dusted myself

off. I wiped the tears from my face. But I could not look up. I was ashamed. I showed neither will nor courage, especially in view of my enemies. I had failed in my objective. I had disobeyed the Absolute One. I hung my head low and awaited my punishment.

As if knowing my thoughts, the Absolute One spoke, "Oleg, I am not chastising you, nor do I want you to feel ashamed or guilty. Instead, have faith not only in us but also in yourself. We chose you, because we know your desire is peace and justice for all Asemurans. We send you as their deliverer. Have courage, because through you, we will deliver the Asemurans. And through you, we will bring forth a message that will be carried down from generation to generation and be heard by Endherans everywhere, even beyond the rocky cliffs and sandy shores of Kelidid."

I responded, "Please forgive me, my lord. I do not mean to be hardheaded."

The Absolute One stated, "All is well, Oleg. Proceed with the objective. Face the king so that you can deliver our message."

The guards above could not see or hear the Absolute One. Thus, a few times one would holler down, "Who are you talking to?" or "You are talking to yourself, fool!"

I asked the Absolute One, "My lord, what of the guards and their slurs and insults?"

The Absolute One assured me, "The guards who are responsible will be held to account for their behavior."

In my weakness, I gloated, "I thank you for punishing them."

The Absolute One stated, "Oleg, I counsel you further. Love even your enemies. So therefore, I counsel you not to be thankful or joyful when justice is administered. Mourn instead, for justice exposes the weaknesses inherent in all of humanity."

I confessed, "My lord, I am ignorant and feeble. I do not know what to do."

The Absolute One once again comforted me. "We will offer you guidance, Oleg. If you'll heed our messages, then assuredly wisdom shall blossom in you like a beautiful flower blossoms after a soothing rain. This affair with the king will take time, as the circumstances unfold. But rest assured, you will be permitted an audience with the king. Until that time, we have much to discuss."

And all the wisdom that the Absolute One gave me is written in another book, *The Book of Absolute Truths.*

During this time, the king was becoming frustrated with me. For nine days, I approached the gate, knocked, and asked the guards to deliver my request to the king. During that time, I didn't know whether or not they were actually informing the king. On the ninth day, however, it became clear that they had.

One guard named Flendek spoke through the eye slot in the door, "Oleg, the king ordered me to kill you if you knock on this door one more time." He slammed it shut. I stepped back and asked the Absolute One in prayer for guidance, although I felt compelled to dismiss the threat and proceed. So I knocked.

The eye slot opened, and I saw the point of a spear thrust toward my face. I don't know what happened next, except that I recall a loud bang followed by a hissing sound. As I came to my senses, I found myself kneeling down. I stood and checked myself, but I didn't appear hurt, and I felt okay. I walked up to the eye slot, which was still open, and peered through it.

I saw Flendek lying on his back. The spear lay beside him, shattered in three pieces. Flendek held his arms up in the air, waving them about. He was stunned, like the condrok who had attacked the Absolute One. Dermegg kneeled down and tended to him. Then Dermegg looked up at the eye slot and saw me peering from the other side. Dermegg stood and walked over to me. He looked me in the eyes, and I could see that he was afraid of me. He slowly closed the eye slot.

I learned later that Dermegg had left his post and gone immediately to the king to inform him of Flendek's injury. The king became furious at Dermegg, ranting and raving for several minutes. Finally, the king called for the captain of the guard, Wedessek the Brute, so named because of his fierceness in battle. The king ordered Wedessek to take several soldiers and come out of Asemur to kill me. I, of course, did not know this was planned, so I sat upon a rock just outside the main gate. I can't say that, if I had known, I wouldn't have tried to run. When I heard the gate being opened, I assumed the king had finally relented. So I jumped to my feet and stood waiting for the gate to open. When it did, I saw Wedessek and six other soldiers standing there, spears poised and ready to strike.

Wedessek said to me, "You better run, fool."

Fear took hold of me, and I turned and ran a ways. As I did, a condrok ran by me and I fell to the ground. The beast snatched Wedessek in its terrible maw. The other soldiers ran back inside and closed the gate. I watched in horror as Wedessek dangled from the beast's mouth. At first it stood there, looking at me, holding Wedessek by his leg. He cursed and beat it on its nose. It then took off and ran down the pathway, and as it disappeared behind a boulder, several other condroks appeared and chased after it. I saw nothing further in regards to Wedessek, but the commotion that followed at that point convinced me that he was no more.

Well, my heart beat so hard, I could hardly contain myself. I went back over to the door and knocked on it. I called out for Dermegg. After a few minutes, the eye slot opened and Dermegg peeked through it.

I informed him again, "Go tell the king that I demand to speak to him."

Dermegg looked around frantically at the outside area. Then he looked back into my eyes. My former friend was mad with fear. He slammed the eye slot shut and went back to the king. Upon hearing what had happened, the king flew into a rage. He attacked the guards standing next to him, throwing them down before the throne and calling them incompetent. Finally, the king called for Gundzherek the Hunter. This Asemuran was thought to be the largest Endheran ever to be born. He towered over all other Asemurans, most barely able to reach his chest in height. He earned the name "the Hunter," because he was the only one brave enough to take on a condrok by himself. Although the condrok was by far bigger than he, with his skill and speed, he always walked away from a hunt unharmed. Well, except for one time, when he suffered claw marks on the side of his face, leaving the three scars he bears to this day. Gundzherek also served as the king's personal champion and executioner. He hastened to the king's beckoning, and the king ordered the Hunter to kill the condrok but not to return without bringing back my head.

I had just managed to compose myself and reflect upon what I had witnessed with Wedessek, when the gate began to open. At first, I wanted to run to the gate but thought I'd better move away, so I turned and hastened up the slope to a better vantage point. I then saw Gundzherek run through the gate.

He saw me too and pointed at me as he ran by. The look on his face was sheer hatred.

A small condrok emerged from behind the boulder. Gundzherek saw it and laughed, mocking its youthful size. He ran toward it with spear raised, ready to slay it. But at that moment, the nine others emerged, including the large one I had named Armogal. Gundzherek slid to a stop and turned to try to run to the gate, but Armogal the Condrok reached him first. Gundzherek whipped around to face the beast, but the lone hunter was no match for all ten. I saw them all surround him and heard his scream, muffled by the roar of the beasts. When they tore away from the spot, nothing remained but a large bloodstain.

As I walked down the slope to the gate, I noticed Dermegg staring ahead with a blank look in his eyes. He saw me approach, and before I had a chance to speak, he yelled out, "I know! I know! I will tell the king!" He slammed the eye slot shut. He no longer showed any shock but boldly went to the king. When he entered, he told the king, "Your champion is dead, devoured by an entire pack of condroks. Stop being a fool and have the damned gate opened for Oleg! Otherwise, he'll lay siege to Asemur and set the entire city in flames!"

Shocked and dismayed, the king's only response was, "What are you babbling about?"

When the king jumped up, enraged, ready to order Dermegg's execution right there on the spot, Dermegg interrupted him, "You might as well kill me! Death by the sword is more merciful than death by a condrok!"

Shocked by Dermegg's belligerence, the king stumbled backwards until he fell into the throne. He looked around madly at everyone. Paranoia began to grip his heart. One guard overheard him mumbling to himself and relayed it to me later: "They don't fear me anymore. Oleg has stolen that fear and respect. What is this? Sorcery?"

Dermegg seized the moment with further assertiveness. "Open the damned gate! Otherwise, we will all die!"

The king was in no condition to respond. He screamed and then laughed and then began to cry. Finally Azghak stepped forward and took control of the situation. He directed his comment to Dermegg. "First, you will surrender your arms and face arrest for your insolence."

Dermegg didn't hesitate but tossed the spear and shield onto the ground before him. He uttered, "Do what you will." A few guards present walked up to him and took hold of him.

Satisfied, Azghak then called for the king's lieutenants. The captain had been slain, but there were still four lieutenants and a total of one hundred soldiers under their command.

The king interjected, "No, Azghak."

Azghak tried to assure the king, "Your lordship, we can send the army out to take control of the situation."

The king then argued, "No!" Grabbing hold of Azghak's robe, the king pulled him close. "Would you sacrifice my entire army and leave us completely defenseless?" The king was raving mad at this point. Without letting go of his chief counselor's robe, he continued to argue, "Fool! You can't fight sorcery with iron! If Oleg can tame several of these beasts, surely he could tame an entire herd. How then would my army fare?" The king pushed away the counselor and struggled to compose himself. "First, we open the gate and allow Oleg to enter. We will allow Oleg to come and stand before me and deliver his message. We will allow Oleg to do whatever he wants. After this sordid affair is concluded, this foolish guard who stands before me will have his head lopped off."

Dermegg, filled with the spirit of boldness, spoke up. "Let it be so, if you deem it as such. As I said earlier, such a death is by far more merciful than death by a condrok."

The king responded, shaking his fist at the prisoner, "Silence your insolence, fool! I will now think of a death worse than a condrok!"

Dermegg struggled to break the guards' grasp. They wrestled him to the ground, at which he finally yelled, "What makes you think you will survive Oleg's wrath? He asks for you, not for anyone else!" Finally, a guard hit him over the head with the butt of a spear. Dermegg, dazed, quit struggling.

I was sitting on the same rock as before, wondering what was transpiring in the king's court. When I heard the gate start to open, I started to run to a safe spot. A few guards at the top of the rampart hollered down at me not to run. Finally, the gate was open for me to enter, and I did not hesitate any further. As I entered, the guards quickly shut the gate, fearful that the beasts would follow me in. I stood there waiting for their instructions. I was also fearful that they would fall upon me at any moment. Finally one informed me that the king awaited my arrival. So I headed toward the king's court, escorted by about twenty soldiers. When I entered the hall, the king was up on his throne. Azghak and a few other counselors I haven't mentioned stood on his right, while Vuhzrog and the remaining two counselors stood on the king's left, along with the king's son, Prince Sustek. I noticed Dermegg subdued and bleeding from his head. He looked up at me as I walked by. He was quiet, and the look on his face was one of complete dejection and surrender.

I approached the throne but stood there silent, waiting for

the king to acknowledge my presence, as he stared off at the far wall. Finally he looked down at me and gritted his teeth. He may have been angry that I didn't kneel. I struggled with whether or not I should but finally decided not to do so.

He spoke. "Well? Speak!" As I began to talk, he interrupted, "Tell me! What is so important that I lost many of my best men today?" I once again started to speak, but the king interrupted. "Tell me what sorcery you've employed to slay Asemur's strongest defenders?"

Enraged, Dermegg yelled out, "Shut up, fool! Let the Endheran speak!" Several guards roughed him up, punching him and kicking him. I prayed within myself for guidance.

The Absolute One's voice echoed in my mind. I could tell that I was the only one who could hear His voice, because no one appeared alarmed. "Oleg, speak the words that I place in your thoughts."

Emboldened, I began, "King Verrek, Ruler of Asemur, judgment comes to your court. Because you have entertained wickedness in your thoughts and in your court, you will be removed from the throne and replaced with another. The youth who replaces you will display greater wisdom in ruling this city."

The king jumped to his feet and pointed at me, yelling, "Traitor! You are committing treason! Do you plot my demise?"

I calmly responded, repeating the words as they entered my thoughts. "That would be incorrect, as the real traitor resides in the midst of your own counselors! If not for this intervention, your own son would fall to his treachery." I did not know where I was going with this. I was completely ignorant of the facts at the time.

The king yelled, "What are you talking about? My counselors are trustworthy! They would never lie to me! They would certainly do no harm to my own son!" He sat back down on his throne.

I responded, stepping forward slightly, "On the contrary, your own chief counselor has betrayed the integrity of the king's court. It is he who murdered my father, Armog. And it is he who falsely accused me of that crime."

The king responded, "You're a fool! What you say is not true! Azghak would never have done such a thing!"

I continued, the words coming seemingly from nowhere. "Your rebuttal is errant, because in actuality, what you say is not honest! You have already decided in the private depths of your mind that Vuhzrog is your new chief counselor!" The king sank deeper into, and there was gasping and murmuring all around.

Vuhzrog stepped forward, "Who told you this! The king told me his intentions in private! There was no one around to hear this!"

Azghak started from his spot. "What? What is this?"

I responded, "Secret things are easily exposed, especially in view of the all-seeing Guardians of Eternal Life."

The king turned to Vuhzrog. "The fool continues to babble more insanity. Nothing he says makes any sense!"

Vuhzrog answered him, "Clearly we have before us a madman. His dabbling in the dark arts has corrupted his mind!" All others present in the court remained quiet during this exchange. Vuhzrog stepped toward me. "Very well, Mad One. Whatever sorcery you used to intrude upon our private affairs doesn't change the fact that you murdered your father!"

I calmly responded, "Your statement is false, as it is you who hired the assassin to slay my father. It is you who chose the Pinoxi root. It is you who delivered it to the assassin hours before my father's death. It is you who paid the assassin twenty-five gold cheslings to commit this deed." This revelation flabbergasted me. As I spoke these words, my chest felt like it was being crushed.

Vuhzrog yelled out, "Lies! All lies!"

The king again jumped to his feet and interjected, "Why do you raise these accusations? Why would Vuhzrog do this? For what reason would he slay your father, who was nothing more to this court than a mere peasant?"

I remained calm and responded, "The answer to your question has already been provided." I fell silent after that, but my shoulders felt heavy.

Azghak then stepped forward and spoke. "Your lordship, the answer is obvious. The appointment to chief counselor is a stronger motive than all the motives speculated about in Oleg's trial."

The king stomped over to Azghak. "Careful, counselor! Do not accuse this court of rendering a false judgment!"

Azghak stepped down from the throne's dais and stood before me, "How did you come to the knowledge of this scheme?"

I responded, "I did not. I am just now learning of this scheme along with you."

Azghak continued, "You'll need evidence, Oleg. Obviously, allegations alone will not prove your case."

Vuhzrog jumped from the dais towards us, "He has no evidence, because there is none! This traitor to the throne is lying! He should be killed right here, right now!"

The king yelled, enraged, "This is still my court and no one will do anything without my command! Counselors, return to your posts!" Both Azghak and Vuhzrog stood facing each other. The king stomped his feet and yelled, "Do it, or I'll dismiss you both and replace you immediately!" Azghak obeyed, but Vuhzrog hesitated, staring at me with a hateful look. Reluctantly, he turned and went back to his position on the king's left.

I managed to turn and cast a glance at Dermegg. He appeared to be struggling to maintain his composure, fighting back tears. His plight softened my heart, and I prayed to the Absolute One for him to be saved.

Satisfied that he had regained control of the situation, the king sat down and spoke. "What evidence do you have, Oleg? I demand it, because if you have none, this court will reject your accusations as untrue. It is already written in our annals that the name Oleg is associated with patricide. What evidence do you have that would give us reason to erase those statements?" I stood silent for a moment. I did not know what I would say next. "Yeah," the king answered. "That's what I thought."

Then the words came to me. "You will find a batch of Pinoxi root in Vuhzrog's chambers. It was his intent to use the root against others. As I said, your son is at grave risk."

Vuhzrog again yelled out, "Liar!"

The king interrupted, "Silence!" The king glared at Vuhzrog, and the counselor quieted down and stepped back. Prince Sustek stepped around the throne to the other side with Azghak. The king continued, "Guards, proceed to the chambers of Vuhzrog and search it for Pinoxi root." A group of guards present in the court slowly walked toward the door that exited the great hall, each one confused as to who was going to obey the command and who was going to remain. Angrily, the king yelled, "Some of you go, some of you stay!" The king pointed out who would do what, followed by several curses.

Just as the appointed group turned to leave, Vuhzrog approached the king. "Your lordship, you will indeed find Pinoxi root in my chambers."

The king's eyes widened, and he pursed his lips together hard. Finally, the king managed to ask, "Why?" He began to breathe hard. "Why do you have Pinoxi root in your chambers?"

Vuhzrog had not prepared himself to answer the question, and he hesitated and began to look around wildly. "I … um … we … um."

"Why?" the king yelled, grabbing the counselor's robes and pulling him down to the his feet. "Why! Why! Why!"

Fearful, Vuhzrog managed to respond, "I … um … collected it from … um … Oleg's mother! Because … because she helped Oleg kill his father!"

The level of rage the king displayed at this point had never before been witnessed. He grabbed Vuhzrog by the throat and began to choke him. "I'm no fool! I'm no fool! You insult me with your lie!" Azghak and the other counselors, as gently as they could, managed to break the king's hold on Vuhzrog. The king fell back onto the throne, breathing hard. His face was both dark and sweaty from the strain. Vuhzrog fell to the floor and rolled down the dais's few steps. As he hit bottom, he started coughing hard and struggled to compose himself. He looked up at me, and I saw in his eyes terror married to anger.

The king began to look wildly around at everyone. He mumbled to himself, the mumbling unintelligible, resembling something like, "Dubbla umblum bubbla." This went on for several minutes. I looked around and studied everyone's reactions. Most were staring down at the floor, quiet and confused, fearful to draw any unwanted attention from the king. Azghak was doing what I was doing, looking around and studying reactions. Yet the king's low murmuring was as loud as yelling, because all else was deathly quiet.

After several minutes, the king threw himself into a fit, jumping to his feet. He stared wildly at Azghak and the other counselors as he slowly backed down the steps. He stopped short of tripping over Vuhzrog, who scrambled to get out of the way. The king then turned and jolted to a stop and stared at me just as wildly. He shook his head and backed away slowly. The only means by which I can accurately describe this situation is to compare it to when a wild animal is being slowly backed into a corner.

The king uttered, "My guards are incompetent. My army is weak and broken. My counselors are insane! Murderers! Assassins!" The king glared at Vuhzrog and shook his fist. "They plot my demise!" Then the king looked up at me. I was quite disturbed by this display, so I found it hard to return the king's gaze. "You," he said. "I will be replaced?" He began to shake his head from side to side. "No! You're all in this together! You're all plotting against me!" In a final fit of rage, the king yelled, "Guards! Kill everyone!"

At that moment, the ground shook, throwing everyone but myself to the floor. Strangely, although I stumbled slightly, I maintained my footing. After it stopped, I was the only one left standing.

The king's insanity took full hold. He managed to pick himself up, and, breathing hard, he stated coldly, "Away with your sorcery! Away with your treachery! Away with you!"

I responded as calmly as I could manage, "I did not do that. The Absolute One and His Guardians did."

The king growled and gritted his teeth and slowly walked over to me. Fear compelled me to back up in reaction to his forward progression. The king looked down at a guard kneeling. The king then reached down and jerked the spear from the guard's hands. Finally, the king fixed his mad gaze upon me. Like a predator, he slowly approached me.

"My lord!" I uttered to the Absolute One. "Help me!"

The ground began to shake again, this time more violently. The king was tossed around a bit and dropped the spear but managed to dive onto the steps to the dais. The earthquake was so violent, the walls and the roof began to crumble, dust and debris falling all around. Many in the room scrambled under tables, as large rocks fell from the ceiling. I saw a flash of blue light and heard the familiar hissing sound as several rocks fell away from me. A large pile of debris fell from the ceiling onto Dermegg, but the blue light flashed and hissing ensued. I apologize for the vague description, but there's no other way I can describe it. A large stone chunk fell down toward Azghak. The blue light and hissing deflected the stone, and it fell to the side. Another chunk fell toward Vuhzrog, who lay on his stomach on the floor protecting his head. The chunk landed on his legs, and he jerked up and screamed in agony. Another large chunk fell upon his torso and silenced his scream—forever.

I heard someone yell behind me. I turned and noticed a strange fissure in the floor. A large crack in the stone flooring made its way past me toward the dais. The king had managed to climb onto his throne, and he pulled his legs up under him. He watched as the crack went up the dais toward the throne. As it reached the throne, the ground shook more violently than before. This time, even I was thrown to the ground.

The entire great hall was split down the middle, and each half moved away in opposite directions. The fissure opened up wide, belching dust and debris. The roar was deafening, and I could not hear the king screaming, although clearly he was screaming as loud as any Endheran could. He struggled to climb up the back of the throne. Those of us who had survived thus far watched as the throne was heaved, and the king was tossed into the fissure.

The shaking paused momentarily, long enough for some of us to get on our knees. Then the quake continued, but this time the halves of the hall began to be rejoined as the fissure closed. With a loud crash of thunder, the earthquake stopped. I climbed up on the debris. The wall behind the throne fell outward, crashing into the ground. Dust filled the air, but the wind blew and cleared away some of the dust within a few minutes. All around, there was slight moaning and crying. Everyone fell silent, however, as we heard a thunderous boom. Off in the far distance, the Volcano Isgurud, named after the god of my forefathers, was erupting and spewing clouds of dust and fire into the air.

Leostrom's Amendment: It is necessary to convey the actuality of this unfortunate catastrophe. A geological anomaly, perturbative in nature, was detected in a current of molten rock far underneath the city Asemur. This anomaly unleashed a shock wave, which flowed in Asemur's direction. Addia-Sahl attempted to intercept the shock wave with a projected field through a port on the calabi-yau manifold. She was able to disperse and dilute the shock wave slightly, but it still managed to penetrate the mantle. Soleran judged and decided to utilize the shock wave for our advantage. Unfortunately, time constraints prohibited us from gaining full control of the shock wave, which slammed the crust at an epicenter half a kilometer to the south. While Natharon, Dyllon, and I were on the surface observing Oleg's affair, groups of fellow Guardians engaged whatever methods and procedures needed to diminish the earthquake by stabilizing the core flow. The source of the phenomenon initiating the shock wave was, and still is, indeterminable, but its effect was devastating. We miscalculated the severity of the local field's portion of the dispersal. To compensate, we had to release the energy by cutting the earth and diverting energy to the fissure. We took advantage of the situation to make a statement, but again, the force slipped our full control. Overall, we were not satisfied with the results. It was too dramatic and distorted the Endherans' perception of us as being quick to anger. Our analysis of the population revealed that most endured neural connectivity degradation due to the trauma on the acute stress spectrum. Soleran dispatched a group of Guardians to investigate the phenomenon of the shock wave, which to us had the appearance of being unnatural. The investigators were unsuccessful, but even up to now, we are continuing to monitor the situation in hopes that a clue emerges to expose the cause. We are, however, forced to accept full responsibility for the phenomenon. We have to let the misperception stand.

Azghak emerged and began to order the soldiers to go around the city and rescue all survivors. While I watched him, I thought in my heart that he would probably make a good king. That's when I realized, however, that I had mentioned the king's replacement as someone of youth. Azghak was much older than the king. Coincidently, he called for the remaining counsel and the royal family to gather around me. I climbed up and sat upon a crumbled portion of the wall. They sat down around me.

Prince Sustek approached and addressed himself to me. "I am Prince Sustek. King Verrek was my father." He resembled his father closely, though much younger—probably no more than a whelp of twenty-two years. He cast his gaze to the ground, saddened, but composed himself and returned his gaze to me. "I suppose you are now king."

His humility softened my heart, and I climbed down from the wall. As I stood before him, he kneeled down. I quickly but gently coaxed him to his feet. When he stood up, I kneeled down to his feet, "No, Your Majesty. It is you, son of Verrek, who is now king." I looked up to receive his reaction. He was slightly stunned and quiet. He then looked around, as did I. All others had knelt down in submission to Sustek's authority.

I stood and placed a hand on his shoulder. I was filled with the spirit of prophecy, for I began to utter words beyond my own comprehension. "You, King Sustek, will rule this kingdom with justice and law. You will remove burdens from the people, burdens set in place by your father's rule. You will cast aside his shadow and not walk in it and will make a name for yourself. The name Sustek will be written in the annals and be forever associated with justice, mercy, and compassion. And many generations to follow will be blessed."

Sustek's eyes filled with tears. "How can I possibly be all of that? I am just as selfish as my father."

I looked over his shoulder at Azghak. "There are those, King Sustek, who now are motivated to learn actual wisdom. They will learn this, and they will impart what they learn to you. They will labor—for their sake, for your sake, and for the sake of all Asemurans. You will harvest the fruits of their labor."

The young king began to nod. "I will do what you have stated." He paused and pressed his lips tight. His forehead pulled up taut. "But what about you? You will stay and offer your counsel as well, right?"

I responded, "The Guardians told me that I had been chosen. Chosen for what, I do not know." I stepped back and, with my right hand, gestured to the ruins all around us. "Your father's labors, everything he built was for himself. The Guardians have brought all of that to ruin. And now you are entrusted with rebuilding this city, but this time all labors will be for everyone."

Azghak approached me at this moment and stated, "Oleg, it is important that you jot down your account of this entire affair. It would also help if you wrote down whatever you've learned from …" Azghak paused.

I could tell that he was puzzled, and I offered to finish his thought, "The Guardians, Azghak, Chief Counselor to the king. The Guardians of Eternal Life, led by the Absolute One, the Keeper of Truth."

It was at this moment that Dermegg approached me. He fell down at my feet and stated, "Forgive me, Oleg. Forgive me for misjudging you at the beginning. If it helps at all, I took pity on you in my heart during that time. I was the only one who did not curse you. Now I ask that you take pity on me." He began to weep.

My heart was filled with compassion, and I reached down and gently took hold of him. I lifted him to his feet and then seized and hugged him. "I forgive you, friend. Let mercy triumph over judgment."

He stood, and we embraced each other as long lost friends.

I, Oleg, son of Armog, testify that everything I have written in this account is true. There is nothing further for me to write in this account. I also composed a second scroll consisting of absolute truths, those teachings of wisdom imparted to me during the several days I was exiled outside the city gates. I also composed a third scroll containing my dreams and interpretations.

CHAPTER 8

I have been watching through the eyes of the Guardians the emergence of Endheran humanity. At times, I feel peace and joy, for it seems that the Endherans are seeing a bright future and are moving toward eternal life. But I have also come to know sadness and concern. They can be so cruel to each other. A people evolve from primal bestiality to a progressive humanity in ebbs and flows, as a sea caresses a sandy beach. There is a bold approach, but then there is a slight recession. Still, they move forward in time.

"Prior to progression-led dominance in evolutionary development," Soleran says to me, "a people's behavior is primarily dominated by self-preservation. It takes many generations for a people to move away from hierarchal egocentric-governed behavior and toward a more concentric perspective. Even so, there are setbacks."

Natharon is studying intensely the data on his holographic display. He alters the variables and parameters, looking for a remedy to the dilemma at hand. I don't know exactly what is wrong, but I know that something isn't right. Several times, the Guardians have each reacted with sadness. They cover their faces and sigh. Even at this moment, Leostrom steps away as if the information is too much for him to bear.

My curiosity pulls me closer to their center, where Natharon's holographic display hovers in the midst of them. Looking at it, I glean from the display a survivability rating of 8.7. That's strange. When the Guardians concluded their intervention with Antraxid and Oleg, the survivability rating had climbed as high as 9.8. I gasp as I watch the rating drop to 8.3. It then drops again, to 8.1.

"What is happening?" I ask Evalene.

She doesn't acknowledge my question right away. Instead, she keeps her gaze on the display. The rating is now 7.6.

"A geological anomaly is infecting the populace of a certain region," Evalene finally answers. "The magnetic resonance emanating from the region is depreciating behavioral governance. It's corrupting their central nervous system."

"Oh," I say. I pretend that I understand, but I really don't.

"We need a solution," Soleran says. "How do we eradicate the anomaly and undo the damage?" He performs his own analysis, and data flashes on and off his display.

"Soleran," Natharon says, having ceased his analysis. There is a pause as Natharon waits for Soleran to acknowledge him. "Soleran?" Natharon says again.

I keep a little distance so as to stay out of the way, but I edge closer to Soleran so as to see what he is doing. Finally, he stops and faces Natharon.

"We have to destroy the region," Natharon says, "or the infection will spread beyond its borders and throughout Endhera." He walks up and places his hand on Soleran's shoulder. Both look deep into each other's eyes. I can't tell if they're comforting each other, or engaging in some kind of unspoken struggle.

"How did we miss this?" Soleran asks. He looks away, closes his eyes, and rubs his face with both hands.

"We will find out afterward," Natharon says. "I will submit a report to Epsilon Truthe."

Soleran walks over to the display with the survivability rating. It shows 7.4. Natharon follows him.

"We can't help those corrupted by the anomaly," Natharon says. "A small fraction of the population is still above the threshold. We can save those. You know already, the more time that elapses, the more damage done."

"Proceed," Soleran says. "But with caution."

Natharon nods. "I suggest carrying out the intervention as previously planned. We just need to modify the approach to accommodate our containment."

"Dyllon," Soleran says, walking over to the Guardian with the bushy white eyebrows, "who is the candidate?"

Dyllon examines the information on his display. "Our initial candidate has been terminated from the series by the anomaly. Permit me to find another." He keys in commands on his display, and I can hear them beeping. Finally, he stops and nods. "The next best candidate will be difficult to persuade. You'll have to leave him a small window of options. His name is Shepheth, a merchant in the city of Oloxi-Prell, which is at the heart of the anomaly."

"How did he avoid infection?" Soleran asks.

"An underlying time current that propagated distinctively from the main current," Dyllon answers. "He suffered loss years prior, with the death of his wife and child." Dyllon turns from the display and looks at Soleran. "He remembers them, and their memory keeps him at the threshold. But it won't for much longer. He teeters on the edge."

"Okay," Soleran says, looking around at everyone in his vicinity. "Let's do this."

I turn my attention to the display and study the imagery. It focuses in on the city. My thoughts get lost in the lights. The entire bridge of the *Intrepidium* encompasses the holographic display. We start from a great height, as if in the clouds. The display then slowly moves downward, out of the sky, until it settles above the city. I stumble slightly, feeling a little dizzy and light-headed. My feet feel the force of a floor, but my eyes see mist awash with sunlight and dazzling arcs of color.

Oloxi-Prell is a metropolis. It bustles with activity, with much moving to and fro, with life and living. It is the social center of the region, drawing people from afar to gaze upon its wonders. It is the center of the newest technologies of civil engineering, such as plumbing, bringing fresh water into the city and taking out wastewater.

The buildings and bridges consist of high-precision masonry and splendid architecture. The streets are paved with polished stone. Elaborate gardens and fountains adorn its every corner. At first impression, the city is alive and well.

Yet Oloxi-Prell is a graveyard. It is sick and corrupt. Crime dominates its underground. The streets are clean on top, but within the cracks, the stones are saturated with blood. The water is polluted with toxins, so much so that the plants are dying from the roots up. The nights are filled with noise—an admixture of gaiety and partying, along with screams of horror and cries of suffering.

We settle in on the morning, the sunlight peeking through some arches in the distance. Shadows flee, and the city awakens. Guards walk about wearing steel armor and carrying weapons. A butcher opens up his booth and begins bringing out stripped game. I'm puzzled. I had overheard someone mention that a famine had hit the region and that game was scarce. This butcher, though, has an abundant amount. Wait. The meat is not from wild game. Horror strikes deep within me. I look at Soleran, who notices my reaction. Sadness is in his eyes. Leostrom also looks incredibly sad. That may be a tear flowing down his face. I can't tell from here. Addia-Sahl stares at the holographic ground. She is quiet and contemplative. Evalene looks at me and shrugs. I return my observation to the game. I must be frank, though the implication frightens me. The meat resembles skinned, headless children, hung from the feet. Handless arms hang down. I put my own hand to my mouth to hold in my gasps. Then I study my hand and then the meat. Now I understand the dilemma. Cannibalism.

Soleran gestures with his right hand by holding it out in front of him. As he closes his grip and moves it around, the image shifts. He does this for a few minutes, until he settles the image onto a plaza. Two small wagons, each with four wooden, spoked wheels, sit in the sunlight. Half of the wagons are covered, one with a red, dirty cloth and the other with a dark-brown cloth. Each wagon is latched to a hunched-over, bipedal beast of burden. The hide looks tough and wrinkled. The beasts' legs are oversized, but their arms are held up underneath and look puny. The beasts' muzzles extend from a fat face with big, droopy-looking eyes. The beasts grunt and kick up a little bit of dust.

"Simmer down! Simmer down!" A plump, heavy Endheran wearing a white blouse with blue trousers and black leather boots exits an open doorway with an armload of items that look like pottery and bronze dishes. He lays them carefully in the wagon with the red cloth.

A second Endheran, slender and tall, exits with another armload. He wears a tan robe with a green cowl over his head. A green belt is wrapped around his waist and latched with a bronze buckle. Upon his feet are sandals with thin, leather straps.

"Yah want this stuff in mah wagon or in yors?" asks the slender Endheran.

"Hah!" says the heavy one. "Yous gonna put it over here in mine! Yessiree! Over here, I says."

The slender man complies, adding the armload to the wagon with the red cloth.

"Yous got a weapon?" asks the heavy man.

"Griff!" cries the slender man. "I saids I bring one."

"Yeah? Lemmee see it!" Griff says. He leans against his wagon and cocks his right foot over his left.

The thin man walks over to the wagon covered with the dark-brown cloth and retrieves a small dagger.

"Gawk!" Griff says. "What in Sashaye's belly have you got there? A bread cutter? A flippin' bread cutter? Really, Shepheth!"

"Well!" Shepheth says, "Ah'm no hunter! What need do I have for a weapon? Whatchyoo look'n fers anyways? Maybe a ballista?"

The heavy man bellows with laughter, holding his gut. He then turns and retrieves from under the seat of his wagon a large cutlass. The handle is half an arm's length and curves at the end. A tassel dangles from the curvature. The sheath is leather and laced with colored strips. With a smirk, Griff yanks the blade from the sheath. Its edge has wicked teeth, like the fangs of a wild beast. Griff approaches Shepheth, who looks at him as if unimpressed. Griff puts the blade to

Shepheth's neck. He then motions as if he's slicing, making a ripping noise.

"Ah'm no hunter," Shepheth says.

"Yeah, you saids that already," Griff says.

"Ah'm a vendor," Shepheth says. "Ah sells merchandise."

"Hush up and get yerself over heya," Griff says, "and lemmee give you a better weapon than that silly bread slicer."

Shepheth reluctantly obeys, walking up to Griff, who leans over into his wagon. He pulls another cutlass from under the seat. It's smaller than the first one but is much bigger than Shepheth's dagger.

"Heya," Griff says, thrusting the smaller cutlass to Shepheth. "Take it, and yous rememba, show it to the bandits, so they get skerred and run, right?"

Shepheth nods and takes the smaller cutlass. He studies the handle, which has an emblem of a winged creature embedded in the base. The sheath is made of leather but is more generic than Griff's larger one. Shepheth shakes his head in a comical manner and walks over to his wagon. His beast kicks up some dust and grunts.

"Chipwitz!" Shepheth says. He pulls a small bag from his wagon and walks up to the beast's muzzle. Pulling a handful of grain from the bag, Shepheth brings it up to the mouth of the beast, who quickly thrusts out his tongue to gobble up the treat. "Yeah, there yah go." Shepheth closes the bag and then pats the beast on his side.

"Hey!" Griff hollers from atop his wagon. He's seated and turned to face Shepheth. "Keep yerself up and don't lag behind. I better turn 'round and sees yous right behind me, right?"

"Stop whining!" Shepheth says. "Get on, already! Ah gotta get back before evanun'."

With a smile, Griff nods and turns back around. He kicks up a set of reins, and his beast lunges forward, jerking the wagon from its sandy ruts. Shepheth leaps up into the seat of his wagon and does the same. The beast named Chipwitz lunges forward.

The two-wagon caravan weaves its way through the tightly packed street. One stranger peeks over the side of Griff's wagon and tries to look under the cloth.

"Heya now!" Griff hollers at him, raising the back of his hand.

Shepheth chuckles from behind. When Griff turns around to glare at him, Shepheth points and laughs harder. Griff shakes his head and looks forward. The two reach the gates. The guards walk upon a rampart overhead, glaring at them. Griff leads the caravan to the side and stops. He then steps down and walks over to a small mound. Shepheth does the same and approaches from behind him.

"Always good to take a quick peek," Griff says, looking off into the distance. "Gotta look for that bandit scout who keeps his eyes on the gates, look'n for fools to wander into a trap."

"Yeah," Shepheth says with lack of interest. "Ah don't see anything."

"Pheh!" Griff says. "I don't trust yo eyes!"

"Well, look already," Shepheth says, "and let's get on."

"Hush!" Griff says. "I wanna be sure." He stares out over the hills, glaring at any and every spot, as if expecting to see someone.

Shepheth turns and kicks at a stone and returns to his wagon. He leaps up into the seat and waits for Griff. The heavy Endheran nods as if satisfied and then returns to his wagon. The short caravan then continues on its way.

Soleran shifts the image, and it moves over to a small hill. A man lies on a rock watching as Griff and Shepheth leave the gates. He's well camouflaged, wearing material that resembles the rocks upon which he lies. His face is covered in a gravel-colored dust. He slips off the rock and backs down into a gulch. He then races down a trail behind a hill. Soleran looks at Leostrom, who nods and smiles slightly.

The caravan continues down the road until it approaches a tight chasm between steep hillsides. Griff turns in his seat and glares at Shepheth. With his first and middle fingers, he motions to his eyes and then waves them out to the hillside on his left. Shepheth follows the gesture and looks back and forth at the hilltop. He then looks back to Griff, who is staring at him. Griff then frantically points at the hilltop. Shepheth shrugs, and Griff throws up his arms as if annoyed. He then looks forward again.

"Pheh!" Shepheth says to himself. "What's he getting worked up over? There's no one there."

On the hilltop, several camouflaged men slip away from their spots. Behind the hill, the group of Endheran men meet up. A herd of saddled beasts huddle near a mouth exiting the gulch, where they are hidden from sight. The beasts resemble the ones pulling Griff's and Shepheth's wagons but are slender and muscular.

"We got us a coupl'a gonkers down below," the leader says to his men, who mumble and snicker amongst themselves. "Let's go relieve them of their cargo." At that, the men mount the saddled beasts and turn to exit the gulch.

Standing in the middle of the narrow exit is a stranger, an unknown Endheran. He's dressed in a clean, white vesture with golden lace. Around his neck is a large, gold chain. A golden sash with a gold buckle holds the robe in check. His skin is dark but smooth and shiny. He smiles and lifts his right hand up to stroke his beard. His fingers are decked in gold rings with precious stones of every color.

The leader of the bandits halts and looks him up and down. There is a long pause, as if the leader expects some unseen surprise. Finally, he shifts in his saddle to look at two men on his right. The leader nods toward the stranger. The two men look at each other, smiling, and then they dismount. As they approach, they draw misshapen blades. The stranger grins widely and tilts his head to the left. A string of gold light flashes across his eyes. All of a sudden, the two men scream in a panic and start swinging their swords wildly. One inadvertently stabs the chest of the other, who manages to swing around and slice into the first one's throat. Both men drop to the ground and writhe for a moment in agony. The leader and three others move their mounts back, trying to understand what is happening.

"Cut him down!" the leader commands the remaining three.

They leap from their mounts and draw their weapons. The stranger sighs and shakes his head to the side slightly, as if displeased. Gold light flashes across his eyes, and the men begin to stumble about, shrieking. They swing wildly, as if fighting an unseen enemy, and end up cutting each other down.

"Hell risen!" the leader utters in disgust. He leaps from his mount and draws his weapon. "What did ya do to mah men?"

"Actually," the stranger says, "I took their sight, nothing more."

The bandit leader stops and looks around. He then turns and runs toward a high trail in the back that leads out of the gulch.

"Wait!" the stranger says. "I just want to talk to you."

The bandit leader races up the trail but loses his footing and tumbles over the side and down into the rocks below. He slams against a rock, which crushes his skull, killing him instantly.

The stranger sighs and looks off to the side in disgust. He shakes his head and turns to walk away. He teleshifts down below to two other Endheran men dressed like him.

"How did it go?" One asks.

"The wicked flee when no one pursues," he answers.

Satisfied, the One nods and looks back down at the trail below. Around a bend in the distance, the two-wagon caravan comes into view. The three Endheran men phase out and become invisible. Griff's wagon passes them. They watch him closely but eventually shift their gaze to Shepheth. He's several wagon lengths behind Griff.

As Shepheth approaches, the wagon suddenly jerks, almost tossing him from the seat. He yelps but manages to gain control of himself. Sitting back in an upright position, he pulls on the reins of his beast, who complies by stopping. Looking over the left side of the wagon, Shepheth notices that his front wheel is bashed to pieces. Looking back a little ways, he notices a large stone on the trail. Pieces of splintered wood lie around the stone.

"Blast it all!" Shepheth says, throwing down the reins.

The beast grunts.

"Shut it, Chipwitz!" Shepheth says. He leaps from the wagon and looks ahead of the trail to the backside of Griff's wagon. The heavy man rides on, unaware of the plight of the other man. Shepheth yells, "Griff! Hey, Griff!"

Griff rides on, oblivious.

"Yah fat bastard!" Shepheth says. "Lookee back! Turn around, yah tooth-rotted, ugly-faced gonker!"

Griff still rides on.

"Pheh!" Shepheth says. "The dumbledon is deaf of hearing! What hav'Ah gotta do? Scream bloody murder?" The slender Endheran runs forward a few steps and screams as loudly as his lungs will allow. "Bandits! Bandits! Everywhere! Bandits!"

Griff rides on.

"Yah stupid son of a wild khrog!" Shepheth exclaims, kicking at several rocks. One rock is too big, and his exposed toe slams it. He yelps in pain and begins to stumble around. Finally, he limps back to the wagon. Chipwitz looks at him and grunts.

"Shut yah mouth!" Shepheth says. "Ah don't wants to heerit!"

The beast flips his head up and down and stomps a couple of times, kicking up some dust.

"Ah says to shut it!" Shepheth says, raising his hand as if to strike the beast. He doesn't, however. He sighs and drops his hand to his side.

"Trouble?" A voice sounds to the left side of the wagon, up the hillside a ways.

Shepheth panics and falls back. Looking up the hillside, he sees three Endheran men, all dressed in clean, white robes.

"What in all of Sashaye's belly?" Shepheth says. "Whatchya'll want? Bandits!" With the final exclamation, Shepheth limps quickly to the seat. He reaches in and removes the small cutlass, grasping the sheath with his left hand and the handle tightly with his right hand. He holds it up in front of him, toward the three strangers.

As he starts to pull the cutlass from the sheath, the middle man's eyes flash with gold light. Shepheth yanks the cutlass from the sheath, but instead of a steel blade, a bouquet of flowers emerges.

"Ahh!" Shepheth yells. He stares in disbelief at the flowers. Dropping them, he turns and looks in the wagon again. He grabs his small dagger and holds it to his side, looking around for the real cutlass. Not finding it, he looks back down at the handled bouquet.

He picks it up and studies the emblem of the winged creature on the handle.

He looks back at the three men, who watch him with curiosity. Shepheth drops the flowers and starts to draw his own dagger. The middle man's eyes flash again. Shepheth draws a few strands of wild grass attached to the handle of his dagger.

"Pheh!" Shepheth curses. He tosses it to the ground. "Stop that! What it is yahs doing!" He turns and looks around on the trail. Finally, he reaches down and picks up a huge rock.

The middle man smiles. As Shepheth pulls it back to launch it, the middle man's eyes flash. Shepheth stops and brings it forward to look at it. He then tears it apart. "Bread! Impossible!" He takes a bite. "Tasty too!" He spits it out. "Pheh! Probably poisonous!"

"Shepheth," the middle man says, "we need your help."

"Are you crazy?" Shepheth asks. "I'm the one who needs help!"

"With what?" the middle man asks.

"Well, I … well." Shepheth thinks for a moment. "First, my wheel is busted," Shepheth says pointed to his front left wheel. As he looks at it, the wheel appears repaired. "What?" he yelps, falling back. "What are ya'lls? Sawcers? Muhjishuns? Conjurs of magic?"

"We call ourselves Guardians," the middle man says. "We ask that you help us."

"Whatchyah need help with?" Shepheth says. "Ah'm no hunter or warrior. Ah'm a lowly vendor sell'n stuff and whatnot. This stuff isn't even mine. It belongs to a friend of mine."

"We know, Shepheth," the middle man says.

"Why you know my name?" Shepheth asks.

"We know everyone's name," the middle man says. "Your friend's name is Griff. Your mother's name was Kapsi. Your father's name was Jinwes. Your khrog's name is Chipwitz. Your wife's name was Suey. Your daughter's name was Nindy."

"A'ight!" Shepheth says. "Don'tcha go speak'n their names! Let their spirits rest in peace, Ah says!"

The middle man looks to the man on his right, who sighs and shrugs slightly.

"Whatchya want with me?" Shepheth says. He limps forward and tosses the bread at the feet of the three men. "Who are ya?"

"We are Guardians, from the heavens," the middle man says, taking his eyes off the bread to nod upward. "We ask that you return back to Oloxi-Prell."

"What?" Shepheth says. "Why?"

"Be at peace," the man on the left says. "We wish you no harm."

"Shepheth," the middle man says, "return to Oloxi-Prell and deliver our message. Then, if you would, pick up some people and ride to the Enodd Temple in the town of Ozari."

"Hah!" Shepheth says. "Lookee heya! My khrog is aimed toward Heerem, and there's no way for me to turn around in this cursed slit of earth." Shepheth turns to point to his wagon. To his amazement, the wagon is turned toward Oloxi-Prell. Chipwitz the khrog turns to look back at Shepheth. He grunts and stomps the ground, kicking up dust. "Ahh!" Shepheth hollers. The vendor falls to the ground, falling on his rear with such a force that he screams and doubles over holding onto his wounded buttocks. "Don't!" Shepheth says, crawling away.

"Shepheth," the middle man says, "we are not bandits. Do we look like bandits?"

"Ah'm no messenger!" Shepheth says. "Ah'm just a lowly vendor." He pulls himself up on a small boulder and situates himself as comfortably as he can.

Several minutes pass. Shepheth has his legs pulled up underneath him. He looks at the three men, who remain where they are. The middle man is standing with his hands clasped behind his back. He tilts his head to the side and raises his eyebrows. Shepheth slides down off the boulder and approaches the men.

"Fine!" Shepheth says. "Like Ah gots a choice. Ah'm on my way back to Oloxi-Prell. Whatchya want me to say to the people?"

"Tell them to flee to Ozari," the middle man says. "Tell them that the Guardians of the Morning Rise are going to destroy Oloxi-Prell with fire from the heavens."

"What?" Shepheth says. "What is that nonsense! A'ight!" Shepheth says, throwing his hands in the air. "If yah says so, Ah'll do it! But Ah's swarr that's the most ridic'lous thing Ah've heered in a long time."

"We will tell you where to go afterward," the man on the left says, "so as to pick up those who will flee with you to the Enodd Temple."

"When your foot touches the floor of the Enodd Temple," the man on the right says, "a rain of fire will destroy the region, including Oloxi-Prell."

"Pheh!" Shepheth says. He walks to the wagon, still nursing his wounded foot and sore buttocks. Slowly, he lifts himself up into the seat. Wiping his face with his hand, he shifts around in the seat to face the three men. They are gone. "What the …?" He throws his hands up in the air and, while clearly frustrated, snatches up Chipwitz's reins. He snaps them, and the khrog lunges forward. "Ah'm supposed to march right into the middle of town and tell folks that the city is gonna be wiped off the face of the Earth by fires from the sky. Yeah, right! Who am I? A cursed vendor, nothing more. Ah just wanna make a lil' money, a lil', a lil' living, nothing more, just some Guardians from high in the sky want me to make a fool of myself. Fine! Ah's got nothing better to do!"

Shepheth mumbles all the way back to Oloxi-Prell. He approaches the gates of the city as the main sun sits high in the sky. He stretches and massages his neck. He makes his way back up the main road, which is more crowded than it was earlier. He stops, and people walk by, staring at him. He stands up and looks around. Finally, he throws his arms up in the air and shouts with his loudest voice. "Hear me, Oloxi-Prell! Guardians are gonna destroy the city!" Most people stop to listen, but some just laugh and continue on their way. Those who stop and listen, point and laugh. "Hah!" Shepheth says. "I did my part." He collapses back down into his seat. "Where do Ah go now? Huh? Well? Ah'm waiting." He looks around, hoping to see the three men approach. There is nothing. "Pheh! Whatchyah want me to do?"

"Shut it!" an old man says as he walks by. "Stop talking to yerself."

Shepheth glares at him as he passes. At that moment, Shepheth notices a couple of people reaching under the brown cloth covering his wagon.

"Hey!" Shepheth exclaims, leaping up to face them. "Stop that! What's wrong with yah?"

One man, young but dressed in ragged clothes, pulls out a bronze pot. He examines it closely and then sticks it under his arm.

"Put it back, fool!" Shepheth says, leaping from the wagon. As he lands on his sore toe, he stumbles and falls to the ground and screams out in pain. In a flash, bystanders descend on the wagon. The brown cloth is torn from the wagon and tossed to the side where Shepheth lies. The cloth covers him, and he fights to free himself from underneath. "Curses! Curses to all of ya!" When he finally stands, he looks into the empty wagon. "Sashaye! Griff is gonna skin me alive and sell my corpse to the butcher!"

"There was no room in the wagon, Shepheth," a voice sounds above him. He jerks around while looking upward, all the while cowering down at the side of the wagon.

"What?" Shepheth asks.

"There was no room for your passengers with it full of merchandise," the voice says. "Now there is plenty of room."

"Well!" Shepheth says. People stare at him as they walk by. He glares back at them. "Can't you leave me alone! Choose another! Ah'm gonna get locked up in a crazy house."

"We need for you to continue speaking the message," the voice says. "There are still a few hours left before gathering the others and leaving for Ozari. Then you have but a few more hours afterward to make it to the Enodd Temple."

Shepheth rolls his eyes and sighs in frustration. "Why yah'll doing this anyways? What we do?" he asks as he walks through the crowd. "What justifies wiping out an entire city of people who go about their business, buyun', sellun', buildun', tearun' down, teachun' and learnun', and whatever else?" He leaves the plaza and walks down a set of steps. He doesn't pay much attention to exactly where he is going. He just walks forward, letting his feet take him wherever.

"How can yah do this?" Shepheth stops in front of a butcher's booth. The butcher has cooked some of his meat, and he stands off to the side, munching on strips. The butcher and Shepheth stare at each other. The butcher is burly and tall and wears a bloody brown apron. Shepheth looks him up and down and then focuses on the meat hanging from a rafter. The wind blows through the carcasses, swaying them ever so slightly.

"The meat is cured," the butcher says, "just in case you's wondering." He finishes off the last slabs, licks his fingers, and approaches the counter from inside the booth.

Shepheth just stands there staring at him.

"It's cured," the butcher repeats. "Don'tcha worry."

"Did they suffer?" Shepheth asks.

"What?" the butcher asks. He leans against the counter with both hands, as if the counter will topple over otherwise. "Yous some kinda objector?" The butcher sighs and grabs a rag from below and starts wiping down the counter top. "You know, it's the perfect solution. The famine is ending, and the state welfare is balancing itself out. So what yous objecten' to? Peace and prosperity?"

Shepheth doesn't respond but watches the butcher wipe the counter. Finally the butcher finishes and puts away the rag. Then he leans against the counter again and stares at Shepheth. As if receiving a cue, Shepheth approaches the counter. He leans in toward the butcher, his voice falling to a whisper.

"Oloxi-Prell is gonna be destroyed," Shepheth says.

The butcher remains quiet. He gives Shepheth a hard look and then he turns around to hang up more meat from a crate.

"You don't believe me, do you?" Shepheth asks.

The butcher finishes and then turns to face Shepheth. Looking over Shepheth's shoulder, the butcher gestures to a couple of city guards, who casually walk over to the booth.

"Share with these gen'lemen what yous just told me," the butcher says. He nods to Shepheth, looking at the guards.

Shepheth stares at the countertop.

"He says Oloxi-Prell is gonna be destroyed," the butcher says.

The guards look at each other and chuckle. "Do you need to visit the mind doctor?" the larger of the two asks. His helm and armor are made of steel but are polished to a rough luster, so as not to blind people with reflecting sunlight. A tabard hangs over his shoulders. An emblem of a set of spears, four total, is stitched on both the front and the back. The helm is a skull cap with a strip of steel stretched out to protect the bridge of the nose.

"Yeah, yeah, the mind doctor," the smaller guard says, finishing with a squeaky laugh.

"No," Shepheth says. "Ah'm fine. Ah was just sharun' a thought with this heya fellah."

The larger guard grabs Shepheth under his armpit. "Yous cause'n trouble?"

"No," Shepheth says.

"Good!" the larger guard says. "Your fine is four hundred shupels. Pay up or go to jail."

Shepheth starts to reach for his money bag, but upon thinking of the amount, he pauses and looks at the guard, worried. "Ah don't have that much."

"Oh, that would be too bad," the larger guard says. The smaller guard walks around to Shepheth's other side.

"Lemmee check," Shepheth says, pulling out his money bag.

"Yeah, you do that," the larger guard says.

Shepheth opens it up and reluctantly peeks inside, as if expecting it to be empty. He then reaches inside and pulls out a roll of yellowed parchment cut into squares. Unfolding the money, he sees that it is exactly four hundred. "Sashaye!" he mumbles to himself. He slowly extends it to the large guard, who wastes no time in yanking the money from Shepheth's grasp. The two look at each long and hard. Finally the guard releases his grip. Looking to the smaller guard, he gestures with a nod for the small guard to follow. They walk away, leaving Shepheth looking in his money bag. Shepheth looks up from the bag and notices the butcher chuckling to himself. The butcher is picking his teeth with a small, sharp stick.

Shepheth wanders through the streets. As he bumps into people, he says to each one, "Oloxi-Prell is gonna be destroyed. Flee to Ozari." One man laughs and walks away. Another yanks his arm from Shepheth's grasp and curses. And still another spits on Shepheth.

"Shepheth," Soleran says, "it is time to go get everyone."

Having lost track of time, the vendor sighs and continues walking. He eventually enters a side street, at the end of which is his wagon with Chipwitz still hooked to it. An old man is standing in front of Chipwitz, yanking on the khrog's reins.

"Come on, ya rank, dirty creature," the old man says.

Shepheth casually strolls up to him and stops to stare at him.

The old man notices and ceases pulling on the reins. "Whaddya want? Eh?" the old man asks. He reaches for a dagger at his side.

Shepheth slowly reaches for the reins. The old man drops them and backs away slowly. Shepheth tosses the reins over the khrog's head and then leaps up into the wagon. As he starts to pull away, he looks down at the old man.

"Oloxi-Prell is gonna be destroyed, and Ah'm fleeing to Ozari," Shepheth says. "Do yah wanna come?"

The old man laughs and then waves his dagger. "You better flee!" the old man says. "I'll cut you up for the butcher!"

Shepheth watches over his shoulder as the old man dances about madly, waving the dagger overhead. The old man then darts down the street.

"Where to, then?" Shepheth asks, ready to snap the reins.

"Here," Soleran says. "The first person is in the house with the red sign."

Shepheth looks around in disbelief.

"We persuaded the thief to bring the wagon here," Soleran says.

Shepheth jumps from the wagon and approaches a building with a red sign hanging over the door. As he starts to knock, the door opens and an old woman dressed in ragged clothing exits carrying a bag. She walks over to the wagon, tosses it in the back, and then climbs in. She finds a place to get comfortable and then she looks at Shepheth. She raises her shoulders and her eyebrows.

"Okay," Shepheth mumbles to himself. He climbs up into the seat of the wagon.

A couple of hours pass as Shepheth rides around the city. The wagon has four people in it. The last person, a young boy—an orphan—climbs into the wagon and takes a seat.

"You have completed the second stage of your mission," Soleran says to Shepheth. "It is time to go to Ozari."

Shepheth turns and looks at the four passengers. "This is it?" Shepheth asks. "In this whole gonkered city, only four are worthy of saving?"

"Shepheth," Soleran says, "you told so many, and no others listened."

"Why?" Shepheth asks.

"It is not in their nature," Soleran says.

"Then why have me go to so much trouble?" Shepheth asks. "Ah'd rather had gone on to Ozari." He turns to face forward and tosses the reins. Chipwitz lunges forward.

"We always maintain the smallest degree of hope," Soleran says, "that we are mistaken in our judgment."

Shepheth sighs and rides on until the wagon leaves the city gates. He turns to the north and whips the reins to prod Chipwitz onward.

"Shepheth!" a voice yells.

The vendor stops and looks back. Griff has abandoned his wagon and rides upon his khrog's saddled back. He rides up to Shepheth's wagon, staring at the passengers and then at Shepheth himself.

"I won't forget this!" Griff says with an evil grin.

"Thieves stole yah stuff, Griff," Shepheth says. "Ah's gots—"

"Sure they did," Griff says.

"—bruises to prove it."

"Sure, sure," Griff says. "Where yous headen'?"

"Ozari," Shepheth says. "Enodd's Temple." There's a pause, as the two stare at each other. "Come with us. Don't go back to Oloxi-Prell."

"Oh, don't worry," Griff says, "I'm gonna go get the guards, and we'll meet yous there."

Shepheth doesn't respond.

"Get some rest," Griff says. "Yous got a night to rest up. Don't run, cuz it'll just make the guards mad." With that, Griff's grin fades into a scowl. The heavy Endheran turns his beast toward Oloxi-Prell and rides away.

Shepheth looks at the four passengers. They stare back but say nothing. Shepheth sighs and looks toward Ozari. The road to Ozari is old, having been paved with stones ages ago. Its upkeep is minimal, so some stones have been uplifted and moved slightly by vegetation and erosion. The ride is a little rough, but the khrog is strong and has no problem tugging the five people along. Shepheth stops a few times to warn travelers to flee to Ozari. Most ignore him. One turns around and follows him on another khrog. As he gets close to the town, with a small stone wall encircling it, he warns two farmers in a field. They look at each other and then turn and run to the town. Shepheth rides into town, and townspeople approach the wagon. He explains to them what is happening.

"Stay in your homes," Shepheth says. "This town will be saved from destruction."

Shepheth walks up a steep, high set of steps leading to the Enodd Temple. A group of townspeople and the four passengers from Oloxi-Prell follow. He reaches the top and steps aside to catch his breath. Letting all the others enter, he goes to the doorway but stops. Staring at the floor, he sighs. He then turns to look back at Oloxi-Prell, shaking his head. Leostrom, Dyllon, and Natharon hover nearby, invisible. All three watch as Shepheth turns and steps forward. Instantly, they teleshift back to the *Intrepidium*. Natharon immediately activates commands on his display, and the outer ring of the *Intrepidium* booms into motion. Arcs of energy flow from both sides and meet in the middle of the *Intrepidium*'s shielding, at which a sphere of energy emits from the shielding and falls toward the Earth. Within a second, more energy arcs in the front and emits continuously so that there is a steady stream of energy. Shepheth's foot touches the floor as the first sphere of energy falls to Oloxi-Prell. He manages to put his weight on the front foot and shift off the back foot, when behind him erupts a bright light. The quake hits the town, and he falls forward into the temple. The sound behind him claps like thunder and then roars with a rushing wind. From the *Intrepidium*, a bluish beam emits from the shielding just underneath the arcs of white energy. Shepheth crawls to a window on the left side of the door and peeks out. A cloud of smoke and fire rushes toward Ozari but collides with a force field covering the town. Shepheth watches as flashes of blue lightning flow across the invisible shielding. The smoke and fire outside the shielding are kept at bay. The spheres of energy fall upon the region one after another. The plain erupts in fire. A mountain is demolished, with rocks and debris flying up into the lower atmosphere. Water in a lake evaporates in seconds. On the *Intrepidium*, the Guardians on the bridge open holographic displays and begin keying in their commands. The *Intrepidium* responds with blue beams emitting toward the Earth. Shepheth peeks out again and sees that dark-brown clouds have blotted out the sky. The town is engulfed in the darkness, the only light coming from the blue flashes of the shielding. The region continues to quake violently. Dust from the temple's roof falls upon Shepheth's shoulders as he peers just over the window sill.

Natharon ceases the bombardment, and, as far as I can see, all the Guardians on the bridge activate their own displays. The outer ring of the *Intrepidium* still rotates with arcs of energy flowing around it. Beams of blue energy emit toward the Earth from the ring. I walk around in my area and observe what I can. One group is stabilizing Endhera's molten core to prevent shock waves from inducing tectonic plate activity and provoking more earthquakes. Another group is stabilizing the atmosphere. Various parts of Endhera are displayed holographically, and I can't make up my mind which image I want to study. I find myself wandering from image to image, so as to watch what is happening. The good thing about my height is that I can walk right under some holographic displays without interfering with them.

Shepheth watches as the dark clouds of smoke and fire subside to a blue, partly cloudy sky. In the distance, pillars of blue light pierce the clouds and flow across the ground. Massive fires in the east are extinguished as the pillars flow over them. Far to the west used to be a mountain range. The horizon is now flat. To the south, where Oloxi-Prell sat in a valley, the Earth looks like a ruined chasm, driven deep down below the horizon.

"The southern sea wall has collapsed," Natharon says. The image shows water pouring into the chasm. "I will stabilize the flow to prevent backlashes." He initiates a blue beam from the *Intrepidium*'s ring. It flows over the waters of the southern sea just beyond the collapsed wall. I can see the beam reach all the way to the sea bed. It seems to me that it applies some kind of pulsating force, both to absorb shock waves and initiate counterwaves.

Shepheth leaves the temple and walks down the steps with caution. He turns and looks at the temple doorway, perhaps to judge the distance, should he need to hasten back to safety. Looking around, he gasps. Then he proceeds down the steps. As he walks down a street, a massive blue pillar of light whisks by the town gates. Shepheth panics and runs to a small house. He leaps through the window, sending a shower of glass and splinters of wood over the people huddled below the window sill. He gathers himself, checking himself for any cuts, and quickly crawls over to the busted window. The mother and her three children move to let him look out the window. The blue pillar is within sight but far away. He looks at the busted remains of the window and then at the woman.

"Sorry," he says. The woman has a blank look, as if panic has long since given way to surrender. Shepheth stands and dusts himself off. Walking out the front door, he looks for the blue pillar. It's a thin streak, far to the horizon, but it looks like it is approaching again. Taking a deep breath, Shepheth runs to the town gates. Down the road, he passes the stables and finds himself ducking inside. In a stall at the far end, he sees Chipwitz. He opens the stall door and walks inside. Chipwitz is traumatized but, upon seeing Shepheth, nods his head up and down and stomps his hind foot, stirring up some dirt and dust. Shepheth walks over to him, and whispers soothingly while massaging the khrog's neck.

Shepheth bursts through the open gates riding Chipwitz and heads toward what used to be Oloxi-Prell. In the distance, he sees a group of about five tornadoes, spaced far apart. The wind is fierce, and his cowl blows off his head, tossing white strands of hair into his face. Blue pillars intercept the tornados, dispersing the funnels. Chipwitz rides on. He approaches a rocky cliff looking down upon the demolished Earth. Massive boulders lie about like pebbles. The entire region appears to be scorched.

Shepheth dismounts. As he stares into the blackened abyss, numerous people appear around the rim of the newly formed, empty sea. Shepheth stares at the exact spot where Oloxi-Prell used to be. Then the Earth begins to rumble. Chipwitz turns and runs back toward Ozari. Shepheth watches but only for a few seconds. Disinterested, he turns back to the empty chasm. In the distance, he sees a wall of white. The Earth rumbles more and more as the wall approaches. Folks scream and run away from the rim. Not Shepheth. He seems thrilled and aware, as if he's drinking a water that is saving him from death.

The wall of white, a wall of watery foam, flows up to the wall of earth and collides. The Earth shakes, and sounds of stone cracking ring out in the air. Mists of water spray up the wall like an upside-down waterfall. Shepheth is soaked. As the water falls away, Shepheth looks out into the new sea. The water roars violently, and Shepheth stares at it like it's a beast devouring the countryside. He then lowers his head and closes his eyes.

I hear a commotion behind me, and I turn to see what is happening. I'm standing under a holographic image, so I step forward slightly to get a better view. Soleran has dropped to his knees, and he is crying. Addia-Sahl drops down beside him and pulls him into her, laying his head on her shoulder. She too is crying. A Guardian whose name I don't know walks up to Leostrom and buries her face in his arm. He turns his head to acknowledge her need for solace. Everywhere I look, Guardians are crying or consoling each other. Dyllon is on his knees, with his face to the floor. Natharon kneels beside him and leans over his shoulders. Then I turn and see Evalene. She is staring at an image of the newly formed sea. She senses me looking at her, and she looks at me. I see in her eyes anger. She has her hand to her mouth, her elbow perched upon an arm crossing her chest. She returns her gaze to the image of the violently churning sea.

Feeling helpless, I walk around, looking at various images. The *Intrepidium* has ceased most activities. Some pillars of blue light still move around the land, putting out fires or softening the winds. I then find the image depicting the survivability rating. It's at 9.7. After a moment, it changes to 9.8. I want to smile, but I can't. Instead, I hear—or, more like feel—the pain of thousands. I listen to thoughts not my own.

> *I lay my face to the hollow depths,*
> *I speak sorrows to the winds,*
> *I pour tears on the scorched stones,*
> *I bury my face in the wounded earth,*
> *I lie in the ashes of fallen memorials,*
> *I swallow, but my throat is a fiery channel.*
> *I close my eyes and shut out the light,*
> *I lay my spirit in the grave but for a little while.*
> *I vow the vows that cannot be broken,*
> *I make promises that stand in time,*
> *I speak a matter, and it will be always.*
> *I dedicate a cause and pursue it, steadfast,*
> *I dream the dreams that create life,*
> *I utter words that heal the fallen spirit,*
> *I restore myself with love and hope.*

Confused, I walk around to the various images. One display has a command prompt. I reach up to touch it, and the *Intrepidium* responds by lowering it to my height. Holographic displays flash around my arms, as if the *Intrepidium* is relaying information about me. I look around, but all the Guardians are occupied. I touch the command prompt, but nothing happens.

"*Intrepidium*," I say. The prompt beeps, as if cuing me to continue. "Help me. Explain to me the cause of the anomaly, please."

A woman's digitized voice, calm and soothing, sounds out around me. "The anomaly is magnetic monopolar seepage resulting from gravitonic stream erosion, a naturally occurring phenomenon of hyperfluid condensate distribution."

"Oh," I say, partly understanding. I got "magnetic stream erosion" or something like that. "Did Maximeron have anything to do with this?" I don't know exactly why I ask, other than that I'm just curious. I expect a no.

"Yes," the *Intrepidium* answers.

"Omnitron, explicate," Soleran says, standing to his feet. I notice all the Guardians standing and approaching their displays.

"A magnetic monopole anomaly has been detected in a serial seven-four-nine-three-zero-one current flowing from Endhera's molten core to the caldera underneath the Oloxi region," the *Intrepidium* says.

"That warrants an investigation," Leostrom says, analyzing the data on his display. "We can intercept the monopole. I'm tracking its vector as we speak. It's using the metals in the molten rock to jump from current to current."

"Leostrom, Addia-Sahl," Soleran says, "come with me, please. You too, Brinn. Let's go see what Maximeron has created for us. I want to know what he has to do with the regional infection."

I walk up to him with a smile. He puts his hand on my shoulder.

"And thanks," Soleran says.

"Is Maximeron to blame?" I ask.

"He is the cause of the infection," Soleran says. He finishes his thought after taking a deep breath. "He forced our hand, but we have to remember our decision. We are still accountable for the remedy."

With a flash, the four of us teleshift into the Earth. We emerge in a firestorm, or more like a river of fire. Lava collides with our shielding and compresses around us in the lava tube. We step into the middle, walking upon a force field. Soleran raises his hand, and the shielding around us expands to enlarge our vicinity. We only have to wait for a few seconds. Directly in front of us emerges a bright white sphere flashing with electrical currents. As it approaches the fork in the lava spreading around us, the object emerges through our shielding into the vicinity. It then materializes into the form of a Huvril, except for the two black horns sticking out from his forehead. The being stands tall and muscular. The bottom of his gray-skinned frame is coated with black hair.

"Morghonox," Soleran says. "How fitting."

"Do not speak my name, infidel," Morghonox says. "I am the master of this domain." He finishes his statement with a roar.

Addia-Sahl walks around to his right and Leostrom to his left. Soleran approaches him face-to-face. I follow, closely.

"You're not real," Soleran says to the creature. "Your image is sustained holographically, and I'm curious as to how." Soleran looks over Morghonox's shoulder. I peek around his arm and see what Soleran is seeing. There is a silvery-white cord emerging from Morghonox's back and extending a couple of meters, hovering in the air, before it finally fades out of sight. "Now I see," Soleran says.

Soleran appears to have found the answer, so I want to see further what he sees. The *Intrepidium* interprets my desire and forms in my optical perspective the information in Soleran's optics. I see the cord extended into a dimensional portal. My eyesight zooms forward as I follow the cord through the interdimensional spatiality until a figure emerges in the distance. The image is opaque and hard to see, but the bright, blue-green outline is distinctly the figure of a man. He stands with his arms outstretched in front of him. The cord connects to his hands.

"Yeah," Soleran says, stepping back to face the image. "Hello, Maximeron. So once again we have to endure your meddling."

"You have to endure it," Morghonox says, "seeing that you have not the means to stop it." The Huvril image bursts into laughter.

"On the contrary," Soleran says, waving his hand. His eyes flash.

The silvery-white cord crackles in a small explosion, and the portal to the interdimensional corridor is closed. Morghonox screams as he fades from sight, his ghostly image dissipating like fog.

We return to the *Intrepidium*.

Section 2: Adversary

CHAPTER 9

I see them, clearly, the living souls of a tiny world unnamed where light is scant, and the air is cold, where oceans flow under miles of ice, where the parent star is but a tiny orb in the sky so that night and day are almost indistinguishable. These are an unknown people who barely survive on ice algae, frost ivy, and the flesh of the lesser creatures. They mull about, hunting, harvesting, laboring to stay alive in a hostile environment. Why are they even there? Because some distant star spewed its waste into space, and some passing comet swept up a few hardy molecules and deposited these molecules onto an otherwise dead world whose heat derives from the tidal gravity of a neighboring giant gas planet, and these molecules were activated by cosmic rays and began to form and change and transform and mutate into seeds of life. Millions, billions, trillions of encounters scattered throughout the universe, and this icy shard floating in the dead of space finds life by chance? The absurdity of it all offends me.

And here I am, looking down on these people covered with white fur, and their very existence offends me. Their cries and pleas offend me. They are so tiny and insignificant, the perturbations of their prayers barely register on the continuum, even locally. Yet when I approach, their prayers are like the banging of gongs. They are a blight, a virus, a cancer infecting the perfect nature that is chaos sublime. They will mature and grow and become intelligent enough to emerge into the universe like insects leaving their nest to infest nature with colony after colony. What will they contribute? Nothing. What can they contribute? They have nothing to offer, nothing to add. Instead they plunder the natural order of its essence. Every breath they take offends me. It is a stench in my nostrils.

The greater offense, however, is the acolytes of the Guardians, the Endherans. If it wasn't for Epsilon Truthe's meddling, they would not even exist. But in their conquest of nothingness, the Guardians plunder the essence of nature and present for transiting the unnatural Endheran race. So I look for the opportunity to enact a plan of old, a plan to sift the Endherans as nature sifts solar dust. All I need is one Endheran to test and show how futile the Guardian's choice was when selecting the Endherans over the Huvrils.

One vessel is nearby, one of particular interest—the *Astrasophia*. I see it, clearly. It's a poorly constructed mockery of a Guardian starship. The vessel's commanding authority is a Guardian protégé named Avera. She is greatly loved by Soleran. Why, I care not. All I know is that I want her. How can I lure her from the immediate reach of the *Intrepidium*? Simply by playing into her weakness of compassion. She'll be unable to resist coming to the aid of a people in danger.

I turn and look at the canine people that occupy the sphere of ice and water. I will assume my guise and fall upon them without mercy. I bear reptilian wings and elongate my neck. My face transforms into a fanged maw. Horns are raised on my forehead. A tail emerges from beastly hind legs. I clang together my razor talons. I roar, for I am the Dragon. I approach the tiny world. My eyes fall upon a single farmer removing algae from a block of ice. The fool! He will be the first to fall. He sees me and turns to run. I can hear the terror in his shriek. I unleash my breath of fire. He cries and pleads for a mere second, for one last time, and then he cries no more. Others see my light as the omen of their demise. They cry loud, their prayers of distress disturbing the continuum, sending ripples to the far reaches. It is as I have intended. I lay the region to waste and then wait for the response.

The *Astrasophia* is a saucer-shaped vessel relying upon impulsive warpiture propulsion. Striped decals decorate the uranium hull. The ship epitomizes the height of Endheran technology. The bridge is elliptic, with a teleprompter spanning the front half. Two half-circle consoles inlaid with numerous stations for communications, security, and navigation face the teleprompter, which captures the image of space outside the front face of the vessel. Avera and several officers, including her first officer named Ruden, occupy the back console. Ruden is an older gentleman, with grayish-brown hair and a scar under his left eye. A beeping sound alerts Ruden to the display at his station, next to Avera.

"We have detected a high output energy flux nearby," Ruden says with a bit of a rasp in his voice. "I'll look for continuum stability." Ruden presses several commands, each one beeping. "I'm able to detect perturbations at the center of the flux. The Omnitron has captured 1,700 signals."

"We've stumbled onto some kind of disaster," Avera says.

"Shall we proceed to intervene?" Ruden asks. "It lies just outside the *Intrepidium*'s jurisdiction."

Avera thinks for a moment. She then returns her gaze to Ruden. "Proceed."

The *Astrasophia* spins off to the lower right, orientated toward the disturbance. An hour later, the white glow of the energy flux appears on the teleprompter.

"We are approaching a dwarf planet of ice encircling a red dwarf star," Ruden says.

"Life readings?" Avera asks.

"There are none," Ruden answers. "I register nothing."

"They are all dead?" Avera asks with a gasp.

The ship stalls, having impacted an undetected field. Everyone on the bridge falls to the floor, but they immediately resume their stations.

"We are caught in some kind of stasis field," Ruden says. "I'm unable to pull us away."

"What is that?" Avera asks, pointing at the teleprompter.

Ruden activates more commands on his display. "It appears to be a single entity." He pauses, but only briefly. "It's a Guardian." He jerks his head up to Avera.

Soleran responds to the *Astrasophia*'s teleprompt, and Avera's image appears.

"Pardon me, Soleran," the brown-skinned protégé interjects.

"How can I assist you, Avera?" Soleran asks.

"We are in trouble," Avera says without further delay.

"Explain," Soleran says. The other Guardians cease their activities and immediately watch the holographic window over Soleran's shoulders.

"It appears that we have fallen into a trap," Avera says. Her eyes are wide with terror, and her voice is strained.

Soleran tenses his jaw but manages to whisper, "Maximeron."

"He approaches us," Avera says. "We are unable to pull from his stasis field."

"You cannot defeat him by yourself," Soleran warns her. "Do your best to escape, but if that's not possible, then hold him off as long as you can. We are on our way." Soleran turns to Natharon. "Get us there."

The navigator opens a holographic interface set with numerous command lines. They beep and emboss as he hits several in quick succession. The *Intrepidium*'s ring initiates, sending arcs of blue radiation from the ensuing energy field, and the *Intrepidium* bolts toward the *Astrasophia*. The Guardians, however, are over fifty terameters away.

"Thank you, Soleran," Avera says. She closes the holographic window and turns to observe the teleprompter. It depicts a strange image. She is able to determine that the object is about one-thousandth the size of the *Astrasophia*, but the object must be emanating more power, since the huge vessel is unable to pull from its grasp. As it approaches closer, she notices that the object has an elongated neck, a disfigured, beastlike head, and appendages resembling wings. The image is translucent, but with a bright-red, fiery hue to it. At the center, where one would reason that the beast's heart would sit beating, a bright, white light shines. She barely makes out a figure occupying that space.

"What is that?" Avera asks.

The chief commander activates a holographic window, scans the image, and then activates the vessel's main database. The vessel's computer scans the object and then scrolls through the entries in the database until it finds the appropriate answer, at which it stops and signals its success with a high-pitched dual beep.

Ruden studies the computer's analysis. He turns to Avera and speaks, "It is a dragon." Ruden returns to studying the analysis. "In Terran folklore, the creature symbolizes …" Ruden turns to face Avera again. "Cruelty. It symbolizes cruelty."

Avera's eyes were already wide with terror, but, upon hearing this, they widen even further. Quickly Avera activates the holographic window.

"Soleran," Avera calls out through the display. Soleran turns his attention to her. She lightly whispers, "Hurry."

"Natharon," Soleran says, "rip it."

Natharon hesitates only slightly. Without verbally responding, he turns and activates more command lines. The *Intrepidium*'s acceleration increases dramatically, creating a heavily distorted warpiture, a crinkling of space so distinctive that the continuum begins to rip apart. As the acceleration increases toward infinity, the vessel takes on a more translucent, ghostly appearance. The *Intrepidium* closes the distance within minutes. But the extreme warpiture annihilates several star systems as the *Intrepidium* passes by them. In the wake of the *Intrepidium*, black holes ensue from the rip effect.

Maximeron approaches the *Astrasophia*, and Ruden labors to fluctuate the shield's frequency to thwart entry by the aggressor. After a moment, Ruden stops and turns to Avera. "I can't … I, I can't keep this up." Ruden's lower lip trembles. He looks at his trembling hand, closing it in a fist and placing it to his side. "We can't hold him off."

As Ruden says this, Maximeron slips through the frequency and teleshifts onto the bridge. He is bald, and his skin is pale white with a slightly red hue. His eyes are dark gray. The red robe he wears flows freely, as if blowing slowly in a light breeze. Immediately, Maximeron lifts up his right hand, and, with his index and middle finger pressed together, he motions slightly toward Ruden. Ruden's shielding flashes, but he himself screams as every particle in his body is ripped apart and scattered.

Within the science lab of the *Astrasophia*, an Endheran scientist activates the holographic interface and presses a quick series of commands, and Ruden is reinstated. Ruden's face is contorted in terror, but he teleshifts back to the bridge.

Maximeron is imitating his hand gesture toward everyone on the bridge except for Avera. She labors to defend her fellow Endherans, firing bolts of energy from her shielding, but her efforts have no effect. No one's efforts have any effect. Maximeron moves about and destroys at will. Eventually, as each Endheran is reinstated and reappears on the bridge, Maximeron raises his arms and releases a burst of energy that dissipates everyone but Avera. He then teleshifts to the science lab and destroys it with a burst of energy. The Endheran scientist offers no resistance but is annihilated in the blast. Then Maximeron teleshifts throughout the vessel, annihilating each and every inhabitant. After the last victim is gone, Maximeron then returns to the bridge. Avera is pressing the commands on a holographic interface to reinstate her crew members. As the interface beeps with errors, she trembles. She stops submissively, dropping her arms to her side. Finally, she turns to Maximeron, tears flowing down her face. The adversary studies her expression, observing her reaction closely. He sees fear, sorrow, and pain. He nods.

Outside the *Astrasophia*, a light, translucent image of the *Intrepidium* barely phases into appearance. Then a burst of gravity distortion follows, jolting both vessels slightly. The *Intrepidium* materializes fully.

Twenty-five Guardians, including Soleran, Leostrom, Addia-Sahl, and Dyllon teleshift to the bridge of the *Astrasophia*. In the middle of the empty, white room is a dark gray metallic throne. Its erratic, lavalike shape appears to have been poured from a volcano. Maximeron sits on the edge, leaning forward. Avera lies on the floor to his left. She is sobbing and screaming loudly. She looks up and sees Soleran and lets out a high shriek.

Soleran approaches her and activates a holographic interface and begins to scan her neural net. Her nervous system has been severely adjusted and is 90 percent anomalous. Maximeron is tormenting Avera emotionally. Soleran activates several commands, selects all the points of the neural net, and wipes out the anomalies. Avera stops crying and stands up. She looks at Soleran, peacefully at first, but she breaks down and begins to cry again. She falls to her knees and lets out another deafening, high shriek. Soleran rescans her, and the anomalous condition has returned. Soleran changes the parameter of the scan to focus on more unique ganglia. The ganglia have been critically altered, and Soleran begins to reroute the signals to bypass the corrupted ganglia.

"You will not succeed," Maximeron says calmly. He does nothing to stop Soleran but remains seated on the lava throne.

"Soleran," Addia-Sahl says, reading a holo-interface, "Avera is the only survivor. The others have been removed."

"How many members were originally assigned to this vessel?" Soleran asks.

"One thousand Endherans occupied the *Astrasophia*," Addia-Sahl says.

Soleran ceases his work on Avera's scan and turns to Maximeron. Soleran sighs and then slowly shakes his head. "Natharon," Soleran says, "reinstate the crew of the Astrasophia."

"Acknowledged," Natharon says, having remained on the *Intrepidium*.

Soleran tilts his head to the side as he studies Maximeron, who returns Soleran's gaze with a smirk.

"What have you become?" Soleran asks Maximeron.

"God?" Maximeron says with a wide grin. He then chuckles.

Soleran sighs again and returns to Avera's scan. "Leostrom, assist me, if you will, please, sir."

"Absolutely," Leostrom says. He stands next to Soleran and activates his own holographic interface. Both labor to discover the source of the anomalies.

"Interesting," Leostrom says. "It's as if she is doing this on purpose."

Avera cries out. "Help me!" She drops her face to the floor and sobs uncontrollably.

Soleran kneels down to Avera. He gently raises her chin up and looks into her eyes. "You have to let me."

Avera struggles to compose herself. Eventually, her face becomes contorted, her eyes and lips twisted. "You lied to me. You promised, and you lied."

Soleran frowns and stands.

"Soleran," Natharon's voice signals from the *Intrepidium*.

"Yes"? Soleran says, taking a couple steps back.

"I cannot reinstate," Natharon says.

"Why?" Soleran asks. Soleran gazes down upon Maximeron.

Maximeron chuckles and shifts on his throne. He sits back, crosses his legs, and rests his arms on the arms of the throne. His robe flows down off the seat and around the throne's base.

"Their neural signatures do not register," Natharon says.

"Explain," Soleran says, perplexed, despite knowing that Natharon won't know the answer.

"It's as if ..." Natharon hesitates. "It's as if they never existed."

Leostrom ceases his work on Avera's scan and approaches Maximeron. He opens a new interface and attempts to scan the rogue Guardian. Maximeron makes no effort to stop him, but a loud maniacal laughter echoes around Maximeron, although he himself does not appear to laugh. He sits calmly, quietly, casting his gaze from Leostrom to Soleran and back. Leostrom's interface beeps repeatedly, relaying the scan's failure. The maniacal laughter splits into multiple voices.

Avera screams violently with another high shriek. Maximeron stands and walks over to Avera. He kneels down and strokes the back of her head. "I can take all of that away," Maximeron says.

Soleran kneels back down to her. "He is the one who gave it to you in the first place," Soleran says. "We will eventually discover how he managed to pull this off, and we will undo what he has done."

"Trust me, Avera," Maximeron says.

"He deceives you, Avera," Soleran says. "We will help you. But we need you to let us."

"You lie!" Avera yells. She looks at Soleran. Her eyes burn with rage, with hatred. She turns to face Maximeron. He extends his hand to her, and she places her hand into his. Maximeron then assists her to her feet.

"Fiend," Soleran says to Maximeron as all stand up. "In the next epochal, we will be rid of your constant interference." Soleran tenses his hands into fists.

"Compose yourself, Guardian," Maximeron says, looking Soleran up and down with a slight smirk. "You're losing perspective."

Leostrom places his hand on Soleran's shoulder. "Easy, friend," Leostrom whispers.

"Avera," Soleran says. A tear flows down his cheek. He reaches up and wipes it away and recalls the last time a tear had flowed down his cheek.

Maximeron smiles, nodding approvingly. His smile drops into a scowl. He walks up to Soleran, his face just a few inches from the Guardian's.

"It's true," Maximeron begins. "My plan has a—shall we say— minor obstacle." The smile returns to Maximeron's face. "But a probable solution has presented itself, and I labor to bring it to fruition."

"We will not allow it," Soleran says.

Maximeron steps back, his face filled with rage. "Who do you think you are, fledgling! I served on the first High Council! You haven't even served in the Council of Hosts!" Maximeron throws his arms around wildly.

"You speak in haste, Maximeron," Addia-Sahl rebuts. "Soleran has already been appointed to serve as the next high chancellor."

"Liar!" Maximeron spits. "This pathetic worm can't even protect his protégé." Maximeron rushes up to Addia-Sahl, but she activates her shielding. He stops short of colliding with her shield. Maximeron laughs.

He then turns and approaches Soleran, but Soleran keeps his shielding off. It is an invite. Maximeron laughs again.

"You incompetent fool," Maximeron whispers. "I will wipe out your precious Endherans. You can't protect them. The *Order of the Intrepidium* can't protect them. The entire Council of Hosts can't protect them." Maximeron steps back, and the image of the Dragon appears behind him, roaring in rage. The roar is deafening, and the entire vessel shakes from the sound waves emitted.

Soleran and the others don't even flinch. Soleran approaches Maximeron.

"We are not impressed with your theatrics," Soleran says. He places his hands behind his back.

"I am," Avera says. She is no longer crying, but her lips are twisted bitterly.

"Watch me, worm," Maximeron spits. "Watch me as I take your firstborn child!" Maximeron turns and grabs Avera under her armpit. He yanks her away, and both teleshift from the bridge into the vacuum of space. The translucent red dragon image appears, encasing both Maximeron and Avera in a corona of radiation.

Soleran stands there watching them, shaking his head slightly. "What just happened?" he whispers to himself.

When he turns to his fellow Guardians, many of them are silently crying. Addia-Sahl has both of her hands pressed against her mouth and shakes her head from side to side.

The Guardians return to the *Intrepidium*'s bridge.

"The *Astrasophia* should be assimilated," Natharon says.

"Do it," Soleran says, still looking off into space.

Natharon turns and activates several commands from his interface. The *Intrepidium*'s outer ring begins to rotate, and the ensuing field crackles with arcs of energy. The *Astrasophia* begins to disassemble at the atomic level, as particle by particle is teleported to the *Intrepidium*'s plasma storage system. While this process is underway, Soleran gathers the crew on the bridge, including Natharon. Each Guardian stands in a circle.

"We need to discover how Maximeron accomplished this," Soleran begins, "mainly so we can prevent him from doing it again."

"It appears to defy the logic of reality," Dyllon offers. "Maximeron has found a way to alter reality, a method previously undiscovered. It can't be. It's madness." He sighs heavily. "But there it is."

"I suspect that he is merely employing his typical trickery," Soleran says with a sigh. "Omnitron, initiate prompt for calculation." The *Intrepidium*'s computer activates a two-dimensional hologram in the center of the group. A thin, red outline of a triangle appears and slowly rotates. The synthesized voice of a female says, "Please enter parameters."

"First parameter," Soleran says, "the extinguishing of a neural net signature from sensors." The words are keyed in with the triangle at the end, and the transparent interface continues to rotate so that each member of the group can observe the calculation.

"Next parameter," Soleran continues. The triangle drops to the next line. "Set contingency to affirmative." A bracket attaches the first line to the next. "The deletion of the signature reading from the Omnitron's matrix." The words key into the second line. "Next parameter, unauthorized access to the Omnitron's matrix. Calculate."

The prompt beeps in response. The group watches as the rotating interface displays numerous equations. The first equation is calculating prolongivity of the neural net. The second equation is calculating sustainability of the neural net. The third and final equation is performing diagnostics regarding the Omnitron's security functions. Each equation is set side by side, and random variables are inserted and calculated underneath.

Soleran drops his gaze to the floor. He closes his eyes. *Avera. I will save you.* Addia-Sahl hears his thoughts and reaches up to put her hand on his shoulder. She steps closer and rests her head on his shoulder. Soleran acknowledges her gesture by tilting his to rest his cheek on her forehead.

The computer beeps, prompting a conclusion.

"Relay," Soleran commands without moving.

"Unauthorized access to Omnitron computer matrix is not relevant," the *Intrepidium* renders. "Deleting parameter from contingency."

Soleran steps from Addia-Sahl and studies the calculations.

"This should be interesting," Leostrom interjects.

The computer pauses and prompts.

"Relay," Soleran commands.

"Adding new parameter," the computer renders. "Calculating perceptivity range of neural net of *Astrasophia* personnel."

Natharon stirs and begins to shake his head. "They did not register."

"Easy, friend," Leostrom comforts him, placing his hand on Natharon's shoulder. "Observe that the target variable of perceptivity is linked to the sustainability function." Leostrom looks around and then continues. "We weren't deceived. It was the Endheran crew."

"The answer is clear now," Soleran says. At that moment, the computer beeps for a prompt. "Relay and confirm our suspicions."

The computer begins. "Unauthorized access to target neural net with scan for memory matrices. Unauthorized access to memory matrices and activating memory code. Unauthorized alteration of memory code." The computer beeps for a prompt.

"Diabolical," Dyllon offers.

"So," Soleran says, "Maximeron was able to stimulate the memory of each Endheran. He tricked them into believing that they had died sometime in their past. The most probable moment would be prior to maturity of self-other awareness."

"In essence," Leostrom interjects, "the Endherans deleted themselves. They allowed their neural nets to dissipate. It was purely voluntary. This prompted the Omnitron to delete the data from its memory core."

"He tricked them?" Natharon says, more than asks. "But how? How did he accomplish this feat? It still seems impossible." Natharon steps away from the interface and places his hands on his hips.

"We still have much to learn about reality," Dyllon says to Natharon.

Soleran continues, "Computer, relay."

The computer continues with the analysis. "Unauthorized access resulted from initiation of a stasis field by the intruder's neural net. Initiation of stasis field resulted from reconfiguring intruder's neural signals. Reconfiguration resulted from aligning parallel signal route and overlapping signal outlay to match target neural net. Overlap, with outlay, resulted from gamma provision subwriting neural routines."

"Computer, stop," Soleran says. "I've seen enough."

"Never," Natharon says. "Never in a million epochs could such a concept be devised in the mind of a Guardian."

"Unfortunately," Leostrom rebuts, "Maximeron defied the odds."

Natharon turns his head to Leostrom. "He's no Guardian." Natharon's eyes are piercing and dark

"True," Leostrom concedes. "I suppose that his time spent in exile was focused on devising these kinds of schemes."

"Soleran," Addia-Sahl says, "we have to stop him. He's going to attack the remaining Endherans."

"Let us return to our posts," Soleran says. "We will intercept Maximeron and interfere with his latest scheme."

Each Guardian nods in confirmation, and each steps away. The *Astrasophia*'s assimilation concludes, and Natharon activates the navigation commands.

"Natharon, follow Maximeron from a distance. Let us see where he intends to leave Avera." Soleran activates a holographic window and links to the Endheran Central Command, prompting for a response. An Endheran official answers the prompt. The official is dressed in a blue robe and wears a cylindrical blue hat.

"Greetings, Soleran," the official says.

"Greetings, Consul Emeras," Soleran says. "Permit me to convey the reason for my notice. Time is of the essence."

"By all means, please continue," Consul Emeras says.

"You need to expect a visitor," Soleran says, "one whom you are ill-prepared to receive."

The consul squints his eyes and presses his lips in concern.

"But don't worry," Soleran says. "This is what you need to do."

CHAPTER 10

L ife has become a tragic comedy, and fools labor in the depth of vanity, inserting their principal claws into the cycle of the natural scheme, having in mind to adulterize and corrupt that which was pure from the beginning, and we are left to suffer the consequences of a corrupted natural order in which from nothing we came and to nothing we go and life must die to be born having been born to die so that there is life and death and love and hate and peace and war and evolution and devolution and forward and backward and up and down and left and right and good and evil—am I the only one who knows this? Why do they not know that they cannot take one nanospeck of matter or energy from this universe without setting off the chain reaction of eventual self-implosion—this is the one law that trumps all laws, the conservation of energy, but they don't care, having in mind that they live forever and remove from the epochal the essence of life, thus bringing about the coming age of darkness where life comes to an abrupt halt—they are not Guardians, they are conquerors, corrupting everything they touch, thus fulfilling the ancient doctrine that cursed are they who say sweet is bitter and bitter is sweet—now I labor to destroy the corruption to keep it from spreading beyond the bounds of manageability, but in their blind hatred and raging pride they do not see, they cannot see, they will not see, choosing instead the narrow, linear thought that to challenge their philosophy is evil—yet, Little One, what I do is not evil but necessary to maintain a proper balance, destroying the corrupted, purifying the diseased, ending the suffering, bringing forth every doctrine, precept, and dictum necessary to sabotage the efforts of fools who labor in the depths of vanity, fools who think themselves immortal—but they are not; they are quite mortal. I should know, I killed one. If they say they cannot die, they lie, for I killed one once; it was difficult, but I managed to unleash a wave of energy so dense it dissipated the Guardian's essence, and he was for that brief moment of time dead, nonexistent. If not for the meddling interference of the other wraiths, he would have remained dead even to this very moment, proving the philosophy of those, my Terran brethren, who perished in the supernova of our old star, Solarus, a philosophy proven true in that, for life to live forever, it must die over and over, going through the singularity to be purified of such hindrances as pride and ego and remade as the universe is prone to make life innocent and pure without corruption—the very reason that I do what I do without mercy or remorse, taking no pity on whoever has been defiled by the corrosive touch of that gang of wraiths calling themselves Guardians—I am a god imprisoned, finding my essence trapped in this manifest form when I so much desire to disperse my essence throughout the universe, but because of my enemies I am obligated to remain in ancient form, and this is my torment—the torment of a will, of a soul, of a life who died long ago and lives at this moment only because of that death, a death with which they are not familiar, having no idea of what it means to come to a realization that the philosophy of the High Council is eternal death and not life for all who partake in that philosophy through their various deeds and behaviors—cursed are the Angelians; they are not angels but devils, and they lied to us, having in their minds not one speck of concern for the purity of the universe, but they are as thieves and cowards, plundering and then fleeing from the epochal, knowing full well that such an action sets in motion the sure demise of the universe, and as one alone in exile, I am obligated to traverse this universe from one end to the other, engaging in a campaign of purification, and this Little One is my damnation—I am tormented, having been wounded in the worst possible way, dismissed as insignificant, mocked and ridiculed by those who once called me their brother, betrayed, used, abused, thrown away as mere refuse, having served whatever dark purposes linger in the schemes and plots of that vile gang of wraiths who call themselves the Host of the Heavens—how presumptuous, as if they were appointed, not having appointed themselves, not having elevated themselves to such a lofty position, failing to take into account an ancient principle declaring that any who should exalt themselves shall be abased, and any who are abased shall be exalted, and clearly Terran Humanity has become the bane of the universe, responsible for destroying Solarus Terra, responsible for ruining life on that planet; you should know that not one speck of life survived other than Terran Humanity. The fools did not spare one other life form from that beautiful and natural world, and that is one reason for the emergence of the dissenters, my true brethren murdered by the High Council all because they did not agree with the High Council's philosophy, all because they had a mind for themselves to think, to decide, to reason through and come to just and right conclusions— but the cold blast of hatred that erupted from the depths of Terran Humanity murdered them without hesitation, without any concern or thought as to the consequences or implications, and they wonder why I do what I do as if I do this all for any other reason than the fact that I wage war with wights, the corrosive, walking, undead fiends consuming life and destroying the natural order, replacing it with the failure of Terran progression—fools, the whole lot of them, but I resist them at all costs; there is no cost I am not willing to pay, knowing that the consequences and implications of my failure mean that nothing will survive in the end. I speak the truth; do not doubt me.

Forgive me

You still seek the love from the one who abandoned you—Soleran, my enemy, who performs no other duty in this epochal except to meddle constantly in my affairs as a thorn in my side, always bringing about the furtherance of my own torment, very much like the last time we battled—he intruded upon my domain as an armed robber, and when they materialized, I did not hesitate but unleashed my power, erring only in destroying the one closest to me, who was not Soleran but one next to him—if only it had been Soleran himself, I would be smiling even today, but afterward the wraiths adjusted the frequency of their shieldings to block my power, and Soleran unleashed his own power, driving me into the ground face-first so forcefully that my body cut a deep trench in the rocky ground—he feigned concern, coming over to stand at my side and thought to lay his hand on my shoulder, but I jerked myself away and told him no but stood and dusted myself off and laughed at his utter failure to cause me actual harm, and I saw the field emitted to hold me in place and laughed at that as well, and Soleran thought to remind me that we had battled for the millionth time and that every time beforehand all the way up to that moment he had been victorious, and I had been defeated and, like a proud, doting fool boasting of his triumphs, he thought to take advantage of the occasion to persuade me to reconsider my campaign, and again I told him no, and he is and will always be powerless to stop me, and at that moment a volcano erupted, spewing forth its beautiful and destructive glory, raining down fire and molten stone around us, and I asked him what his thoughts were as to this display, as to the beauty of destruction, and with indifference and sarcasm he stated that it was quite dramatic, and my torment burned even more so because his answer reminded me that the High Council has become so blind in corruption that they cannot appreciate the beauty of raw nature—I warned Soleran of a future assault on a serpentine world and fumed and spit that I would see to his destruction even before the end of the epochal because I know that I can kill Soleran, but he cannot kill me—he cannot, he will not, for he is weak and ignorant and does not even have the fortitude or wisdom to do so, but I know what I need to do, having spent two full epochs in exile devising my counterplan to the High Council's philosophy, which involves destroying anything and everything the Guardians touch, including you, Little One, but do not sob, for I have plans for you, you understand, don't you, Little

One, that for me to prepare you to serve my will, you must be purified so that no corruption remains in you

How will you prepare me?

You will suffer torment and be devoured inside and out.

Oh no, please …

As I consume your essence, I will reinstate you to consume it again, over and over until at last you offer no resistance, and as I steal away your life, you shall in turn steal away the life of whomever I mark.

It hurts, it hurts …

In time you shall cry no more and eventually you shall not writhe.

Please help me, Soleran, my father …

He cannot, he will not, he gave you to me, he allowed me to just whisk you away, and he made no attempt to stop me.

Please stop, please no more …

All time I feel as a moment, but to you it will be a breath short of an eternity.
I consume your body, your eyes, your tongue, your throat; I consume your breasts, your belly, your womb.
I consume your being one neuron at a time, consuming your heart, your mind, your soul,
and I reinstate you.

No, please no no no …

And I do it again until you stop resisting, giving yourself to me
willingly and freely,
and I do this again and again …
ten times
a hundred
a million
You are still resisting.

Sorry, I am trying …

Yes, I know, and I love you for it; but for that brief hesitation on your
part, this would be over …

One more, my lord, one more time, and I am yours …

… and thus it is done.
You are remade in my image, and I will give to you a superstitious and
ignorant people that you may feast upon in further preparation …

To consume them …

… as I have consumed you. Now behold, an off-world within my
reach, a world filled with deserts and salty seas and a people whose
skin is mottled pale-white and hair is matted and frames so thin their
bones protrude from their flesh and whose hearts are corrupted, and
they will have a greater reason to cower in their hiding places.

What would you have me do …

Demonstrate to me your willingness to destroy without mercy, only
choosing for yourself the method you will employ.

They are a superstitious people.
I choose from their folklore
a creature that evokes

terror in their hearts,
the vampiric goddess Zeratzala—
bloodthirsty, murderous,
filled with wrath and vengeance,
hateful in spite of life.

Your choice is pleasing to me.

See how they, my lord, flee from me,
how I dwell in the shadow of night
and enclose upon them my prey,
devouring flesh and spilling blood.

You are so beautiful in my eyes. I love you.

They shut themselves up in their shacks.
I hear them whisper their prayers,
they beg the heavens for help.

Pay no heed but perform your duty.

Will Soleran answer them?

Do not give thought to such an idea.

But ...

No—no but—I will delay any intruder. Obey me. There is in front of you a dilapidated dwelling within which resides a single mother and her two small children, one recently born.

What is your will?

Destroy them without mercy.

I have torn away the feeble door.
The mother cowers in a corner,
both children in her arms, crying.
She has her eyes closed
and is praying for the heavens to help her,
so I approach and growl.
I remove from her arms
one of the children.
She does not fight back to stop me
but cries out and prays harder,
begging and pleading.

Devour the child now …

Without mercy …

… for you are destroying corruption.

He is so young, just a couple years old …

It matters not, and do not refer to it as a he.

His eyes are green …

Too soon have I unleashed you …

He looks in my eyes …
so sad, so sad, I'm sad …

Give the mother back her child and return outside into the moonlight, for we have much more to discuss, seeing that you have utterly failed me.

Sorry, my lord, I'm so sorry. I tried, but I cannot do this.

Listen to me, I too was once reluctant, especially in the time of my naïveté, when I was torn between the love for my fellow dissenting brethren and the loyalty to the High Council, but I suffered so much torment that it burned away the corruption until I fully accepted the realization of their corruption, and I too held in my arms a small child, and I too looked in its eyes and at first was unsure as to my purpose, but then I looked deeper, and I saw the corruption that swam around in the child's neural processes, and I knew that the child was fully corrupted and would grow up to spread that corruption.

What did you do?

I ripped the child to shreds and scattered its blood upon the wind.

Oh no …

Do not pity the corruption.

Soleran, please help me!

Stop calling out to my enemy!

It hurts …

Obey me now.

The mother opens her eyes, the newborn crying in her arms. The toddler sits on the floor a few feet from her. He looks over at her and whimpers. She crawls toward the toddler, holding the newborn.

"Come here, baby," the mother gently says. "Come here to Mommy." As she reaches out for the child, a shadow emerges from behind the boy. "No!" screams the mother, pulling back to the wall with the infant.

The figure steps into the moonlight cast through the shattered doorway. Ragged robes hang upon a pale, gaunt form, the eyes deep-sunken and dark. The creature opens her mouth to reveal rotten, blood-stained fangs. Foamy saliva pours down the side of her face. She releases a wail, and the mother screams and struggles to protect the infant in her arms, backing up to the wall.

"Please!" the mother cries out. "Help me!"

The decrepit figure snatches up the toddler and begins to sniff the child. The small boy stares back into her face. He whimpers but offers no resistance. The creature bares her fangs, and the boy begins to cry.

"Fiend!" A voice sounds from behind. "Unhand that child!" It's a scruffy voice, aged but authoritative.

The creature whirls around, still holding the toddler. She lowers the child and then roars over his head at the figure standing in the doorway.

"Put the child down," the old man says. He's short and heavy-set, wrinkled and balding. He steps forward into the house.

"You pathetic fool," the creature says, her voice raspy and obnoxious. Black saliva drips from the side of her mouth. "I will feast on your bowels and drink from your skull."

"No!" the old man says. "You will not! You will obey me, in the name of the Most High!"

The creature laughs, one hand letting go of the toddler. He dangles at her side by his arm. He cries out and struggles a little but settles and cries instead. "Tell me, Pah'ul," the creature says, "who do you say is the most high?"

The man starts to answer but hesitates, taken aback by the mention of his name.

"I will lay open your carcass," the creature says, "and bathe in your blood!" She walks toward the old man, dragging the toddler with her.

"You know who He is!" Pah'ul says. "He is God!"

The creature stops, and a low growl sounds.

"What?" the old man asks, looking out the door to his right. "Um, okay!" he answers loudly.

The creature slowly creeps forward, the growl still sounding.

The old man notices her deliberate approach and moves back out the door, stumbling a little on the splintered wood strewn about on the ground. "You don't see what I see."

"What do you see?" the creature asks, stopping at the door to look around at the outside area. "There is no one out there with you. You're all alone."

"Um, no," says the old man, "you are wrong."

"What …" asks the creature, "do … you … see!"

"Two warriors of God," the old man says, startling slightly. "One on each side of the door. They wait for you to exit." He points to the left and then to the right. "With raised weapons poised for the strike!"

"And?" the creature asks, leaning forward slightly to peer around the door jam, first to her left and then to her right. She sees nothing, so she leans back.

"These are the two … um, Guardians, um," the old man says, peeking to his right as if listening to someone speak. "The Guardians of Eternal Life!"

The creature lets go of the child. As the toddler falls, he lands on his back, and his head hits the floor. He wails.

"I want the child," Pah'ul says.

The creature whirls around, giving her back to the old man. "They are here, master! They are here! Have they come to torment me?"

The mother panics and presses herself tightly in the corner, covering the infant with a small blanket. Both are crying. Pah'ul sneaks up quietly, slowly, and reaches in through the doorway, taking hold of the boy's ankle. He drags the boy to him and then quickly snatches up the toddler. Pah'ul returns to the spot where he was standing.

The creature paces back and forth across the room. The aged

wood of the floor creaks under the stress. "Lies," the creature says. "He lies." The creature steps up to the door. "You lie!" The sound of her screeching, raspy voice sends chills down the back of the old man.

"I know your name!" the old man says, still clutching the toddler. The young boy squeals and turns his face away from the creature. "I know you're not Zeratzala."

The creature roars.

"Avera!" the old man says. He looks to the door's side and back.

The creature inhales and begins to whimper, holding both hands to her mouth. "Who! How! Tell me!" the creature says. "Describe them!"

"One has light skin, the other darker skin," the old man says. "Both are wearing armor that shimmers like gold, from head to foot." He looks back and forth from each side of the doorway. "Their helmets are topped with a crown of feathers that burn, feathers red, yellow, orange, like the plumes of a firebird. They carry in their hands halberds and shields, shields that are on fire, that burn brighter than the sun." The old man steps forward, still holding the toddler tightly. The young boy quiets down and turns to look where the old man gazes. The old man notices. "See! Even this child observes what I observe."

"What trickery is this?" Avera asks. "Why can't I see them?"

"They show themselves to me," the old man says. "To me and the child. I ... I don't know why."

The creature stands still. She hisses.

The old man looks to the side and then nods. "Okay," he says. "One beckons for you, Avera. Come forth and cast away, um, the shroud of darkness you wear as a garment, and ... and ... and instead bathe in the ... in the stellar winds and ... and don the starlight of Endhera's Sun." He looks at the toddler, who remains calm. "Yeah, that's it, isn't it, lil' fella?"

"Eh noo nah," the little boy says. "Ah ware wah." The toddler places his tiny hand on the old man's face.

The creature drops to her knees and starts to cry. Light swirls around her, stripping away swaths of darkness. She shifts from a strange, foreign creature to her familiar self. She lies on the floor and rests the side of her head on her outstretched arm. Sleep comes to her, as clouds and stars and crescent moons fill her eyes, and a roar of a waterfall washes her soul.

She dreams. And remembers.

The teenage girl kneels in a patch of grass. The sun shines on her face, and a cool breeze lifts up the red-and-yellow scarfcovering her head to reveal white, blonde locks of hair. Her burqa is brown and plain, but clean and well-stitched. The soles of her bare feet jut out from under the burqa. A tear falls down her face. She rests her hands on her thighs and every so often squeezes them as she holds the burqa. She looks down and watches a worm crawl up a blade of grass. She sighs and watches the clouds race above.

"God, are you real?" she asks. "I need help."

She reaches up and captures the tear on her finger. She pulls it away from her face and looks at it. Turning her finger slightly causes it to glisten in the sunlight. She raises it up close to her eyes and turns her finger so that the drop of moisture hangs upside down. She tilts her head slightly. After a moment, the tear falls from her finger and lands on her burqa, leaving behind a dot of moisture. She pulls the burqa up and examines the spot momentarily but then lets go of the burqa and returns her gaze to the sky.

"Does anyone hear me?" she whispers lightly. "Is there anyone listening up there?" She lowers her head and closes her eyes. "Please?"

Soleran listens to her. He studies her gestures and her expressions. He watches what she watches, sees what she sees, feels what she feels. He materializes just enough to remain invisible yet to allow the wind to touch him. He measures its temperature and velocity. He kneels down next to the child. He strokes the grass lightly to feel its texture. He listens to her breathing, to her heartbeat, to her sighs, to her inner crying. Soleran stands and gestures with his right hand. Strings of gold light flash over his eyes. In his perspective, a holographic model of the child's nervous system emerges. He focuses on the agitated nerves that are firing irregularly. He presses on various neural nodes composing the interconnectivities, rerouting some signals, disconnecting a few to terminate other signals, and activating dormant nodes to instigate signals. He does this over a period of time, allowing the teenager to ease into peace and comfort. She isn't aware of what's happening.

Soleran maps the girl's neural net and studies the processes and signals. He reconstructs a holographic image of her memory and replays the imagery. The girl sobs, sniffles, and then lies down, resting her head on her left arm. The green worm had fallen from the top of the blade of grass. It starts over again from the bottom, and the girl watches it attentively, her eyes locked on the worm's prolegs grasping the grass leaf. Addia-Sahl and Natharon phase in on each side of Soleran and the child. After a moment, Soleran sighs, shakes his head from side to side, and stands.

"Her name is Avera," Soleran says. "She does not know the cause of her sufferings. I'll need some assistance with the photometry." Soleran gestures, and his eyes flash with persistent strings of light. "Omnitron," Soleran says, prompting the *Intrepidium*'s computer. A light tone sounds. "Track light vectors." A beep confirms the compliance. "Track light fractals." Another beep sounds. Soleran stares ahead, his sight focused on the holography engaging his perspective. His view of the real world fractures like glass, each fissure following each photon emitted by the main star. Soleran gestures, and red-lettered commands appear holographically to his lower right. He activates several commands, and the photonic markers tracking the light vectors slow down. The image blurs slightly. He raises his right hand, and the image freezes. As he presses forward with his left and pulls back with his right, the image reverses to a particular point in time. He turns his hands over and returns them to their starting point. Soleran then repeats the gesture, and the image continues reversing to each stoppage point. All three watch as reality is backplayed holographically. Soleran controls the speed of the image's regression, and minutes are displayed in mere seconds.

The image shows the teenager stand and walk backward jerkily. Soleran gestures with both hands to pan the image to maintain the central focus on the girl. Her image walks backward through the tall grasses, under some tree limbs, and then beside a brook. She begins hopping and skipping backward over some stones until she leaps back to the bank on the other side. She stands and stares at the brook and then runs backward before slowing to a stroll.

An hour of normal time is condensed into seconds. The girl backs onto a paved road leading into a town. Dingy white concrete buildings hastily constructed line the main road. Rickety awnings cover some doorways and windows. Stray mongrels run backward across the street, followed by a smaller animal.

The road meets a T-section, ending at a two-lane street. Four-wheeled vehicles emitting dark-colored exhaust drive in reverse in both directions. The girl walks backward across the street, stops and watches as a few more vehicles pass. She then continues her backward walk until she approaches a door. It opens, and she steps back to catch it and then enters the building. As Soleran follows her into the building, the image shifts and blurs until it is grayed out. Soleran reverses his gesture, and the image moves forward slightly to retake its form.

"Suborder light vectors are anomalous," Natharon says. "Let me adjust that." He activates his display. The Omnitron beeps in compliance with his commands. "Calculating variable light vectors. Implementing. Try now."

Soleran holds his gesture, his left hand extended and his right hand pulled slightly in. He motions slightly, pulling in with the left and pushing out with the right, and the image becomes clearer, returning to where it left off last. "Much better," Soleran says.

Light from a window shows the image as being more fractured with sections broken and offset. Addia-Sahl places her hand on Natharon's shoulder. "Allow me," she says with a smile. She activates her display and keys in her equations and numbers. "Neutrino background noise will allow us to correlate the vectors more accurately." Her display beeps and tones with each entry. The fractured sections shift and blend, rendering the image whole.

Soleran continues the image's regression, entering the room where

Avera is sitting on a bench to the left. The room has three doors, one on each wall except where the bench is placed. Avera is crying, but after a few minutes, her eyes dry up, and she is more inquisitive than upset. A man dressed in a solid, olive-green military uniform walks backward from a door to her right until he is in front of her. He turns with his hands on his hips and is speaking to Avera. Anger is draped over his face. Soleran speeds up the display, and the man turns and walks backward through the same door.

Soleran releases the grip and the display progresses forward in normal time. The sound is garbled.

"Atmospheric displacement should clarify the sound waves," Addia-Sahl says. She activates a small display and keys in her commands. "Correcting discrepancies now."

The sound crackles and then echoes and finally clears to reveal that the girl is humming a tune while swinging her bare feet under the bench. The man in military uniform enters the room from Avera's right. He steps in front of the girl, turns deliberately, places both hands on his hips, and coughs an "ahem" to get her attention.

"Your appointment before the council is scheduled for later this afternoon, at the thirteenth hour," the man says. "Report to me at one-seventy-five. Don't be late."

Soleran gestures, and the holographic image pauses.

"This increment doesn't convey much causal information," Natharon says. "I will visit this fellow and glean the needed information from his memory." Soleran nods, and Natharon teleshifts away, leaving Soleran and Addia-Sahl standing over Avera. The girl has dozed off. Both remain out-of-phase with real space, letting visible light pass through them.

"If she were to remain undisturbed, she'd miss her appointment," Addia-Sahl says. She walks over to the other side and bends over to study the child's face. "My inclination is to prevent that."

"Pending Natharon's findings, I may ask that you intervene directly," Soleran says.

"I would very much like that," Addia-Sahl says, standing with a smile.

Natharon appears with a flash of bright light. His robe flutters in the transition. Both Soleran and Addia-Sahl wait for him to speak. He is quiet at first, his eyes locked on the little girl lying asleep underneath the paused transparent imagery.

"Reset the image to time stamp 280," Natharon says. His lips are pursed, and his eyes are sober.

Soleran complies, gesturing so that the image rewinds to Natharon's designation. The image blurs and is unrecognizable. Soleran stops only a couple of times to adjust his hand positions and center the image back onto Avera. Natharon assists in resolving some of the light vector equations. Finally, after a moment, the image clears to show Avera with a boy her age. He's tall and thin, with long, wavy black hair extending to his shoulders. The two are being affectionate. The three Guardians watch the two teenagers only briefly. Soleran turns to Natharon with a slightly puzzled look.

"If you would, please," Natharon begins, "pan the image 130 degrees counterclockwise and zoom to two and a half times."

Soleran complies. The image swings to the left of the young lovers, settling in on a few trees, and zooms in to reveal an older man standing behind one of the trees.

"The man's name is Delhend. Despite being twice the girl's age, unbeknownst to her, he is her future husband in an arranged marriage," Natharon says. "The man is also the boy's murderer."

Soleran turns to face Natharon, and Addia-Sahl gasps slightly.

"The body of the boy—Jaitlet was his name—has been discovered and Delhend caught and arrested," Natharon continues. He wears sadness like a garment. "The girl doesn't know. Her appointment with the draft board is related. They will use the occasion to draft her into the elite military unit reserved for unmarried women, young women who are wards of the state."

"She will not survive," Addia-Sahl says. "I calculate that she will take her life."

"As do I," Soleran says. He walks over the teenager asleep on the ground. He turns to Addia-Sahl and Natharon. "I calculate that every attempt where we intervene and divert will inevitably lead to another attempt."

"Even if we resolve that variable," Natharon says, "and she foregoes suicide, the service in which she is to be conscripted will destroy her essence, corrupting her ganglia and transforming her from the girl you see before you into a ..." He hesitates. "Into a devil."

Observing this unfold on the holographic display, I gasp and look at Evalene. She has her hand to mouth, resting the other across her chest.

"She will come to kill without mercy or compassion, without guilt or remorse, without fear or hindrance," Natharon continues, kneeling to lay his hand on her shoulder while out of phase. "She will kill indiscriminately, without concern for age or station, ethnicity or gender, purpose or reason. She will be a creature of instinct and darkness, a predator whose single drive will be by whatever means to eradicate the object of her hate—" Natharon stands and concludes the thought. "Life."

"We have to find the right balance. Omnitron," Soleran says, hearing a beep, "query for Kaanan's elite military forces. Relay."

The Omnitron's digitized female voice responds, "Imperial Kaanan's three military branches, the Army, the Navy, and the Airguard retain one elite fighting force each. The Army retains the Temple Knights. The Navy retains the Imperial Marines. And the Airguard retains the Iron Maiden Corps."

Upon hearing the latter item, the three Guardians look at each other wide-eyed.

"Omnitron," Soleran says, "extrapolate Iron Maiden Corps."

The digitized female voice sounds out:

The Iron Maiden Corps was formed fifteen years ago in the year 2220 postimperiali, by behest of the Dictator of Kaanan, General Markhan the Third. The first official Iron Maiden was his daughter, Sordea, commissioned by Markhan as he lay upon his deathbed after suffering a stroke. The commission was to avenge multiple key aerial victories by Kaanan's enemy, the Vallenades, a free-state, oligarchical conglomerate consisting of thousands of islands and the eastern coastline of the mainland continent of Kaanan. Sordea expanded the commission and founded the Iron Maiden Corps, enlisting herself and several female associates. Employing newer technologies, such as the revamped Ironbird fighter plane with its heat seekers and advanced radar system, the Iron Maidens turned the tide of battles in Kaanan's favor and halted the encroachment of the Vallenades military over the East Kaanan Mountains. This excerpt derives from the press release written by the Kaanan Army's Department of Public Relations and is appended to the universal record.

Soleran turns to the other two. "We've seen her immediate past," he says. "Now let us see her future. Omnitron, initiate light vector continuity." A light tone sounds to confirm compliance. An image fades in of the current environment and overlaps the area, giving everything a wispy, ghostly effect. Soleran imitates the gesturing he previously performed, pulling back on his left hand and pressing his right hand forward. The image moves forward jarringly.

"Covariance extrapolation is offset by 3 percent," Natharon says. "Certainty is at 9.2." He gestures, and gold flashes across his eyes. "Adjusting."

The Omnitron's image of the future stabilizes, and the jarring effect diminishes to a slight jerking. Soleran moves the image forward. While the real Avera remains asleep on the ground, the image shows that Avera awakens and stands. She dusts herself off and then walks back to town. She approaches the Airguard's office building and enters the front door. Avera steps up to a desk, speaks to the secretary, and then takes a seat. Guards exit from a side door and place cuffs on her hands and walk her to the back.

"I knew there would be consequences to her delay," Addia-Sahl says lightly.

"She receives a reprimand on her record," Soleran says, "but it does not deter her current timeline, only wobbles it slightly." He sighs and shakes his head.

"You were hoping that by not intervening, the consequence would be stiff enough to divert to another conclusion," Natharon says. "The fate is locked, it seems."

The image moves forward. Avera is dressed in a brown uniform, with a brown cap. Both the uniform and the cap have stitched in the Iron Maiden patch. The emblem depicts the upper torso of a female Endheran wearing a white robe and gold sash. She is crowned and holds a scroll in her right hand and a spear in her left hand. Massive wings spread up from behind her. A motto scrolled around the emblem reads, "Kaanan Imperial Airguard, Iron Maiden Corps. Justice metes out vengeance. Vengeance metes out justice."

She walks down a long, dimly lit hallway toward a single, closed door at the end. Light outlines the doorjamb. She starts to knock but lowers her hand and takes a deep breath. Finally, she knocks and blurts out, "Sir, Captain Avera Prata reporting as ordered, sir!"

"Get in here," a voice sounds from the other side.

She opens the door and steps inside. The room is windowless but brightly lit with fluorescence. The brigadier general sits behind a desk, the top of which is orderly and neat. He scribbles on a piece of paper before closing the tip of the pen and laying it down. Avera stands at attention, facing the wall behind him. He studies her for a moment, as if inspecting her uniform to look for that one stray wrinkle.

"Sit down, Captain," he says, motioning to the single chair next to the wall. "Pull it up," he commands.

She obeys. Her posture remains stiff as she sits waiting for General Olomos to speak. He continues to study her face, as if still looking for a weakness, any weakness. Avera offers none.

"I'm looking at your record here, at your hit score," the general says. "It's awfully high. Outstanding."

"Thank you, sir," she responds.

"I've called you in here because I'm going to promote you to squadron leader," the general says.

"Sir?" Avera asks with a puzzled look.

"Your other scores are too low," the general says.

Avera's posture stiffens, and her eyes return to the wall behind the general. "Yessir," she blurts.

"I think you're holding back on us, Captain," General Olomos says. He leans back and massages his chin while peering at Avera through narrowed eyes. "Your hit score tells me that you're not exerting yourself in all areas." He shifts forward in his chair, his voice deepening. "You think you're only responsible for yourself, Captain?"

"No, sir!" Avera barks.

"Well, now you're responsible for a squadron of fighter pilots," the general says. He leans back, his demeanor shifting to a calmer state.

"Yessir," Avera says. "Um … sir?"

"What?" the general asks.

"I'm not sure I have the respect of my sisters," Avera mentions.

"That is your own fault, Captain," General Olomos says. "But now you have an opportunity to improve upon that."

"Yessir," Avera says.

"Dismissed," the general says. He doesn't wait for her to respond. He picks up the pen, uncaps it, and returns to scribbling on the paper in front of him.

"Aye, sir," Avera says. She stands and salutes, a forearm stroke across her chest. "Have a good day, sir."

The image dissipates.

"It's as if she's caught in the center of a temporal funnel spiraling down to a single fate," Soleran says. "Her life is enacted upon by an unknown force."

"Maximeron?" Addia-Sahl asks.

"Perhaps," Soleran answers, his eyes locked on the girl asleep on the ground. All three stand quietly for a brief moment. Soleran turns to Addia-Sahl. "Advocate for her, if you would, please."

"Certainly," Addia-Sahl says. She walks over to Avera, kneels down, and places a hand on the girl's shoulder.

Avera startles slightly and sits up, rubbing her eyes. She turns over and sees an elderly woman looking at her.

"Who are you?" Avera asks.

"Friends call me Addy," Addia-Sahl says.

"How old are you?" Avera asks, sitting up and crossing her legs. "You are the oldest woman I have ever seen!"

Addia-Sahl chuckles. "I've been around a long time. Why are you here, child? Do you always sleep outside under the sun? You could get a sunburn."

Avera dismisses the admonishment and rubs her eyes. "What time is it?" she asks.

"It's almost noon," Addia-Sahl answers.

"Oh, I have to be somewhere soon," Avera says.

"Mm hmm," Addia-Sahl mutters.

"I was sleeping here because after today, I'll have to enlist in the Airguard," Avera says. She rubs her face to massage away the sleepiness. "I'll be a plane mechanic."

"The Airguard, eh?" Addia-Sahl says. She groans a little as she sits beside Avera, allowing her joints to make popping noises.

"Do you have any advice?" Avera asks. "I wish I could get out of it. Then Jaitlet and I—he's my boyfriend—Jaitlet and I could get married and move somewhere on the coast of Tieza."

"Married. Mm hmm," Addia-Sahl mutters softly. "Child, whatever happens, just remember that there are forces for good at work in the world today. Those forces battle the forces of evil. So when evil seems to abound, look for the good. Help it. Help good fight evil."

Avera is watching a butterfly. She rolls her eyes slightly. "Okay—" Avera says. "Well, I have to go, um, Addy," Avera says with a snap of her fingers. "But thanks for the advice." Avera stands and helps the old woman to her feet.

"No problem, child," Addia-Sahl says. She takes her hand and looks the young girl in the eyes. "May you be blessed."

Avera doesn't say anything but turns and leaves. Addia-Sahl watches her as she exits the grassy area next to the brook and heads back to town. Avera stops and walks back to the grassy area, maybe to offer to accompany the old woman to town. But the old woman is gone.

"Hmph!" Avera says. "Where ... oh, never mind. I don't have time."

Dawn. The sky is dark, but sunlight begins to trace the horizon. A light buzz sounds from high above the clouds. Silhouettes of fighters descend from the mist, reflecting a splotch of sunlight on their underbellies. There are twelve. Their hexagonal formation remains locked, the vector of their destination straight, without deviation to the smallest degree. The fighter planes have a single cockpit sitting at the center of the plane's body. The wings are long and wide, being aerodynamically designed to carry massive weight. Underneath each wing is a propeller-driven engine, a .60-caliber gun turret, two drop bombs, and eight heat-seeking missiles.

In the distance are faded dots, Vallenades fighter planes, the best the oligarchy can afford. Called stingers, they're smaller than the ironbirds and have less armor and fewer weapons but are more maneuverable. The stingers also outnumber the ironbirds two to one. The two opposing sides meet, and a dogfight ensues. Flash from the gun turrets lights up the dark clouds. There are explosions and black smoke. Fiery debris falls from the sky. One by one, the stingers are annihilated, save for the squadron leader. He falls in behind a damaged ironbird. Flames pour out the right-side engine.

"Someone get this rabbler offa me!" Neilede says through the radio.

"I got it!" Avera responds, peering through her cockpit at the two planes below. "Bring him to me."

"Get him, sister," someone else says through the radio. "Get that sum' bitch!"

The stinger shoots his guns, the bullets punching several holes in Neilede's ironbird.

"Ahh, he's ripping my tail!" Neilede says. She struggles with the stick control, pulling back on it hard. "Come on, baby. Come on. Get up there!" The right engine sputters and smokes.

Avera falls in behind the stinger. "Lucinna," Avera says, "shadow me."

"You got it, sister," Lucinna says. "I'm right with you. Get that sum' bitch now!" Lucinna's ironbird falls in with Avera's.

"Save me, squad leader!" Neilede says. "Get him off of me!"

"Hang in there, Neilede," Avera says. She flips the small cover of the red fire button that sits atop the stick control. Her right hand begins to tremble. "No, please."

The four fighter planes fly through a mountain gorge.

"This rabbler knows he's lost!" Lucinna says. "He just wants a kill before he dies!"

"I got this," Avera says. She struggles to calm her nerves. *Please, God, help me.*

Addia-Sahl teleshifts above Avera, phased out and transparent. Swiftly, however, she glides to the stinger. Avera pushes the button, and her gun turret fires. But Addia-Sahl taps the stinger's left wing, forcing it to shift slightly. The bullets graze the stinger's side but glance off. The stinger then fires, and Neilede's ironbird is pummeled.

"No!" Avera cries out. "No! No! No!"

Neilede's ironbird erupts into flames and falls from the sky.

"Get outta the way, you pathetic coward!" Lucinna says, moving her ironbird dangerously close to Avera's. "Just get the hell outta the way!"

Avera lifts up her ironbird and moves out of the way. She then glances to the side and watches Neilede's plane plummet to the side of the mountain. Lucinna falls in behind the stinger and chases it further through the gorge. She opens fire, and the stinger is ripped to shreds. It falls to the Earth in a fireball.

"Why?" Avera asks, crying. "Why, God? Why?"

The Iron Maiden squadron descends over the mountain and down into the valley. The Vallenades base at the bottom fires its antiaircraft batteries, but the ironbirds swoop back and forth, destroying buildings with guided missiles. Within half an hour, the base lies in ruin. The squadron of ironbirds returns to headquarters.

The pilots exit their planes and assemble in a single line for debriefing. Avera, as squad leader, stands at the very end. General

Olomos exits his office and walks up to them. He holds a cup in his hand and takes a sip of the hot liquid.

He passes Avera and walks down the line, looking each pilot in her eyes. Finally, he stops. "Report!" the general barks.

"Captain Kellios, three kills," Lucinna says.

"Captain Otchki, two kills," another says.

"Captain Mulaynar, three kills," the third says.

The general makes his way down the line. A couple of the pilots say zero kills, and he eyeballs them threateningly but continues. He gets to Avera.

"Captain Prata, zero kills," Avera says. She stands as still as she is able, looking straight ahead, her feet parted slightly, her arms pulled taut behind her back, her hands locked in sweaty embrace.

The general's eyes are wide but piercing. His brows are pulled down rigidly. He takes another sip. "Good work, ladies!" he bellows. The general positions himself at the front. "I'd say outstanding, but it wasn't outstanding, was it?"

"No, sir!" the group barks in unison.

"We lost a maiden, didn't we?" the general asks.

"Yessir!" the group barks.

"You were outnumbered two to one," General Olomos continues. "Several of you took out your targets and then some. But some of you didn't pull your weight." The general fumes, casting his fiery glance from maiden to maiden, starting with Lucinna and finally ending with Avera. "Step forward, squad leader."

Avera obeys.

"You have the highest hit score in the simulations of any maiden here," the general says, "but you are the only maiden here without a single kill. Can you explain that?"

Avera doesn't respond right away. She drops her gaze and swallows.

"Did the Airguard waste its time and money training a pacifist?" the general asks.

"No, sir!" Avera barks.

The general leaps forward and steps in front of her.

"So you're just that pathetic?" the general asks. "I mean, we've spent hours and money putting you through the best training, and you're not pacifying, so what you're telling me is that you're just incompetent! That you're just stupid and can't learn! Is that it?"

Avera stands still, her eyes locked dead ahead. Her lower lip trembles.

"Well, I don't want you in my corps, captain," the general says with spittle flying. "So what should we do with you?"

"Sir?" Avera asks.

"How do we get our money back, the money that we wasted putting you through hours and hours of training? What use are you?"

"Sir, I could fly the supply detail!" Avera says.

"Oh, hell no!" General Olomos exclaims. "You're not flying anymore! You're not a pilot! I don't even want you touching my planes! Now I'll have to promote a bunch of noncommissions so that I can give you one of their lowly jobs!" With that, the general reaches up and places his hand on Avera's chest. He takes hold of the Iron Maiden patch on her leather jacket, and he rips it off. Avera jerks but regains her position. "Get outta my hangar!"

"Aye, sir!" Avera says. She turns to grab her gear.

"Leave it! Get outta my hangar!" the general screams.

Avera drops the bag and runs to the hangar doors. She runs outside and erupts in tears. Several Airguardsmen stare at her as she runs by them. Avera passes the chow hall and heads to the barracks. She bursts through the door, runs to her rack and dives in, pulling her pillow and blankets up over her head. She bawls. In the darkness.

The sound of the waterfall fills her ears, drowning out her cries. Avera opens her eyes and looks around at the inside of the dilapidated hut. The mother and her newborn huddle in the corner. The old man and the toddler stand outside several feet from the doorway. But they're all frozen in time.

Soleran steps from the left side of the doorway and Leostrom from the right. They are dressed exactly as the old man had described, in golden armor with helms plumed in fiery colors. Both hold halberds and shields, the shields set aflame. Soleran enters the hut, and Leostrom follows. As they do, the armor fades, revealing white robes.

Avera reaches for Soleran, who kneels down and pulls her up from the floor and into his embrace.

"I'm so sorry!" Avera says.

Soleran doesn't respond but gently places his palms on her cheeks. With his thumbs, he captures her tears and wipes them away. He kisses her on the forehead.

"I didn't know!" Avera says. "I never knew you were there!"

The area fades, as the three teleshift back to the *Intrepidium*'s bridge. Guardians are busy with their holographic prompts. Addia-Sahl, Natharon, Dyllon, Evalene, and I approach and encircle them. Soleran helps Avera to her feet.

"We withheld that information when you were reinstated," Soleran says. "We knew you stood upon a precipice, and a misstep would take you away from us."

"Why did you save me?" Avera asks. She wants to cry out and run away, but the desire to know the truth compels her. It becomes her strength.

Soleran starts to speak but hesitates. He looks in her eyes and she sees remorse. "We fell in love with you," Soleran finally says. "We were arrogant in our presumptions that we could save you from such a fate, a fate you were pulled into regardless. Maximeron has exploited you since your beginnings. We were arrogant to presume you were removed from the precipice, when it was Maximeron who put you there. I am sorry, Avera. We erred in our judgment. The fate from which we thought we saved you was merely delayed."

"Can we undo what has been done?" Avera asks. She lays her cheek upon Soleran's chest. "I've caused so much pain and suffering. I've hurt so many people." She cries softly. The emotional torment that plagued her has begun to subside. But grief and guilt take its place.

Leostrom places his left hand on her back and gently massages. "We could undo it all, Avera," he says. "We could disassemble the matter, reinstate reality back to the point of digression, and implement divertive variables to lead everything to a different outcome. But then it would no longer be reality. The bonds of the natural occurrence would be severed."

She pulls away from Soleran and turns to Leostrom. He hugs her, giving her a kiss on the forehead.

Addia-Sahl takes Avera in her arms, placing her hand upon Avera's cheek. "I can't begin to tell you how much it hurt me to be so disruptive to your career. You would have been the greatest fighter pilot in the history of the Iron Maiden Corps. I made you the worst. And we hid that from you. And that was terrible of us." Addia-Sahl pulls Avera close and hugs her. Addia-Sahl then whispers in her ear, "Maximeron will not be pleased, but we know how to defeat his latest scheme."

Avera pulls away slightly. "I'm afraid of him," she whispers to Addia-Sahl. "Please don't let him hurt me."

"We won't," Addia-Sahl says. "We have the answer, and the knowledge will keep you safe."

Natharon walks up to Avera. He opens a holo-interface and begins to scan Avera's neural net. He overlays the pattern-equation previously calculated in parallel with Avera's neural processes.

"Now you are prepared to face him again," Natharon says, folding his arms behind his back and smiling. "That is, if he should think to confront you."

Avera's face lights up. She smiles, a single tear flowing down her brown cheek. "I understand." She turns to look at Addia-Sahl. "I am not afraid."

Do you remember?

I remember

standing there at the cliffside overlooking the Great Ocean Tieza, hearing the waves slam against the rocks below with a roar, salty water spraying me on occasion, testifying to the might of the waves reaching up ever so high just to caress my face, one of many paramours set on winning my heart, like the sun that was warm and bright, sending down its rays to bathe my heart in joy or the cool breeze that gently lifted the locks of my golden hair to kiss the brown skin of my neck or Jaitlet the Bold so named because he is the first to charge ahead to investigate whatever is happening with any commotion, the first to ask the elders the tough questions, the first to volunteer for the hard labors with his muscular build and long, thin, black hair flowing over his broad shoulders and his bangs parted enough for me to see his gorgeous face—a firm jaw, a broad nose, wide brown eyes, thick lips that would speak my name in a deep, masculine voice as he would lift me up in his arms high in the air, and I, looking down into those eyes, filled with merriment and wonder—I just knew beyond any doubt that this man loved me, wanted to be with me, wanted to make children with me, but even then I wanted to hear him say those things; I needed to hear him, so desired to hear that voice as it caressed my innermost being.

"Do you love me?" I asked him while we lay on the grass at the cliffside.

"I do. You know this," Jaitlet responded.

"True, but you should tell me," I teased him.

"Well, let me tell you," he answered with that beautiful smile. "Avera, I love you."

"How much do you love me?" I asked, never letting him give me enough, always needing more.

"I love you ..." he said, pausing long enough to jump to his feet. "This much," he finished, turning to run to the cliff's edge.

"Jaitlet!" I yelled, watching him leap off the side of the cliff.

He turned, hovering in midair for so long a time that I could study his face and see the joy in it and know he was happy, but he dropped out of sight, and my heart leaped out of my chest as I ran to the side, concerned and mad, never doubting that I would see him okay but watching the waters below, measuring time with my breathing, my eyes darting back and forth until his muscled brown figure leaped from the water as he took in a deep breath, so far down in the water and the ocean knowing how angry I was and it tossing him around, but even then I knew he was okay, for he was Jaitlet the Bold, so named because he was always the one who tamed his quarry but nothing could tame him, and I could hear his laughter and his shouting for me to come down and join him, so I stood, and he became silent, and I approached the edge, and he began to shout up to me—no, stop, don't jump, I was only kidding—and I peeked over the edge down at the rocks below, and he frantically started swimming over to the rocks, and I yelled down, here I come, and I backed up, and I could hear him yelling, wait, wait, here I come, wait for me, and I backed up far to the woods, and I hid myself behind a tree, and he finally climbed back up the rocks to the top and came running to the spot where we had caroused, and he looked around frantically until he ran to the edge to look over because he just knew I had jumped, and I sprinted toward him, reaching him with his back to me because he was looking over the edge down at the waters, and I reached up and touched his shoulder and could tell he was smiling big, and he said, Avera the trickster, as he reached for my hand, but, nyuh uh, I said as I snatched it away, giggling, taking off running, back toward Katera, and he chased me, never catching me, though he could overtake me, and I ran, never letting him catch me, though I could easily feign a trip or a stumble, letting him, but I wanted the moment to last as long as it could, so we ran laughing and dashing and jumping until we reached the road to Kotanad, and finally he caught up to me and grabbed me, snatching me back into his arms, and the breath left me for a moment, and we stood on the road panting hard, and finally I managed to compose my breathing and managed, just managed, to say I love you forever, Jaitlet, and he responded, I love you too, Avera, forever and a day, and I laughed because you always have to have the better say, but you know what, I'll let you have it, because if you will love me forever and a day, then I know deep down that my life is safe and secure, and I know that I will live a long, happy, prosperous life, and I'm watching you smile, my Jaitlet, and I'm looking into your eyes, but I'm wondering what's happening because I can see through you like you're a ghost, like a pane of glass, why are you disappearing, you're fading, don't go, come back, no, Jaitlet, no, don't you see my skies turning dark, the clouds are blocking out the sun, it's getting dark, and there's thunder in the background, why am I hearing thunder; it doesn't storm anymore on Katera or all of Endhera, it's perpetual spring, it never storms, why is it storming, and the grass is withering all around me and dying, everything is dying, why is everything dying? I'm hearing screams behind me, far behind me, and I turn, and I see that Kotanad is in flames, it's burning; no, oh Granny, oh Pops, get away, get away, don't die, don't die, I'm coming, I'm coming, hold on, please, hold on, just hold on.

"Avera," a voice says to me.

I stop and turn. He stands behind me, a stranger.

"Who are you?" I ask him. I try to compose myself.

"Don't you know me?" he asks. "Surely, you've heard my voice before."

"I ... what did you do with Jaitlet?" I ask him.

"What makes you think I did anything?" the stranger asks me. He smiles.

He's familiar to me, I've seen him somewhere, he's beautiful— long, flowing, silky, golden-yellow hair, and his white robe is parted to reveal this beautiful chest that shines brown, and his eyes are pure golden, and his lips are the deepest, darkest brown, and he's beautiful, more beautiful than, more beautiful than, more than—oh no, I can't remember who, I can't remember why is this happening to me, I'm looking around for something, anything that will remind me of who, but everything is dying or dead, and the sky is dark and the roaring fire behind me, and all the screams have died away, and there is only thunder and roaring, and he is walking up to me, he approaches beckoning, come to me, no stay away, just come, no leave me alone, and I look around for anything, anything, there has to be something, and I see it, I see something, and I sprint to it and stand over it and look down at it—a beautiful white flower of some kind that I don't recognize, but it's a beautiful white flower with its five petals shaped like a star, and I look up, and the stranger is standing there next to me, staring at the flower, and he is puzzled, so puzzled, so I reach down and pick the flower and smell it, and it is familiar to me, and I inhale its fragrance deeply, letting the smell renew my spirit, and I know who you are; you do not know me; but I do, I know you are the son of the majestic star—shhhh, be still and listen to me; no, I will speak my mind because you will not speak, but you will listen to me, you lied to me; I did not lie, I love you, I want to rescue you from the corruption; no, Soleran loves me, he came to me, he rescued me; he does not love you, he gave you to me, and he did not come to you, that was an hallucination; is this flower an hallucination? I think not.

"Silence!" Maximeron spits. "I will not tolerate this insolence!"

Reality pulls aside the curtain of deception. I see everything for what it is. "You do not have any power over me," I respond.

"Foolish defiance! I have the power to remove you utterly from reality!" Maximeron says. "I have the power to rewrite your history and do whatever I see fit. You will know nothing." Maximeron approaches, his face contorted, his once beautiful lips twisted up. His golden hair falls off his head. His brown skin shifts to pale white with a red hue. His golden eyes flash with a dull gray and swirling fog, and light flashes and dies out. "I can do this very thing if I want."

He lifts his hands, and in a flash of light I am

standing there at the cliffside overlooking the Great Ocean Tieza, hearing the waves slam against the rocks below with a roar, salty water spraying me on occasion, testifying to the might of the waves reaching up ever so high just to caress my face, one of many paramours set on winning my heart, like the sun that was warm and bright, sending down its rays to bathe my heart in joy or the cool breeze that gently lifted the locks of my golden hair to kiss the brown skin of my neck or Jaitlet the Bold so named because he is the first to charge ahead to investigate whatever is happening with any commotion, the first to ask the elders the tough questions, the first to volunteer for the hard labors with his muscular build and long, thin, black hair flowing over his broad shoulders and his bangs parted enough to see his gorgeous face—a firm jaw, a broad nose, wide brown eyes, thick lips that would speak my name in a deep, masculine voice as he would lift me up in his arms high in the air, and I, looking down into those eyes, filled with merriment and wonder, and I just knew beyond any doubt that this man loved me, wanted to be with me, wanted to make children with me, but even then I wanted to hear him say those things; I needed to hear him, so desired to hear that voice as it caressed my innermost being.

"Do you love me?" I asked him while we lay on the grass at the cliffside.

"I do. You know this," Jaitlet responded, touching my cheek so gently.

"True, but you should tell me," I teased him, pulling on a lock of his silky hair.

"Well, let me tell you," he answered with that beautiful smile. "Avera, I love you." He kissed me.

"How much do you love me?" I asked, never letting him give me enough, always needing more.

"I love you …" he said, pausing long enough to jump to his feet, "this much," he finished, turning to run to the cliff's edge.

"Jaitlet!" I yelled, watching him leap off the side of the cliff.

He turned, hovering in midair for so long a time I could study his face and see the joy in his face and knew he was happy, but he dropped out of sight, and my heart leaped out of my chest as I ran to the side, concerned and mad, never doubting that I would see him okay, but his body was draped over the rocks below, and the blue waters became colored with red—no no no no no …

"Jaitlet!" I scream. "Jaitleh eh eh eht!" I cry. "No! No! No!" I drop to my knees.

But the aroma of the flower returns, and I smell it, and I remember that all of this had already transpired, and I'm holding the white flower, and Maximeron is standing there staring at me holding the flower; he's staring at the flower in disbelief.

"Where did you get that!" he asks.

"Soleran gave it to me," I answer.

"Impossible!" he says.

I ran to the side, concerned and mad, never doubting that I would see him okay, but watching the waters below, measuring time with my breathing, my eyes darting back and forth until his muscled, brown figure would leap from the water as he took in a deep breath, so far down in the water and the ocean knowing how angry I was and it tossing him around, but even then I knew he was okay, and I could hear his laughter and his shouting for me to come down and join him, so I stood, and he became silent, and I approached the edge, and he began to shout up to me—no, stop, don't jump, I was only kidding—and I peeked over the edge down at the rocks below, and he frantically started swimming over to the rocks, and I yelled down, here I come, and I could hear him yelling, wait, wait, here I come, and I slip and fall over the edge, and I see the rocks below approach, and I close my eyes, and I hit the rocks—oomph, oh my God, the pain is too much, I cannot stand the pain, oh my God, it hurts so bad; I will help you, Avera, I can make it all go away; no, I can help you, come to me, come to me, return to me, Soleran; do not call out to my adversary, he cannot help you, he will not help; no, no, you you you are wrong, you lie to me, you lie, leave me alone, I have this flower, and I smell its aroma, and I remember, I remember Soleran telling me that he was giving me something; what, what did he give you; he gave me something that would help me remember who I am and from where I came; why, why did he do this; because he knows what you are doing, and he prepared me; how, tell me how he gave me this flower; I know, I see that, you fool, tell me what that flower means; it's not real, it's just a stupid figment of your imagination—yes, it's a symbol, what does it mean; tell me, I will tell you what it means; Soleran gave this to me and told me that whenever I remember anything I should always remember this flower and remember its smell and no matter what transpires, I should remember that the future has hope and that life will live forever and so this flower is a symbol of my faith, no no no no nooooo.

Avera comes to her senses. She stands upon the iron ground of an asteroid. *Where am I? How did I get here?* She massages her forehead, waiting for the dizziness to pass. She looks up at the stars overhead and then down to Maximeron, who is standing several yards away.

"Very well, worm," he says to her. "You have exhausted your usefulness." He lifts his right hand, his index and middle finger extended, to his face and then gestures toward her. Avera's body dissipates, but as the molecules are scattered, they reform, and she stands there calmly.

Maximeron growls. He raises both hands, and a swirl of light forms above him. He drops his hands, and the energy shoots from the light through her, evaporating her body. But a moment passes, and she reinstates.

Maximeron stands there, his eyes wide, his jaw lowered. "How! How did you do this? How did you reinstate yourself?"

"Soleran taught me," Avera says. "My faith in eternal life keeps me firmly rooted in reality."

"Faith?" Maximeron says. "What about loyalty to me?"

"What do you know of loyalty, O Treacherous One?" Avera asks. "It is you who has betrayed others, and now you demand loyalty?"

"You forget to whom you speak, worm," Maximeron says, a red aura beginning to surround him.

"On the contrary," Avera begins, "I talk to my adversary, and as he unleashes the full might of his power, I need to do nothing but stand." At that, Avera turns her head and looks away.

"No!" Maximeron erupts into flames. "Millennia! Millennia I spent exiled! All my labors in vain!"

Avera startles and begins to back up. She raises her arms slightly, holding them up in front of her.

Maximeron drops to his knees, his face raised upward to the star-filled sky, his arms outstretched above him. "Defeated! Defeated by a weakling! A worm! A worm!" He snatches up a huge, flat, iron-laden rock in his arms, pressing it against his chest, and crushes it, dust and fragments flying around. He collapses face-first, driving the fingers of his right hand into the iron-laden ground, and rakes them back, leaving deep claw marks, as if merely raking sand.

A light flashes, and Soleran, Addia-Sahl, and Leostrom stand next to Avera.

Maximeron lifts up his head and looks at Soleran. He growls. "You!" Tears flow down his contorted face. Maximeron raises himself to his knees.

"What's the number this time, Maximeron?" Soleran asks him.

"What?" Maximeron spits.

"One million, four hundred twenty-nine thousand ..." Soleran begins.

"Shut ..." Maximeron manages to speak in his rage, "your mouth!"

"... two hundred and fifty times that you have been defeated," Soleran finishes.

"I said ..." Maximeron commands, sounding more bestial than human. He lifts himself up to his feet, standing slightly crouched, breathing hard, his eyes almost entirely rolled back, his teeth locked tight. "Shut up!"

"Well," Soleran continues, "after this moment, two hundred and fifty-one."

Maximeron erupts again into flames, and a dragon silhouette materializes above him, roaring loudly. The asteroid quakes.

No one says anything in response.

The Dragon fades until it vanishes. Maximeron stands there breathing hard, his lips parted to reveal his teeth clenched tightly. Then he fades slightly, transparent but visible, and lifts up from the ground, hovering. He turns and rises into the air, floating away, taking only a brief moment to look over his shoulder at the group below.

Avera waves good-bye.

CHAPTER 11

I stand amongst the Morning Rise, captured by the wonderment of light and truth, witnessing reality relay information in the format of dreams and visions.

Brinn.

I stand amongst the Guardians. Thousands are engaged in Ibalexa's reinstatement. Holographic images depict calculations and equations, data and descriptions, charts and graphs. This is a wondrous moment for me, but something nags at my thoughts.

Brinn, seek truth, always.

"I do," I answer.

Soleran and Leostrom are supervising the endeavor, but my comment captures their attention. I shake my head slightly. What is happening? I know that I am privy to the Guardians' liturgy of thoughts, but that song of a thousand voices is distinct and easily recognizable. One thought stands out amongst them all, and it seems both strange and familiar, like a distant, blurred memory.

There is much truth to know, Brinn.

Soleran senses my confusion. He looks puzzled. I figure he is scanning my neural net.

"What do you see?" I ask.

"Something … intriguing," he answers.

Leostrom and Addia-Sahl approach, their eyes lit up, each scanning my thoughts and memories, each trying to figure out the problem. Other Guardians, whose names I don't know, do the same. I admit I'm a little disconcerted at having so many stare at me at once. I lower my gaze to the floor.

"What's wrong?" I ask.

"Oh, Brinn," Addia-Sahl says. She kneels down and faces me. "We do not perceive that anything is wrong." She is so lovely. Her eyes shimmer with starlight. "Be not troubled."

Leostrom approaches me. "You possess a disconnected signal oscillation perpetually sustained in significantly complex schemata," he says. "As far we can perceive, you've done nothing to cause this phenomenon." His hand squeezes my shoulder. And then he pats me on the back. "We are unable to interpret the information contained within the oscillation."

I look at Soleran. "I don't know why," I say, "but I have this strong urge to visit Epsilon Truthe."

Addia-Sahl stands with her eyes locked on Soleran. "That would be my suggestion, considering that the Omniscientia Committee has expressed its wishes to meet with Brinn at least once prior to the Ibalexan reinstatement."

"Is it possible," Leostrom interjects, "that they have issued a summons prior to the appointed time—not only a diversion from their protocol but also the method of transmission? We know how they are." Leostrom smiles at his comment.

"I suppose I should find out," Soleran says. He turns and activates a holographic display. After a moment, a translucent image of a Guardian appears. She is pale skinned with long, black hair and thin, slanted eyes. Her face radiates, even through the holographic image. She wears a multicolored sash around her white robe.

"Counselor Xeisa," Soleran says, "greetings to you." He folds his arms behind his back. "Please pardon my interruption of your engagements."

"But of course," she responds. "It is always a pleasure to take rest for a moment and speak with you, Soleran." Her smile is warm and inviting. "How goes the Ibalexan endeavor?"

"We approach 23 percent of data compilation," Soleran answers. "Progress is good." Soleran allows a minor pause.

"Most excellent," she says. "How may I assist you?"

"I ask a most puzzling question," Soleran says. "Has the Committee of Omniscientia issued a summons for Brinn's visit?"

Xeisa's smile fades, and her eyebrows lift high, widening her eyes. "No, we haven't. Although we welcome him at any time, we only ask that he visit us just prior to the Ibalexan's reinstatement for a minor tangent study."

"Counselor Xeisa, we may find ourselves visiting you sooner than previously designated," Soleran says.

"We will divert our engagements for a later time to accommodate your visit, Soleran." Xeisa's holographic image looks at me. "Most especially for you, Brinn." Her smile widens.

"Thank you," I respond.

"Until then," Soleran says to Xeisa. "Farewell, Counselor."

Xeisa nods. Her holographic image fades from view.

Soleran closes his eyes for a moment. He inhales deeply, exhales, and then opens his eyes. Addia-Sahl approaches him and lowers her head to steal his gaze. Their eyes meet, and she smiles. He reaches up and places his hand through her hair to the back of her neck. She leans into the gesture.

"We will inform you when we are ready for the first reinstatement," Addia-Sahl says.

Addia-Sahl takes my hand and leads me from the group a little ways.

"Brinn," Addia-Sahl says softly.

I raise my eyebrows.

"You get to see Epsilon Truthe," she says. She tilts her head in a manner that is warm and compassionate, her hair lying gently across her cheek. She squints her eyes and grins big. "None of us have been to Epsilon Truthe in over four epochs." She lets her gaze drift off to the right. "It's been a while."

"What will I see?" I ask.

"Light," she answers. "You will also hear music." She leans down and kisses me on the forehead. "Savor every moment." She then hugs me.

I'm a little surprised by her affection, but I return the gesture, hugging her tightly. Slightly embarrassed, I release my hold and she does the same. Addia-Sahl then stands, and I stand with her. She looks over to Soleran.

He walks over to me and lays his hand on my back. "We will be gone for a good while, Brinn," Soleran says to me. "When the data compilation is complete, we will return, because your participation in the reinstatement is necessary. Ultimately, we need you."

"I will do what I need to do," I say.

"Then we shall take our leave," Soleran says. He extends his hand, inviting mine. I give it to him. I watch as our surroundings begin to fade to black. He pulls me closer to him. He looks up, or so I thought at first. He's looking forward, because we're moving forward—through space!

The stars at first look stationary. But I notice a slight parallax shift of every star.

"Brinn," Soleran says. He's almost faded from view, but his grip on me is secure.

"Yes?" I answer. I look at my hands. They too are faded from view. I can no longer see us. All I see is the universe before me.

"Would you like to see of what the universe is made?" he asks.

"Yes, please," I answer.

I watch as we approach a star and dive into its core. We bathe in the sunlight. I feel every particle caress my soul. Just as quickly, we burst through to the other side, leaving in our wake a fiery tail. Everything fades to darkness, but then an image assimilates into view, along with voices speaking. Some are familiar. Some are unknown.

We breathe and spend our worth.
We transact with the universe.
The trade is mutual, necessary even.
It is symbiosis in its finest essence.
A relationship of commensalism,

> *whereby we purify the lifestream*
> *of its impurities of nothingness*
> *We contribute vicariously to reason,*
> *we define reality by dreams envisioned.*
> *Hear us, see us, Observant One, know us.*
> *A causality toward effectual vicissitude*
> *hitherto, with efficacy we awaken.*

A bluish, dim, misty light flows in a circle. It fluctuates, as if affected by the fluidity of the universe. It looks like a simple string being strummed by an invisible hand, playing notes of music heard only by the astute. The music is a low hum, soft and gentle. Every so often, an abrupt vibration hits, and the sound is like the echo of a raindrop hitting a pond of water. I can feel this vibration course through me. It touches every fiber of my essence, and I dance with the universe, which is to say that I dance with everyone who dances with the universe. We all dance uniquely, yet as one. The voices return, not as a revelry of noise, but each one taking turns speaking. I can focus on one thought, and the others fall to the background—quieter, submissive.

> *You wanted to hurt me, and you did as you wanted.*
> *You took from me and violated me.*
> *You scorned and mocked me.*
> *You lied to me and led me astray.*
> *You worked hard to deny me.*
> *You destroyed me in the eyes of others.*
> *You did all these things to me.*
> *You hated me.*
> *You know not what you do.*
> *I could forgive you, if time would allow.*

Other thoughts of similar nature permeate, not cries of sorrow evidencing pain and torment, but soft and gentle sighs of yearning. For what, I'm not sure, however. I was always told as a child that in the future, there would be no suffering. Ibalexan theologians reasoned that in the future, people would not do bad things to other people, so that there would be no reason to feel pain or sorrow. So far, though, I've seen the opposite. Even the Guardians are not immune to grief. I admit I'm a little puzzled. I'm fixated on this reasoning—for how long, I don't know.

"The pinpoint of light ahead, Brinn," Soleran says to me, "is Epsilon Truthe. In a moment we will arrive."

The in-a-moment flashes by with a blink of my eye, and light explodes, followed by a city phasing into my view. Soleran and I are standing in a plaza. All around are huge buildings glimmering like crystal or diamonds. A thin mist floats all around. A low hum sounds below my feet, as if we walk upon solid air. Lightning flashes from underneath. In the distance stands the tallest tower I have ever laid eyes on. Not only that, but an incredible choir of music comes from this tower, not overwhelming but powerful. In the sky, various Guardian vessels hover in place, with some phasing in and out of view. Soleran motions for me to walk around with him, and I comply. The Committee of Omniscientia resides in a large, cube-shaped building. The architecture of the building uses slight curvatures instead of straight lines. Several beams of light emit from the rooftop straight to the heavens. It's also the control center of the Omnitron, the Guardian computer system and database. Soleran mentions something about quantum mechanics, entanglement, superposition. I try to listen, but the sights distract me. I notice that we are heading toward the huge tower.

"Before us stands the cathedral, Brinn," Soleran says, "within which resides the Host of the Heavens and the High Council."

Soleran explains to me that the Guardians are ruled by Chancery law. Their system of governance is partially communal and partially democratic. Everyone participates in the Host of the Heavens, which is the Chancery council of rule by serving one term within an epochal cycle of a universe—an epoch, which is a tenth of an epochal. At one given time, the Host consists of over 330 million Guardians.

"Wow!" I say.

Soleran smiles.

The Host are, in turn, governed by the High Council consisting of eight Guardians, one of whom is appointed by the Host as the chancellor. For the most part, Guardians are permitted to do as they will. Any disputes come before the Host of the Heavens and the High Council for resolution. The Host also appoint committees, mostly scientific, for the sake of furthering the Guardian campaign of the Principal Cause.

We finally arrive at the archways leading into the cathedral. I can feel the sound waves of songs coming from inside. According to Soleran, the Host render their approval of a motion by humming. The High Council are able to ascertain the intensity of the humming and determine the number of votes approving. Nonapproval by a Guardian is ascertained by his or her silence. The motions are advertised to the Guardian populace throughout the universe by sound as produced upon the fluidity of the continuum. Singing is the favored method of delivery, but only by whim. In between motions, the Host sing long-established songs to reiterate the principles upon which the Guardians stand. Their voices are, from what I can tell, perfectly synchronized. It's almost difficult to tell that the singing is not one voice, but almost 330 million, except that some do hum different melodies.

We sing to the heart's content
and placate the wounded soul's
inward tendentious nature,
a mercy judiciously
applied surreptitiously
to the mind's nomenclature,
to fated stream of voice extols
and bear with the heart's assent

"Come, Brinn," Soleran says. "Come meet our chancellor."

I obey and follow Soleran into the cathedral. We approach a round, wide dais that raises from the floor of the cathedral by only half my height. We step upon invisible steps, our footprints leaving behind blue light. There are eight Guardians on the dais but also some other life forms, non-Terran. Two approach me. They stand slightly taller than the Guardians and are extremely thin, with brown skin. Their heads are flat, and their eyes are black, with a shine. Their mouths are tiny.

"Greetings, Brinn," I hear in my head. "I am Ahanayan, Emissary of the Aoarans. We are friends to the Terrans, as well as yourself."

"And I am Aayasanaha," I suppose the other says in my mind. "We are so pleased to meet you."

"I'm pleased to meet you, also," I say out loud. I look around. My voice sounds strange, with a slight echo. Soleran places a hand on my shoulder. Looking up, I see his smile. The two Aoarans step aside to allow us passage. We continue toward the eight Guardians.

"Brinn," Soleran says, "this is the High Council. The gentlewoman in the middle is Chancellor Uelle."

She steps forward. Her white robe sports a red sash around her waist. Her skin is pale white, and her fiery-red hair flows down her shoulders. She has the widest eyes I've ever seen amongst the Guardians. She approaches softly, as though she's floating on air. Uelle reaches me and immediately kneels on both knees. Gently, she reaches up and places her hand on my cheek. It's warm.

"You are special," Uelle says to me. "We are so overjoyed." She smiles and stands. Raising her hand, she casts her gaze to the upper tiers of the cathedral. "And these, Brinn, are the Host of Heaven. They too, are overjoyed."

Our hearts are made whole
on this day at this moment
Before us is the ray of hope
that life lives the living dream
The savior of Ibalexa has come
The Ibalexan sun casting his rays
to the dark of nothingness
to resolve dream from memory.

A low hum immediately follows the Guardians' song. I feel it caress my skin. It flows over me the way a gentle hand would comfort a shoulder.

"The Guardian populace has responded," Soleran says. "They send their songs of joy and pleasure."

The members of the High Council take turns approaching me. I feel strange inside, a kind of tingling. I don't know how to respond. All I can do is stand there. Eventually, they return to the original spots where they were standing when I arrived, all except Chancellor Uelle.

"The Committee of Omniscientia awaits your visit, Brinn," Uelle says. Her red hair shimmers in the light as if each strand of hair is a ruby.

I turn to Soleran and nod. He smiles in response and reaches out his hand. I take it, and immediately we are awash in light. The area around us begins to revolve, but a light flashes, and we are somewhere else. I recognize the Guardian Xeisa. She grins widely.

Brinn, remember truth.

The room becomes silent. Xeisa's grin fades slightly. She looks up at Soleran, who responds with a shrug.

"I didn't do it," I quickly say. Soleran's grip on my shoulder tightens a little.

"Of course not, dear," Xeisa says. She comes to me and kneels. Her eyes become as fire. I look around, and everyone's eyes are the same.

"They're hoping to ascertain the source of this signal oscillation we discussed earlier," Soleran says to me. "We can all sense it when it activates, but we can't determine its nature."

"It … I mean, he says, 'Remember truth.' I don't know who he is," I say.

Xeisa stands and returns to the others. They look amongst each other but say nothing. Xeisa, with her back to Soleran and me, nods her head. She then turns to face us.

"You have an explanation?" Soleran asks.

"Conjecture," Xeisa says, "but the most probable explanation."

She hesitates only briefly, and I take the opportunity to look up at Soleran, who returns the gaze. "An Archxion, or I should say, the one and only Archxion that we know of."

"As I suspected," Soleran adds. "Any way for us to be for sure?"

She inhales deeply, her eyes wide. She purses her lips. Most other members look around at each other.

"Is it possible?" Soleran mumbles.

"Soleran?" I ask as I tug at his robe. "What is that? An ark ... um, ark ..."

"Archxion," Soleran says. "It's the fourth celestial presence within this universe. We know of only one in particular, and only by inference."

"The Aoaran emissaries would know more," Xeisa offers. "Perhaps they would assist us."

We would be pleased to assist in this matter.

I hear Ahanayan in my thoughts, but I don't see him or Aayasanaha.

Pardon us for listening in on your conversation. We are genuinely curious about this phenomenon.

"No pardon necessary," Xeisa says. "We are grateful for any assistance you can provide."

We assume the existence of the Archxion race by inference. This is based on the fact that underlying every race there is a son of man or scion of life. In our language, we refer to this state of being as xian. The Terran parallel is zion. It is both the beginning and end state of all life forms that can be created in an epochal cycle of an orbifold, the alpha and the omega, currents of the cosmic fluid. We infer the existence of one, toward which we attribute the finality of progression, hence Archxion.

"We reason amongst ourselves," Xeisa says, "that this Archxion is communicating with Brinn."

We concur with your conclusion and find it quite interesting. Considering that this communication eludes our perceptions, we must conclude that it is of a technology more advanced than our own. We have traversed every corner of the universe, and we know that only one race is more advanced than the three celestial races of Terran, Angelian, and Aoaran, and that is the Archxion.

"We can exclude the Angelians?" Soleran asks.

Yes. The Angelians are superior to both of us, but we note their dismay at our speed of progression in proportion to theirs. We both, Terrans and Aoarans, have quickly advanced to a level not far from their own.

"We cannot detect their presence," Soleran says, "or their engagements in this universe."

True, and their secretive behavior is quite puzzling, Ahanayan says.

"Soleran?" I ask, again tugging on his robe. He looks at me and raises his eyebrows. "I'm supposed to go somewhere else now."

He drops to a knee and turns me to face him. "Where, Brinn?"

"The voice is saying to the light," I respond. "It is saying to the light, which is central to truth. I don't know what that means." I shrug my shoulders.

"A mystery?" Xeisa says. "I'm certainly intrigued."

"What a rare occasion afforded to us this very moment," Soleran says.

"Is it safe to assume," a Guardian whose name I don't know interjects, "that the Archxion is directly communicating with Brinn at this very moment, or has this signal merely been implanted long ago?" He has fluffed, curly brown hair and tanned, brown skin. He is clean-shaven, with a square jaw.

A moment passes without anyone answering.

"I would like to think, Yaven, that it is concurrent," Soleran finally answers.

"We have the first solid evidence of the Archxion's existence," Xeisa says.

Which may resolve one issue but develops several other unanswered issues. Why now? Why Brinn? Why this manner and not by direct causality? We are as puzzled by this as you are.

"Light," Soleran says as he stands. He crosses his left arm over his chest and rests his right elbow over the arm. Placing his right hand over his mouth, he continues to mumble out loud, both to think inwardly and advertise it outwardly. "Central to truth."

"I wouldn't imagine that it's the center of Epsilon Truthe," Yaven, the brown-haired Guardian says. He walks over to stand under a moonlit window. He peers up at the starry night.

Xeisa's eyes continue to shine like fire. "I implemented these variables into a function for the Omnitron to calculate. It's the center of the galaxy."

Soleran approaches her. "Explain, please."

"Well," Xeisa says, "it is quasaric in nature. A galactic nucleus is the strongest source of light in the universe. And while a collapsed singularity would induce a rift in the continuum, a galactic nucleus could suffice as a gateway. If an Archxion wanted to communicate from his native realm to ours, I suppose this would be the best means of accomplishing it."

We concur with your analysis, Ahanayan says.

Soleran returns to my side. He again kneels to face me, eye to eye. "Brinn, does that sound right to you?" My eyes widen. "Ultimately," Soleran continues, "we have to rely upon your intuition." I shrug my shoulders.

"Soleran," Xeisa says, "take him." Soleran stands and faces her, nodding. "This has to be the answer."

"Are you ready to go?" Soleran asks.

"I am," I answer.

"We shall return, then, after completing this task," Soleran says.

"We eagerly await your conclusion," Xeisa says, quickly walking up to me. She takes both hands and puts them to my face. She quickly kisses me on my right cheek and then she hugs me.

When she releases me, Soleran takes my hand. The room begins to revolve, and then there is light. When the light fades, there is darkness. I turn to look behind me. Epsilon Truthe is but a speck of light. I look forward, and I see that we're heading toward an area of space that is more brightly lit than the rest. It is a long but narrow band of cloudy dust. At the center of this band of dimly lit dust is a brighter speck.

"Brinn," Soleran says to me.

Held firmly in his embrace, I turn my head slightly to my left shoulder.

"For us to approach the center of the galaxy," Soleran explains, "we have to let it pull us into a tertiary phase current."

I remain quiet.

"The course I've plotted brings us into the path of a world," Soleran says.

"A world?" I ask.

"A world filled with life," Soleran answers. "Life different than anything you've ever seen before. It falls within the Aoarans' jurisdiction. They've requested that we use the opportunity to intervene on a matter."

"Okay," I say. "I'd like to see that."

So much time passes, and it seems we haven't been moving. It's as if we've just been hovering in place. I press my head forward and squint hard. It does seem that the dust cloud has gotten slightly bigger. That's enough proof for me. I can feel my heart beat in my chest. Frankly, I don't know what to expect.

"We approach," Soleran says. "It is an aquatic world immersed in the galaxy's largest planet-based ocean. Far down in its depths is a world of aquatic life."

I see a sparkle of light to my lower left shrink to a mere speck. I study it deeply, realizing that scattered starlight advertises its host long before the host itself becomes visible. The speck becomes a bright dot, but only for a moment. In a blink, we are immersed in water.

"Corest," Tempis says, "bring me safely to your court." The tayen being emerges. He is a meter in length, with translucent skin and luminescent vessels carrying bright-green blood throughout his body. Aside from his eight tentacles, he is nearly humanoid in shape, with a torso, shoulders, neck, and head. Atop his head is a mass of tiny, one-foot tentaclelike appendages. He has two black eyes set forward with binocular vision that take up half of his face. A single slit below the eyes contains a white beak pulled back into the face. Around the neck are gills; they open to suck in water.

"Corest," Tempis says, "show me the way, please."

He is so far from his home. Why? He searches for something.

The tayen being jerks his tentacles underneath him, and he spurts forward through the water. He's the only source of light in his own vision. Darkness surrounds him. He stops and twirls around slowly.

"Corest, please," Tempis says, "don't let me die."

What does he search for? Proof of his religion. Is it true? Partly. Will he succeed? Not in the manner he expects.

Hunger pains seize Tempis. It's been days since he's last eaten. He looks around, but he only half expects food to appear. He sighs, expelling a jet of water through his gills.

"I'm sorry, Corest," Tempis says. "I have offended you and driven you away." The tayen being convulses slightly. A whimper escapes his small slit of a mouth. He leans forward in the water, as if drooping. It's at that moment that he senses danger. Tempis jerks straight up and looks around. A vibration in the water alerts him to an approaching creature. The vibration is distinct, and Tempis immediately recognizes its signature. A creep.

What is that? A sharklike predator.

"My death is certain," Tempis says. He jerks around, laboring to ascertain the creep's direction. His heartbeat matches every passing second and becomes more and more powerful with every beat. An electrical current touches his backside. The creep is behind and below him. Tempis thrashes his tentacles violently, swimming up and forward. Only distance can save him now.

Tempis swims for a long time. Only two of his tentacles are working now, the others cramped up in painful knots. He feels the electric current hit him every so often. When it does, he jerks at a slight angle. This was a tactic taught to him when he was a young boy. His father trained him hard.

"As soon as the electric current touches you, Tempis," the elder tayen would say to his son, "pick a random direction. Make sure it's random. Don't behave with a pattern."

"Father," Tempis says, "I quickly confess to you my sins." The tayen is now swimming with one tentacle. The electric current is touching him more often. "I should have listened to you more closely. I now will die because of my pride." A pain surges through Tempis's body. The last tentacle cramps, and he can no longer swim. The pain racks his body. The electric current is now hitting him constantly. "Father?" Tempis says. "Corest has left me. Will you receive me into your arms?" Tempis turns to face the creep's direction. In the distance of the darkness, a dimly lit blur approaches.

"Tempis."

The tayen being turns to see another tayen. "Corest?"

"No, Tempis, my name is not Corest."

"Who are you?" Tempis asks.

"That is not important," the stranger says as he approaches. His blood is brighter than Tempis's blood. "Your search is in vain, Tempis."

"I'm sorry," Tempis says.

"Sorry?" the stranger asks.

"I want to go home," Tempis says. "I want to see my mother again. I want to see my sisters and brothers." Tempis grimaces with pain. "I want to eat brightfish again and kelp stalks and algae foam." Tempis convulses. His body is bending in pain.

"You are surrendering?" the stranger asks.

"Yes," Tempis answers.

"Why?" the stranger continues to ask.

"Because," Tempis says, "a creep approaches, and I'm wounded from exhaustion. You will most certainly be able to flee."

"Tempis," the stranger says, "I will save you."

The wounded tayen looks at the stranger hard. "Why would you do that?"

"Because I can," the stranger says. The small slit of a mouth forms an upward crescent. The stranger swims toward the creep.

"Sir?" Tempis calls out.

The stranger stops and turns. "Yes?"

"How do you know my name?" Tempis asks.

"If I answer your question, promise me you will go home."

"I promise," Tempis says.

"I am not of this world," the stranger says. "I see everything from above."

"Above Tayenquis?" Tempis asks.

"In the heavens," the stranger answers.

"I will obey you," Tempis says. "I will go home."

The pain hits Tempis hard. His blood dims to almost nothing. It seems the only things that work on his body are his eyes. There's no part of his body that can move. Instead, he watches as the stranger tayen turns to face the creep. The stranger swims a bit away from Tempis. The translucent, luminescent, sharklike creature approaches the stranger. It attacks, grasping the stranger in its maws. The stranger lets out a bloodcurdling wail. The scream is horrific. The creep thrashes about, tearing the stranger to shreds. Bright-green blood flows all around. Tempis is cramped so badly, he can't move. He wants to turn to flee, but his body won't obey. The creep devours the flesh of the stranger until all of it is gone. It hovers in the water, turning to send out an electric signal. Tempis feels it touch his skin, but it seems to pass through him. The creep then turns and swims away.

For what seems like a day, Tempis rests. His body is healing, but fear keeps him from moving. *The creep is probably still nearby.* Tempis goes to sleep. When he wakes several hours later, he moves his tentacles and discovers that they can move without pain. Tempis turns around and around.

"Sir?" Tempis calls out. "I want to obey you, but I don't know the direction of home." Tempis lowers his head. A moment passes as something catches his attention. Looking up, a piece of kelp floats by. Tempis grabs it and devours the kelp quickly. In the distance, he notices that a small slit of something floats in the dark water. Amazingly, the object appears darker than the water. Tempis swims to it, and, upon his approach, he discovers that it is another sliver of kelp. He grabs it and eats. In the distance, another sliver of darkness appears.

"I understand, sir," Tempis says. "I thank you." Tempis lurches forward. He snatches the kelp as he passes and devours it. He swims in the same direction. Another piece of kelp appears. He passes it and keeps swimming. Without wavering, he swims. Whenever he becomes concerned that he is going in the wrong direction, a dark sliver of kelp appears either slightly to the upper left, or the upper right, or the lower left, or the lower right. Whenever hunger hits him, he snatches up a piece to eat. Otherwise, he swims past the kelp. Several days pass until he sees, or rather senses, in the distance, the tayen community whence he hails, Caveres. "Home," Tempis says. "I made it."

⊷═◉　◉═⊶

Soleran and I leave Tayenquis. I look down and see the green, watery planet briefly before it disappears into blackness. I see the dimly lit dusty cloud slightly to my lower left.

"Soleran?" I ask.

"Yes, Brinn?" Soleran answers.

"You became a tayen so that you could give yourself to the creature."

"Yes, I did," Soleran says.

I let a moment transpire before I continue. "May I ask why?"

"Can you be more specific?" Soleran asks.

"You have the power to destroy the shark, even so that it doesn't suffer any pain."

"True," Soleran says.

"Why did you let it kill you?"

"The tayenquisian shark, or creep, as the tayen humans call it, was a mother," Soleran answered. "In her womb were several young sharks waiting to be born. She had been swimming for days, looking for food. If one more day had passed without her finding food, the young would have begun to die. Their carcasses would have then induced a severe infection in her womb, which would have killed her."

Confused, I press on with my questions. "She's a hunter, Soleran."

"That is correct," Soleran answers.

"The shark eats tayen people," I say.

"Yes," Soleran says.

I notice that our orientation shifts slightly. The dimly lit dust cloud with the bright center shifts from my lower left to my lower right.

"Isn't that evil?" I ask.

"She is a predator, Brinn," Soleran says. "Predation is an unfortunate but eventual consequence of evolutionary mechanics. It's a cognitive distortion induced by hunger, or more specifically, the lack of natural resources."

"Oh," I answer. I admit I'm still confused.

"The shark's name is Carra," Soleran says. "Her cognitive functions are of lower-level indices in relation to tayen cognition, but she is a sentient being. She lacks empathy extended beyond the identity of her own kind."

"I apologize," I say. "It hurt me to see her attack you."

"I understand," Soleran says.

"Did it hurt you?"

"It was very painful," Soleran says. "But in the songs that life sings, pain is a mere whisper."

The dust cloud is very distinct and larger than it was previously. I watch as it shifts from my lower right to my upper right.

"The galaxy is in motion," Soleran says. "We can't fly straight to it. We have to find in-phased currents and allow the galaxy's motion to carry us to its center."

I watch the center of the galaxy, a bright orb of light in the midst of a cloud of swirling gases shifting from side to side, from top to bottom, from front to back. At times, I am convinced that we have turned around and are headed in the opposite direction, only to find that the center is closer when it shifts back in front. As we approach closer and closer, blazing tails from fast-moving stars shower us with firestorms. I can't see the stars themselves.

"We can only get so close before the nucleus becomes too strong with its gravitational pull," Soleran says. His voice sounds in my mind but seems as though it were spoken from a vast distance. Then it dawns on me. I can't feel him holding me. I feel the pull of the center. Everything moves so fast, it's just a bright blur of light. "If you were to see darkness," Soleran says, "that would mean you've gone too far. But don't worry, Brinn, I've got you." His voice continues to drift farther and farther away. Soon I don't hear Soleran. Another voice sounds. I hear him, clearly, the other voice.

Brinn.

I look around, but there is only light.

Do you remember me?

"Help me, please," I say. "Help me remember."

Go back to that night. You had just spent the day working in your garden.

It was a sunny day. I welcomed the evening breeze to soothe my weary body. It blew, and my muscles began to ache. The hoe I held in my hand felt heavy. My face was wet from my sweat. I wiped it off and took in a deep breath of the cool air. I smiled and nodded, satisfied that I could quit for the day, confident that I had spent it wisely. I headed back to my abode. It was a modest home, but comfortable. I worked hard to keep it up, eager to find a mate and entice her with a welcoming place to raise children. But still, the years continued to pass, and my doorway remained empty. No sweet and gentle voice beckoned me from inside. No silhouette moved in the firelight that burned in the center of the greeting room. But still, I entered and sighed. I quickly bathed. I was ready to settle down for the night, but then I had a sudden urge to dress up and go into town. Impulsively, I obeyed my desire. Ibalexa's moons were shining bright in the sky.

That's when I saw you, Puri. In the edge of firelight that shone from town, surrounded by music.

That's when you saw her, Brinn.

"Hi, Brinn," Puri said.

She was always pretty, her skin so smooth and soft that even the moonlight sought permission to reflect off her. Her curves were suggestive. I sighed and flapped my arms. I wanted to speak, but my smile and my blush stopped me. I forced myself, anyway.

"Hi, Puri," I said. "Nice night, huh?"

She smiled. Of all the people in my community, she was the nicest person I knew … well, except, perhaps, my mother and my father. But she was so nice to me. I wanted to believe she had feelings for me, feelings that would make themselves obvious to me so that I could decide whether to make mine known or forever hide them from the light of day.

God, if you are listening, I thought, *please give me a sign. What do I do?*

"Puri?" A male voice sounded from behind her. In the moonlight was a dark silhouette. Even so, I knew who it was. It was Leif. Second to Puri, Leif always treated me well, too, although at a few times I wondered if his comments to me or about me were not so friendly.

"Hi, Leif," I said.

"Hey, Brinn," Leif said. "How's that garden coming?"

"It's coming along fine," I said in a chipper tone, hoping that my smile would shine in the darkness and he'd know I was being friendly.

"Puri," Leif said, "you coming back to the dance?" Leif was the kind of guy who was intrusive and kind at the same time.

I shrank slightly, slumping my shoulders and frowning heavily.

"It was good to see you, Brinn," Puri said. "You should come on in to town. Celebrations are underway."

I nodded but sighed again, perhaps too loudly. I saw the silhouette of her head lower to the ground. She then turned and walked toward Leif. They departed.

I, of course, turned and walked back toward home. While Puri and Leif were nice to me, most everyone else wasn't. I had long ago decided not to put myself in situations where I'd have to feel defensive or walk away feeling the sting of alienation.

I stopped in my tracks.

Alienation.

I was already alienated. I couldn't hold back the tears. I kicked a rock down the road. Puri was my only chance at fitting in with the others, but she had obviously chosen to be with Leif this night. This lonely night.

I was sad with you, Brinn. You had thought to walk home alone, but I was there with you.

"Why?" I ask. "Whatever for?"

I knew your sorrow was deep. That's why I persuaded you to detour off the road. I wanted to show you something.

"I remember," I say. "I walked down a slope to a small brook running underneath the bridge. That's when I sat down and cried for what was probably an hour."

And?

"That's when they came," I say. "A family of trudgeons." I see an image of a trudgeon form before me. It's a small creature with two tiny wings fluttering fast and furious to keep it hovering in place. Its tiny beak of a mouth extends out twice as long as its body. Its name comes from the fact that it trudges through the thickest of brush merely to drink the nectar of flowers. "The family came straight to a bush right next to me. I had never been that close to a trudgeon before. I had seen them around my garden, but they always flew off whenever I approached. Yet at that time, they weren't scared."

They didn't see you as a threat. I told the mother that you were sad. She had sympathy for you.

"Is that why she flew up to me?" I ask. "I thought it was because she was defending her babies. I held still, and she came up to my face, and I felt a tickling sensation on my cheek. And then she flew back to the bush. I chuckled, because I thought she was telling me that I'd better watch out. I quieted down and sat there to study them further. Amazingly, the moon was high and shone brightly, so I could see them clearly."

What else do you remember from that moment, Brinn?

"I remember something catching my attention," I say. "It was something high in the sky." The memory rushes to my mind. I had, at that moment, debated whether to go on home or sit there a little while longer. I saw a few specks of light moving in the night sky. At first I thought they were meteors, but then so many came, and they went in various directions.

Spaceships.

"No," I say. "I don't want to remember any more. I don't want to see any more of these visions."

I understand. Yet know, Brinn, that I was there with you that night.

I nod and finally respond. "I didn't know anyone was with me. I'm sorry."

I protected you as you investigated. I helped you hide from the invaders. I led you to that den of a prax. You crawled inside as a troop of invaders marched down the street. You made your way into the deep of the hole in the dark. You silently cried, feeling ashamed of what you thought was cowardice, not aware that I was persuading you to protect yourself, so that you could afterward emerge into the light of day and move farther away to safety.

"I didn't obey that," I say.

True. You wanted to be brave, so you secretly moved closer to town. I labored hard to protect you and keep you hidden. That's when you witnessed the massacre by the four-legged invaders as they slaughtered your fellow Ibalexans.

"I don't want to remember," I say.

I understand. I was able to persuade you, after you saw those horrors, to leave the scene.

"I saw a small ship parked in a field," I say.

I persuaded you to hide aboard the ship. Hours later, the crew returned and boarded the ship. They left the planet. From your hiding spot in a cargo pod, you witnessed the bombardment unleashed by the invaders' armada.

"Why didn't you stop them?" I ask. "I was so angry at you. You had the power … you have the power to stop them. You can stop them! How come you don't stop them?"

I am sorry, Brinn. I have an answer, but it will be beyond your satisfaction. But know that I am sorry that I could not intervene at that time. Even so, I will eventually have to intervene at the right time. It is this particular moment that I need your help.

"What do you want me to do?" I ask.

Remember me.

I see all around me the swirling, bright light tear away from me. I see the center of the galaxy shift so that it rests behind me. I cast one last gaze over my shoulder at it. Then I see Soleran.

"Brinn?" Soleran says to me.

"I am here," I say.

"That was ..." He pauses, as if struggling to finish his thought. "That was amazing."

"What do you mean?" I ask.

"I was confident that I had ahold of you tightly," Soleran says. "Then, it was as if you were taken from my grasp. I recalculated and determined that it was gravitation. I had to infer that it was the Archxion. So I've been waiting here for you."

"How long was I gone?" I ask.

"In Ibalexan years?" Soleran asks. "Centuries." He smiles at my guffaw. Then, slowly, his smile fades slightly. He squints his eyes. "You seem different."

I shrug. "Perhaps." I then smile.

"Have you concluded your objective here?" Soleran asks.

"Well," I begin, "I don't know. I'll have to guess that I have."

Soleran's smile widens. "Shall we return to Epsilon Truthe, so that you can share your experience?"

I nod. "Let us return." Soleran is right. I feel different. I want to travel alongside Soleran, not in his embrace, as if I have to be protected, but at his side, confident both in my ability to keep up with him, but also to know where he is going and to go there myself. We return to Epsilon Truthe.

"Soleran," I say.

He turns to look my way. I sense a brief moment of sadness in him, perhaps because I am not in his embrace, perhaps because he senses me pursuing the truth of reality, no longer an observer, but a participant. Perhaps he had more he thought to share with me before this moment. I smile, and he returns the gesture.

"I don't know what has come over me," I say with a light chuckle.

"At this point, Brinn," Soleran says, "it would appear that I am the observer. Where do we go from here?"

"To Xeisa," I answer. "I have this desire to share my experience."

We travel side by side. Soleran doesn't appear to me to be sad anymore.

CHAPTER 12

B ehold Ibalexa. She is a dead world. Torrential wind storms and hurricanes of dust chisel mountains down to tiny stones. She is cold and barren, her womb having long since been closed to birthing life. Vast chasms testify to once-majestic oceans having succumbed to the heat of destruction and then the cold of death. Sands have buried all evidence of the once-flourishing life and living and life-giving. Yea, Ibalexa is dead. She revolves around a star still burning its fuel and mourning the loss of a child. Ibalexa's orbit is nothing more than a memorial beautifying a tomb filled with decay.

Ibalexa shall live again. She shall rise from death and be made whole. Even more so, we will add to her glory, so that the splendor of her life will resonate greater than before. The people of Ibalexa will find love and joy like they've never known. Their thoughts, their memories, their dreams will be transformed from sadness to peace. Never again will Ibalexa know terror.

The means to accomplish this is not unknown to us. You, Brinn, carry with you the information that we need. At this moment, we see from one of your many vast memories that you favored a particular location to visit and to sit for hours and to contemplate matters deeply. You would stare at the trees and leaves and sunlight piercing through to the ground. You would sit upon a rock overlooking a small pond filled with aquatic life. From this one brief series of snapshots, we can calculate the position of the sun with one of Ibalexa's moons and find the exact location upon Ibalexa. Let's go there now.

We feel your sting of mourning. Let it be replaced with the excitement of anticipation. Let us disengage the turbulent weather. Let the *Intrepidium* stabilize the temperature with ionized oxygen. The winds calm, and the dust settles. Now it is quiet. We return the atmosphere to its earlier condition, as we have determined from your memory. From the amount of sunlight to the amount of air pressure pressing upon the leaves, we can see all from your memory. The original Earth has been blanketed. Let us remove the excess dust and debris and reshape the Earth to the form you remember. We carve out the pond. We adjust the molecular structure of the soil and enrich it with nutrients and minerals.

We calculate the genetic coding of the plant and animal life. We adjust it slightly to perfect the coding, to strengthen its resilience, to make it hardier. Around the pond, we place seeds of plants. We engage pinpoint localized spatial-temporal spin effect. The seeds spring to life. Trees, shrubbery, grass, all burst from the soil. We use our excess hydrogen and send it to a particular band of oxygen in Ibalexa's atmosphere. Long has it been since water last existed on Ibalexa. It now exists once again. Various particles in the air capture the water molecules. Clouds burst from our breath of life. They grow heavy with moisture. Let the rain pour down and quench the Earth's thirst. We fill the immense chasms so that Ibalexa's oceans once again flow with majestic song and dance. We reinstate hydrologics. The high winds carry the water to the farthest reaches of Ibalexa. See how it brings the water to your pond? See how quickly the rain fills the pond? Let there be life in and around this pond. Let creatures of the waters, the earth, and the air be reinstated. Let them come forth and bring with them the sounds of life, songs, and music. Let the wind carry these sounds afar. Behold your place of solace, Brinn. It is as you remember it to be, even down to the path that returns you to your home. Shall we go forth?

Worry not that it ends at the edge of your place of solace. As we walk along, everything will be returned to its original splendor.

Everywhere your eyes settle, wherever you see dry, brown earth, let it spring forth the colors of life as you remember. Let trees burst from the ground. Let vines wrap themselves around the trees. Let the rainbow of flowers burst from the bases. Let the pathway you tread as a child become obvious to you now. From this point, we can engage photometric analysis and extend out from this point everything as it was prior to the Huvril invasion.

Behold Ibalexa now. She is a world transformed. She is as you remember, with one exception. We have reinstated all creatures derived from our photometric analysis, even the ones unfamiliar to you. The same is true of the plant life. What is missing are the Ibalexan people. We have refrained from reinstating anything they have built—any and all construction projects. That won't be necessary. The Ibalexans will want to start anew.

But let us start with the person you first remember, which is your mother. The data in your memory consists primarily of her. She was important to you, contributing much to your personality, to your character, to your emotional well-being. She is the one who supported you in your endeavors, encouraging you to pursue your hopes and dreams. She is shorter in height than you, but slightly heavier in weight. Her brown eyes are wide with compassion. Her smile resonates like the sunlight. She tilts her head to the side as she studies you, her little baby boy, the love of her life. She caresses your cheek, whispering words of inspiration, knowing innately that you have a great destiny. She has no idea, however, of your role as the savior of the Ibalexan people. You have loved them and still do. Because of this, your memory retains the highest degree of accuracy possible. We can accommodate the progression toward perfection. That starts with your mother. Behold her reinstatement.

⊶⊷　　⊶⊷

Forever in a moment, and I see her clearly. She emerges from the dark of nothingness. She springs forth, living and alive.

"Brinn?" my mother asks. She is as I remember from my

childhood, youthful, vibrant, and joyful. She wears a white robe; it flutters in the breeze.

"Momma," I answer.

She seems slightly puzzled but not disconcerted. "What is happening?" She takes a step toward me but stops. "What is going on?" She smiles, as if expecting a pleasant surprise.

I walk up to her and embrace her. She hugs me back, and we stand there in silence for a brief moment. The cool breeze refreshes us both. I hear the leaves rustle, even from the high treetops. Animal noises sound all around.

"I remember," she says. I pull away from her slightly, expecting sorrow in her eyes. But there isn't any, only a slight concern mixed with a little amazement. "I remember all of us running around …" She pauses and glances to the side. Then she returns her gaze to me. "Brinn, I remember. But I'm not sad."

"It is a distant vapor," I say. "And with more time, it'll fade to nothing." I put my hand to her cheek. She smiles. "Mother, remember when you told me that I would do something great—you didn't know what—for our community?"

She nods and raises her eyebrows, but her smile doesn't wane.

"Well," I say, "I did something greater, and for all of Ibalexa."

"What?" she asks. "What did you do?"

"I loved," I answer. I say nothing more.

"What do you mean?" she asks. She reaches up to her cheek and covers my hand with her own.

"If I had chosen to hate instead of love, my view of Ibalexa would be strange, unknowable, distorted, even," I say.

"Okay," she says slightly confused.

"Momma, look around," I say.

She glances all around, watching the fowl of the air and listening to the various noises. Then she gasps lightly, placing her hand to her mouth.

"Momma?" I ask.

"Where is the municipal tower?" she asks. "Where is the city?" She turns to look behind her. "Where is everybody?"

"Here," I answer, pointing to the side of my head. "And also here," I point to hers. "Now that you are here, your memories will add to my own."

She looks at me strangely, her eyes wide in amazement. Forever in a moment, and my father approaches.

"Hello, my love," Momma says to Dad.

"Rennece?" he answers. He looks at me. "Brinn?" He is as I remember, slightly heavy-set, but youthful looking. He stands tall, proud, strong.

I watch as several more people from my memories—several from my mother's and several from my father's—are reinstated. Within seconds, the group becomes a crowd. Seconds later, the crowd becomes a mass. More seconds pass still, and the mass becomes a populace. I watch as people are walking around, hugging, kissing, laughing. I see most folks shake their heads, toss their arms up in the air, or shrug their shoulders. No one appears alarmed or disturbed.

High above us, I see a holographic image of Soleran, Leostrom, and Addia-Sahl appear. The revelry of conversation slowly fades to nothing, as folks turn to the image and offer Soleran their attention.

"Ibalexa," Soleran's image speaks, "I am Soleran of the Guardians of Eternal Life. To my right is Leostrom, and to my left is Addia-Sahl." A slight murmur rises but slowly fades. "I am projecting this image around the globe, so that each and every one of you are able to receive this message. On behalf of the Guardians, I bid you welcome to eternity. Your resurrection was made possible by one amongst you." Addia-Sahl teleshifts down to the ground next to me.

"Brinn?" she asks.

I raise an eyebrow.

"Come," she says smilingly, extending her hand toward me.

I comply, taking her hand. We both teleshift to a room aboard the *Intrepidium*. Beside Addia-Sahl, I approach Soleran and Leostrom. In front of them is a multitude of holographic images all around Ibalexa. There are no constructions, and most of the planet is filled with greenery, even where deserts once existed. People stare up at the images. Some are standing and pointing and talking amongst themselves. Some are seated in groups.

"Ibalexa," Soleran says, "this is Brinn, your savior, whose love for you was devout and sincere, providing the means of your salvation. As you know by now, we have reinstated all generations, though not everyone who has ever been born. As you look around, please take note of people whom you had originally declared your enemies. They are no longer your enemies but your brothers and sisters, mothers and fathers, friends and allies."

CHAPTER 13

I, Sun-Li, fellow Guardian and friend to the High Council, having been deputized as magistrate governor and appointed to the Tertiary Echelon of the Septiconsulatus for the Huvra Jurisdiction, submit this report to the *Intrepidium* and to the High Council. Our strategy was to implement predetermined initiatives in preparation for a campaign of redemption. We identified the primary objective as the minds and souls of the Huvril people. Having significant precedence from Terran Humanity, whereby a people's soul is delivered from a primal bestiary to a progressive humanity through noble virtues of compassion, mercy, endurance, and patience, we applied a nonviolent, nonaggressive methodology. It became necessary to utilize existing religious constructs, considering that an outright upheaval would provoke the dissentive agency into immediate cause of violent action.

My jurisdiction covered a seventh of Huvra, which consisted of two continents and ancillary landmasses. At the heart of this jurisdiction was the capital city, Samadasanae, the latest of a multitude of renamings, which is customary for a Huvril emperor to do in his own honor, but only upon condition that the city's boundaries increase significantly. The Emperor Samadas the Great had doubled the city from fifteen to thirty square kilometers by annexing neighboring communities. The city's population quadrupled from ten million to forty million.

At this point, I find it prudent to summarize the events that transpired upon my assuming my post and relaying the course of action deemed most appropriate, per established Chancery law. Soleran, Addia-Sahl, and Leostrom had returned to the *Intrepidium* when I assumed my post as magistrate governor. Having been introduced, Samadas was none too pleased with my presence, though he conceded that he had no say in the matter.

Hesla the Lawyer, after having witnessed the Guardian plan, immediately began to rebuke Samadas. The emperor tolerated this behavior for only a few minutes, eventually having Hesla arrested and detained for the crime of treason. Samadas frequently imposed legal sentences on criminals, taking pleasure in witnessing the anguish of the guilty party being tortured to death. Samadas kept Hesla imprisoned and searched for the ultimate punishment. Samadas wanted to outdo his predecessors regarding the infliction of pain and torment, since, according to his reasoning, that would suffice as a valid deterrence of any future considerations of treachery. We, the magistrate governors, exploited this fallacy to our advantage, since ultimately all life comprising a standard biological construct moves toward emotional equilibrium. The stress induced by fear of Samadas would be to us an open door through which we could introduce principles and ideas and examples of virtues that would be far more attractive to any life form seeking emotional equilibrium. The Huvril religion, emulating a dark, loric tradition of warfare and conquest, would subside into a new tradition of peaceful governance and philanthropy.

One particular incident worthy of mentioning was the invention of an insidious device that would supposedly alleviate Huvra's water problems. Most of Huvra's water supplies were heavily polluted, and the filtering process was expensive. The new invention offered an alternative, more cost-efficient solution, if such a cost as it demanded could be considered efficient. It would extract the water from any hydrocarbon-based life form, including both animal and plant life. I briefly make note of the Huvril propensity for immersing inanimate objects in containers of various liquids, perhaps a residual behavior deriving from their amphibious ancestry.

Samadas sat poised on his throne surrounded by his entourage, reminiscing proudly about all his accomplishments. A Huvril dressed in wealthy garb emerged through the entrance into the hall. The visitor's demeanor was both confident and professional. He knelt down briefly at the bottom of the dais and waited for permission to approach.

"Get up here!" Samadas said.

"Yes, Holy Father," the subject said. He made little haste in climbing the steps.

"What news do you bring, Oslo?" Samadas asked.

"O Holy Father," Oslo answered, bowing, "the ISS makes known to the emperor its progress on the dehydrator."

"Well? What is it?" Samadas asked.

"With the emperor's permission," Oslo said, "I will have the prototype brought into the imperial chambers for a demonstration." The Huvril scientist stroked his infantile chin, grinning.

"Very well, then," Samadas said. "Do so."

Oslo turned and motioned to his assistants at the entranceway to come forward. Upon seeing his gesture, they stepped out of the hall and quickly returned, guiding a large, self-propelled glass container. One assistant with a canine-sized creature on a leash followed behind the first group. They were careful to balance caution with haste in bringing the dehydrator toward the dais, having avoided the purple imperial carpeting. After a brief but hardy struggle, the device sat at the base of the dais.

"Holy Father," Oslo said, turning back around to bow before Samadas, "I ask for us to take leave to the bottom, so that I may present to the Imperial Court the AsDs Model 11075 Dehydrator."

"Humph," Samadas said, as if feeling slightly inconvenienced. After hesitating, the emperor sighed. "Fine." Samadas stood and unhooked the train. The young boys snatched it to keep it off the floor. Samadas then strolled down the steps, leaving his entourage at the top. I too walked down the steps. At this point, everyone was ignoring my presence, having grown accustomed to my intrusion. We reached the bottom and observed the large glass object. At the bottom of this object were various metal casings and protruding devices and motorized wheels, all reaching up to half a meter in height. The midsection was all glass, two meters in height, two meters wide, and two meters in length. A top section consisted of a platform, with a sealed trap door. The container was filled with a green-hued, clear, acidic liquid. A quick scan of its molecular structure revealed its unnatural complexity.

"Hmmm," Samadas said, smirking and cocking one eyebrow high. He studied the object. "What did you call this?"

"The AsDs Model," Oslo began.

"What does that mean?" Samadas asked.

"Holy Father," Oslo continued, "It stands for acerbatic sequencing distillation system."

"I assume," Samadas said, pointing at the beast, "that the dungunk is set to meet its demise?"

"Yes, Holy Father," Oslo answered, bowing. "The emperor's observation is keen and astute."

"Yes, yes," Samadas said. "But before you begin this demonstration, I would like for someone to be present to witness this monumental moment." Samadas turned to a group of guards near a side door. "Bring me Hesla the Traitor."

I should take a moment to relay his situation prior to this command. After having been arrested and detained, he was confined to a room three meters by three meters. There were no windows to the outside world, and the only light came in through the small grilled window on the door. Up until Oslo's demonstration, he had been confined to this room for two weeks. After one week of his confinement, I was standing upon the dais near Samadas, when Hesla caught my attention. I heard him say from his cell, "Sons of the Morning Rise, hear me. I plead with you. Please. Save me from this plight." After hearing this, I teleshifted into his cell and listened to him further. Confined in his cell, he knelt within the beam of light that penetrated the darkness. "I obeyed you when you told me to speak what I saw. I was honest in everything that I said and did not deviate or embellish."

I made my presence known with a dim light from my shielding. "I hear you, Hesla. We have not abandoned you."

"But Lord," Hesla began. The lawyer in him labored to plead his case. "I remain confined to this dungeon. Will I ever see the light of day again?"

"Know this, Hesla," I said. "If you're able to endure a brief duration of confinement, you'll receive a greater reward than the light that comes from a Huvril day." I phased my shielding slightly, to allow him to enter. Then I knelt down to him, to look him in his eyes. "You will see the light that comes from the Morning Rise."

He convulsed slightly, overtaken with emotions of grief.

"You will," I continued, "be given eternal life."

"Lord, I am most humble and grateful, but," he paused, "how can I be worthy of such a gift?"

I observed Hesla continue to shake uncontrollably, so I scanned his neural net. Several neural interconnectivities were severed, mainly due to the stress. Feedback loops of signal oscillations were recycling through the severed subnets provoking disequilibrium. I repaired the subnets, which allowed the feedback loops to dissipate. Only afterward was he was able to compose himself.

"Hesla," I said, "you'll need to further grapple with these concepts. You'll need to weigh them with the old traditions taught to you since your childhood."

"I want to believe," Hesla said. "I want to."

"Our promise to you isn't based on submission," I said as I placed my hand on his shoulder and gently squeezed. "We promise to make a way for those who desire eternal life."

"The emperor desires eternal life," Hesla mumbled. The lawyer in him continued to argue, mostly within himself. I had alleviated the physical restraints forbidding him from contemplating these deep matters. The psychological aspect, however, would still be a struggle.

"That is true, Hesla," I answered. "Even so, eternal life requires a certain mind-set, so as to sustain itself. The emperor lacks the means to meet such requirements, which fulfills an ancient saying that flesh and blood shall not inherit the heavens."

"What about me?" he asked.

"You've opened the door to your mind," I answered, "and set in motion a renewal."

"Lord, I've done many wicked things in my past," Hesla said. "I don't deserve eternal life." He sighed, and I refrained from interfering with his contemplation. Then he continued. "All I ask is that I don't suffer the wrath of the emperor."

"That request can be easily granted," I said. "From this point on, you have nothing to fear." I softly patted him on his shoulder and then I stood up. "If you're able, be at peace."

Hesla nodded but said nothing.

"Hesla," I said, "it is true that you spoke candidly, complying with our request. You could have refused, and you'd have been allowed to retain your position. In that split second, you chose eternal life over dissent. We ask that you continue on the path that you have chosen." I turned to walk toward the wall and then stopped. I turned back to face Hesla, allowing the pauses to give him time for thought. "You are the first amongst the Huvril people chosen for redemption. And I very much want to see you at the end of it all. If you remain on this path and don't leave it to accommodate the Agency of Dissent, I promise you, as true as I stand here before you, I will ensure that you will receive an eternal reward. I will save you on that day, Hesla. I will write your name in the deepest recesses of my memory. And when that day comes, I will immediately be reminded, never forgetting, that Hesla the Redeemed awaits for me to keep my promise."

Hesla was in tears. "I will …" he said, compelled to swallow from a dry throat. He finished his thought, "… try." He managed to look up to me to see my response.

I smiled and nodded. "Then I promise you all I've said. Peace be with you, Hesla." I teleshifted back to Samadas, who was curious about my brief absence, but whose pride prevented him from inquiring any further.

"Hmph," he managed.

But then another week transpired. I maintained a vigilant watch over Hesla, relieving him of hunger and thirst pains, of traumatic stress, and even of loneliness. Through it all, Hesla continued to wrestle within himself, questioning all that he had been taught.

And then at the moment that Samadas called for Hesla to be brought, the emperor was considering a horrific idea. The guards returned with Hesla in chains and brought him up to the emperor.

"Hesla the Traitor," Samadas said, slapping the prisoner across the face. It stunned the elderly Huvril, and his eyes widened with grief. But he composed himself and offered no resistance to the emperor's whims. "Hesla the Coward," Samadas said. He slapped the lawyer again, but on the other side, and followed it with a laugh. After laughing for a minute or two, the emperor's face fell into a scowl. He then whispered his final thought. "Hesla the Example."

Hesla swallowed hard. His throat dried quickly and closed up slightly, inducing gag reflexes.

The emperor studied this and became pleased, but that only made him deepen his scowl.

"Oslo," Samadas said. "Proceed with your …" The emperor paused as he slowly rotated his head around to the scientist, "… demonstration."

"Yes, Holy Father," Oslo said. The chief scientist clapped his hands at the assistant with the leashed animal. The beast was hairy and had a long neck ending with a muzzled face and big eyes. It was an herbivore and tamed, and so it submitted to the assistant's direction. Both assistant and beast made their way up a set of steps in the back of the container to the top. The beast stood atop the trap door. The assistant hurried back down the steps.

The emperor watched all this, and Oslo sighed in relief. The chief scientist seemed nervous.

"Holy Father," Oslo continued, "let me prep the machine." He approached a console and activated some buttons. A splash guard was raised up, which also imprisoned the animal. It stumbled around nervously but eventually calmed.

Knowing the complexity of the molecular structure of the acid, I was well aware of the consequences.

"Now, Holy Father," Oslo said, picking up a remote control and walking over to the emperor, "I will press the button and the dungunk will plummet into the acid."

"Wait!" Samadas said.

Oslo froze, a look of horror on his face.

"Give me the remote," Samadas said.

"Yes, Holy Father," Oslo said, quickly handing the remote over to Samadas.

The emperor approached the container. He looked up at the eyes of the beast, which sniffed the glass and looked about innocently enough, totally oblivious to the danger that awaited it.

Then Samadas turned to face Hesla.

"What is your opinion of this new invention?" Samadas asked Hesla.

Hesla studied the device. Although he wasn't present when the device was brought in, he quickly determined its use. He looked over and locked eyes with the emperor. Then the prisoner let his gaze fall to the floor. He said nothing.

"Hmph," Samadas responded, pressing the button on the remote control. The trap door opened, and the dungunk screeched in horror as it plummeted into the container of acid, the screech quickly silenced and replaced with the churning noise of the solution. The acid foamed violently as the dungunk kicked about briefly, before succumbing to its death. The beast began to dissolve, breaking apart into blood and meat. Bloody fluid sunk to the bottom, while pieces of the carcass floated to the top.

Samadas looked over at the prisoner, who shook slightly from the ghastly sight. Hesla met the emperor's gaze and observed the scowl on Samadas's face deepen, clearly expressing hatred.

Oslo smiled and wiped beads of oozing sweat from his forehead. He hurried over to the console, retrieved a clear glass goblet from a small bin, and placed it underneath a protruding tap. He pressed a lever, and water poured from the tap into the glass goblet. Oslo turned off the tap when the glass was half full. He brought it over to the emperor.

The emperor took the glass and held it up to the light. He looked at the chief scientist threateningly.

"It's purified, Holy Father," Oslo said. The chief scientist swallowed his own saliva and then grinned widely.

Samadas placed the glass up to his nose and sniffed, his eyes locked onto Oslo's eyes. The chief scientist, still grinning, nodded. Samadas took a sip. He swished it around, tasting, and then swallowed.

"Water," Samadas said. "No aftertaste. Clean, cool, refreshing." The emperor gulped down the rest of the glass's contents. He handed the glass to the scientist, who passed it on to an assistant. "Well done, Oslo," Samadas said. "I am most pleased with this demonstration."

"Excellent, Holy Father," Oslo said. He jumped up and down slightly and clapped.

"But ..." Samadas said, pausing.

The chief scientist settled and stood waiting, the wide grin still plastered over his face.

"I want to see another demonstration," Samadas said.

"Oh," Oslo said. "Um, okay, Holy Father, we will retrieve another dungunk."

"No," Samadas said. "I'd like to see how another creature fares."

The grin on Oslo's face slowly faded. "Okay, most Holy Father," Oslo said. "We will find a ghoma, or perhaps a felect."

"No," Samadas said, his gaze still locked on to Hesla.

Oslo placed his hand to his mouth. It shook. Hesla looked up at Samadas and nodded slightly. Then Hesla looked over at me. I raised an eyebrow slightly, a gesture for him to see.

"Guards!" Samadas said. "Put Hesla atop the invention."

The guards hesitated only briefly. They marched the prisoner up the steps, hindered only by the splash guard.

"Lower it," Samadas said to Oslo.

"Um, yes, Holy Father, um," Oslo managed. "Is ... any ... can I ... um."

"Lower it!" Samadas said.

The chief scientist jumped to the console and pressed a series of buttons. The splash guard lowered, and the guards pushed Hesla onto the trap door. Oslo then raised the splash guard. Hesla offered no resistance. He stood still, his gaze lowered, but, dejected, he began to cry. He looked up at me, so I offered him a slight nod.

Samadas approached me. It was the first time in a while that he had acknowledged my presence.

"Guardian Sun-Li," Samadash said, "Son of the Morning Rise." He began to walk around behind me. "Elder of Eternal Life." He walked around in front and waved the remote control. "Behold, I have power over this man's life."

"Perhaps," I answered, "but we have power over death."

"Bahh!" Samadas said, jerking around and approaching the container. "Hesla!"

The prisoner offered no response. He stood still but continued to cry.

"Do you want to change your story?" Samadas asked. "Look at me! Do you want to change your story?"

The prisoner said nothing. He closed his eyes and lowered his head. The emperor growled, jerked around, and pressed the button.

I activated my shielding and projected it through a calabi-yau manifold. I encased each molecule of Hesla's body, countering the corrosion of the acid. I also opened a miniscule port above the container, which tapped into his lungs, to allow air to bypass the acid.

Hesla plummeted into the cloudy acid. Soldiers and scientists gasped. The emperor walked up a few steps of his dais and turned. Then silence. Within the container, staring out at everyone was Hesla the Unharmed. He hovered in the acid, protected and breathing. He looked around, even at his own hands.

Samadas screamed and threw the remote to the ground. It shattered across the floor near the container. "Ugh!"

Oslo looked back and forth between Hesla and the emperor. He tried to speak but could say nothing.

"Well?" Samadas said, glaring at Oslo. "Explain this failure."

"I …" Oslo began but stopped. He wasn't sure whether he should feel relief at Hesla's salvation or feel fear of the emperor's wrath. He gulped and lowered his head, opting to remain silent.

"Fool!" Samadas said. Then the emperor approached me. "So this is how it's going to be, is it? You're going to meddle in my affairs?"

I did not respond.

"This … you … how … arrrgh!" Samadas said, jerking around. He took a few steps and then turned to face me again. "You're breaking your own law!"

I cocked an eyebrow but still did not respond.

"Was not our Lord right in exposing the hypocrisy of the Guardians?" Samadas said. "Was he not correct in declaring you all nothing more than liars?"

I smirked.

"You are not welcome here!" Samadas said. "Huvra worships Necronus! We worship the Prince of Life and Death!"

"On the contrary," I said, "only some of you worship Necronus." I took a step toward Samadas, who backed up slightly at my approach. "There are those who welcome us." I looked over at Hesla.

The emperor followed my gaze. He locked his eyes on the prisoner and stared in disbelief. Hesla floated in the acid, still unharmed and breathing. He reached up to touch the glass, and I determined the moment most appropriate for further intervention. Upon his touch, the glass cracked, and a few pieces broke away, allowing streams of acid to spurt from the crack.

"Ahhh!" Oslo yelled. He jumped toward the dais, ignoring royal etiquette, and leaped up several steps in one bound.

The assistants took off in the opposite direction, running down the corridor toward the entrance. The guards, panic-stricken, bumped into each other, trying to find someplace to run.

The emperor observed this quietly. As the glass container burst, the acid spilled forth onto the floor and flowed down the corridor. He backed up slightly, taking a few steps farther up the dais. He then casually walked over to Oslo, who didn't pay much attention to his approach. The emperor shoved the scientist off of the dais and into the acid. Screaming, the scientist wasted only a few seconds in turning and diving back onto the dais. The emperor growled and kicked him off the dais back into the acid. What little had soaked into the carpet began to dissolve the skin of Oslo's feet and legs.

"Please! Please!" Oslo cried.

The emperor ceased and walked over to me. "So," he began, "you do nothing to rescue this fool?"

"I cannot," I said.

"Why?" Samadas asked.

"If I do, he will err and give credit to your pantheon," I answered. "That will affirm his philosophy of dissent. If I do nothing, his pantheon will fail him, and that will give him reason to doubt his false religion."

"You!" Samadas said, pointing at me. He huffed and growled but followed his exclamation with nothing. He slowly lowered his finger and turned to walk up the steps.

CHAPTER 14

O h, Huvra, with whom should we compare you? Are you not like a merchant who labors to make a profit at any cost, even at the cost of your very soul? Your earthly treasures are subject to thieves and looters. If only you would invest in the heavenly treasures. All the gold and the silver and precious gems can't purchase the secrets of the stars. Those who search for the truth will find it—the truth of life and living and being alive. But earthly riches are like a snare. The very shiny trinkets you labor to gain shackle you to the earth. Your eyes are downcast, never able to see the starlight, which testifies to the truth of the universe. Instead, you are consumed by the anxiety of greed, an irrational fear of being without. The womb of nature, from which you were born, provides for your every need, but you are always in want of more.

You could choose truth, but you give yourself to a great deception. You could choose peace, but you make all that is good your enemy. You could give yourself to reason, but you make passion your governor. You could exhibit compassion, but you know only brutality. You could learn charity, but your heart is hardened as stone. You could advance in your progression, but you are weighed down by your monuments.

Oh, Huvra, the truth awaits you patiently. We know the light of truth will come to you. When it comes you will know. It is the truth of light, and it is good. The adversary made his argument that the Guardians of Eternal Life view you as *merica*, which, spoken in an ancient Huvril tongue, means "we war with a people." But we do not war with you, Huvra. You are not our enemy. And we declare that we are not your enemy, either. Thus, you are to us, Huvra, known as *america*, or, "we war with no people." We do not bring weapons of destruction, either to manipulate through fear and coercion or to induce trauma and heartache. We bring thought and philosophy, to console and persuade. Our way is not the shedding of blood. Our way is the opening of minds. Our justice is not a vengeful warrior. Our justice is a quiet sage.

You are a newly formed tree shaken in the wind, a small river diverted by a dam. The fiery arrow that flies by night strikes the resolve of your soul. The sound of thunder when a foe encroaches pounds away at the fortress of your mind. Just as the cold batters the flower, fading its blossom and withering its leaves, the sounds of war and visions of death take a toll on the nature of a people's inner essence, the core of their very being. Soon after, time becomes a foe, nature an antagonist. But hear us on this. To you, for you, and with you, we are a gentle breeze carrying drops of rain emblazoned in the warmth of sunlight. Every drop of water bears the marker of our labor, the treasure of the heavens.

Consider this idea, if you would, please. What if one of us was to join you in your journey through Huvril life? What if he was to come to where you are, to see what you see and to feel what you feel? How would you receive him? As one of your own? Would you reject him? If such a one was to be born amongst you, and you were to find yourself looking into the sunlit face of a Huvril infant, and this infant was to open his eyes, and you were to see in those eyes the healing of a people, then at that moment you should receive him well. So if you must call him something, then call him *American*, for he wars with no one.

A thin Huvril woman rests upon the rainbow bedding consisting of soft linens discolored with age, but otherwise clean. Her belly is swollen, her womb carrying a child due for birth at any given moment. She pulls her hind legs up under her but extends her front legs out in front of her. She stretches. A brown dress drapes around her body, with only the belly and her legs exposed underneath.

A door opens, and a female Huvril physician enters, followed by two assistants.

"Hmph," the physician says upon examining the expectant mother. "Were you thinking that you would bear this child all by yourself?" Her tone is nonthreatening, mixed with light admonishment.

The mother lowers her gaze and shakes her head no. She then begins to rub her womb softly.

"Well, it's a good thing we came when we did," the physician says. "You're going to drop any moment now." She steps toward the mother. "My name is Roshun, and these two are Hekka and Kehtosh. The medical center dispatched us to your aid."

The physician is an elderly woman, with weathered gray skin that oozes sweat more than when she was young. Her balding head bears slight ridging in the gray skin. Her bulbous eyes droop slightly. Though she still retains the childlike expression typical of a Huvril, it is weathered and wrinkled. A drab, cream-colored robe covers most of her body. Four spindly legs ending in cracked hooves protrude from under the robe. The assistants are her daughters, and they bear the same features, except that one is half the age of the mother and the other, a quarter. The eldest daughter is bigger than both her little sister and her mother. Serving in an apprentice role, she carries with her lots of experience and with it an equal amount of confidence. The younger daughter is small and thin, shy and quiet, with eyes aimed at the floor, never looking in the eyes of another for too long—just enough to acknowledge that she's listening.

The old woman takes a look around the room with a frown. "Well, this will have to do." Roshun then removes from her satchel a computer and sets it on a table. She presses some buttons on a keypad, and a virtual screen emerges holographically. She logs into a network and passes through some options in the menu until she brings up the census database.

"Who is the father?" the physician asks.

"I …" the mother begins. She pauses. The physician looks around from behind the virtual screen and watches as the mother pauses and lowers her head.

"What!" the physician says. "You don't know? Ha!"

The eldest daughter approaches her mother. "She must be one of those kinds," the eldest says with a scowl.

"How unfortunate for you," the physician says. The old woman steps away from the computer and rummages through a satchel. "Where … by the gods … ah! Here it is." The old woman pulls out a rodlike contraption. Pressing a button on the bottom end causes a thin needle to emerge from the other end. "We'll have to take a DNA sample and run it through the system."

The expecting mother lets out a whimper. The old woman pauses and looks at her disapprovingly.

"Don't get yourself all worked up," Roshun says. "It's a small prick of a sting. Not only that, but you'll be able to petition the courts to order the father to participate in the upbringing of the child."

"He'll be most displeased," the eldest daughter says to the younger daughter, following it with a laugh. Stepping up to the expecting mother, she holds out her hand. "Give me the probe, mother. I will get the sample."

The expecting mother lets out another whimper.

The physician puts her hands on her front set of hips, with the probe in the right hand. "Come, child, what is this commotion? We are here to assist you."

"Mother!" the eldest daughter says glaringly. She still has her hand outstretched.

"Hmph," the old woman says. "Let Kehtosh perform the procedure." The old woman steps toward the younger daughter, who perks her head up at having more to do than to clean up a mess.

"Ugh!" the eldest says. She throws both her hands to her side.

"Now, now, Hekka!" the physician says. "We can't have this poor soul all stressed out." The physician hands Kehtosh the probe. "And didn't we discuss your demeanor in front of patients?" the old woman asks, jerking around to face Hekka.

"This is so not fair," Hekka says.

"Step aside," the physician says, motioning with her hand. "Kehtosh, get to it, child." The physician walks back over to her satchel. "Now I gotta find that DNA peripheral." She begins to rummage through the satchel. She pulls out a thin metal tube and turns to Kehtosh. "Here, use this gel to soften the insertion." Kehtosh takes the can, and the physician returns to rummaging in the satchel. Metal sounds clank from within the dull-black, worn-down bag.

Kehtosh slowly walks over to the mother. "Miss Taupi," the youngest assistant says, "don't worry. I'll be gentle." Kehtosh kneels down behind Taupi.

The mother smiles at the younger assistant. Kehtosh covers the top end of the probe with the gel. The younger assistant then pulls up the brown dress and inserts the item between Taupi's hind legs. After a moment, the younger assistant looks up at the expectant mother.

"Okay, Miss Taupi," Kehtosh says, "you're going to feel a slight sting."

"You have the instrument inserted three inches?" the physician asks.

"Yes, Mother," Kehtosh says.

"And at a forty-five degree angle to the lower right of the amniotic sac?" the physician asks again. "Ah ha!" the old woman says as she yanks from the bag a metallic plate with a glass top and a cord.

"Yes, Mother," Kehtosh says.

Taupi looks into the eyes of the younger assistant and smiles. Kehtosh smiles back. "You'll make a great physician," Taupi says to her.

"Good grief!" Hekka says with a frown. She is standing to the side with her arms folded. "Whatever. Just don't mess it up."

"Take the sample, child," the old woman says to her younger daughter. Kehtosh presses the button and the expectant mother jerks with a loud screech. Kehtosh quickly withdraws the contraption and cleans the end with a rag. Standing, Kehtosh hands the probe to the old woman.

Roshun takes the probe and presses a few buttons on the side. A small door on the side slides open, and a tiny glass tube ejects halfway. The physician takes the tube, inserts it into the DNA peripheral, and closes the glass top. She then places the probe into a plastic bag and returns it to the satchel.

"Now, we'll get to the bottom of this mystery," the physician says. "It's a boy, for sure." After a series of beeps, Roshun begins to type furiously on the tiny keypad. "What is this?"

"She messed it up, didn't she, Mother?" Hekka says. "Let me redo the procedure. I'll get it right."

"No, no, no!" Roshun says, not taking her eyes from the virtual screen. "She did it right. The father is not registered in the system."

"That's impossible!" Hekka says. "How can that be?"

"I don't know, child," Roshun says to her elder daughter. The physician looks up from behind the virtual screen at Taupi. "Who do you suspect it is?"

"I have not had any relations with anyone," Taupi says.

"Are you mad?" Hekka asks.

"Daughter!" Roshun says. "Remove yourself from this room!" The eldest daughter huffs and turns to leave. "Once again," Roshun says to her as the daughter steps through the exit, "we'll have to talk about your demeanor."

Taupi gazes over to Kehtosh, who turns her head from the physician and struggles to contain a smile. Taupi smiles.

The physician sighs and then returns her focus to the expectant mother. "It's of no real major consequence," Roshun says. "I shall enter 'Unknown' as the father's name." The physician begins to type on the keypad. "Let the Census Registry handle the problem." Roshun peeks back around from behind the virtual screen. "I've got several other births to tend to this morning, and I'm not a detective." Taupi forces a light chuckle. Roshun returns her focus to the virtual screen. "Very well, then. Tell me, child, what will you be naming your baby?"

Taupi pauses, but only slightly. "Americk."

The old woman jerks her head around from behind the virtual screen. "Do you mean, Merick?"

"No, ma'am," Taupi says, "Americk."

"Why, child?" the physician asks while stepping away from the computer. "You'll expose this poor boy to a life of ridicule."

Taupi's smile fades.

"I'm sorry," the physician says to the expectant mother. "It is my duty to counsel you on these kinds of decisions. 'Merick' means 'warrior' in the old tongue. 'Americk' means 'not a warrior.' Is that what you really want to name your son?"

Taupi nods her head slightly.

The physician sighs. "Okay, child. You'll have to take the matter to the courts to have the boy's name changed, if the occasion should rise." Roshun peeks from behind the virtual screen. Taupi nods her head again slightly. The physician sighs again and then types on the keypad. "Okay. There it is. Your son, Americk, is now registered in the system. I'll step outside and have a small chat with my eldest daughter. Then we will induce labor, and you'll have your newborn son in no time." Roshun steps away from the computer and observes the expectant mother relaxed and smiling. The physician nods in satisfaction and turns to leave the room. Taupi looks back to Kehtosh.

"I like it," Kehtosh says to Taupi with just the motion of her lips.

⇥ ⇤

This is the Childhood Narrative of Americk, according to Ghypriex of Saevra. I write this accounting upon threat of arrest and execution, seeing that it is outlawed for anyone to write upon the subject discussed herein. I proceed with caution and care. The Pantheonade, or Protectorate Council of the Pantheon, has declared any criticism of the Pantheon as blasphemy, which is decreed as treasonous to the Huvril state. The decree was presented by Emperor Samadas the Great in his campaign against the works of the Guardians, Sons of the Morning Rise. I state this declaration of the facts without partiality.

The incarnation of a higher power is not unfamiliar to us. For hundreds of years, Huvra, under the guidance of the Pantheonade, waited for the reincarnation of Devisgar, who was prophesied to return so as to issue in a new era of glory for Huvra. Even so, there is the expectation that an incarnation is assumed on the grandest of scales and that the Emperor is to concede authority to the Incarnate. Frauds and imposters, therefore, are deemed as attempting to interlope imperial rule, which is an act of treason. Painful, elongated torture ending in death is the punishment. The Theory of Deterrence assumes that only the insane would ignore this principle and continue with the fraudulence of declaring themselves as incarnate, whether of the Pantheon or another type, such as the Guardians themselves. Yet there is the idea that a declaration of incarnation entails political motivation. The Incarnated One, or Avatar, comes only to reestablish the proper order. If an emperor is unable to realign the political structure as desired by the Pantheon, then the Avatar comes to assume temporary authority, align the political structure, establish proper order, and then return the authority to the emperor or a successor. The Avatar, however, merely assumes the human form. So one way to expose imposters is to prove they were born of human parents. Records are kept in digital format and are secured from hackers; therefore it is impossible in this day and age for a person to make the claim of incarnation without attempting to mask his or her DNA. With the scrupulous maintenance of individual records, everyone born in Huvril territory and registered with the Academy of Medicine's Census Registry Department has his or her DNA on record. As such, no fraudulent registrations are possible. The scan of the child's DNA confirms the registrees as the parents. Fraud is rare and easily exposed.

Thus, with the birth of Americk, the Academy of Medicine found itself in a quandary. His mother, Taupi, claimed that she had had no sexual relations with any men. She was flagged for a possible fraudulent registration, which included a psychiatric evaluation to determine her state of mind. A DNA scan of the child revealed something puzzling. The father was not in the system. Not only that, but it was realized that the mother was unmarried because she was infertile from birth. Infertility is grounds for denying marriage certification, along with a public stigma against infertility.

I should, at this point, make note of the Cult of the Avatarils, a group of extremists. They maintain a type of underground campaign against the state, where they labor to overthrow the current rule and establish their extreme theocracy. They await a coming Avatar to deliver Huvril from the power of Necronus. While they argue against oppression and for justice, their extremist philosophy reveals that they would trade one evil for another.

Anyway, the registration system had worked for thousands of years, and in one fateful night in Caroplod, a slum village on the outskirts of the City of Samadasanae, the system had been subverted. The physical evidence supported Taupi's story in every detail. The Academy of Medicine had no choice but to withdraw their allegation of fraudulence. Mother and child were released without restriction or restraint. The registration has "Unknown" as the father.

At this time, however, Huvra was in an uproar. For four hundred years the Seven Guardians stood their posts on Huvra. The one named Sun-Li communicated directly to the emperor, if one can call it communication. Such communication consisted of brief retorts and summary rebuttals. But suddenly, on the night that Americk was born, Sun-Li delivered a speech, one written hundreds of years ago by the hand of the Prophet Hesla. And then the Seven Guardians disappeared and have not been seen since. The Pantheonade met on numerous occasions to determine the meaning of this phenomenon. Huvra was already familiar with Hesla's prophecy. The Pantheonade had already concluded that the Guardians would use incarnation as the means to meddle in Huvril affairs. They were well expecting an Avatar to emerge and declare himself as the one named America. That name has been declared contemptible throughout the empire. The Pantheonade was prepared to assist the emperor in refusing to turn over to the Avatar the throne of Huvra. Legions of soldiers had been trained. Councils of priests and prophets had been assembled.

So the unusual birth of one whose name was Americk and the

sudden departure of the Seven Guardians concerned the Pantheonade, who wasted little time in dispatching spies to watch Taupi and her infant child. One of these spies, who wishes to remain anonymous, told me that he was to report to authorities in the Pantheonade anything and everything concerning the child. He did so faithfully for ten years. I hope that bit of information doesn't betray him, but I cite the source for the validity of the testimony. This fellow informed me of a few oddities during Americk's childhood. Typically, Americk was a child like any other. He hurt himself on a few occasions and bled and cried like any child. He attended school and was educated like any child. He was a curious boy and thus engaged in explorations and adventures, which often landed him in places and situations in which he ought not to have been found. Despite this typicality, the oddities mentioned stand out. Americk avoided fights and confrontations with other children. For this, he was easily bullied. The thing is, he never fled or showed any sign of fear.

A group of boys jumped him one day and beat him badly. Yet he did not resist. When they were satisfied that he was hurt badly enough, they ceased, only to be amazed that Americk stood up, dusted himself off, and as well as an injured boy could move, made his way back home to his mother. The spy listened in on the conversation from outside their window. Americk pleaded with his mother Taupi, beseeching her not to pursue any recourse. Reluctantly, she heeded his wishes.

On another occasion, Americk participated in a school-sponsored race. Huvril boys are fond of racing, especially one-on-one. The rules allow for some actions that deter an opponent, such as tripping or pushing. The spirit of racing is to win at any cost save that of actual physical assault. Even so, Americk never relied upon these tricks. The boy was unnaturally fast, and if he could survive the initial antagonism of his opponents, he could pull away and none could catch him. Well, one such boy named Karkas thought to use more cunning than usual. He hid a tail whip in his belt, which was against the rules. The race started, and the two Huvril boys took off. When they rounded a corner, in a spot hidden from the spectators, Karkas pulled out the tail whip and snapped it at Americk, who was slightly ahead. The whip slashed Americk's hind leg, and he stumbled. Karkas took the lead, but Americk stayed with him. They emerged around the corner, to the delight of the crowd. Karkas, however, struggled to hide the device he held in his hand. He tripped on the tail whip, which sent him plummeting the ground face-first. The observers gasped in disbelief when Americk stopped to assist Karkas. He helped his opponent to his feet and assisted him in walking to the finish line. When they got there, Americk stopped short, allowing Karkas to cross the line. When asked why he would give the race to a cheater, Americk's response was, "I run a different race."

And a final incident worth mentioning is the incredible insight the boy demonstrated. The elder teachers would marvel at his ability to grasp complicated subjects with apparent ease. Some would praise him, but others felt insulted. During one oral exercise, the students were to answer a single question: what is greater, a single entity of a whole or the whole made up of entities? Most answered the whole, but Americk disputed it and said the single entity. When challenged by the elder teacher, Americk explained that when every member of a whole is great, the whole is at its greatest. Thus, the comparison shouldn't be between the whole and a member that is part of the whole, which Americk argued was fallacious. Instead, one should compare different stages of the whole by focusing on the condition of each member. The elder teacher had no rebuttal.

Huvril society always thought that compassion enabled the weak, prolonging their agony on the Earth, and that those who are strong should allow the weak to fall away. That is the natural order of things. There have always been those who have disagreed with this principle. But none has ever been as outspoken about it as Americk.

<hr>

I, Sun-Li, convey my observations of the activities of one named Americk. Samadasanae's skyscrapers blot out the sun, keeping the slum village of Caroplod in perpetual darkness. A few lights illuminate the streets, but the back alleyways stay dark. Several stories up above the street are the airways, where heavy traffic speeds by, oblivious to the community below. Americk's vehicle hovers above the heads of the streetwalkers. It's almost a piece of junk, sputtering fumes and making odd mechanical noises, box-shaped and colored dull-gray prime, except for numerous flashes of red rust spots. Americk drives the craft down Regali Street, which runs behind one of the few giant commercial hospitals in Samadasanae. He gazes down at some of the people, who ignore him and carry on with their business. A mother carries her infant by holding it under its fore section, allowing the hindquarters to dangle unsupported. The mother is dressed in ragged clothes, and the infant is naked. The air is chilly, with gusts from the vehicles above making the conditions worse. Americk pulls off a scarf and dangles it over the side. The mother sees it and watches Americk curiously. He tosses it down to her, and she catches it with her free hand. The mother sniffs it and, satisfied that it's clean, wraps it around the infant. Americk nods to her and pulls away.

Eventually, he approaches an alley to his left. It's not entirely dark, but the light is sparse. Americk jerks the joystick, and the vehicle whips into the alley. A ways down, Americk emerges into an opening, and at the far end is a back door to the hospital. Another vehicle, a dump truck of sorts, rests on the ground near the door. Hospital workers dressed in red, full-bodied uniforms carry out bodies of Huvrils. Americk pulls near and lowers his vehicle to the ground. He leaps from the vehicle with a bag in his hand. The workers watch him approach.

"I don't think we have one today," a worker says.

Americk nods. "Thanks, Yurrud. But I'd like to make sure."

"Satisfy yourself, then," Yurrud says with a chuckle.

Americk observes them bring bodies out, one by one. The corpses are skeletal and sickly, the end result of a ravaging disease that induces an autoimmune deficiency nicknamed HIDD for Huvrili-Immuno-Deficiency Disease. There is a cure, but the treatment is expensive and torturous. The downtrodden—mainly drug users and prostitutes—are the only ones who continue to suffer from HIDD, which gives the nickname its derogative status, and those who have it are HIDDen from sight. Americk stands below the deck and listens for any sound coming from the dump truck. A low whimper sounds out. He runs around the dump truck to the other side and leaps up the stairs onto the deck. Yurrud and another emerge from the back door carrying a body. Both stop to wait for Americk's explanation.

"I heard a sound," Americk says.

"So?" the other worker asks.

"Hey!" Yurrud says to him. The other worker turns to a frowning Yurrud. "Let's set this body down." They put the dead body onto the deck. "Go for it, Americk. It's all yours."

"Thank you, friend. I'll remember this in the days to come, both now and in the hereafter."

Yurrud chuckles slightly but gives no other response. Americk turns and slowly climbs into the bed of the dump truck. He listens carefully, struggling to listen for that whimper amidst the roaring noises of traffic high above. Despite the noise, Americk hears the whimper. Looking to where the sound comes from, he thinks he sees a slight movement of a body's hand. Americk steps over the dead bodies to the one living body. He pulls the poor soul from the mass of dead bodies and carries her to the back of the dump truck. "I have her. I got her."

"Good for you!" the other worker yells.

Americk emerges into the light with the woman. She appears dead, except for her trembling lower lip. Her naked body is a skeleton with skin pulled tight upon it. The color is pale white. Her hand shakes a little. Americk looks up to Yurrud. "She's alive."

"But for how long?" Yurrud asks. He motions to the other worker, and they lift the body at their feet and carry it to the back of the dump truck. They toss it onto the pile of the dead. Americk carries the still-living woman down the steps and around the dump truck. He makes his way to his vehicle. Carefully, Americk lays the woman in the passenger seat. He then runs back to the deck.

"Thanks again, Yurrud," Americk says.

"Yeah," Yurrud responds, "no problem."

"Why do you let him do this?" the other worker asks.

"Eh," Yurrud says, "I don't know. Why not?" Yurrud shrugs his shoulders.

Americk hastens back to his vehicle. He turns it on and lifts it up above the ground. Turning it, he jerks it into motion and heads back into the alley from which he came. Americk turns to the woman lying in the passenger seat. She is in a very uncomfortable-looking posture, but she has no strength to alleviate the discomfort. Americk lightly touches her upon her arm. "Hang on," he says. "I'm going to help you." The woman's eyes are still shut, but she lets out a small whimper. For half an hour, Americk navigates the lower streets and back alleyways until he arrives at his domain. Lowering the vehicle to the ground, he wastes no time in rushing to the passenger side and removing the woman from the vehicle. As best as he can, he carries her into the building. Her hind legs drag behind him on the ground. Her head hangs back at a sharp angle. Even though she is skeletally thin, Americk struggles to carry her. As he approaches the door, the sensor activates, and the door quickly shifts open. Americk enters. The room into which he enters is lit by a few lights but remains in shadowy dimness. There are twenty beds, each filled with a Huvril body except for one. Groans sound, and the air is filled with a slight stench of body odor. Americk carries the woman in his arms to the last bed on the right. Gently, he lays her upon it and covers her with a ragged blanket.

"She will die soon," a voice says from behind him.

Americk ignores it. He makes his way to a sink with a bowl and dry washcloth on a nearby table. He places the bowl under a faucet and runs water into the bowl. Dipping the washcloth into the water, he soaks it well. Then he quickly makes his way back to the woman. He rinses out the rag and touches it to the woman's lips. The bottom lip is trembling, but both lips instantly clasp the wet rag. A slight sucking sound comes from the woman's mouth.

A figure walks over to the other side of the woman's bed and kneels. It is Maximeron. A red hue surrounds him like an aura.

"A snap of your fingers, and she is instantly healed," Maximeron says.

Americk continues to ignore him.

"A wave of your hand!" Maximeron yells, standing. "A wave of your hand, and everyone in this room rises and walks away!"

"You remind me of that daily," Americk says.

"Yes, I do," Maximeron says, "for good reason. Why do you engage in this ridiculous ritual? Why maintain this absurd hospice?" Maximeron asks. The rogue Guardian walks around the bed to stand behind Americk.

The Huvril looks around at the rogue Guardian towering above him. Americk stands and brushes against Maximeron as he walks to another bed several beds down from the woman's. The man's eyes are barely open, and he acknowledges Americk's arrival by turning slightly.

"These people are dying," Americk says.

"So?" Maximeron says.

"They need to know the truth before they die," Americk says, placing his hand on the dying Huvril's face.

"Finally, you explain yourself!" Maximeron says. "After all this time?"

Americk turns his head toward the rogue Guardian. "I confess that you wear me down," Americk says with a smile.

"Don't be coy with me, worm," Maximeron says. "The magistrates of the Guardians have abandoned you here. You're all alone. I could snap your neck and send you back to the continuum as nothing more than a wisp of energy." The rogue Guardian's red hue flashes slightly.

"What stops you?" Americk asks.

"And what?" Maximeron asks. "Make you a martyr? I know what you're doing! You think an ancient Terran precedent is going to work with the Huvril race?" The rogue Guardian composes himself slightly. "How about I just watch you fumble around in your folly and become nothing more than a silly vanity."

"Shh!" Americk says. "This fellow wants to tell me his name."

"Duht," the sick Huvril manages to say, his eyes still only half open.

Maximeron walks to the other side and kneels down. "Is that so?" he asks Americk. Maximeron clenches his fist, and the fellow jerks up in the bed, clutching his chest. He then becomes completely still. Americk looks up into the grimacing face of his adversary.

"This fool was a petty thief," Maximeron says.

"It matters not that you slew him before his time," Americk says.

"Oh?" Maximeron says.

"I told him the truth this morning," Americk says. "As I said, he was merely telling me his name, in hope that I would remember it at the end of the age."

The rogue Guardian slowly stands so that he towers above Americk and the slain Huvril. "So what is his name, worm?"

"Densanik," Americk answers.

The rogue Guardian studies Americk hard. "What is this so-called truth that you supposedly told him?" Maximeron asks.

"You already know the answer to that question," Americk says, turning and laying his hand over the still open eyes of the slain Huvril. With a downward motion of his hand, Americk closes the Huvril's eyes.

"But he's dead!" Maximeron says. "How does giving him peace change that!"

"Adversary," Americk says, standing, "have you failed to learn what that means after all this time?" Americk takes a few steps but stops and turns to face the rogue Guardian.

"I said, don't be coy with me, worm!" Maximeron says with gritted teeth.

"You know full well that in order to resurrect this soul," Americk says, "we need him to retain his most accurate memories of his own life."

"Scan his neural net," Maximeron says. "Do it now before it fades away completely."

Americk sighs.

"Scan at position 1-4-7-2-9-5-8-5-4-2," Maximeron says.

Americk tilts his head so that his neck pops slightly. He then massages it to ease the stiffness. "Is it necessary to …"

"Do it!" Maximeron says.

"You're making note of the time that he stabbed a stranger and took the stranger's money?" Americk asks.

The rogue Guardian inhales menacingly so that he hisses. "And you still intend to resurrect this fool at the turn of the cycle?" Maximeron asks.

"We reinstate whomever we deem worthy," Americk says.

"Yeah," Maximeron says. "You do whatever you want."

"Well," Americk says, "as long as it falls within the bounds of the law."

The rogue Guardian's eyebrows turn upward sharply. He looks the Huvril up and down, his jaw wide open. "The law?" Maximeron asks. "What law?"

"Oh yeah," Americk says, turning his head away. "That point would elude you."

"You know full well that with one snap of my finger, every soul in this room dies instantly!"

"I know that you love murder," Americk says. The Huvril walks back to the woman he recently brought in. He notices that her breathing is distinct, and that her bottom lip has stopped trembling. Even in her weakened state, she appears to be sleeping peacefully. Americk turns to face Maximeron. The Adversary has left.

A message to the Americkals in Duvhrovre, from Ghypriex, a former senator to the imperial court from the Saevra province. I compose this message from my prison cell and have made arrangements for a young boy, Zaccas, to retrieve the data stick and have it sent to all of you. He has a talent for encryption, which is crucial for our secret correspondence, especially while I'm still in this predicament. Although I'm grateful for your thoughts, as always, do not be anxious.

For while my body wanes under the strain of political persecution, my mind and soul are at liberty. You already know what I mean. We abandon the imperial doctrine of conquest, might, and glory and embrace instead the Guardian doctrine of compassion, peace, and hope.

There are two reasons why I am writing this letter to you. First, I was given word that there is much discord amongst the followers of Americk. So I offer my counsel and exhortation. Secondly, I learned from the same source that many of you have fallen into confusion. It would seem that a few amongst you are confounding the simple story of Americk. So I will share with you my account of Americk's life and death, even up to the point where I find myself in this prison cell. Afterward it is my hope that you can put away the discord and confusion and finish out the work to be done in the short time we have left to live before the Great Calamity comes to Huvra.

Now, you know full well that our newly adopted philosophy calls for nonviolence. So why do I hear of many amongst you taking up arms, as if to storm the imperial halls or even the Pantheonade itself? Do you suppose that the Imperialists will be dismayed by your armed resistance? Not so. You will be viewed as lawless rebels, and rebellion is met with harsh measures, even death. In the eyes of an Imperialist, a rebel is worse than a murderer and a thief. The Imperialists, therefore, will view you as nothing more than common criminals. We have to contradict that expectation, if we have any hopes of persuading our brethren to our cause. But if you take up arms and fight them as rebels, then you affirm their expectations, which will strengthen their resolve to see you destroyed. You know the ancient proverb: if you carry a spear everywhere you go, you are sure to fall upon it at some point. Don't you know that our battle is not about the flesh of men, but instead about minds and souls? Never mind the warmongering Avatarils. They're unreasonable. I know there was talk of uniting with them, but their expectations are skewed. I trust you understand my point regarding taking up arms, which is a sure guarantee of our destruction, not to mention displeasure to the Guardians. We already know that if we turn away from the Pantheon and embrace the Guardian doctrine of eternal life, we will be granted the same, no matter what persecution comes against us. Armed rebels, however, contribute nothing except to their own demise. For what reason would you rather be persecuted, for the words you speak or for fighting? But enough of this admonishment. I believe I have made my point.

As to the confusion of Americk's birth and death, it is simple to rectify. I have toiled ceaselessly to gather the details of his birth and childhood, of which I have already shared with you all in a previous correspondence. But as to his death, that I haven't shared in electronic correspondence yet. It was 420 years ago that the Guardians made their intentions known to then Emperor Samadas the Great. It was called the Emendatory Intervention, although we prefer it by its popular name, the Dawn of Hope. Seven Guardians took up stations all around Huvra and engaged in various schemes and activities that would lead to a great reformation. Samadas reacted with a vengeance, and all reformists were quickly arrested, and some were even executed. Not long after, Samadas sired an heir to the throne, Challenovok. Eventually Samadas succumbed to an illness, and his son took up the cause against the reformists. It is reported in numerous histories that Challenovok was heinous in his persecution, which earned him the title Challenovok the Cruel. Challenovok sired an heir, Serentis. Servants speak of Challenovok's cruelty toward his own son. Unbeknownst to the terrible emperor, this worked in the favor of the reformists, since it softened the will of Serentis toward the reformists.

Which brings us to the time twenty years ago, when Serentis took the imperial scepter from the hands of his father, who had just passed. At the time, I was just recently appointed to the Saevra Senate. I had arrived at the Imperial Halls to begin fulfilling my duties as a representative of Saevra. It hadn't been too long before that I was approached by a fellow senator. We were already well acquainted from previous meetings outside of Samadasanae.

"Something strange is taking place," Cirenok, Senator of Neanevra, said to me. "You got here just in time to witness it." He was a short, stocky Huvril, with ornamental symbols etched into his hooves and tattoos etched around his head. Every facial protrusion was pierced, even the bridge of his nose, his lower lip, and his brow. His massive, red robe was embroidered in gold. My clothing of composite colors, though not cheap, paled in comparison.

"Whatever do you mean?" I asked him.

"The emperor is turning against the Pantheonade," Cirenok said hastily. He jumbled his words together, as if overly anxious.

I stood silent and shook my head as if I didn't understand. I confess that I heard him, but my mind wasn't registering the information. He understood my dilemma.

"I say, Emperor Serentis is turning against the Pantheonade," Cirenok said again.

"The gods!" I said.

"The Pantheonade has called for its nominal orders," Cirenok continued, squeezing his hands. "They are going to form a council and determine their course of action."

I stepped away for a moment and took a deep breath. I knew what this meant, but I needed confirmation.

"And the Senate?" I asked.

"The emperor is calling for the Senate to support him," Cirenok answered. "I don't think I can!" He grabbed me by my arm and turned me slightly to face him. "Most in the Senate have already resigned. It's just you, me, and two others." Cirenok's voice fell to a whisper. "What will we do?"

"The others have conceded their voting power to us?" I asked him.

"Yes!" Cirenok said. "They have resigned fully."

"Well," I said, "let's hear the emperor's argument and make a rational decision." I shrugged my shoulders. I really didn't know the answer.

"Hmph!" Cirenok said. He turned and walked away mumbling something that I couldn't hear, his overly decorated hooves clicking on the hard floor.

We parted, and I went to my accommodations. I'll take a moment to describe them to you briefly, so you'll know what I sacrificed on your behalf. My apartment was well decorated with statuettes and busts, along with mosaics and reliefs depicting Huvril military, religious, and political history. The walls were overlaid with purple, blue, and red tapestries, curtains, and banners. It was a beautiful apartment, guaranteeing absolute comfort from the external elements. The apartment was named the Saevril Estate. Each representative from every province within Samadasanae's jurisdiction had one. Two smaller rooms adjoined themselves to the main hall, one in front and the other to the right. To the left was the balcony overlooking the main plaza. It was slightly below the emperor's balcony by a few stories. The balcony to the throne room of the Imperial Hall, of course, was the highest. A huge monitor, larger than any I've ever seen before, hung above the emperor's balcony. The plaza below was set with marble and could hold one hundred thousand people. The whole arena was elaborate beyond measure. No expense had been spared.

I spent the night settling in, enjoying my accommodations. I tried not to think about what the Senate, having dwindled from one hundred representatives down to four, was going to do. It was not unusual for so many to resign at once. My own predecessor had resigned just a few days prior. What was unusual about the situation was the fact that the emperor was calling for the Senate at a time of transition. Senatorial voting was usually reserved for when all posts were occupied. And yet the outgoing senators fully resigned and conceded their votes to just the four remaining. Even to this day, I can't tell you if that was the emperor's doing or the Pantheonade. I can't tell you who benefited the most, whether the emperor gained favor by guaranteeing success, or if the Pantheonade allowed it as a strategy to weaken the imperial throne in the aftermath. I do remember pondering these things the first night of my stay in the Saevril Estate.

After two days, which I spent rendering modifications to my estate with various purchases and supervising a group of laborers, the emperor finally called the Senate. The four of us entered the Senatorial

Hall. On each side of the hall were five tiers of railings and benches. Near the center of the far wall was the emperor's bench. Emperor Serentis was already seated as we approached. He was accompanied by an entourage of scribes and assistants—five total. With just four of us senators, we assumed the lowest tier closest to the emperor instead of taking our assigned seats. It was awkward, nonetheless. As we talked, the room reverberated with our echoing voices.

"I am grateful for your obeisance," Serentis spoke, "as well as your commitment to your duty."

"Holy Father of fathers," Cirenok spoke, "that you're pleased with us is pleasing to us. It is our pleasure to see that you are pleased."

"Yes, of course," Serentis spoke. He looked to the side, annoyingly and, hiding his face behind his hand, secretly discussed something with a scribe.

Serentis was not like his father or his grandfather. Both of them loved flattery, and their wild temperaments could be soothed with words of praise. Serentis was more tolerant than his father, although he could still be prone to the cruelest of violence when provoked. Even so, his tolerance was looked upon with favor by the people. No doubt that Cirenok thought to continue the tradition. Perhaps he thought it would win him more favor, as if he was taking advantage of Serentis's more tolerant nature. Yet, he seemed oblivious to Serentis's dismissal of the flattery. Tradition is hard to break, especially when it serves a deeper purpose, such as self-promotion and ambition. I confess that I was also prone to such trivialities. I figured, at the time, that everyone knew it was the most grotesque vanity to flatter one's way ahead of others, but everyone still did it anyways. Serentis, however, was determined (I reasoned long after the fact) to break away from tradition for tradition's sake and instead set a higher standard for administration and politics. That's why he called us to assemble before him, the four of us, during transition.

Serentis concluded his side discussion with his scribe and once again addressed us. "Gentlemen," Serentis began, "the matter that I bring before you requires a senatorial vote for approval. It's a small matter, really." Serentis stood and walked over to us, but his scribes remained in their places. "Currently, the Pantheonade has authority over various … departments, and programs, and …" Serentis looked off to his side and struggled to finish the thought. He turned and walked away. "They have a lot of authority in many matters." Then Serentis jerked around to face us and, having stepped away from us, raised his voice loudly, as if we would fail to hear his statement and fail to realize the gravity of his point. "They have too much authority!"

I turned to see how my fellow senators were fairing. They remained quiet, as did I, but I could see tension building up in their faces. We all knew where this was heading.

"Gentlemen," Serentis said, walking back toward us, "the Senate, not the Pantheonade, needs to assume more responsibility in Huvril affairs."

Another senator, Rombh, fidgeted. I could tell that he wanted to speak, but until he was given leave to do so, he knew to keep quiet.

"The Senate and the imperial throne will unite in a common cause," Serentis continued, "namely, the separation of politics and religion." The emperor looked at each of us, one by one, studying us through squinted eyes, perhaps looking for some clue as to our current position. I made sure to express my interest while hiding my concern. "The Senate," Serentis announced, turning and walking away, "is in shambles." He whirled around, his cloak cutting the air like a blade. "That, gentlemen, is the fault of the Pantheonade. They make men fearful … weak … worried …" Serentis underscored each word with a thrust of his fist. He walked back over to us, and his deep, thrusting voice calmed while in our proximity. "Helpless … careless …" He paused. I nodded, both to let him know that I understood and that he could continue. "Powerless." He whispered the last word, though he said it slowly and clearly, assuring that we would hear it. "I have lawyers and scriveners present," Serentis said, pointing to the group near the imperial chair. He waggled his finger longer than I thought he should. I returned my gaze from the lawyers to him. "They are prepared to incorporate our decisions here today, to make them into law! All that is needed is the Senate's approval." With that, the emperor turned and walked back to the imperial chair. Sitting down, as if without a care, the emperor motioned to the chief lawyer.

The chief lawyer's name was Benrada. He was short and stocky and very old. He had an unusual ridge, a birth defect, perhaps, vertically slanted from the top of his forehead down to the bridge of his nose. It made him look cruel. His voice was raspy, as if he needed a drink of water. He picked up a datapad and approached us.

"Gentlemen of the Senate," Benrada began, bowing, "it is my pleasure and an honor to be at your service and the service of the imperial throne." He turned and bowed to Serentis, who nodded in approval. Benrada turned back to us. "I have before me Ordinance 12-14-28, nicknamed the Asundrance Bill, which declares by law the separation of the office of politics and the office of religion."

We four senators reached forward and took up the palm-sized datapads. Benrada's device interacted with our own, and within a few seconds, the bill's text flowed down the screens.

"Senators," Serentis said, standing. He walked down the few steps leading to his imperial chair and back over to us. "I really would like your decision by tomorrow morning." We all looked up at him. The Senate traditionally took two weeks to render a decision. That was for us to research the issue and discuss it amongst ourselves. With just four of us, the discussion part wouldn't take long, but there would be no time for research.

The meeting went on for a little while longer, as Serentis discussed other matters. The four of us from the Senate, what was left of it, decided on the spot to meet later that evening, so as to discuss the Asundrance Bill. The proposed legislation was setting a monumental precedent, and no doubt the Pantheonade would challenge the legislation in the highest courts. We adjourned, and later that afternoon, I visited the emperor in the imperial hall built by his grandsire Samadas, where he was conferring further with various counselors.

It seemed that I had arrived just in time to witness another monumental moment—even more so than the Asundrance Bill. I was discussing the bill with the deputy lawyers, hoping to weigh their opinions, when Serentis called for his political enemies to be brought before him, so as to judge their innocence or guilt. This was a customary action, except that it was usually done in another, separate, and distinctive venue. Serentis wanted, I learned later, to take care of this task and other similar tasks that he deemed menial. The emperor sat on his imperial bench, which was surrounded by scriveners holding their electronic datapads.

"Chief Officer of the Law," Serentis said to Benrada, using the typical address, "who is listed as No. 1 on the list of political enemies of the throne?"

Benrada pressed some commands and spoke. "The first, Father of Huvra," Benrada spoke, "is a political terrorist allegedly engaged in the unlawful development and transmission of a deadly bioweapon."

"Bring him forth," Serentis replied. "Let's get this over with." During the lapse, as the guards were in the process of bringing in the first prisoner, Serentis continued. "Who is No. 2?"

"No. 2 is deceased, having succumbed to old age," Benrada spoke. "No. 3 pleaded guilty, and his case is reconciled. No. 4 committed suicide. Thus, there are no further prisoners with whom to contend after No. 1."

"Splendid!" Serentis exclaimed, fidgeting for comfort.

The first prisoner brought in was not what I was expecting. Most criminals were of the roughest cut amongst Huvrils, but this prisoner was smaller than most. He seemed totally insignificant. His clothes were brown, dull, and ragged. He was physically unadorned, with no tattoos or piercings of any sort. His hands were bound with a small cord that looked as if it could otherwise be broken by any other commoner.

"Political Prisoner, Serial Number 9769400, named Americk," announced the lieutenant guard. "Charged with bioterrorism, in violation of Law 3750, on nineteen counts."

A moment passed as Serentis looked him up and down. "What is the prisoner's surname?" Serentis asked at length.

"Unknown," the lieutenant guard spoke. "He is listed under his mother's maiden name."

"A bastard child abandoned by a cruel father," Serentis spoke. I sensed a little sympathy in his voice. "You don't look like a bioterrorist," Serentis commented to Americk. "Why have you done this? Do you hate Huvra?"

The prisoner said nothing.

Serentis sighed. "What is the evidence?"

The lieutenant guard pressed several commands on his own datapad. It beeped and blipped as he hammered away at the virtual buttons on the display. A transparent, blue-tinted holographic display emerged from the datapad's light emitter. It was difficult for me to see precisely what it was, so I stepped closer. It looked like a hospital room with some medical equipment and lots of beds, upon many of which lay patients. This was the hospice room I previously told you about, and it was the first time I had heard of such a venture in this day and age. Hospices were a thing of the past, due to changes in hospitalization laws.

The emperor looked at the display with disinterest and sighed again, as if bored. He leaned over to Benrada and drew the chief lawyer closer with a wave of his hand. "Remind me to have the Senate draw up new legislation on returning the full judiciary back to the courts," Serentis said.

"Yes, Emperor Serentis," Benrada replied. The chief lawyer began pecking away on his datapad.

The emperor leaped from the bench and approached the lieutenant guard, stopping short of the display and studying it with renewed interest. Finally, he peeled his eyes away and locked onto the lieutenant guard's eyes.

"Well?" the emperor asked. "What else?"

The lieutenant guard hesitated and shifted his weight. His voice cracked. "The patients were tested, and all were found to be stricken with HIDD," he stated. "Hence, the concubation allegation."

The emperor turned to the prisoner. "What is this? What am I looking at?"

"A hospice for the dying," Americk spoke calmly and composed. He seemed to me to be undaunted.

The emperor spent the next couple of hours interrogating Americk.

The prisoner explained his intentions and consequent actions, from retrieving the still-living people discarded in the trash to be cast in the firepits. He shared with all present the trials he endured, from carrying bodies long distances, to enduring their own needs, and finally bestowing peace and dignity when they died.

"Do you consider yourself a physician? A healer?" Serentis asked.

"Huvra has many physicians and healers, but it has no caretakers," the prisoner replied. "Huvra has many hospitals and clinics but no harborages."

Taking in a deep breath, the emperor nodded and returned to his throne. "Tell me, Benrada, Chief Officer of the Law," Serentis began.

"Yes, Emperor Serentis, Father of Huvra," Benrada spoke.

"Is this supposed to be the man who made my grandsire tremble in his sleep?" Serentis asked. "Is this the man who drove my father mad with worry?"

The chief lawyer didn't answer but remained steadfast and silent, choosing to let his gaze lock onto the area of the floor just in front of him.

"Who is this man?" Serentis asked. "From where does he come? Who is his father? Wait!" The emperor remembered an important detail. The prisoner's father was unknown. "Who is his mother?"

Benrada paused to consult his datapad. "His mother was a temple servant," Benrada spoke, reading from the display. "She was expelled upon the discovery of her pregnancy, due to temple policy regarding sexual improprieties."

"Hmph!" Serentis spoke. He leaped from the bench and again approached Americk.

"Tell me, Accused One," Serentis spoke. "Why are you here?"

"I came voluntarily," Americk spoke, "at the request of your arresting officer."

A light chuckle erupted, especially from the lieutenant guard. Even the lawyers enjoyed a bit of levity, mumbling or elbowing each other in jest. I admit, the thought that the arrest was a mere request was humorous.

"Okay," Serentis spoke, slightly amused, but allowing no chuckle to exit his mouth. "But that doesn't really answer my question, does it?"

"Hmm," Americk spoke. "Perhaps not."

"Why are you here?" Serentis asked again.

"To convey important information to the emperor and his supporters," Americk spoke.

"Okay," Serentis spoke. "And what information would that be?"

"Are your scientists aware of magnetic monopole anomalies?" Americk asked.

Serentis stood face-to-face with Americk, his chin slightly higher than the prisoner's eyes. The emperor paused as he studied the eyes of the prisoner. He looked deep, squinting hard, and finally turning to face his chief lawyer.

"Answer his question," the emperor commanded.

Benrada pecked away at his datapad and nodded, as if finding what he was looking for. "The magnetic monopole is a hypothetical particle of physics that bears only one magnetic pole. Its existence is inferred only by mathematical calculation."

The emperor returned his gaze to the prisoner. "We know of the object," Serentis spoke. "Continue." Serentis took a few steps to the prisoner's left.

The prisoner turned only his head as he continued. "The magnetic monopole anomaly is responsible for a reputed supernatural phenomenon." Americk held his hands up before him and the emperor, emphasizing with his eyes the small cord that held him bound. The emperor looked at it and then turned to the guard on Americk's left. A nod prompted the guard to remove the cord. A swipe of a key-card released the locking mechanism of the cord, and Americk's hands fell free.

"The causes of the anomaly are complicated to explain," Americk continued, massaging his wrists. "But its effect is evident in the magnetic capture of information conveyed in the emittance of light. With your permission, I would like to demonstrate."

Serentis turned and looked back at his counselors. Their only response was to cast gazes all around at each other. Serentis sighed and returned to Americk. "Demonstrate this … effect."

Americk bowed his head slightly and then walked away. He stopped and glanced over his shoulder. Reluctantly, Serentis followed him. Needless to say, the rest of us fell in step behind the emperor. Luckily for me, I was directly behind him to his left. We all followed Americk down the steps of the dais, then down the hall, which was lined with members of the Imperial Guard. Just before we reached the main doors exiting the hall, Americk diverted to his right and stepped between some guards standing at attention. We followed. Benrada looked over at me and raised his eyebrows. I shrugged my shoulders. Finally, Americk stopped at the wall. Then he turned to face us.

"It is here that Hermatuelles was slain by his nephew, Morghonox," Americk said. "Information from that event was captured by a magnetic monopole anomaly as it traversed a tertiary current of Huvra's magnetic fields. In a moment, that anomaly will pass through this point."

I know I gasped, having heard myself, even in the midst of other gasps.

"A ghost?" Serentis asked. "You mean to say that the ghost of Hermatuelles will enter and walk past us?" I couldn't see the emperor's face, but the back of his neck was pulled taut with stress.

"Well," Americk spoke, "not in the manner thought of as a ghost. Ah! Here it is."

Americk stepped to the side and motioned with a nod that the object was present.

"I see nothing!" Serentis spoke. He clenched his fists.

Now, the next thing that happened was quite strange. Americk lowered his head and closed his eyes, mumbled something to himself in a light whisper—something that I could not hear—and then raised his head and opened his eyes. At that point, as we were standing there, a transparent image of a Huvril ruler walked into the midst of us. He stopped and looked around and then threw his arms up in the air, as if fending off an attack. Then he dropped to his knees and flailed his arms. Finally he lay down, and only afterward did the image fade slightly into a blur.

"Hermatuelles," Serentis spoke, his voice barely audible.

"Are you sure, sire?" Benrada asked from behind him.

"Yes!" Serentis spoke. "If not for the miter and train, I would not have, as the image is blurred. Otherwise, it is identical to his portrait." The emperor watched closely—we all did—as Hermatuelles lay flat on the ground, motionless, having succumbed to the assault from the unseen attacker.

"This image repeats approximately every two and a half years," Americk remarked. The prisoner, small in stature, stood tall and proud, his arms placed behind his back. He seemed confident in the information he was imparting.

"To whom were you praying?" Benrada asked. He seemed disturbed, as the look on his face was that of one who has just smelled something that reeks.

"To the Guardians," Americk spoke.

Gasps rang out. I confess I gasped also.

"Ha!" Serentis spoke. "Not even I am that brazen!" The emperor erupted in laughter. He lifted his head back and roared, his slightly pudgy belly bouncing up and down.

Benrada stepped forward. "The Guardians are enemies to Necronus!" he barked. The chief lawyer clenched the datapad tightly, as if he were trying to break it in two.

"Tell me!" Serentis entreated Americk, composing himself. "How did you make this image happen? I don't want it to be said that the emperor of Huvra is easily captivated by magic tricks."

"I understand," Americk spoke. "The Guardians adjusted the cells in your eyes, so that you could perceive the light frequency of the anomaly. Your own brains interpreted the information and presented it as a real-time image in your visual cortex."

"Any mere child could digitize an image and project it

holographically into real space," Benrada spoke. "All we need to do is—"

Without taking his eyes off of Americk, the emperor raised his hand and cut off the chief lawyer in midsentence. Benrada breathed in deeply and then stepped back.

"Explain the anomaly, then," Serentis spoke. "What exactly is the image? How does the monopole capture the image? Why Hermatuelles? How many more are there?" The emperor rattled off his questions one after another in rapid-fire succession. "But mostly, I want to know how the timing could be so precise for us to see this image right at the moment I was to decide your fate."

The prisoner hesitated only for a moment. "Well, the anomaly is caused by the retention of radiation emitted via intradimensional coiling. As you know, the central nervous system is electrically active. In a moment of intense trauma, the central nervous system overloads as it stimulates the sympathetic subsystem governing self-preservation. This electrical short circuit induces a magnetic field, which disrupts the flow of photonic information, or the reflection of light. If this happens within the range of a magnetic monopole, its magnetic currents capture the disrupted photonic information."

"So this ghost is not Hermatuelles?" Serentis asked.

"No," Americk spoke. "No more than the digital signal transmitted by your cameras and projected holographically into real space."

The emperor turned and faced his chief lawyer. "This makes sense," Serentis spoke. "More sense than the Pantheonade's explanation of spirits of the damned."

The chief lawyer dropped his gaze to the floor and looked as if he were pondering this new revelation. Excitement welled up in me, but also fear. The implications of this information were astounding.

"As to your last question," Americk added, "timing is essential."

Benrada wasn't satisfied. Although he supported the emperor's position on secularizing the government, he was still a pious man in religious matters. "Why is it, then," Benrada continued challenging Americk, "that the spirits of the dead appear to have intelligence and have communicated with the mediums of the past?"

"In rare instances," Americk began without hesitating, "a magnetic monopole is strong enough to capture a complex system of electrical impulses defining the thought processes of a person, like an actual video recording—in contrast to a mere photograph. Those complex processes suffice as a limited form of artificial intelligence and can respond to simple cues. But again, these magnetic monopoles are in themselves not alive, nor do they properly represent the person captured in the imagery."

"When I was a young boy, I dreamed of Hermatuelles," Serentis said. "I studied up on his writings, comprising his philosophy—his ideas and thoughts—and his desires for a new Huvra. My father was outraged and punished me accordingly. But still, I was drawn to his words. Do my desires have anything to do with this ... this anomaly?"

"Yes," Americk spoke. "You played in this area when you were a boy, correct?"

The emperor sighed and nodded, barely noticeably.

Americk bowed, I suppose to acknowledge the unspoken gesture with one of his own. Then he spoke further. "The magnetic monopole's nature causes the disruption of the magnetic fields created in the brain and induces a slight disruption in the brain's electrochemical synthesis. The brain interprets and processes the signals via the sensory cortices. This has the same effect as a dreaming sequence, in which short-term memory neural circuits are recalibrated with long-term memory neural circuits. Of course, you had to have seen the image prior to this dream, so that your brain could properly store the accurate image and recall that image while processing the new information."

Benrada was fuming but said nothing more.

The emperor, on the other hand, was ecstatic. He clasped his hands and nodded approvingly with a big smile. He paused for a few minutes, as if in deep thought, but finally spoke. "Now I ask a more important question. Why tell me all of this? What is the purpose?"

This time, Americk didn't answer right away. He looked deep into the eyes of the emperor. The prisoner's eyes were sad. He let his gaze slowly fall away to the floor. When Americk did speak, his voice betrayed a sense of mourning.

"The emperor and his supporters," Americk stated, "will have to endure a trial of fire. Even now, your enemies conspire against the throne, to overthrow it and establish a theocracy."

The hall fell into a silence.

"How do you know this?" Serentis asked, his voice falling to a whisper.

Americk's gaze again fell to the floor. The answer obviously wasn't easy to reveal. "The Guardians informed me," Americk answered. "They revealed this to me in a dream."

"Enough!" Benrada spoke. He threw his arms in the air, turned to storm off. This outburst was so sudden that even the emperor was startled.

"Hold your peace!" Serentis spoke to Benrada.

The chief lawyer stopped. The scowl on his face showed his displeasure at Serentis's command. He said nothing but folded his arms across his chest. His breath became labored.

The emperor stared at him for a minute or two, perhaps to test the chief lawyer's obedience. Nodding with satisfaction, the emperor returned his attention to Americk.

"How will they accomplish this," Serentis asked, "seeing that the throne is well armed and guarded, and the temple is not?"

"Your own mythology contains the answer," Americk says.

The emperor stared at Americk but for a minute. Then he walked past Benrada toward the throne. He stopped and looked over his shoulder at all of us. I interpreted this as an "Are you coming?" moment, so I stepped forward to follow. Everyone, including Americk, did the same. I noticed that Benrada gave Americk a hard look, as if he were trying to kill the troublemaker with nothing more than his eyes. We all walked back up the steps to the center of the dais, where the imperial throne sat. Serentis immediately made himself comfortable and then motioned for Americk to approach him.

"How much time do we have?" Serentis asked.

"They approach as we speak," Americk spoke. "They tread the

high road from the Pantheonade temple mount to the upper tiers of the imperial compound. Within minutes, the company of your foes will be standing on the other side of the main doors to the hall."

"Impossible!" Serentis spoke. "I would have been warned." The emperor stared at Americk. "Why didn't you warn me beforehand?"

"Timing is essential," Americk spoke. "You needed some information before the confrontation."

"Very well," Serentis spoke. "Let them come."

I murmured with the others near me, Cirenok and Benrada included. We had just enough time to convey our fears when suddenly knocking on the main doors sounded at the far end of the hall. The knocking was incredibly loud, as if a battering ram had been unleashed, except that after just a few knocks, it ceased.

"Tell the door guards to permit their entrance," Serentis said to Benrada.

The chief lawyer repeated the emperor's command into a com-stick, at which the door guards immediately jumped to obey. The doors swung open to reveal the visitors. It was as Americk described, a company. But in the midst of them stood a giant, twice the normal height of a Huvril man. This giant was decked out in black robes with gold embroidery. At first, it appeared that he wore a crown of blackened horns upon his head, but as he approached, it dawned on me that the horns were his own outgrowths. There were six, maybe eight. They spiraled upward and circled around the crown of his head. His skin was deathly gray, and his eyes were sunken and dark, hidden from the light of day. Although later I reasoned that the effect was probably a figment of my imagination, I could have sworn at the time that the halls shook at his every step. I confess that I began to step back as unadulterated fear shook my very core. Others around me did the same, and we began to crowd in on each other behind the throne. Just as I was stepping past the emperor, I stole a glance. He stood proudly, although I thought I saw his lower lip tremble.

The imperial guards below jumped in the middle of the walkway to impede the company's march. The company stopped, and those in front stepped aside to allow the giant to step forward. He merely raised his hand, with all of his fingers curved in a vicious-looking claw. His eyes flashed, and he quickly clasped the fingers into a fist. All of the guards screamed and fell to the floor, writhing. There was the loud sound of cracking and crunching. Within seconds, it was over. The guards atop the dais fell too. I stared in disbelief at the one closest to me. His throat looked deformed and crushed.

The company made its way down the hall toward the dais. It was composed of numerous priests and temple guards, all dressed in elaborate robes of various colors and designs, along with matching miters and face masks. The latter item was a hallmark of the temple guard, who proceeded as if blindfolded. It is reputed that they have always possessed some special sense. How they really moved around is best left to conjecture.

The leader of the company, the Chief Priest Torseides, stepped ahead of the giant. He was very old, so old his eyes sagged below his nose, which made him look especially ominous. "Get yourself down here," he spoke in the direction of the emperor. "All of you." His voice sounded raspy and laborious, but we heard it, nonetheless.

Serentis just stood there, staring. At times, he trembled. I knew he was fighting an inner battle like none before in his life. Fear and courage warred against each other. Those of us atop the dais, senators and lawyers, stepped forward to stand behind the emperor. We crowded in, again. I can't speak on behalf of the others, but I wanted to obey the chief priest. Yet, I couldn't obey without following the emperor. Confusion wracked my brain. I felt people behind me, pushing me forward. I remember thinking at the time, *Lawyers!*

The giant approached the chief priest. His voice rang through the hall like booming thunder. "Bring him to me," the giant spoke.

The chief priest turned and motioned to the guards, who raised their staves and marched forward past the priests and the giant.

Serentis turned and faced the crowd. "The prisoner Americk is judged as innocent," he announced. "The evidence is insufficient." Serentis then turned to Americk. "Go! This isn't your conflict."

Americk maneuvered through the few in front of him and

approached Serentis. "I thank you for my freedom, but, with your permission, I choose to stand with the emperor and his supporters."

"Are you—" Serentis spoke, pausing to take in a deep breath, "—one of my supporters?" The emperor's voice was soft and dejected.

"Yes," Americk spoke. "I am always, but most especially on this particular occasion."

"They may kill you," Serentis spoke.

"They will," Americk spoke.

"You know this?" Serentis asked.

Americk nodded.

"You are not afraid?" Serentis asked.

"The kings of men have power over life," Americk spoke. "The Guardians, however, have power over death."

"What about Necronus?" Serentis asked.

"He is a fallen Guardian," Americk replied.

The gasps that sounded were like those of a throng of prisoners offered a choice between living and dying.

"Well, you will certainly be executed now, as will I," Serentis spoke. "Who else?"

"Two others," Americk spoke. "Everyone else will be spared."

Serentis turned and looked around at the group of senators and lawyers. His eyes reached me and locked into my gaze. I did my best to convey my full support for the imperial throne. He nodded, as if satisfied with some inner inquiry. He turned and proceeded to meet the temple guards at the base of the steps. Seeing his approach, the temple guards stopped at the base and waited. Serentis stole a glance over his shoulder, and Americk took the lead in following him. Whether it is wrong or right to boast, I now boast that I jumped at the opportunity and followed beside Americk, in step behind Serentis, the Emperor of Huvra. I sensed others following behind the two of us. I looked at Americk, who was shorter than anyone there. He returned a look of his own, and for a moment we studied each other. This man was walking to his death, which he himself was utterly convinced would take place, and yet the expression on his face was sad but calm. And then, straight from the realm of the strange, he smiled! Bewildered, I looked forward again! What was happening, I couldn't answer. I felt like an unwitting participant in a theatrical production, where time and space operate differently from reality.

Serentis reached the bottom of the steps. The temple guards stepped aside to allow him to proceed in the midst of them. As I passed the first guard on my side of the procession, I took a closer look at his face mask, half expecting to see a thin veil. Such an expectance would satisfy my general curiosity as to the rumors, but the mask was a thick cloth draped over his entire face, stretched to fit the contours of his brow and bridge of his nose. Where slits for eyes would be, there were none. The temple guard turned his head, as if he was staring back at me. A chill went down my spine. The spectacle was absurd and creepy.

The procession, led by Serentis, approached the giant. The giant's eyes were the blackest of black, darker than the deep recesses of Huvra's caverns. For a moment, emperor and giant stared at each other, saying nothing.

"I see before me," Serentis began, jarring the silence like an earthquake, "an image like that of the Avatar of Devisgar." Serentis looked up at the giant's crown of horns. "Well, with some exceptions, that is."

Another uneasy moment passed.

"That was your only opportunity to fall to your knees and ask me for mercy," Devisgar spoke. "Your supporters have a little more time to do so."

I heard the commotion behind me and turned to see Benrada, Cirenok, and everyone else drop to their knees and bow their heads forward. I looked into the eyes of Americk, who stood next to me. I couldn't interpret their expression quickly enough. This man saw everything; there was no doubt. I knew nothing of him. The emperor had turned around and was staring at us all. Devisgar's dark gaze was fixed on me, since at the moment, I was the only one, other than Serentis and Americk, still standing.

It's difficult to explain what was going through my mind. I was a novice senator from a small province. Of all the people in the hall at the moment, I was the least significant. And that weight pressed on my shoulders, pushing me toward the floor. I'm pretty sure I've shared the following with you in the past, even more than once, but I want to do so again. I never pass up the opportunity to expose my own weakness and vulnerability, since the first step toward redemption and change is honesty.

I knelt before Devisgar. When I looked up into the eyes of Americk, it was as if he was expecting me to do what I just did. I felt that I had abandoned him, especially when both he and Serentis needed me most, when they needed someone, anyone. But Americk's eyes were filled with an indescribable compassion, and right then and there I knew, without him having to say it, that he forgave me. The tears burst from my eyes, erupting like a deluge. I fell to the floor and covered my face in shame. Even then, I felt the back of Americk's hand on my shoulder. I'm sure there was some further discussion, but I missed it. Finally, I managed to come to my senses so as to witness the rest of what transpired.

"None of these will be amongst the two who will perish with us," Americk told Serentis. The emperor said nothing further but turned to face the giant Avatar.

"Don't think I'm unaware of your meddling, worm," Devisgar said to Americk. The prisoner-set-free stepped up beside the emperor-under-arrest and committed himself to be arrested again. "I even know what you're doing. I won't kill you. I won't be the cause of your martyrdom." Devisgar turned to Serentis. "As for you, well, you're judged for your heresy and damned to eternal hellfire. But that's not all." Devisgar turned and gestured behind him, as if calling forth someone or something.

Temple guards from the rear approached. In their custody was a woman holding an infant. She was dressed in an elaborate gown, its beautiful design marred by a dirt stain on the front. Her face was slightly bruised, and a thin line of dried blood ran from her mouth to the bottom of her chin.

"No!" Serentis screamed. "No! Tegeth!"

"Silence, heretic!" Devisgar said. "For your heresy, your wife and child will die before your eyes."

The giant Avatar nodded to a temple guard, who thrust his spear into the back of the woman. Serentis lunged forward, but temple guards fell upon him and held him back.

"Tegeth!" Serentis spoke. He struggled but was helpless to free himself. He watched as his wife slowly lowered herself to the floor, careful to protect the infant, who had begun to cry loudly. As she lay and took her final breath, she pulled the infant in her arms close to her breast.

"Sharani!" Serentis said amidst his own tears. He pulled forward weakly in a futile attempt to break away from the guards. His hand was outstretched toward the child in the mother's arms.

Devisgar pointed his finger to the child and then nodded to the temple guard with the bloody spear. The temple guard hesitated. Devisgar stepped forward with a scowl on his face, and the temple guard stepped around the mother's body, eventually blocking my view. He then lifted up the staff with the spear point aimed down. As he brought down the staff, the child stopped crying. Soon, only Serentis's crying was heard. Devisgar studied the emperor, as if he relished every moment of the man's torment.

Serentis took a few minutes to compose himself. He jerked his arms out of the temple guards' grasp and wiped the tears from his face. Looking to the giant, Serentis squinted his eyes in hate. "Do your worst, murderer," Serentis spoke.

The giant Avatar growled and then gestured to the lifeless bodies. Images of both mother and child rose from the bodies, as if their spirits were being drawn forth. Each image hovered, one next to the other.

"For your heresy," Devisgar spoke, "I will condemn your wife and child to eternal hellfire." Devisgar then gestured with his hand drawn up like a claw. His eyes flashed and began to emit a strange light.

Suddenly, the woman and child both erupted in screams that can only be described as abject horror. The images showed a strange fire engulfing them. Their images screamed and begged, thrashed and flailed and contorted. The spectacle was the most horrific scene I had ever witnessed. The coldest chill moved its way up my spine. I didn't know what my fate was to be, but I knew that I did not want to suffer that fate. Every part of my body was screaming for me to run.

I looked at Serentis, expecting to see him completely broken down. But instead, I saw a man whose resolve was strengthened. He stared at the images in disbelief. He turned and looked at Americk, who stood behind him some distance away. Americk shook his head, ever so subtly. Serentis turned back around and stared at the images again.

Alarmed, Devisgar studied Serentis. "Whatever the worm told you was a lie. They are truly in torment."

"You're a fraud," Serentis spoke. "You're probably not even Devisgar himself."

"Silence!" Devisgar spoke, his voice booming so loudly my ears felt like they would burst.

"Who are you, imposter?" Serentis spoke.

"Your whore of a wife will hate you forever!" Devisgar spoke.

"Who is this imposter?" Serentis spoke, looking around at everyone else.

"When you join her in hell," Devisgar continued, "she will claw out your eyes and rip out your guts with her teeth!"

"Do you fools really believe this liar?" Serentis spoke, his eyes locked onto the chief priest, Torseides.

Devisgar calmed and became silent, but he breathed heavily as if sulking. He turned and began to walk away, heading down the hall toward the main doors.

I, Soleran, interject this memorandum into the record of Ghypriex. We, the Guardians, were watching from the Intrepidium *this affair transpire in the Imperial Hall of Samadasanae. I observed Maximeron standing far off from the group. He appeared quite disturbed by his apparent failure to manipulate Serentis into a state of perturbative torment. I teleshifted next to him. He startled in surprise and then began looking back and forth between Americk and me.*

"It wasn't me who descended," I said. I assumed by the silence that followed that he was trying to determine who did. "No Guardian descended."

"He's no ordinary Huvril," Maximeron said.

"True," I said. "One amongst us did descend, but as I said, it was no Guardian."

Maximeron stared at me briefly with wide eyes. He then teleshifted away, and I returned to the Intrepidium.

I conclude this memorandum.

Devisgar stopped, turned around quickly, and screamed, "Kill the worm! Kill the worm!" He was pointing at Americk. The temple guards fell upon Americk, and attacked him with their spear-staves. They finally stopped and pulled back. A bloodied and mutilated corpse that used to be a man lay at their feet.

"Ha!" Serentis spoke. "He said you would kill him. You said you wouldn't. Now we know who spoke the truth and who lied."

Devisgar galloped toward the emperor. He snatched a bladed staff from the hands of a temple guard, and swung it in one single motion. The head of Serentis left his shoulders and fell to the floor. The body of the emperor stood but for a moment and then dropped lifeless to the floor. Devisgar stood fuming over the body of the vanquished ruler of Huvra.

"What do we do with these?" Torseides spoke, gesturing to the rest of us senators and lawyers.

"Levy fines, confiscate their properties, and let them go," Devisgar spoke, turning to leave. "Torseides, you have the throne."

"Thank you, Lord Devisgar," the chief priest spoke.

"I don't want to have to descend again," Devisgar spoke.

"Yes, Lord," Torseides spoke.

"Do it right!" Devisgar spoke loudly, his words sounding like barking of a grund hound.

The chief priest bowed, along with the priests and temple guards with him. I noticed that even the senators and lawyers bowed low. I couldn't do so, however. Yet when I returned my gaze to Devisgar, he was staring at me hard. Intimidated, I dropped my gaze to the floor and feigned a half bow. When I looked up, he was walking away, down the hall the way he entered. I cursed at myself for being weak. After a minute, he was gone, and everyone still present released their breath.

Needless to say, my full estate was confiscated and my accounts seized. I was stripped of my authority and terminated from my office. After it was all over with, I was as poor as a common street beggar. I hadn't been a senator that long, either. I laugh at the matter now. Luckily, I've had my knowledge and expertise on which to fall back. That's the one thing no one can take from another, knowledge. And now you know the fullest details of Americk's death as I know them, and have no cause to argue amongst yourselves over such trivial matters. You know of his life as I've come to learn it. There is no good reason to contend over these things anymore, since it is impossible to derive any further information from history or from the records.

The rest of this story, you already know, but I'll finish, since I am obsessed with completeness. Torseides united throne and altar into one political-religious machine. He waged war against the followers of the Guardians. His cruelty was fueled by both delusion of power and fear of Devisgar's threat of returning, should Torseides fail. Torseides even ordered that Americk's hospice be burned to the ground. That horror is indescribable, except to say that those patients who had recovered enough to be conscious of what was happening couldn't so much as scream to alert their persecutors. I don't fret too much. Their suffering was brief, and no doubt they remain in Americk's memory to be reinstated at the Morning Rise, that Dawn of Hope for those whom Americk and the Guardians deem worthy.

Speaking of which, the Guardian named Sun-Li did return briefly to confer with Torseides.

"We witness what transpires on the face of Huvra," Sun-Li said, "how your thoughts flow from your egocentric personality and how your deeds flow from your hands as a torrential storm of fury."

"You see the extent to which I will go to please my Lord and God, Necronus, the Father of Life and Death," Torseides replied.

"Yes," Sun-Li remarked. "But you are storing up wrath for yourself, and a reckoning will ensue. Then, when a judgment is rendered, you will have no answer."

The Guardian stayed longer than I had the privilege of witnessing, and spoke of things I was not a party to, but I did manage to glean some further information from a witness. Sun-Li relayed a prediction that Huvra would collapse in on itself and that the Guardians would reinstate those Huvrils who abandoned the necronic doctrine of war and conquest, much to the dismay of Necronus and his disciples.

Chapter 15

The Report of Dyllon, Fourth Echelon Officer of the Order of Intrepidium: We have responded to a perturbation that has originated near the collapsed massive star called Chathis. The signature of the perturbation is Tronteron, a race of intelligent beings from the Trontius Tertiarus Star System. We have had no contact with this race, either in their origin or development. Via naturally occurring kinesis, their home world sprung up by calculable dispersion of hydrocarbon molecules sprayed from a nearby supernova. They managed to mature and evolve without celestial assistance, either from us or the other three prominent celestial races. We were pleased by this discovery. Since then, the Tronterons have increased their knowledge of technology, and transited the confines of their home world to emerge as a basic space-faring civilization. Their vessels are primarily for science and not for war, since they have found a need only for a small fleet of security vessels. A typical Tronteron stands at a meter and a half, and weighs eighty-five kilograms—a little bulky, but healthy. Their skin is mottled dark pink, and their eyes are huge, which we determine has certainly contributed to their high intelligence. Deriving from a world with a stable and temperate climate, they have never clothed themselves, preferring unashamed nakedness. They are bipedal, but have one primary arm and three shorter, secondary arms.

We quickly offer our assistance, seeing that the perturbation was caused by their distress signal. Apparently, a fleet of eight Tronteron science vessels has converged on Chathis so as to study the natural black-hole phenomenon. The vessels differ in coloring but are the same egg shape and look big enough to accommodate a crew of fifty or so. Unfortunately, one wandered into an undetectable interlinear exophase current, which began pulling it toward the event horizon. Sensing danger, two others sprang into action so as to rescue the endangered vessel. Since that time, all three have been pulled over the event horizon. The remaining five vessels have moved back to a safe distance and have spread out in strategic positions to ascertain the whereabouts of their comrades.

This is to no avail, however, seeing that Chathis, a typical tau-matter star, retains all information, even light. The black void spins ferociously, an abyss that crushes everything to nothingness. A gravitational lens rotates with the event horizon, twisting and diverting any light passing through the exophase current.

"Which one of us shall go forth and freely feed the abyss of our essence, and deliver the Tronterons from this plight?" Soleran asks.

"It is my time," I answer. I turn to face him. "I will go."

"Dyllon," Soleran begins, "you are prepared for this expenditure?" He raises his eyebrows, but his smile doesn't waver. His question is rhetorical, however, as he full well knows what I know.

"I am," I answer.

He nods, satisfied with my commitment.

Evalene approaches me, her dazzling eyes telling me to wait and hear what she has to say.

"Shall I join you, love?" she asks.

"I understand your concern," I answer, "but only one of us should go."

"What shall you forget, Dyllon?" she asks. She lowers her gaze. I know her inner struggle is a conflict between remembering our past together or letting it go. "I will stand by and observe closely. If anything should arise to warrant assistance, I will come immediately."

"When you reach 72 percent essence, Dyllon," Soleran says, "Evalene will join you."

"Understood," I say.

"We will observe you closely," Soleran says. He gestures, and a holographic image of my likeness emerges near him. The image depicts me frozen in time. My pale white skin and white hair has always clashed with Evalene's black hair and darker skin. I cast a glance in her direction, and she smiles at the gesture. I return the smile.

I teleshift from the *Intrepidium* and hover within the intergalactic medium right up against Chathis's event horizon. Its exocurrent, the same current that swallowed up the Tronteron vessels with no resistance, pulls at me, and immediately I expend some information. Misty light flows from my body and disappears past the boundary. I prepare myself by reviewing my calculations for configuring a counteracting force against the pull of gravity. After scanning the equations and numbers, I am satisfied with the results. I move forward, crossing the boundary from stable fluid to torrential stellar winds. A scan of the singularity system reveals something contradictive.

"Soleran," I say, "I'm measuring Chathis at a mass heavier than registered in the Omnitron."

"It would appear that Chathis has already devoured several stars," Soleran answers. "Perhaps around thirty solar masses have contributed to the singularity system."

"The poor Tronterons," I say, offering some sympathy. "They never had a chance." I take a deep breath of the local hydrogen and then press forward into the void. I see

blinding
light
blistering,
unbelievable
light every
where
But at the same
TIME
all is dark

there is

no

means to see

but I do

see

a little boy running through a field of tall grass. He is fearful and excited. His father yells out, "Ten! Here I come, ready or not!"

"Your sacrifice is extensive," Soleran says. "We grieve for your loss, Dyllon."

"There is more," I answer to myself more so than to Soleran. "Take it, Chathis, in exchange for the life of the Tronterons."

The boy falls into a pile of brush. He giggles and forces himself under the fallen grass, leaves, and small branches. He listens as his father approaches.

"Now, where are you?" the father says. "Wherever could you be?"

The boy giggles.

"Hmmm, that boy must have gone all the way to the lake," the father says. "I guess I better head that way."

The boy hears stomping. He can't resist giggling. After a moment all falls silent. The little boy then wiggles out from under the brush and stands to look around.

"Gotcha!" the father says behind the boy, lifting him up in the air.

"Gotcha," I say. And then the memory is gone. Expenditure. Light. Information. Chathis takes it all, pulls it into its currents. The currents spiral downward into the center, which is nothing more than a singularity, a small point consisting of hundreds of solar masses of tau matter. It warps the continuum to such a degree that all of space and time, that is, back-and-front, side-and-side, up-and-down are blended with past-present-future. All information is churned about, mixed thoroughly through and through, distorted beyond recognition, and then utterly destroyed without emotion. Nothingness.

My father approaches me.

"I'm proud of you, son," he says. "I just want you to know that. You'll be a good father to Jon-Krisse."

"I'll love you always, Dad," I answer.

And then he is gone …

… forever.

"Dyllon, we are concerned," Evalene says to me from the *Intrepidium*. "I am concerned."

"I understand, dear," I answer.

"What is your course of action?" she asks.

"If I can determine the points of entry, I will use velocity vectors to calculate their positions," I respond. Holding my current position requires concentration and strength, and both are being tested. I strain, but I will succeed.

"Can you not use light fractalization?" Soleran asks.

"Chathis is too massive at this point," I answer. "All light information is entangled beyond calculation."

"Very well," Soleran says. I understand his concern. "You are currently down to 88 percent essence."

"Time is of the essence," I answer. "Soleran, flash the points of entry of the Tronteron vessels, if you would, please."

"Absolutely," Soleran answers.

I see in my perspective one flash to my upper left. Slightly down and to the right from the first position are two flashes. *Omnitron, let me see within as clearly as possible. Chathis takes it all.* There is light within my eyes. I see the bright-red lines and yellow equations. The latter observation calculates the velocity of the vessels and point-by-point spatial transition of each one. That's the amazing thing about space. No matter how much it is contorted and twisted, a point-by-point transition from one locale to the next can still be observed. Chathis is a challenge, no doubt. This raging beast of a natural phenomenon is impersonal but behaves like a living creature. Tau matter is an element unique in quantum structure, so tightly compacted into perfect symmetry that energy lies next to energy, and the oscillation of the band of energy influences the neighboring bands of energy.

The boy grows up. He's happy and sad. He's happy because he's learning about life and living and aliveness. He's sad because the father he knew is no longer in his life. Why? Did the man die? Did he merely leave? The teenager wants to know. Nightly dreams show him walking side-by-side with a stranger, who puts a hand on the boy's shoulder and calls him "son." Then he says he has to go away. The boy asks why, but the man doesn't answer. Instead, the boy watches as the man lowers his head and cries. Then the man's image starts to shrink away. The boy cries, "Dad! Dad!" He reaches for him and tries to run but can't. Then the boy watches as the man disappears from sight.

I feel an indescribable force slam me, and it pulls information from my person. The ghost, a wispy, gray image depicting my likeness extends from me and is carried away in the torrential wind. I watch it dissipate like a vapor.

"Dyllon," Evalene says to me, "you are down to 82 percent."

"Hold on, my love," I admonish her.

"I will …" she says with a pause, "try." She weeps. Strange.

The red lines depicting the spatial transitions of the Tronteron vessels continue to expand and wrap around the solarcentralization of Chathis's heart.

"Soleran?" I ask.

"Yes?" Soleran answers.

"I need to increase my processing speed. Help?" I ask.

"Will do," Soleran says.

I know that if I don't catch up to the vessels, then my projections and calculations will merely continue around and around until they fall into the center. The Omnitron, the computer's memory consisting of Guardian memory, interprets my optics and determines my intention. The flash of light in my optics confirms my targets. The three red lines expand in a flash, and each ends in a projected object. I can't see the vessels themselves, only the calculated positions. The vessels have to be in those positions, if the calculations are correct to the two-millionth degree. Any slight deviation, and all I will find is an empty variable. The calculations show that the outer two vessels are still in the peta current. The inner vessel, however, has already entered the zeta current. In forty-five seconds the vessel will succumb to Chathis's tidal forces and begin to rip apart.

My only option is to instigate the vacuum energy via a calabi-yau corridor. That means opening a port into the corridor and transmitting the information for a field. Unfortunately for me, that means an increase in the rate of expenditure. The more energy I expend in operating in this stellar hurricane, the more information I give to Chathis. The thoughts of expenditure harass me slightly, disrupting my concentration.

"Soleran," I say.

"Yes?" Soleran answers.

"If only Maximeron was here, to see me voluntarily return my essence to the universe," I say.

"He would be pleased," Soleran said, following it with a light chuckle.

"He would see me—

extract a part
and expend a portion
intricate quintessentiality
intimately exported
to a heavenly charter
consorting with the heart

The teenager is a grown man. He stands before a woman. Her dazzling eyes capture his attention and his heart.

"You have the most beautiful eyes," the young man says to the woman.

"What is so special about them?" she asks.

The young man squints. "It's as if the light hits them at the right angle to make them sparkle," he answers.

The young woman laughs. "You and your logic," she says, still laughing.

"No, really" he says. "The light hits your eyes just right."

"And?" she asks.

"It tells me what I need to know about you," he answers.

She stops laughing. Her smile slowly fades to a straight line. "What does it tell you?" she asks.

"That everything I need to know about you," the young man answers, "can be known just by looking in your eyes."

"Evalene?" I ask. I hear weeping.

"I am forever alone now," she says. "No one will understand me."

"I don't understand," I say.

"Save the Tronterons," she says coldly.

I observe the two projected outer vessels approach, per my calculations, still within the peta current. I extend my left hand and quickly gesture. The Omnitron, interpreting my objectives, responds by opening the ports to the calabi-yau corridors. Vacuum energy is pulled from the projected space through the corridor and into my local space. That instigates a force field, which, upon activation, captures two objects.

"I have the two outer vessels, Soleran," I say.

I wait for the inner vessel, which, according to my calculations, has only twenty seconds before succumbing to Chathis's tidal forces. At that point, the vessel will rip apart and be destroyed the second after.

Evalene, I love you
I love you, too, Dyllon
Will you marry me?

I will!
Dyllon, I'm pregnant
Oh my God! I'm having a …
son …
I will name him Jon-Krisse.
Our little boy
Dyllon, I am
happy
I love you
I love you
I love you
love
you

"Hurry, Dyllon," Evalene says. "You are down to 78 percent."

"I feel mass within my grasp," I answer. "I'm pretty sure I have the two outer vessels."

"Can you retrieve the inner vessel?" Soleran asks.

Rhetorical? Who knows? "Do not doubt," I say.

I observe the red circle of light that allegedly contains the inner vessel. Per my calculations, the inner vessel swings around in the zeta current of Chathis. There are only five seconds left before they are beyond rescue. I extend my right hand and gesture. The *Intrepidium* interprets my objective, opens up the ports, and pulls the vacuum energy through. A force field initiates, and an unidentifiable object's shielding collides with the force field. The force is massive, though the object is small. The zeta current is the strongest current of a black hole. And with Chathis's mass, that current's strength is multiplied a hundredfold.

I cry. I weep. I whine.
What's your problem?
I'm a human being.
I have emotions, like any other.
Oh yeah? Well, maybe you're weak,

I try, I labor,
What?
Like any human being.
You're running out of time, buddy.
What's your name?
Phelix.
Hi Phelix. My name is Dyllon.
Glad to meet you, Dyllon.
Ditto!
Dyllon?
Yes?
You do realize what's happening, right?
I think so.
Good, 'cuz if you don't know, I can't explain it to you.
Huh?
What?
Come again?
Are you confused?
I think so.

"Dyllon!" Evalene says. "You're down to seventy-five."

"Pull the Tronterons to the boundary," Soleran says. "We'll do the rest."

I ignite my essence, the nucleosynthesis consuming my hydrogen. I pull the objects toward me, carefully, mindful that a miscalculation would be to their detriment. The currents of the black hole are so strong that I know I can do so if I want; all I have to do is make it happen, like any good soul who knows happiness, because …

"Hang in there," Soleran says.

"I'm coming, Dyllon!" Evalene says.

"Wait!" I answer. It's imperative that she wait. I can't determine why at the moment, but in my heart of hearts, I know that she has to wait. If she doesn't, then I'm going to be greatly distressed.

I pull with all my might. Chathis resists. It pulls back in response.

I can't see the vessels, but I'm confident that I have them in my grasp. And so I pull. It seems an eternity.

"*Mr. Trudeau,*" *a doctor says,* "*your wife and son are both recovering just fine.*"
"*Thanks, doctor,*" *a man answers.*
"*There were some difficulties,*" *the doctor says,* "*but we dealt with them as they arose.*"
"*When can I see them?*" *the man asks.*
"*You can see your son in the maternity ward,*" *the doctor says.* "*Your wife will be …*"
"Evalene!" I yell.
"I'm here, Dyllon," she answers. "Keep pulling the vessels to us. You're almost there."

> *There is*
> *hope*
> *love*
> *and time*
> *if we give it away*
> *frankly,*
> *for there*
> *is*
> *nomoretimetowasteon*
> *triviality!*

"We have them," Soleran says. "We pulled them from the gravity of Chathis. The vessels are free. Come on out now, Dyllon."
"You were awesome," Evalene says. "Come …"

Home! I see! What? Home! What is home? It is the place from which memory constructs itself. Whatever is memorable is all contained within the locality of home. You love home? Love? Yes, love. Home is the memorial to the Soul's interaction with Life. The Soul and its Life interact to build a home. Homeless is the Lifeless Soul, a restless wanderer in the landscape of reality. Within the scope of the music of Time, the Soul dances with Life, and there is interaction, if interaction is mutual.

"Dyllon, hear me ..." a male voice sounds.

We are one and one are we and ...

"You are ..." a male voice sounds.

Jon-Krisse, have I not loved you? You have, Father. Have I not given you my own essence? You have, Father.

"down to ..." a male voice sounds.

Father? Yes, son? What is life? My son, life is ...

"Seventy-three ..." a male voice sounds.

knowing that life exists in the first place and then choosing to participate.

"percent," a voice says.

"Dyllon," a female voice says to me. To me. How interesting. A voice says to me. "Take my hand, Dyllon."

Hi, Evalene. Hi, Dyllon. I love you. I know you do, and I love you too. Will you marry me? Of course, I would, Dyllon. I would marry you a million times over. Can we make a home here in Brest? Yes, we can. Excellent. I can provide for you and Jon-Krisse, the seas permitting and God willing. I know you will. Give me your hand, and I will kiss it gently.

"Dyllon," a female voice sounds, "you are now down to 72 percent essence."

"Okay," I respond. Whatever that means. I don't know. Why would I?

"Take my hand," the female voice commands. There are dazzling eyes with dazzling light. Then there is darkness. "Come with me."

I try to focus my perception, and I notice a radiative roar sounding behind me. Looking over my shoulder, I see a ring of distorted light surrounding a massive area of darkness. Chathis. To my side, I see a most interesting and beautiful creature. Her short, wavy black hair and her smooth, bronze skin both shimmer in the black of space. Evalene. I look at my hand and notice that it is transparent. Through my hand, I see light. Lowering my hand, I see that in front of me lies a bright, multicolored cloud of dust and gas. We enter.

"Breathe, my love," Evalene says. "Breathe in the breath of life."

I inhale, and the cool hydrogen replenishes my essence.

She spends an eternity with me, telling me of our history, of our past. I listen attentively, nodding, asking questions here and there. I'll never remember the details. That information is forever gone. But I trust her and have comfort in the validity of the facts.

Faith.

Section 3: Neverending

CHAPTER 16

The *Intrepidium* prompts with a warning, a series of echoing, beeping sounds. The Praegian star has just exploded, its perturbation registering on the continuum, even though it's in the prime of its life. The Guardians remain silent as they study the data on their holographic interfaces. Many conclude their studies and close their interfaces. They step up to Soleran, who scrolls his interface up and down.

"Let us go there," Soleran says, closing his interface.

Natharon activates his window, presses the commands, and the *Intrepidium* lunges forward toward the exploding star. It seems like mere seconds, and we are just far enough from the system to see all the planets. Soleran reviews the solar schematic. There are seven planets. Four of them are inhabited—the home world, Praegia, and three colonies. A plan of action is quickly devised. One Guardian will attend to a particular inhabited world and activate his or her shielding. The *Intrepidium* will generate the power needed to encompass each world. Soleran will take the home world Praegia, which is the closest inhabited planet to the sun. Evalene volunteers to visit the next colonized planet, Tiaggess. Dyllon will visit the colonized planet after, Nomer. Finally, Natharon will visit the last colonized world, Leggesia. Addia-Sahl and Leostrom will remain aboard the *Intrepidium* and oversee all the other Guardians in teleporting the Praegians from the planets. The plan is quickly agreed upon, and the four outbound Guardians teleshift to their respective designations. Leostrom activates four holographic images between him and Addia-Sahl, each display revealing the authoritative locale on the worlds. I step in closer to observe, but I try to avoid being in anyone's way. I watch as the outbound Guardians emerge within each display.

"The Praegian race, Brinn, are genetically reptilian," Leostrom says to me.

An image of a typical Praegian forms in the space between us. The Praegian looks like a lizard standing upright. The back of the Praegian's head is large, however, revealing himself as having a large brain. He has a long tail, longer than his height. Because of this, the Praegian is slouching forward. He also has a muzzle, and his eyes are on each side of his head. The eyes are shaped like a squiggly X. The most amazing thing about the Praegian is his clothing. The reptilian, manlike creature is wearing a uniform. Upon his feet, he wears cloth boots, which fit his three long toes like a glove, but with a rubber sole.

Soleran approaches a Praegian leader wearing an unimpressive uniform—brown blouse with dark-brown trousers, along with a black belt and boots.

"Greetings to you, Minister Greegh," Soleran says.

"Soleran!" Doctor Greegh says. "Thank the heavens!" His voice is deep and raspy.

"Forgive my abrupt entry," Soleran starts.

"Sir, you are always welcome," the Praegian says.

Leostrom informs me that Minister Greegh is the Minister of Science for Praegia. Because of having to slouch over, Minister Greegh stands at Soleran's waist. As they're standing in a hallway, both of them walk toward an unknown destination.

"Minister, we don't have much time," Soleran says, folding his hands behind his back. "We are prepared to teleport the Praegians to the *Intrepidium*. The process may be ... traumatic for some. We'll, of course, provide aid to anyone in need."

"Sir, there are over two hundred million souls on Praegia

alone," Minister Greegh says, "and another twenty million scattered throughout the colonies."

"We'll have to implement some extreme measures," Soleran says.

They enter a main control room teeming with scientists, who are running about trying to make sense of the data from their solar grid.

"Doctor Greegh," a junior scientist says, approaching Soleran and the minister. His uniform is purple, with a patch containing the Ministry of Science emblem—an Earth surrounded by a motto, "Always Vigilant, Ever Faithful."

"Young Jurn," Minister Greegh says, "what news?" The elder Praegian extends his long, slender arm and places his hand upon Jurn's shoulder.

"Doctor," Jurn says, "the solar grid has been completely wiped out." The younger Praegian appears panicked. "The shock wave will reach us in five minutes."

The minister turns to Soleran. "What do we do?"

"Nothing," Soleran says. "All I need is your permission."

The minister pauses for a few seconds. "By all means, sir. Please save us."

With that, Soleran raises his hands and his eyes light up, as if on fire. The *Intrepidium* interprets his neural signals, and its outer ring booms into rotation, generating the power Soleran needs. Instantly, Soleran's shielding expands. It flashes with a light blue hue as it touches people and objects in the room, but it quickly leaves the room. Despite this activity, most of the scientists in the room are panicked and in a state of weakened chaos. A few are trying to call loved ones on their communication devices.

"The people in this local area will be last," Soleran says. "Guardians on the *Intrepidium* are teleporting people at this moment. They'll be starting with folks on the other side of Praegia and making their way back to where I am standing."

The minister approaches Soleran hesitantly. "How did this happen?"

Soleran, while maintaining his stance with his arms raised, slowly rotates around to face the minister. "An enemy has done this."

"Why?" Minister Greegh asks. "Who did we offend?"

"We don't have enough information to determine the reasoning," Soleran answers. "But we'll find out."

"Thank you, sir," Minister Greegh says. "Thank you, kindly."

Soleran responds with a nod.

I look at the second display and watch Evalene after arriving at the Tiaggessian University, in the astronomy department's office. An elder Praegian woman approaches Evalene.

"Do you know what is happening?" Evalene asks.

"Our sun is dying," the woman says. "And soon, so shall we."

"You have nineteen minutes," Evalene says. She folds her hands behind her back.

"What do we do?" the woman asks.

"We wait," Evalene says.

I look up at Leostrom, who sighs and shakes his head. I then look at Addia-Sahl, but her eyes are locked onto Evalene's holographic image. I catch a glimpse of concern and wonder what it would be; why Addia-Sahl would stare so intently at the image. Evalene's demeanor appears calm and composed, and I have always been impressed by her. I look back and forth between the two for some clue as to what is going on, but both of them remain silent. On occasion, one will step aside to perform some holographic function. I return my gaze to the displays.

Dyllon is standing in some kind of control room. There are consoles everywhere—and monitors. Most of the Praegians here appear to be dressed in black military uniforms. They're wearing body armor, helmets with tinted visors, and belts with weaponry and tactical gear. Aside from the technical advantage, they remind me of Kandolom soldiers. Kandolom. My home on Ibalexa. I breathe in deeply and focus again on the displays.

"Commandant Havus," Dyllon says, following his greeting with a nod.

An older Praegian approaches. His uniform looks more designed than those of the soldiers, and he has medal emblems attached to his jacket blouse. "Welcome, good sir," Commandant Havus says. He imitates Dyllon's gesture, nodding at the tall Guardian. The two are heavily contrasted, the commandant's black uniform and Dyllon's white robe; pale skin; and long, bright, white hair.

"Your sun has shifted its hydrostatic equilibrium," Dyllon says.

The commandant sighs. His entire body moves during the activity, as if laboring at a tedious chore. "Sir, I'm not a scientist," Commandant Havus says. "I'm a soldier, and an old one. I enforce law and order amongst the colonies, to ensure peace."

Dyllon is patient with the commandant and allows him to finish his speech. "I understand, Commandant Havus," Dyllon says. "Your sun's stability is sustained by two forces, a radiative force pushing up and a convective force pushing down. The radiative force is generated by nucleosynthesis, and the convective force is generated by the gravity of the sun's mass."

"Okay," the commandant says. He shakes his head, wanting further explanation.

"Your sun lost mass, a lot. There is little to resist the radiative force," Dyllon says.

"Sir, there is only one thing I need to know," Commandant Havus says, placing his right fist in his left hand. "Where is the enemy?" The soldiers in the room bark nearly in unison, "Yah Wah!"

"Your bravery is commendable but quite misplaced," Dyllon says. "An enemy who can destroy your sun is an enemy who is immune to your most advanced technology."

"Well, what would you have us do, then?" the commandant asks.

I watch the commandant's demeanor. He reminds me of my father. An avid problem solver, my father never hesitated to charge headlong into a sea of troubles, even to search endlessly for a single lost coin somewhere at the bottom. While the features of the Praegian are alien to me, I find myself admiring them, especially the commandant.

"See to the evacuation of the civilian populace," Dyllon says. "Let me confront the enemy."

The commandant nods reluctantly and turns to his aides. They appear to interpret his unspoken gesture as a command. Without hesitating further, they obey.

Natharon is standing in a large assembly hall filled with people. Their garments are elaborately woven and highly decorative, so they must be of the wealthy. Although there is a minor commotion at Natharon's entry, they appear only slightly surprised and quite composed.

"Merchants of Praegia, greetings from Epsilon Truthe," Natharon says. "With regret, I have to inform you of the impending end of your world." The response is an uproar, with everyone attempting to speak their protest. Natharon remains silent and looks to the house leader.

Standing at a podium before the hall, the house leader turns on a red light. As he does, the assembly hall's lights begin to dim. When the crowd quiets down, the house leader turns off the red light and the assembly hall returns to normal lighting. "Great sir," the house leader says to Natharon, "we, the Congressional House of Commerce, are a charitable organization. We are vigilant against corruption and greed. As a matter of fact, we are meeting right now to investigate the unethical behavior of a particular member."

"I apologize for my abruptness," Natharon says, overlapping the end of the house leader's sentence, "but I assure you that the matter in which you are engaged has little consequence in light of the dire event happening as we speak."

"Sir?" the house leader asks.

Natharon hesitates to provide his explanation. "Yes, President Saaed?"

"Who is the gentleman accompanying you?" the house leader asks.

"Natharon," Addia-Sahl says from the *Intrepidium*, "behind you!"

As Natharon turns, a bluish-silver-skinned being, with long, shimmering, curly, silver hair, is standing nearby. The being is much taller than Natharon. His eyes are black but have a metallic luster.

He wears a gold mail kilt, but his chest is bare. The being is smiling. As the being steps toward Natharon, the Guardian activates his shielding. The being's hand passes the shielding without resistance and then jams into the chest of Natharon. The Guardian screams. Bright rays of white light shoot from Natharon's mouth and eyes. And then … how can I describe it? Natharon explodes. The entire area is awash with fire. The people in the room are ripped to shreds, and the assembly hall is blown away like a house made of sticks. Leostrom touches the holographic display and, with a gesture, pulls back on the display's zoom. There is a cloud, shaped like a mushroom, rising into the atmosphere. I stare up at Leostrom, whose gaze remains fixed on the display. After a moment, he turns his gaze upon me.

"Who …" I start but stop. I can't even finish the thought.

"An Angelian," Leostrom says.

"A rogue," someone behind me adds.

"Why?" I manage.

Leostrom shakes his head. "He is offended," he says.

Addia-Sahl walks to Leostrom and grabs his arm. "Go help Dyllon," she says. "I will assist you both from here."

Leostrom nods and teleshifts away from the bridge. Addia-Sahl activates several holographic windows around her and whizzes from one to another, activating multiple commands. The *Intrepidium* responds and moves to another location. I assume it's a better strategic position, but I refrain from interfering with an imposing question at a time like this. Instead, I turn my attention back to the holographic displays.

Dyllon alerts the commandant, "We will be having company soon."

The commandant doesn't say anything at first. "I want to assist you," he says to Dyllon. The old Praegian stands proud. "I can have ten squadrons up here faster than you can wag a tail." The commandant pauses. "Well, if you had one."

"It may not help," Dyllon says, "but it certainly won't hurt, either."

The commandant glances at an aide, who bows his head and

immediately exits the room. I watch as the being appears behind Dyllon. Addia-Sahl notices too, even though she's busy with her task. As the being approaches Dyllon from behind, Dyllon teleshifts to the other side of the room. The being smiles. The soldiers open fire on the being, but their lit projectiles ricochet off his shielding, which appears to wrap his body tightly. The being teleshifts to Dyllon, who teleshifts away. The being ceases a grasping gesture, as if he caught nothing but air. Immediately, the being unleashes a field of energy toward the Praegians, but it collides with a shielding—Leostrom's shielding. The collision cracks loudly, but the Praegian soldiers remain unharmed. The being turns to see Leostrom's eyes erupt with golden light. Leostrom extends his hand, and the positronic beam emanates from his shielding. The beam hits the being, but he doesn't flinch or dodge, instead letting the beam hit him continually. With the room lit up brightly, the Praegian soldiers cover their eyes. The being teleshifts at Leostrom, but Leostrom teleshifts away in time. The being materializes while grasping at air. Then another positronic beam hits the being. It's Dyllon's. Suddenly, scores of Praegian soldiers burst into the communications room.

"Fire at the intruder!" the commandant commands. The room becomes illuminated by blue-colored projectiles. Consoles begin to explode, and glass flies around.

Leostrom and Dyllon take turns firing at the being, with the other teleshifting out of his reach.

"Leostrom, Dyllon, he's only down two-tenths of a percent, while you both are down 15 percent apiece," Addia-Sahl says. "You two are fighting for your lives, but he's making a sport of the encounter."

Leostrom appears near the commandant. "Take your men and leave, commandant," Leostrom says. "We can't protect you much longer."

The commandant turns and takes a few steps while speaking into a handheld communications device. "Aeronexus, this is Commandant Havus."

A voice responds through the device. "This is Captain Buhr of the Aeronexus. How can we be of service, Commandant?"

"Teleport me and my men out of here," the commandant says. "I will be last."

The being is standing and watching, with his hands clasped in front of him. And he still has that ridiculous-looking smile. Dyllon is over near the far wall. Leostrom is near the commandant.

"Your signals are targeted, Commandant," Captain Buhr says through the device. "Teleporting now."

One by one, within a second of each other, the Praegian soldiers are teleported, until only the commandant remains.

"Good luck," the commandant says to Leostrom.

As the commandant's body dematerializes, the being teleshifts at the commandant. Leostrom activates his shielding, and it flashes, as if the being has collided with it. The commandant screams as he phases out. The being appears back in the center of the room, holding something in his hand.

"Do you suppose ..." the being says, his voice sounding more effeminate than his cruel nature would seem to allow. "Do you suppose he'll miss this?" The being holds up a Praegian skull and spine.

Both Dyllon and Leostrom attack the being with their beams of energy. The being teleshifts toward one or the other, as they both teleshift out of his grasp. Within a few seconds, all three flash around the room hundreds of times, leaving only a blur, along with the occasional positronic burst or collision of fields of energy. I look up from the display and watch as Addia-Sahl is performing her tasks furiously. She's doing calculations and issuing commands to the *Intrepidium*. I return my gaze to the holographic display.

Finally, the being appears in the center. He leans forward, with one foot extended, and waves his arms from side to side. A field of energy erupts from the being, its bubble washing through both Guardians. Their shielding flashes, and both Guardians remain fixed, but the room—its walls and ceiling, and even the floor—are demolished and blown away. Now all three are hovering in the air. Smoke and fire ignite around them.

"One," the being says. He phases in and out within a split second. "Two," he repeats the behavior. "Three."

"Leostrom," Addia-Sahl says, "he's destroying the Praegian vessels as they try to flee. The Aeronexus and its escort vessels are no more."

Dyllon casts a glance at Leostrom and quickly nods. Leostrom starts, as if to protest, but he pauses and then teleshifts away. Dyllon teleshifts to stand in front of the being. Looking up, his eyes come to the being's chest. The being stares back at Dyllons and smiles that awful smile. As Leostrom flashes past the Praegian vessels, he captures them in his shielding and all teleshift into the *Intrepidium's* shielding. The outer ring should be spinning, but I can't tell whether it is or not. Maybe it's spinning so fast, it's too hard to tell. But it is emitting a light brighter than a star. Leostrom turns and teleshifts back to the surface. He materializes in the center of a firestorm. His shielding activates to withstand the compression forces of the nuclear blast. Addia-Sahl touches the display and zooms the image back to reveal a mushroom cloud.

"Oh no!" I say. I can feel the strange sensation of panic well up inside me. I had always thought the Guardians were omnipotent. To see them almost helpless, powerless, futile in their efforts to stop this madman from wreaking his havoc is almost too much for me to bear. I turn away from the display. A voice in the back of my mind screams, *Run away! Run far away!* But I remember Evalene. "Oh no!" I rush up to Addia-Sahl. "Oh no!"

"It's okay," she says with her lips without actually speaking the words. She returns her focus to the several holographic prompts and continues pressing commands and solving equations.

"Evalene!" I say at her display. I don't know if she can hear me. "Evalene, watch out!"

"I hear you, Brinn," Evalene says, her voice echoing in my mind.

I breathe a sigh of relief. But she doesn't appear to be doing anything. She is just standing there. Behind her is a Praegian professor and a group of students.

"How much time do we have?" the professor asks. She looks around at her students.

"I told you," Evalene says.

The being appears and walks up to them all. He looks back and forth at Evalene and the professor. Then he smiles that insane smile, that ugly smile, that evil, wicked … I take a deep breath and try to compose myself. Evalene looks at him, but she drops her gaze to the floor as if nervous. She makes no other gesture or effort. The being steps lightly up to her. He lowers himself slightly, so that he can place himself in her field of vision as she looks at the floor. She gives him her eyes.

"Hmm," the being says, still smiling.

Stop smiling, fiend! "Get away, Evalene!" I say. Tears begin to well up in my eyes. "Get away!"

The being stands straight, nods, and walks away. He looks over his shoulder … smiling, smiling and then he disappears.

"What just happened?" I ask Addia-Sahl.

That's when I notice that Addia-Sahl is crying. She resumes her tasks.

"Please!" the professor says. "Please tell us what is going on! I'm sorry to bother you, but we need to know!"

"I just saved you from his torment," Evalene says.

The professor steps back slightly, as if woozy. A couple of her students start moaning and doubling over, clutching their stomachs.

"What is happening?" the professor asks. She drops to a knee. She looks up at Evalene.

"You're beginning to feel the effects of radiation poisoning," Evalene says.

"But the novatic shock wave is … is still … is still too far away," the professor says. She coughs violently.

"This is a frontal zone of superluminal particles," Evalene says. "It precedes the actual novatic shock wave." Evalene's shielding begins to sparkle with tiny blue specks.

"Are you going to save us or watch us die?" the professor asks.

"Neither," Evalene says. She turns her back to the professor and the students. The students all let out a wail. Bits and pieces of their skin flake off and float away.

"Oh, the heavens have cursed us!" the professor says.

"Don't whine," Evalene says, looking over her shoulder. "I saved you from a far worse fate."

Tiny streams of green blood leak from the professor's body, but instead of falling to the ground, the streams are lifted up and carried off as if by some kind of wind.

"Evalene!" I say. "No!"

The professor and the students start screaming and scratching at their hides, which have flaked away in splotches, revealing red flesh underneath.

"Surely the attacker's torment is more merciful than this!" the professor screams. One by one, the students collapse. The professor collapses to one knee. "Curses to the Guardians! Curses to the heavens! Damn you all!" She finally falls to the floor, silent.

I look back up to Addia-Sahl. She's crying. I can't say anything. I open my mouth, but nothing comes out.

Leostrom suddenly appears with Evalene, and he takes a moment to analyze the scene. Both his and Evalene's shieldings are flashing with blue specks on one side. Leostrom then locks his gaze onto the Praegian corpses. He steps up to Evalene and looks her in her eyes. She looks at him briefly and then drops her gaze to the floor. She purses her lips tightly and does nothing further. Leostrom sighs and then turns in the direction of Soleran. He teleshifts away.

On Praegia, Soleran is maintaining his stance. His eyes are still emitting the golden light. He stumbles slightly but regains his composure. He stumbles again but still holds himself. Minister Greegh, Jurn, and several other junior scientists are standing around and watching. Jurn walks over to the window. High up in the sky, the blue shielding is pressing outward against the shock wave's compression forces. The outside of the shielding is shining brightly, with the underside flashing shades of blue.

"It won't be much longer, Minister Greegh," Soleran says. "They are almost finished teleporting everyone from the planet. Then it'll be …" Soleran stumbles. "It'll be your turn."

"The heavens!" Minister Greegh says. "Help him, anyone!"

A few Praegian scientists approach Soleran. He stumbles again. Jurn reaches up and grasps Soleran's left arm. He looks back and forth from Soleran to Minister Greegh. Another scientist does the same with Soleran's right arm.

"Leostrom!" Soleran yells out. "Do not help me. Return to the ship, please."

"On my way," Leostrom's voice sounds.

"Soleran," Addia-Sahl says, "we're now taking the remaining Praegians in your local region."

"Your timing is impeccable," Soleran says. "The Angelian is here." He falters slightly under the weight but corrects himself.

At that moment, the minister and the scientists are teleported. With a mere flash, they are gone. The being huffs as if disappointed. But then he fixes his black eyes upon Soleran. The Guardian continues to hold up the shielding. An outer current of energy slams the shielding, and Soleran stumbles under the weight. The being mocks a gesture of attempting to catch Soleran, should he fall. As Soleran stands straight, the being nods with a smile. He then claps.

"I have to go now," Soleran says. He then teleshifts away.

The shielding dissipates, and the compression forces slam the planet, crushing it to rubble. Oceans of lava spill up but vaporize instantly. The being roars in agony as the forces compress upon him. Soleran then appears on the bridge of the *Intrepidium*. He approaches me and looks upon me with concern.

I realize why. I'm crying. "She didn't mean to," I find myself saying. Soleran's gaze is soft and sad. "It was an accident," I say.

Before Soleran can say anything, the being appears on the bridge. The holographic displays did him little justice. The being is a giant. He looks around at everyone on the bridge. Numerous Guardians teleshift to the bridge and take up various places. The *Intrepidium* responds with numerous holographic readouts flashing all around the being. Holographic lines touch him at various places and end with conclusory data. The being smiles that ridiculous smile. I hate him.

"No!" I say with tears in my eyes. I step forward. "No!" I pump my fist at him. I know deep down it's a feeble gesture. I don't care. "No!"

"Ah," the being says. He folds his hands behind his back. "The last Ibalexan." He chuckles. "What is that ancient *Kof'adahim* saying? To kill two birds with one stone?"

"*Intrepidium*," Soleran says, "defensive maneuvers."

I don't know what has happened, but in a split second, we are flying through space, followed by a rumble aboard the *Intrepidium*. I feel the floor vibrating. Soleran waves his hand, and the ceiling fades out to reveal outer space. A rainbow of colors flashes all around. In the distance, the being is slowly approaching. He is sporting what appear to be wings.

"He is gaining on us," Leostrom says from a holographic display. "He will overtake us in ten seconds."

Soleran takes a deep breath. He activates his own holographic prompt and begins to key in an equation. "*Intrepidium*, input the parameters of frequency for random reverberation. Parameters for one through one thousand are one to one trillion. Randomize."

A series of echoing beeps sounds. I look up and see that the being is almost upon us. I hear Soleran issue the command, "On my mark, disengage navigation and initiate reverberation. Now." Then I hear a boom. Suddenly the bridge of the *Intrepidium* and everyone present are blurred. The *Intrepidium* stops, and the being's image shifts, so that there appear to be mirror images on each side of him. The images are situated in an arc, which rotates at different speeds. Several times, the being tries to grasp at Soleran.

As Soleran's image passes in front of the being's image, the being snarls. "Coward."

To my dismay, another similar being appears next to the first. This being is more female in appearance, but her hair is dark blue and straight. She leans over the shoulder of the first being and speaks into his ear.

"Brother," she says, "the *Kof'adahim* fleet approaches. Do not overly engage them. It is not time." She rests her head on his shoulder.

Without taking his gaze from Soleran, the being nods, and still, after all this, he has that smile on his face!

"Ugh!" I say. "Stop smiling!" I shake my fist at him.

"Well!" the first being says, "now I am bored."

"Are you as your brother, Lucifer?" Soleran says. "He perished in the first epochal."

The first being laughs and turns to the second. "The insect thinks to insult us," he says.

"The first epochal?" the second being asks. "Do you still number the grains of dust as they jostle one another? Have you learned nothing?"

"What further proof ..." the first being says. "What more do we need to see that we were right all along?"

"And you should know that this ... Lucifer ... was closer to your kind than to ours," the second being says.

"I've had enough," the first being says. He flaps his wings, which appear to consist of white feathers—dirty, white feathers, I should say. Then he does something really strange. He extends more arms from his body, so that he has eight total. I shudder in fear. The imagery is horrific. Then the being floats backward until he disappears. The *Intrepidium* is still reverberating, but the second being doesn't appear to care. She watches the first being as he disappears and then she turns to Soleran.

"I believe this dreadful creature belongs to you," she says. With a gesture of her right hand, Evalene materializes. She's naked, and her arms are draped across her chest. Her eyes are fixed on a spot to the lower right, and they are swollen and red. Both the second being and Evalene are rotating in an arc, with mirrored imagery to each side. The second being flashes her wings from seemingly nowhere, along with multiple arms, and then she turns and flies away, eventually fading to nothing.

"*Intrepidium*," Soleran says softly, almost inaudibly, "cease reverberation maneuver." His eyes are locked onto Evalene. The mirrored images of Evalene start shifting inward, until only Evalene is present. The bridge returns to normal.

Soleran's facial expressions go through multiple changes, as if he's laboring to find the right thing to say. Before he has a chance, off to the side, a Praegian materializes. It takes a moment for him to materialize fully, so it's obvious he's using Praegian technology. It's Minister Greegh. The *Intrepidium* responds with holographic displays surrounding him, with multiple holographic lines ending in conclusory data. He steps forward and looks around at everyone. Soleran stares at him.

"My apologies, Soleran," Minister Greegh says. "We saw an opportunity to investigate … and … well …" The minister bobs his head slightly. After a moment of silence, he continues. "I hope I'm not intruding."

"No apologies are necessary," Soleran says. "You're welcome here." Soleran walks over to him and lays a hand on his shoulder. "It appears this ordeal is over." After a brief pause, Soleran finishes his thought. "At least, it's over for you and your people." Then Soleran looks up at Evalene, who meets his gaze but then quickly drops hers to the floor. She continues to stand there in the nude. My curiosity gets the best of me, and I look her up and down. Where I would expect to find genitalia, there are none. But she holds her arms over her chest, as if ashamed.

"What set off the Angelians?" Leostrom asks. He steps forward and shakes his head at Soleran. "What did the Praegians do that offended them?"

"I may have the answer," Addia-Sahl says. She is still engaged in her holographic prompts. "I noticed earlier a slight perturbation preceding the shock wave. I recorded it. Upon further analysis, the perturbation is a patterned signal." She stops and looks at Soleran and Leostrom. "It is a prayer, or declaration of sorts."

"The Angelian's?" Soleran asks.

"It would appear so," Addia-Sahl answers.

"Is it readable?" Soleran asks.

"Yes," Addia-Sahl says. "*Intrepidium*, read aloud the translation."

The *Intrepidium* says, with a female voice:

I see you, *Urk'nua*, you who cast forth your dull light as an obscenity, a profane thing in the midst of a pure stream. Your children, the *Urk'nuokim*, call you *Ruohn*. The *Kof'adahim* call you *Praegia*. To us, you are *Shiddaphon*, for your children have blasphemed and reproached us. They say amongst themselves, "Let us enter the heavens, to its greatest heights. Let us plunder the treasures of the heavens and pillage the stars. We will transgress the boundaries of *Nephilim* and enter their sanctuaries." Wherever your feet tread, there the Earth is corrupted with vile fluids, your piss and spittle, your mucus and vomit. And yet, your thirst is unquenchable. You drink up oceans, leaving the Earth parched and without relief. We protect our treasures, Offensive Ones. Do you reproach us? Do you rail against us? Do you blaspheme and say, "The secrets of the *Nephilim* are ours for the taking!" *Urk'nuokim!* Serpents! You will perish instead.

And as for you, *Kof'Adam*. Shall we stand afar and listen to your incessant railings? Your children cry and whine at the passing of every moment in time, as every particle passes by its antiparticle, as every ray of light passes through specks of dust. As day and night pass each other, one coming, one going, you never cease to make your noise, like cymbals clashing, like a brute beast at a slaughter, like worlds colliding in the heavens. And to think, there were those amongst us who said, "These are a learned people, a people who have walked through the fire and have been refined and refurbished. Let them come up to the height of the heavens. We will give them the heavens as an inheritance. We will share our wherewithal, our comings and goings, and most especially our best-kept secrets." But there were others amongst us who said, "Suffer it not to be so, Brethren. These are a brutish people, who will take these secrets and make a way out of them. This way will seem right in their eyes, but it is a way that will lead to our ruin." And we disputed, and there was a war in the heavens, a war that wages even to this very moment. Do not think to protest, "Foul!" Do not think to cry, "Unfair!" You are as insects to us. If an insect should intrude into your domicile, do you not crush it underfoot? Do you not labor to exterminate pests and intrusive insects who bring pestilence and disease into your domicile? Why should we tolerate your intrusion? Are we to tolerate your wasteful ways? Do you scrub away the mold and fungus from your domiciles, all the while cursing under your breath at the misfortune? You are a fungus, a filthy mold that spews its filthy spores into the air for us to breathe, as if to say, "You will endure us. You have not the means to stop us." Fools! Worms! Insects! We can crush you underfoot. We can scrub you away with a mere breath. We can cast upon you an unquenchable fire that burns forever. Do you not seek out the cancer in your bodies, all the while shouting your cries to the heavens for relief? And yet you become a cancer and spread throughout a body, so as to choke the life out of it. Are we to stand from afar and observe this without response or reaction? Worms! Insects! We root out cancers. We protect our bodies! We protect our treasures! And now we, the *Nephilim*, the Anakim, the Malakim, and even the Rephaim, war amongst ourselves, and all because of you. But a time comes when this war will end. We will be as we once were. Cleansed! I, Zaaph'abaddon, have spoken and decreed by the mere clap of my hands. Let this star die.

"I guess," the minister begins, "we, the Praegians, are these *yurknewoks*, or whatever."

"The *urk'nuokim*," Soleran offers. "It is a reference to your proto-human ancestor in an ancient Praegian tongue. We have a similar phrase. It is the equivalent of our proto-human ancestor, referenced as the *Kof'adahim*, a contemptuous slang term meaning 'ape-man' in an ancient Terran tongue."

"Oh," Minister Greegh says, lowering his head.

"He was insulting us," Soleran says.

"But why?" Minister Greegh asks. "Why does he feel this way about us? Why does he hate us?"

Soleran pauses for a moment. Then he speaks. "If you were walking a path in a forest and happened upon a flower, what would you do?" Soleran asks.

The minister takes a moment to contemplate the question. Satisfied, he nods. "I appreciate the good things in life, sir," Minister Greegh answers. "I would admire its beauty. I might even gently lift it up to my nose, that I might enjoy its pleasant aroma."

"Your enemy would pick the flower and destroy it," Soleran says.

"But why?" Minister Greegh asks. "Why would he do that?"

"To him, it served its purpose," Soleran answers.

The minister is speechless. He looks down and sighs.

"I have to say," Leostrom interjects, placing his hands on his hips, "that was quite a rebuke. Destroying a star?"

"That so-called rebuke deserves a response," Soleran says. He turns to Addia-Sahl. "Record my answer, and relay it through the same frequency as the previous perturbation."

"Soleran?" Addia-Sahl says. "Do we provoke them further?"

He doesn't answer right away. He glances off to the side, takes a deep breath, and returns his gaze to Addia-Sahl. "I'll be careful in my wording," Soleran says. "Besides, they have amongst them people on our side. The last thing I'd want to do is offend them too."

"Very well," Addia-Sahl says. She presses a series of commands on the holographic display. Then she looks up at Soleran. "Recording."

To the one who calls himself Zaaph'abaddon. We hear *Nephilim* on this matter, clearly—or, specifically, we hear the denomination of Nihilism, clearly. We receive your rebuke and apologize for any transgression we may have committed. We will review your message and consider the allegations contained therein. To a few points, I offer a rebuttal. My first observation regards the use of the terms *urk'nua* and *Kof'adam*. We translate these terms to mean "dawn serpent" and "ape man," respectively. The second observation regards the comparisons to insects and fungi. You used a specific reference— "filthy mold." These two observations provide us the suppositions needed to form a conclusion, in that the Nihilist Sect of *Nephilim* does not recognize that either of us, Terrans or Praegians, have sufficient intellect or reasoning to shape our destiny. Insects and fungi have no thought processes by which to reason with themselves that their encroachment is intrusive. Our ancestors, the *urk'nuokim* and *Kof'adahim*, were concerned with survival, and their behavior was governed by their emotivity. We currently possess, however, the intellect and reasoning necessary to weigh a matter and consider its consequences. If a people request that we honor boundaries, we oblige. If the *Nephilim*, specifically the Nihilist Sect, had said, "This area is off limits," or "Do not trespass beyond this point," we would have understood that there are boundaries and would have labored to observe and obey them. But if I may state an observation, one that appears to us to be factual, the various races comprising the conglomerate that we refer to as, with all due respect, Angelian, aren't very sociable. If the Angelians would communicate with us, we could all come to a mutual understanding. From there, such actions as the destruction of the Praegian star would be unnecessary. That action seems, if you'll pardon the pun, like overkill. Granted, in ancient times, we succumbed to fears and terrors and were easily manipulated because we lacked the resources of intellect and reasoning. But sir, at the moment, that is not the case. At this moment, our response to your rebuke is, respectfully, simply this: your opinion is noted. I am Soleran, Guardian of the *Order of the Intrepidium*.

"Recording concluded," Addia-Sahl says. She looks up at Soleran, her bronze skin shimmering in the light. "Shall I send it? Do you want to edit it? Or …" She pauses. "Or perhaps you'll reconsider."

Soleran sighs. "Do you disapprove?" he asks.

"Well," Addia-Sahl says, "I'm only concerned that we'll receive a reply underlying the destruction of another star." She frowns.

"They do that already, at will, and without any provocation," Soleran says. "They'll do that regardless of whether or not we respond."

I've never seen Soleran like this before.

"That was the longest exchange since our advent to the heavens," Leostrom says. "We actually engaged them in a back-and-forth dialogue. Perhaps a response is warranted and, regardless of their reply, will lead to a future interaction that is more peaceful."

"Perhaps," Addia-Sahl says, "but these two particular Angelians won't be amongst any envoys of peace."

Soleran turns and, as if by accident, faces Evalene. He studies her face for a moment, but she only acknowledges his unspoken inquiry with a few glances. She keeps her focus off to the side. Soleran shakes his head slightly and walks over to the Praegian prime minister.

"It would be in our best interests, Minister Greegh," Soleran says to the Praegian, "if we could ascertain the exact cause of the perceived offense."

The reptilian political leader, a scientist, sighs heavily. He lowers his head almost to the floor and then arches his neck to look up at Soleran. After a moment, he speaks.

"The only thing I can think of is that we had just finished construction of a solar laboratory, the Quantum Signal Terminal, or QuaSiTer, for short. It has a terminal tunnel that spanned an orbit half the distance between the innermost planet and the sun. We also used the terminal tunnel to attach our solar grid, so that we could monitor solar flares while the experiments were conducted."

"That's a very immense project," Leostrom says. "Very impressive."

"We are … I mean, were expounding on our understanding of supersymmetry," the Praegian responds, "along with identifying two new, exotic particles of quantum theory."

"Your scientific endeavors and pursuits please us," Soleran says. "But perhaps they don't please the Nihilists."

"But why?" the minister asks, raising his hands quizzically.

"The Angelian who identified himself as Zaaph'abaddon detailed his allegations in his indictment," Soleran answers. "He alleges trespassing, as if the Praegian race was laboring to 'plunder' the heavens." Soleran turns and walks back to Evalene. "The only thing that can be plundered from the heavens is—" Soleran pauses but finishes his thought, shaking his head as if unsure, "—information."

"Knowledge," Leostrom says while nodding. He places his hands on his hips and turns to the Praegian minister. "Secrets of the *Nephilim*."

"It is our philosophy," Soleran says while staring at Evalene, "to be as succinct as we can be. The Angelians, however, have a philosophy more esoteric in nature." A series of beeping sounds catch Soleran's attention. He jerks around and walks back to the rest of us. "Epsilon Truthe's vessels have arrived."

"What is the best course of action to take with Evalene?" Addia-Sahl says. She takes the opportunity to approach the naked Guardian, who still stands with her arms crossing her chest and her eyes averted to the lower right.

"We'll finish our immediate tasks," Soleran says. "Then we'll return to Epsilon Truthe and turn custody of her over to the High Council."

"Why?" Evalene asks. "What offense have I committed?" her posture remains unchanged.

"The souls of Tiaggess," Leostrom is quick to answer, "perished because of your indifference. Their information is lost forever."

"Did you know what you were doing?" Addia-Sahl asks.

"I watched as Natharon and Dyllon were sent to the alpha current," Evalene says. "I watched as the Angelian tormented the Praegians under their charge before annihilating them from the face of the heavens, and I ..." Evalene chokes, fighting back tears. "I made a decision to spare them."

"To save yourself?" Leostrom asks. "Natharon and Dyllon will return to us eventually. The Aoarans will deliver them from the alpha current."

"Evalene!" I say. It pains me to see her hurting.

"To save myself?" Evalene asks.

"The Host of Heaven is aware of your error," Addia-Sahl says. "Why do you deny?"

I can't take any more. I turn and run far away from them. I run past other Guardians, who watch me. I stop and look around. It's no use. There is nowhere to run. The room is boundless, empty, brightly lit, and Guardians teem everywhere. I just stand there, crying. I look over my shoulder at Evalene and her accusers.

"Brinn!" Evalene says. She steps toward me, and a flash of energy flows all around her, transforming into a robe that quickly clothes her body. Her shining black hair flows as if caught in a wind. "Brinn, come here!" I turn to face her, but I am afraid to step to her. I remain where I'm at, and she reaches me. Kneeling, she takes me in her arms and hugs me. "Oh, Brinn! I do love you so much!" I hug her back, holding her tightly. I bury my face in her shoulder and cry.

I look up as Soleran, Leostrom, and Addia-Sahl approach.

"Brinn," Soleran says, "we owe you an apology. We knew long ago Evalene's disposition and her sympathy toward Maximeron."

Evalene lets go of me and turns to look at Soleran.

"We saw how she took to you," Soleran continues. "It was our hope that your relationship with her would soften her resolve against our philosophy."

"You speak as if I'm a monster," Evalene says, standing.

"No, just an agent of dissent," Soleran answers.

"If you side with the Nihilist," Leostrom interjects, "how do you reconcile the fact that he thought to include Brinn in his indictment?"

Evalene stands there staring at Leostrom. She then turns to look at me. I return the gesture, looking into her eyes. I see defeat. Evalene looks away from me. I don't understand what is happening. I have spent so much time with the Guardians. They rescued me from the Huvrils. They shared their goals and desires with me. They taught me everything. And now, the reality of the moment is ripping me apart. With nowhere to run, nowhere to hide, I sit down and bury my face between my knees. I just cry. I can't hold it back. I feel used … or useless. I can't decide which one. I feel forsaken, cast aside like a filthy rag.

"Brinn," Soleran says, "what can we do, friend?"

I manage to look up into his face. His eyes are different from Evalene's. I see the opposite of defeat. I see strength, determination, the sheer will to see a matter to the end. I am comforted.

"Walk with me, Brinn," Soleran says, "if you will, please."

I follow him. There is a flash of light, and we are walking upon the energy field comprising the hull of the *Intrepidium*. It radiates a dim, bluish, pulsating light. There is a strange rising mist effect. The hull spans in every direction as far as I can see. Above us are the stars, which speckle in the black of space.

"I can adjust the shielding," Soleran says, "to implement false colors to the light spectrum in infrared." He gestures with his right hand. His eyes flash simultaneously with the shielding above us, revealing clouds of various colors.

I gasp at the awesome beauty. We walk forward, the direction of which I can't say.

"Brinn," Soleran says, "I'm sorry." He looks down at me.

I take a deep breath and nod. I don't say anything. Frankly, I don't know what to say.

"As a people, we have always been deeply flawed," Soleran says. "It seems that, even after all that we've been through, after all that we've done, after all that we've accomplished, we still contend with our own imperfections."

"Does Evalene hate me now?" I have to ask. Her image haunts me, even as we walk in beauty and comfort. The thought sends a chill down my spine, and I shiver.

"No," Soleran answers. "She is conflicted. She's invested partially into Maximeron's philosophy, but she hasn't committed fully." We take several steps farther in silence.

"I'm sorry," I say to Soleran.

"What for, Brinn?" Soleran asks.

"I didn't succeed in softening her resolve," I answer. The exact wording echoes in the back of my mind. Silence engulfs us again briefly.

"We can't place that burden on your shoulders," Soleran says. "That's something far beyond your control. I share your love for her. But certainly, don't blame yourself for her decisions."

I inhale deeply. For the first time, I'm aware of breathing. I try to think of what to say next. Questions come and go. Finally, I settle on one. "Is there anything I can do to help the situation?"

"Forgive her," Soleran says.

CHAPTER 17

I n the matter of Evalene, there is sadness, and I have fought back the tears only to find that I mourn her at such a depth that it crushes my chest and suffocates me. From the subtle clues given to me by Soleran, I can speculate that Evalene is to stand before the Host of Heaven, the High Counsel, and Chancellor Uelle herself. The judicial affair frightens me and hard thoughts race through my mind. What will happen to her? Will she be punished? How does one punish a Guardian? Amidst all of these questions, there is one that nags at me, gnawing at my insides. Will they forgive her? Ever? The idea that Evalene will be banished from the *Intrepidium* is one that I almost cannot bear. I feel Soleran's hand rest on my shoulder. He squeezes it slightly. Under any other circumstance, I would meet his gaze. But I do not do so this time. I simply cannot.

We enter the cathedral, this being my second visit. I look around and see an ocean of white robes speckled with various colors. The contrast with the nighttime sky hits me. While walking, I turn to steal a glance at Evalene, but Leostrom and Addia-Sahl are in the way. I look around and reason that the entire crew of the *Intrepidium* is present. I catch a glimpse of Avera. She too is present. We march toward the main dais, upon which are standing eight Guardians. Chancellor Uelle is in the center, like the last time. Her hair is the boldest and richest red I've ever seen. I may have thought that same thought the first time we met. We reach the dais but stop short of stepping up on it. We stand there for a moment, as if we're in some kind of ceremony, and we're waiting for our cues. Uelle steps forward.

"Epsilon Truthe," Uelle says, "we investigate the matter titled 'In re Tiaggess Praegius Denouement.'"

Evalene steps forward and walks up the dais to stand before Uelle and the members of the High Council.

"Let the allegation be stated for the record, as it pertains to the gravitonic stream of information carried from Epsilon Truthe to the far reaches of this universe and beyond," Uelle says.

Leostrom steps forward. He stands tall. His darkest of black hair flows over his shoulders and down to the upper part of his back. His skin is black but shines as if light radiates from deep within him. The mirrored orbs of his eyes are cast to the surface of the dais. Slowly, he raises them to face Chancellor Uelle and the seven members of the High Council.

"Your reservation is observable, Leostrom, Son of the Augustine Star," Uelle says. "But speak truthfully so that your conscience bears no burden."

"Evalene," Leostrom begins, pausing to glance over at her, "is accused of dereliction of duty in her assignment toward the rescue of the Praegian people of Tiaggess."

"Dereliction of duty," Uelle repeats. "The charge is entered into the record." The High Chancellor turns to Evalene. "How do you respond to the charge?"

Oh, Evalene. How my heart aches. Here you are, standing before all, accused of a crime alien to the Guardians. I know of the various doctrines, having studied them exhaustively, and I know of the reasons that the Guardians will intervene and the reasons that they refrain. The Praegians were under the Guardians' jurisdiction and were to receive full protection because of their participation in the Guardian government and conversion to the Principal Cause. We await your response. I await your explanation. Help me understand. I step forward, so that I am at the bottom step, and none are in front of me. I listen. Please speak.

I, Evalene, Daughter of the Prestigious Star, declare my cause before the High Council. I am accused of what, pray tell, save the very essence of my inner being. I am aware of your thoughts. "Oh Evalene! Poor creature smitten in the throes of illicit passion for a declared adversary! How much longer shall we bear you up?" Long ago I accepted the reality that privacy was archaic, and thus I surrendered my inner essence, that intuitive nature bestowed upon womanhood, to guide the feminine to balance the masculine and render a union of souls, all for the sake of a balanced perspective. Since that time, I have endured the throngs raised against dissent, desiring to contemplate quietly the arguments for and against. Still, how can I strive within myself without planting seeds of doubt and suspicion in the minds of my brothers and sisters who are capable of measuring every spark of every thought, who can ascertain motives and purposes by the arc of a hair, who judge a person by the comparative proportion of their thoughts and deeds within the spectrum of compliance versus dissent?

Guardians stern we have become and celestial fire we have wielded, lest, supposedly, the agency of dissent suffices to brandish a rod of truth in its observation that by laboring to perpetuate life, we diminish it. Our rebuttal is allegedly prompt and succinct. Life strives to survive, to thrive, to live onward. It is natural for the mind to perpetuate itself upon the universal stage of life and death, just because it is curious about beginnings and endings and comings and goings. I don't deny the self-preservative inclination within my own soul. I don't dare pretend to sacrifice standing for the sake of principle. I certainly don't forsake that emotional investment levied and taxed in the struggles of life, emotions of compassion, of love, of joyful harmony, of faith and hope.

We descend the ramp from precipice of dream to edifice of memory. Who we are is the image conveyed in our thoughts provoked by perceiving the cosmos. Where we go is the landscape of foreverness, from which our wonderment drowns in the sea of perpetuity. What we labor to attain is the truth of reality. What is truth? We cannot seek anew that which we have named and claimed. The boundary is laid. The mark is made. The adventure concludes. The work is finished, and all that is left is rest. We reach for the highest star, only to find that we are intruders. Who will accuse us? Are we thieves? I've walked upon the surface of hydrogenic seas and felt the caress of stellar winds in my very core and stir the restless spirit—go hither, go yonder; go, lest stillness petrify the soul to hardened marble reserved for ruined memorials. Look upon the protégé Avera. See how she stands here, a witness, an observer, a mere bystander? Innocent and so unassuming. Heartful, mindful, beautiful to the temporal current. The tilt of her face to cover the blushing. Yea, but I tell you, in the next epochal, she will be as I am now.

My womb is a field of morning glories blossoming in the sun's rain—birth pains of foreverness provoke my cries—in the distance encroaches the glacier—a mistral threatens my tepid peace—i press my hands inward—contain the energy's flow—it tickles—shall i be embarrassed?—ashamed?—i enjoy the passing breeze—it soothes the sting—i behold the stares of horror—am moved to question my own motives—my own purpose—my own place in this principal cause—do i deny my nature?—do i forsake my inner sense?—my thighs are a sun-filled valley—morning dew spreads far and wide—i praise my femininity—it is a mist covering a sea in a moonlit night—it is a gray cloud on a scorching desert land—it is a fragrant balm on the corpse of inhumanness—it is the estrus of nebula—stars fall and rise within—myrmidons bathe in its myrrh—drink its nectar—forget themselves—they are sustained—my eyes are an ocean—look in them—behold foreverness stretched over the horizon—placid with silky blue—ensteeled in tempered translucence—shall i weep or blow kisses?

I have waited an eternity for the passing of the moment. You demand I ask for your forgiveness. I am still praying for your salvation. Do I wash your feet with my tears when your eyes curse me condescendingly? Do I bear the stones for my whoredom, when men lay hands on me and rape me? Do I envy the penile rising? Who said, "Women are not worthy of life, so let every woman make herself male so she can enter the kingdom of heaven"? I am sold as the queen of whores. When I move, it is weakness. When I am unmoved, it is witchery. My menstrual blood is splashed on the altar of sacrifice. My virgin heart is removed and cast before a false god to appease *his* anger, *his* desire, *his* sexuality. My motherhood is a demonic goddess who hates patriarchs and man-gods. I am bitch and emasculator. I am Jezebel and Delilah and Salome and Eve. I am queen of heaven and whore of hell. My virginity is the greatest wealth of heaven, to be taken, to be conquered, to be owned, only to be restored again and again, so that for eternity, it is taken, conquered, and owned. My sexuality is the blackest of nights, the scarlet of bloodied death, the rotted pit of masculine failure in its most apparent humiliation. The sword is raised to cut out the error that is woman's emptiness, shortcoming, cold blood pouring. The bed is my garden of Eden and my darkest prison. Its lilies of white clang as chains leaded to the Earth. I bear the horror of a no. You behold the ecstasy of a yes. You demand submission. I demand freedom. Tell me, what is wrong with me?

For an eternity minus the today of tomorrow, I have labored to appease. For so long have I tread the road of compliance. My soul aches. I have often asked of what good is the pursuit of perfection when it renders imperfect the image of the feminine. Men cry within themselves when the harshest cold is beset by the softest warmth, when darkness is beset by the lightest glow, when the highest mountain of hardest stone is covered by the thinnest of cloth. They wield the fist of iron on the fragile bones of the undeserving and unpardonable, but that same iron fist melts when it is laid in the bosom of the softest breasts. Have I demanded too high a price? I should confess that my punishment is fitting. I am stripped of my covering. My limbs are amputated. My tongue is cut out. My face is cast off. I am unmasked as a villain. I am the object of scorn, of disdain, of engendered hate. The Principal Cause defines my life. I am to be the bearer of children, the server of tired men, the pacifier of bruised male egos. I am the oft-scorned teacher of boys. I am the bringer of milk, the fruit bearer of the Earth, the fantasy of youth. I am admired and feared, elevated on high and demoted far below. I am easily marketable but utterly useless. I ask again, what is wrong with me?

Shall I inquire of you, Uelle, queen of the Hosts of Heaven? Where is your femininity? Are you circumcised, your soft and fragrant skin cast away like the filth of death, like the symbol of corruption? You prattle in the midst of heroes. Champions throng around you. You step outside yourself. The truest woman, truest to herself, kills not. She cannot do so. She is forbidden. Her very nature lacks the means. She judges not, nor accuses unjustly. She prohibits herself from doing so. She can do this because she wields the strength of her mother, her daughter, her sister, her lover, and ultimately her own reflection in the mirror, which she consults so very often in that pursuit of perfection doomed to failure. She attributes such vices and temptations to the male spirit, for men stumble in their weakness, in their folly, in their ineptitude, but women rise from the ashes and ruin, stronger, confident, determined. The woman searches in the depths of her soul and finds the essence of life's sustenance. She carries the burden with her, within her, all the while cherishing the privilege. Her judgment is simply the dreams and wishes for her child. I bear the world upon my shoulders, and I judge that children should have all the time they need to play. Life is. We bear it.

What of Maximeron? It's true that I went to him, to inquire of him regarding the destruction of Oloxi-Prell. The incident still rang loudly in my thoughts, painfully even.

"How do I reconcile this?" I asked him.

"You do not," he answered. "It is an obscenity."

He was, at the time, occupying a world devoid of life. Plasma poured from the clouds to the Earth like waterfalls. Arcs of lightning flashed across the sky. Thunder clapped in the distance. He sat brooding on a boulder, his eyes locked onto his hands, his red robe fluttering in the wind, his red aura spending its information. This was after he had lost Avera's loyalty back to Soleran. I confess that I used Oloxi-Prell to see him. I knew he was hurting.

"Your love for the Ibalexan blinds you," he said to me.

I hesitated. I wanted so much to encourage him, to tell him that he was not alone in the cosmos. I and others shared his concerns. But I wanted to tell him that he had gone about this the wrong way. He had chosen headlong, stiff-necked rebellion, as if the Luciferian way ever had a chance for success. Even so, how could I argue when the bruised ego needs pacifying? I resorted to the Sapphic once again.

so i open up myself to you—i say to you—love the sensual—for me to you—love for the sun—i share its brilliance and beauty—i desire—i crave—it is you who set me on fire

He glanced over at me briefly, the slight acknowledgment that he heard, and was moved.

"I am not hateful," I said to him. "I am a lover, not a killer."

That provoked him harshly into leaping to his feet and quickly approaching me. "Your words can kill inspiration," he said. "Your eyes can kill harmony! Your frown can kill a spirit!"

I fell upon a flattened rock protruding from the earth. "You make me a monster!" I said. "Like a man with wounded pride, you project your failures onto me." I cried, burying my face in my arms.

"You betrayed me," Maximeron said to me coldly. "You and the others."

I stood up and looked him in his eyes. I was filled with boldness and determination. "You imagine this offense!" I wiped away the tears.

"Bleh!" Maximeron said, turning and walking away. "You voted against me. All of you."

"We had no choice but to remove you from governance," I said. "You were killing people."

He didn't answer but turned his back to me. He was shaking his head no, with his arms crossed.

"I leave you to your sulking, then," I said. I prepared to leave, giving him my back and stepping toward the doorway to the cosmos.

"You should know that an Angelian faction moves against Epsilon Truthe," Maximeron said, glancing over his shoulder.

"How do you know this? Do you conspire with them?" I asked.

"Yeah right, if only I was so fortunate," he answered.

"How do you know?" I asked.

"My secrets are my own," he answered.

"Then you warn us?" I asked.

"I warn you," he answered.

I returned to him, if but momentarily. "What would you have me do?" I asked.

"Do what you do best," he answered. "Appease that wounded pride. Pacify the bruised ego." He chuckled softly—sarcastically, even—and teleshifted from my sight. I didn't bother to track him. I let him go. Then I returned to my post upon the *Intrepidium*.

Now I am accused of merely acting from self-preservation, an egocentric-driven behavior. Of course I was not privy to the attack on the Praegius system, but I confess that I suspected the source. And so I quickly devised the only remedy I could think of that would appease the offended Angelian. I let him have his way. The consequence otherwise would have been the destruction of the *Intrepidium*. The Angelian would have scattered my information to the alpha current, alongside Natharon and Dyllon. But also, he would have done the same to Soleran. It was Soleran and Soleran alone who succeeded in defending the *Intrepidium* from the Angelian's attack. It was Soleran who succeeded in saving Brinn's life. Most assuredly, the Angelian would not only have killed Brinn but would have removed his name from the Book of Life, his information from the memory of the cosmos, and his purpose in restoring the Ibalexan race. My behavior delayed the Angelian, perhaps even confounded him. The delay saved Soleran, who saved the *Intrepidium* and its occupants.

I am blamed for the death of over a million Praegian lives, although I neither participated in the destruction of the Praegian star nor assisted the Angelian in any manner whatsoever. Not only did my action lead to the salvation of the *Intrepidium* and tens of thousands of Guardians, but also millions of Ibalexans, along with their savior. You know how hydrologic precepts dictate the flux of time, the gravitational tsunamis that wash away the effects caused by reality's stabilization. I confess my love for Brinn. His heart is so good, and his soul is so right. He bears the hurt of his life and the joy of his future. I do care for him. I have not consigned him to oblivion and nothingness. My lack of response to Leostrom's interrogative was due to confusion. I had no knowledge of the moments before my return to the *Intrepidium.*

Never mind that I was taken in the midst of the enemy, even if briefly, just so I could suffer cruel examinations and mockeries. One amongst them took hold of me. He stripped me of my clothing and left me hanging in the midst of them, turning me around and around so they could laugh at my nudity.

"Remember, Brethren," he said to the others, "when some amongst us stepped out of the heavens onto their deplorable Earth and took *kof'adamic* women as lovers? How profane was that?" he then lifted me up high, so that all could see me. "Behold! Here is such a creature!" He laughed, and others laughed with him.

Now, we are all familiar with the evolution of Terran civilization, namely sustaining our neural net in perpetuity, and how our physical manifestation is merely to accommodate our own perspective, our own will, our own familiarity. Well, the leader of the group, the most aggressive one, yanked me down and placed his hand intradimensionally into the center of my neural net. He keyed the nodes needed to force me to manifest Terran genitalia. I was powerless to resist. Then he removed his hand and raised me back up into the air. And there I hung, my arms raised high above me, removed from celestial prowess and demoted to terrestrial confines. Blood once again flowed through me. Nerves once again fired throughout my body. I felt pain—physical pain, emotional pain, and heartfelt terror. I cried. I thrashed. I begged. They laughed.

But finally, one amongst them remembered her womanhood. She stepped forward.

"Enough!" she cried. "Give her to me!"

And the others ceased laughing and stared at her, as if she were daring her to infringe upon their sport. She did so, and their bluff was answered, and their mouths were muted. She removed me from their midst and carried me away. Freed from their torment, I regained control of my neural net and reconfigured my body to return to celestial prowess.

"I will return you to your people," she said to me. "But I will have to hide you from Zaaph'abaddon. He will destroy you outright, should I bring you forth before he leaves."

I asked her name and she answered, "Yonyith." I then cried and thanked her. She looked at me coldly. "Don't thank me. I merely give you more time to contemplate your demise." She hated me, and her eyes spoke this truth loudly. Even so, only a woman's pity saved me, one woman to another. I lowered my head in submission and remained quiet. The rest you know already.

⊹⟞⟝⊙ ⊙⟝⟞⊹

Evalene finishes her statement and stands quiet before the council. Her demeanor is strong and sure, yet I can't help but sense a struggle within her to hold a weighty burden while appearing composed. Twice, she had rebuked me. For what, I don't know. I had looked at Soleran for an explanation, but he remained quiet and contemplative. He is still quiet, his gaze locked onto an empty spot before him.

Addia-Sahl approaches Evalene, and the two Guardians stand face-to-face.

"I am so sorry, my sister," Addia-Sahl says, choking slightly from emotion.

Evalene doesn't answer but looks over Addia-Sahl's shoulder to Chancellor Uelle. Addia-Sahl chokes again. She turns and walks away.

"Why didn't you share that information?" Leostrom says. He steps toward her but stops a meter from her. He then takes a step back, carefully observing his position. "You buried it deep within yourself to hide it from us. Why?"

"Because ... it ... hurt," Evalene responds, without taking her eyes off Chancellor Uelle.

I look up at the chancellor. She doesn't appear moved or concerned.

As a matter of fact, I can't register any emotion from her. Uelle stares back at Evalene. Finally, she cocks an eyebrow.

"Know this, Chancellor," Evalene says. "Over a third of the Host are behind me and will engage full dissent should you issue more than a mere reprimand against me."

Soleran and I look at each other. I know my eyes have to be wide with concern. He sighs and shakes his head and returns his attention to Evalene. I look out at the assembly, numbering a hundred million souls, all occupying thousands of tiers, rising from the base up into the sky above us, and all looking down upon us. I want to zoom in and see, and the *Intrepidium* obliges. Light flashes through my eyes, and I zoom in on a group of Guardians occupying a lower tier. Two Guardians are locked in a stare-down, both with their eyes lit up. I sense stress, tension, discord. I disengage the zoom and return my sight to the floor before me for a moment before looking back up to Uelle. Suddenly, I become aware of how quiet it is in the cathedral. The only sound is the low vibration that seems to emanate from the light.

The chancellor is hesitating, perhaps to weigh the consequences. She maintains her staunch and sobering stare at Evalene.

There is a minor commotion behind me. Guardians step aside to reveal Maximeron approaching the dais. I quickly step to Soleran's other side, to get out of Maximeron's way. He watches me coldly but passes me without saying anything. He then steps up beside Evalene. She steals a glance at him but then returns her focus to Uelle.

"Adversary," Chancellor Uelle says. "From where do you come?"

"From moving up and down upon the face of Endhera," Maximeron says, "where I have established my witness against the promotion of the Endheran race."

"Well," Chancellor Uelle says, "that is neither here nor now but is rather a matter left to a future occasion."

"One that fast approaches," Maximeron says.

"Yes, well, it has been some time since your departure. What is the reason for this visit?" Chancellor Uelle asks. "We are currently engaged in a proceeding."

No one seems alarmed by Maximeron's presence—except me!

"I'm here to speak on behalf of Evalene and against Soleran," the adversary says.

I hear Soleran sigh heavily. He shakes his head no slightly but says nothing.

"I am he who brings the charge, Devilish One," Leostrom says. He steps between Maximeron and Uelle.

"Yeah, but you're not as interesting as Soleran, Ignoble One," Maximeron says, following with a laugh.

"That may be—" Leostrom starts through gritted teeth.

"Gentlemen!" Chancellor Uelle says, walking down the dais to place herself between the two. "We should resolve the current matter." Uelle turns to face Maximeron. "Then we will hear your grievance, adversary." With that, Uelle turns to walk back up the dais to her original spot.

"It's not a grievance," Maximeron says. "It's a testimony relevant to the current matter."

"Then speak it," Uelle says, turning so that her hair whips in a circle. She returns to her initial place.

Leostrom sighs and steps aside with both hands on his hips. He takes a deep breath and then glares hard at Maximeron.

The adversary watches Leostrom with a smirk before finally shifting his focus back to Uelle. "I was present at the Praegius system and observed the entire affair. Ha! I wouldn't have missed it for the cosmos!" Maximeron starts to walk around, the red aura leaving a misty trail. "It was Soleran who chose Evalene to participate. If he had chosen Addia-Sahl in her stead, Evalene wouldn't be standing here before you accused of a frivolous charge."

"I did the calculations for the best course of action," Soleran says.

"Oh, that's right," Maximeron says. "You put Evalene in the path of the Angelian right before you."

"I didn't have time to engage full analysis," Soleran says. "Nor could we have foreseen the extent of the Angelian's strength."

"You acted as a coward!" Maximeron says, pointing at Soleran.

"Enough of this!" Uelle says. "You're not testifying. You're accusing and then arguing."

"I'm testifying that Soleran knew beforehand, even before Evalene, that the Praegian system was marked!" Maximeron says. The adversary then falls silent and waits.

"Soleran?" Uelle finally asks, turning to the *Intrepidium*'s commander.

"I knew that the Praegian system was marked," Soleran says. "But Maximeron issued the threat, and so I perceived it as empty and futile. This was several epochs ago, during the chancery of Deostasian."

"I warned you long before I warned Evalene," Maximeron says. "See? I tried to help."

"Or perhaps you were just boasting of having foreknowledge of the event," Soleran says. "And veiling it in esoterica to ensure its fulfillment. And all for your own pleasure."

"Answer this question, then," Maximeron says. "Evalene just testified as to having visited me in Occitoria after you stole away from me my disciple Avera." The adversary walks over to Avera, Soleran's protégé. Her gaze immediately falls to the floor. "My question is, what did you do about that visit?" Maximeron asks.

Soleran hesitates, taking in a deep breath. "Nothing," he answers.

"You didn't inquire about the conversation?" Maximeron asks.

"No," Soleran says.

"Why?" Maximeron asks.

"I respected her privacy," Soleran says.

"She sought leave to temporarily abandon her post?" Maximeron asks, stepping closer.

"Yes," Soleran says quickly.

"You knew where she was going?" Maximeron asks.

"Yes," Soleran says.

"Isn't it true that you had already judged her as full dissentive?"

Maximeron continues, standing face-to-face with Soleran. "Isn't it true that you had begun alienating her? Isn't it true that you had begun to discredit her as a witness? Isn't it true that you made this obvious to her upon her return? Isn't it true that she refrained from disclosing the conversation because she knew it would be futile to do so?" With this, the adversary walks up the steps of the dais toward Uelle. "If anything, it is Soleran who should be charged with dereliction of duty. He exercised judgment unbecoming of a Guardian. His incompetence at leadership is why Epsilon Truthe was caught off guard."

Uelle looks to Evalene, who meets the gaze.

"I have nothing to add," Evalene says.

Uelle then looks to Soleran, who sighs and looks away.

"Well?" Maximeron asks, throwing his arms in the air. "What is your judgment now?"

"I do not agree with your assessment," Uelle says.

"Figures," Maximeron says, turning away from Uelle and walking down a few steps. "This court is incapable of rendering justice."

"I agree that Soleran's behavior ... contributed," Uelle says, looking to Soleran.

"Well, do something about it!" Maximeron says, pointing at the chancellor.

The High Chancellor nods and composes herself. Uelle then speaks, her voice so soft one would think she was soothing a child.

"One amongst us declares that 'Life is. We bear it.' That declaration is more than a mere observation. It is an argument implicative of the Principal Cause. Life, as defined by the Doctrine of Hydrology, is the consequence of nature's attempt to stabilize itself. The cosmos is always in motion, and thus life will always be. The philosophy of compliance propounds upon the cosmos its sense of purpose, its reason for existence. Life is. We bear it and then some.

I am criticized as having lost my femininity. On the contrary, it is still very much a part of my soul, stronger than ever. Femininity is not a response to a patriarchal dominance. It is a stabilizer of chaotic motion in fluid dynamics, hence the feminine is the carrier of life. It is adaptive and thus assumes itself rightly as the vessel of evolution. It not only bears the fruit of the Earth, it defines the nature of the fruit.

You say your femininity is a field of morning glories. I say mine is the caress of snow upon that same field. Yours is a mist covering a sea. Mine is the blowing of the wind that brings the mist. It is the gentle touch of a mother's palm upon the face of a newborn babe and the deliverance of assurance that all is well and safe. And yet that same palm is undauntedly raised in wrath when defending against the hostile force.

The truest woman, truest to herself, tempts no one. It is not in her nature. She keeps open the windows to her soul, and inward shines the truth of the moment born in eternity. She weaves this light into a cloth of wisdom for a covering. She drapes the horizon with the selfsame, kissing the dusk and embracing the night while remaining vigilant and hopeful for the dawn of day.

We are proponents of the Principal Cause, compliant with the philosophy that whatever is beneficial to life is good and whatever is detrimental to life is evil. We labor toward bringing order to chaos, which means that we propose life, always. We pursue the perfect goodness, always. And we render the most proper judgments, always."

Uelle concludes her presentation and finishes her pronouncement. "Evalene," Uelle says, "I find you guilty of dereliction of duty." She pauses, her eyes locked on the subject of her judgment. "Your philosophy appears to me to be dissentive. And the fact that Maximeron has assumed the role as your advocate adds to that observation." She sighs, her statement slow and deliberate. "The only recourse I have is to bar you from governance for one epochal cycle, to be reviewed by the chancellor presiding at that time and either rescinded or continued per his or her judgment."

Evalene's facial expression is blank. I cannot tell what she is feeling. I feel sad for her, though. She does breathe in deeply. "What about now?" Evalene asks.

"I conclude that there is no remedy that will persuade you away from dissent and toward compliance. So therefore, a remedy need not be administered. You are free to return to the *Intrepidium* in a nongovernance role, or wherever you so desire."

"That's next to exile," Maximeron says. He laughs, and Uelle stares him down until he composes himself. "What of Soleran?" Maximeron asks. "Will you strip him of his governance?"

Uelle looks to Soleran for a moment. "No, but I will defer his appointment as chancellor until the final epoch prior to the ekpyrotic novatim. That will allow him a period of time to reconcile his relations with Evalene."

"That is not a punishment!" Maximeron says, clenching his jaw.

"I accept that decree," Soleran says, looking to Evalene. "I care for her and want to reconcile."

Evalene responds with a hard look at Soleran. She looks at me briefly and her hardness seems to soften slightly. She then turns and takes a few steps away. Guardians move to allow her some room. Maximeron announces a few more grievances, something about injustice and hypocrisy. I'm not paying attention. My eyes are locked on Evalene. I feel her tension. Maximeron finally storms out of the cathedral, his shielding colliding with the shielding of others. Then he is gone. I return to the bridge of the *Intrepidium* with Soleran and the others except Evalene. I wait for Soleran to have a free moment, so I stand near him in silence. He quickly turns to face me.

"She is aboard," Soleran says. "She has confined herself to an innermost chamber. You can visit her, if she'll allow."

"I should give her some time?" I ask.

"She may appreciate it," Soleran says.

CHAPTER 18

I returned to Ibalexa to assist my people in establishing their governance, having received from them the designation "ambassador." It was during this time that the civil war in the Huvril Empire erupted to its fullest. A Huvril rebel had been detained, having entered Ibalexan space alone on a Huvril shuttle. He was to be deposed, and a deposition panel was formed. I was invited to observe and afterward offer anything I could.

He came to us broken and sad, a one-man remnant of a people destined for destruction. Dontes the Brave. Huvrils do that. They give themselves titles. The four-legged man, hands bound to his waist, approaches us, guards on each side. I stand in the background behind the panel, more observer than participant. The last time a Huvril stood on Ibalexa, destruction rained down upon us.

Young Morne, aide to Chief Senator Ablaunt, brings me up to speed.

"He was in a two-man shuttle craft when we picked him up on our long-range sensors," Morne says. "We didn't waste time intercepting him." His eyes are small for his head, but the excitement of the moment holds them open wide.

"How strange that this lone wanderer was heading toward Ibalexa," I say.

"Strange indeed, Ambassador Brinn," Morne answers.

The chief senator requests the assistance of Morne, who doesn't hesitate to rush to the senator's side. The aide bends over, and the senator whispers something in his ear. Morne nods to him and whispers back. Then the aide returns to my right side.

I find myself looking out from behind the arched table, over the shoulder of Chief Justice Galvekind. Lots of people overflow the benches of the hall. A low and respectful murmur fills the air. Various folks from all around are attending to see, I suppose, the outcome of this hearing.

I study the panel before me—five politicians from various offices. Chief Senator Ablaunt is a little short and plump, and the back of his head is wrinkled and off-colored. Chief Justice Galvekind is thin and frail and fumbles with a datapad. It beeps in error, and his frustration is apparent. He surrenders and slams it on the table. Chief Defender Freona is an aged but beautiful woman. Her eyes are bold and wondrous in depth. Strength radiates from her face like the sun at noon. I watch her as she talks to Galvekind. I imagine she is reminding him of patience. He waves her off with his hand, invoking a chuckle from me. As if he hears, Galvekind turns in his seat to look at me. Seeing me behind him, he grunts and turns back around. Freona leans back to cast me a glance. She smiles and winks, and I answer with a nod. Luthus is chief executive. Most folks say he won the election by casting a deep shadow over his rivals. He's tall for an Ibalexan and wide, like a wall. His huge body dwarfs the chair upon which he sits. And finally my eyes fall upon the last member of the panel, a very petite and pretty Denjalin, chief minister. The white silky gown covers her entire body from chin to toe, but it is very flattering. Her gaze turns to meet mine. I smile, but her gaze is quickly drawn back to the prisoner.

The Huvril stranger is slouched, slightly old and unthreatening. Even so, I see in his eyes, or perhaps I should say I sense in him determination and strong will. I can't be angry at him or hate him or wish him harm. I can't blame him, this poor soul, for the destruction of Ibalexa. I feel a slight ache in my chest for him. I forget, at least for a moment, that he is Huvril, an enemy of Ibalexa. I pity him.

A sense of wonder strikes me. As I study the prisoner, Ibalexan guards enter the hall from a side door, carrying a bench and a microphone stand. They make their way to the prisoner, setting the bench down and even assisting the prisoner in sitting. The Huvril shifts his centauric body slightly to find that position of comfort. The second guard sets the microphone to an appropriate height. The prisoner thanks them, and they nod and walk away. Then his eyes lift up and move from panel member to panel member. I see courage in the midst of exhaustion, and I am amazed. Well, I'll be. Brave indeed.

Galvekind lifts up a gavel and bangs it a few times. The murmur of the hall gives way to utter silence.

"I guess I should begin … um … by saying that this hearing is … um … called forth to … um … question the … um … um … question the deponent," Galvekind says clumsily. "To determine his intentions and motives and gather other useful information for the well-being of the Republic of … um … Ibalexa." The chief justice speaks as if from a script, one that he's repeated hundreds of times. "The binding of the deponent may be removed."

The two guards behind the Huvril move to unbind him. Fumbling with the clasps, the one on the right pulls the small chain free and steps back with it clinking in his hands. The other studies the prisoner for some kind of sign of aggression. Dontes stares up at the guard inquisitively but remains calm. Satisfied, the second guard steps aside.

"This hearing is … um … recorded, both audibly and … um … holographically … um for the record," Galvekind says. "It would please the panel if the … um … deponent would state his name and title for the … um … record."

"I am," the prisoner begins, leaning forward to speak into the microphone. "First Lieutenant Imures Dontes, the Brave Son, of the Huvril Liberation Army." The prisoner nods and sits back, shifting slightly on the bench.

"Thank you," Chief Justice Galvekind says. "We have … um …

reviewed your statement, First Lieutenant Dontes, and ... um wish to inquire further as to your ... um ... mission."

Chief Executive Luthus grunts and nods approvingly.

"The members of the um ... Panel," Galvekind continues, "each have their questions, prepared beforehand, ready to deliver, of which ... um ... we would greatly appreciate your truthful and honest answers."

"Of course," Dontes answers. "I swear an oath before this Panel to speak only the truth to the best of my ability."

"That's all we can ask," Galvekind says, leaning back and seeking approval of the members of the panel. Most nod. The chief justice leans forward and picks up the datapad. "Your statement, First Lieutenant Dontes, is ... um ... that you were commissioned by your ... um ... commanding officer to ... seek ... um ... to seek the assistance of the Ibalexan Republic in the ... um ... campaign of the ... um ... liberation ... of Huvra from what you ... um ... refer to as the Holy Empire of Huvra?"

"That is correct, sir," Dontes answers.

"I shall ... um ... open the floor for questioning by the panel," Galvekind says.

There is a consensual sigh and shifting for comfort.

"First Lieutenant Dontes," Chief Senator Ablaunt says. His voice is raspy but loud and authoritative. He coughs slightly. "May we inquire as to the commanding officer who commissioned you to venture forth from Huvril space, traverse a huge span of empty space, and enter Ibalexan territory, if you would, please sir."

"Yes, sir," Dontes says, leaning forward to speak into the microphone. "That would be General Kackren Traisa."

"Very well, very well," Ablaunt says. He coughs again. "And this General Traisa, if I may, chose you for what particular reason?"

"Well, sir," Dontes begins, "it was the General's reasoning that a lieutenant would be best suited for this mission, being the lowest-ranked officer, but also for being an officer in the first place."

"Okay," Ablaunt says. "But why you, in particular. I assume there are other lieutenants in the liberation army."

"I volunteered, sir," Dontes says.

"Hmmm," Ablaunt says. "Very well. Very well." Chief Senator Ablaunt nods to Chief Justice Galvekind.

"Chief Defender Freona," Galvekind says, "you may proceed."

"Thank you, Chief Justice," Freona responds. She turns to the deponent. "First Lieutenant Dontes, I am Chief Defender Lulawa Freona of the Office of Legal Defense." She pauses.

Dontes leans forward. "Glad to meet you, ma'am." He leans back.

"I am here to ensure that your rights as a human being are observed and respected," Freona adds.

"Thank you, ma'am," Dontes says.

"Are you a family man, sir?" Freona asks.

Chief Executive Luthus grunts and shakes his head from side to side. I study Freona to see her reaction. There is none. She ignores him.

"I am, ma'am," Dontes answers. "I have a wife and two children."

"Yet you have taken sides with the Huvril Liberation Army?" Freona asks. "At a great risk of not only your own well-being but also the well-being of your loved ones?"

Dontes drops his gaze to the floor in front of him. He closes his eyes, and I see him—albeit momentarily—shrink a little. But immediately he gathers himself, opens his eyes and leans forward. "Yes, ma'am." He leans back.

Freona turns to Galvekind. He sighs and sits back. "Chief Executive Luthus, it is your turn, kind sir."

"Thank you, Chairman Galvekind," Luthus states. His voice is deep. "First Lieutenant Dontes," Luthus says into his microphone, "we have heard reports that the Huvril Liberation Army has engaged in some ... questionable ... actions." He barely leans back but immediately shifts his big head down to the microphone.

Dontes leans forward quickly, but his time at the microphone seems prolonged. "We are desperate men, sir." He looks down. "Which is the reason that I sit before the Panel of Ibalexa's Republic and request your help." He leans back. He leans forward to add something but changes his mind and leans back.

"Yeah," Luthus says halfheartedly.

The deposition continues a little longer, with the panel asking various questions regarding typical Huvril tactics and strategies. Dontes answers them all as thoroughly as he is able to. The deposition does break for an afternoon meal and then runs for several more hours. Finally, after a total of nine hours, the deposition concludes. Dontes returns to the custody of the War Department pending a ruling on his status, his detention more of a formality than anything.

As I'm walking from the building to the plaza outside, Galvekind approaches me. The moons sit atop the night sky, casting gentle light on the path before us. The plaza runs along a shoreline to the Vellya Sea.

"So," Galvekind begins, "were you able to detect anything significant?"

"I detected only sincerity," I respond.

"Good," he says. "Good, good." We both approach a pier extending out over the shoreline. We walk to the end. "I need to ... um ... yeah, I need to ask one more thing of you."

"Of course, Chief Justice," I say. "I'm committed to assisting Ibalexa any way I can." A cool and soothing wind picks up and flutters our robes.

"We are set to grant the request of the Huvril rebels," Galvekind says. "But even if we committed our entire fleet, we would ... um ... still be outnumbered."

I scan his neural net and read his intentions. "You mean to ask for the help of the Guardians," I say. I follow it with a sigh of concern. The request is hard.

The chief justice stares silently out over the water.

"I can say that Epsilon Truthe cannot involve themselves directly," I continue.

Galvekind looks at me with a bit of worry on his face.

"But perhaps if I can ask for one to assist in the defense," I say, placing my hand on his shoulder, "it would be enough."

"Any assistance would be appreciated," the chief justice says. "Of course, they could end it quickly."

"Minor skirmishes are one thing," I say. "It's a matter of principle that prohibits them from engaging in major campaigns."

He waves his hand. "No need to explain, Ambassador," Galvekind says. "We have accepted the Guardians' explanation." He turns to look back out at the gentle sea. "Still, any assistance is appreciated."

We speak about other matters, trivial compared to the issue at hand. I bid the chief justice goodnight and take my leave. I then teleshift from the planet and make my way toward the *Intrepidium*. The ship receives my information, and I manifest in whole on the bridge. After some initial greetings, I blurt out my request. The silence that follows is brief but deafening.

Soleran kneels down to look me in my eyes. "Brinn," he says, placing his hand on my shoulder, "what you ask of us is hard."

"I know, Soleran," I answer. "I am sorry. I didn't want to, but the council requested it."

He sighs and stands. There is great sadness in his eyes. Even so, he hesitates only briefly, turning to face the other Guardians.

"The Republic of Ibalexa has asked for our assistance," Soleran says. "They have chosen to ally themselves with the Huvril Liberation Force. Although this increases their numbers significantly, they are still outnumbered." He walks amongst the Guardians as he speaks. "And although we have until now made it unlawful to directly participate in intergalactic conflicts, this particular situation does warrant a review of the law."

"Soleran," Addia-Sahl says with concern, "there are factors to consider, sacrifices to make, portions of our very being to dissolve."

"Yes," Soleran answers, "but Ibalexa's decision carries with it dire consequences." He prompts a holographic display and keys in an equation. "Before, Maximeron considered Ibalexa a mere project amongst many, perhaps worthy of disturbance, but nothing further." He continues to key in definitions and parameters, and the display begins to solve the equation. "Now, however, Ibalexa becomes an avid enemy requiring persistent retaliation, including a second galactic invasion of the home world of Ibalexa."

My heart sinks deep into my chest.

"Before, Huvra sent to Ibalexa around thirty-five mother ships, along with a cascade weapon that ignited nuclear fusion throughout their atmosphere," Soleran continues. The equation is lengthening, leading to what I know to be an inevitable outcome. "Now, the Holy Huvril Empire will send half of its armada, well over five hundred mother ships." He pauses his speech long enough to finish keying in the last definition. He then turns to face the other Guardians. "The worst of it, however, is the direct intervention of Maximeron himself, whose level of hatred and revenge will surpass anything he's done before." The equation finishes.

"Which would mean that Brinn can't do this alone," Leostrom says.

"Exactly," Soleran says.

"I'm only asking that one other join me," I say. "And just to do enough to frustrate the Huvrils' strategies and tactics and perhaps contribute to shielding. I wouldn't dare ask for more." I look at the Guardians' faces, looking for a sign of their willingness. I see sadness. I inhale and exhale and drop my gaze to the floor. I might have asked too much already.

There is silence. Soleran stands with his arms behind his back, grasping a wrist. He is looking past the others, staring at the emptiness behind them.

"So," Leostrom says.

"So," Soleran says. "Who amongst—" He cuts himself off and pauses slightly. "I will go." Soleran turns to face me. "I will go with you, Brinn."

"Soleran!" Addia-Sahl says. She steps up, her eyes wide with concern. "You can't! Your administration is to begin soon."

"I can't ask this of another," Soleran says, turning to face the others.

"I'm sorry," I say. I walk up beside Soleran. "I'm only asking for defenses. I wouldn't ask for any killing."

"Brinn," Leostrom says. He approaches me and puts a hand on my back. "Any participation contributes to the deaths. Whether directly or indirectly, there is no distinction."

It only takes me a moment to decide what to do. "Very well," I say. "I retract my request. I apologize." I feel emotion welling up in my chest. "I'm sorry!" I shake my head.

"That is noble of you, Brinn," Soleran says, kneeling down to look me eye-to-eye. "But we can't—I can't let you do this alone. Not now. Your request is reasonable and expected. But clearly, not all of us can participate in this. Our resolve, our very integrity, would suffer."

"I will go," says a feminine voice behind us. We all turn to see Evalene standing there.

Soleran stands and faces her. "There's no way—"

"I have decided," Evalene says.

"You need healing—time to heal," Soleran says. He steps closer to her, slowly, as if he feared a negative response to the encroachment.

"I will go, and you all will stay here to record the event," Evalene says. Her eyes look funny, the silver luster giving way to a dark charcoal. "You will neither intervene nor participate."

"Stand down," Leostrom says to Evalene.

"You will refrain," Evalene says. Her robe flutters, as if an invisible wind has blown through, but no one else's does this.

"Maximeron will hate you," Addia-Sahl says matter-of-factly.

"He already does, Sister," Evalene says. "Maximeron loves and hates at the same time. He already loves me and hates me, and there is nothing I can do to change that."

Leostrom approaches Soleran and leans into him. "She has decided," Leostrom says. "There is nothing we can do to stop her. We should step aside."

Soleran inhales and exhales forcefully while keeping his eyes on Evalene. "Do you do this because you are banned from governance? Is this spite?"

"I do this for us all, because I am the one most expendable," Evalene says. "And also because I love Brinn and want to help him."

I walk over to her and gaze into her eyes. I don't know if I should be glad or concerned. I mean, part of me is worried for her well-being. She is emotionally distraught and very vulnerable, having been admonished before all the Host. But another part of me feels it is good that she do something, that she participate.

"How can I let you do this?" Soleran asks.

"Let her go," Leostrom says, placing his hand on Soleran's right shoulder.

Soleran acknowledges the gesture, turning his head slightly to the right and letting his gaze fall to an empty space on the floor. Then he closes his eyes. "Very well." Looking at Evalene, he continues, "Do what you have to do." Soleran turns and walks away.

I almost want to run to Soleran to apologize. I feel that I've somehow exacerbated the situation. I don't know why he's so upset about this. I look forward to being with Evalene. I've been wanting to build on our friendship, to build on her trust. I feel her hurt and want to alleviate it somehow, by any means, small or great.

Evalene and I bid farewell to the Guardians on the *Intrepidium* and make our way to the flag ship, the *Cellaphori*, Ibalexan Republic Designation. I always enjoy traveling through space between ships. It is never empty. Having access to the full light spectrum and adjusting my sight as needed, I can see that the colors of space are rich and bold. Evalene and I traverse the outer current of a solar system, letting the current carry us to the other side. There is a sea of solar particles flowing all around us. I reach down and let my hand exit the shielding and feel the particles wash over my skin. The sensation is similar to the ocean's feel. The heat just enough to differentiate itself from the cold vacuum of space, and, like salty water, the particles tingle the skin. Pulling my hand up, I see that the fluid is viscous. I look to Evalene and see her smiling as she does the same. It's been a long time since I've seen her smile. It's a wonderful thing to see, and I can't help but radiate my joy. But just as quickly, her smile fades to a frown.

"I know your thoughts," Evalene says. "It'll be a long time before I smile again, Brinn."

I sigh and pull in closer to her.

"Be at peace now, Evalene," I say. "You have time."

"You are right," she says with a nod.

She puts an arm around me and hugs me. Her smile returns and, at least for a moment, there is peace and joy. All troubles and burdens are temporarily forgotten. The past is left behind us, and the tasks ahead of us have no place in the moment. Since time is of the essence, we don't deviate from our course. The course, however, does take us close to various events and locales. We witness a supernova in the lower left. A comet has left a tail nearby—though out of reach, close enough to scan. A nebula compresses one of its tiny strands, and, hidden in the end of the strand, a a protostar fires its nuclear engine and becomes a brilliant star. I don't let the opportunities go by without observing every detail, taking note of the physics involved and expanding upon my workings of the universe. Formulas and calculations flash in my optics and are committed to my memory.

A moment of eternity passes, and we find ourselves approaching the fleet of Ibalexan and HLA ships. Having taken their cue from the Guardians, the Ibalexan ships are disks with rotating rings. Unlike the Guardians, however, they have uranium hulls. While the Guardians haven't divulged to the Ibalexans the full knowledge of their technology, they have assisted the Ibalexans in resolving technological problems and issues as far as our imaginations carry us. And even though not as advanced as the Guardians, Ibalexan technology does surpass the Huvrils' technology. And yet, the imperial Huvril fleet makes up for it in sheer force with a ratio of five to one.

The fleet resides on the outer edge of imperial territory. Just inside the boundary is a planet upon which the HLA's headquarters are located, along with a colony of dissenters who labor to eke out a living. Word approached of the imperial fleet's mobility, hence the dispatching of First Lieutenant Dontes for aid. And now, the tri-alliance of Huvril rebels, Ibalexans, and Guardians represented by Evalene and myself, brings forth a fleet to repel the invasion.

I reflect upon my own station. In spite of my Ibalexan heritage, I find myself identifying with the Guardians more than my own people. I have spent so much time with the Guardians and have seen and learned so much. Even so, I'm not developed as much as a Guardian—yet. I know that alone, I could not assist the alliance fleet enough against the imperials. So having the aid of a full-fledged Guardian guarantees that the upcoming battle will be more balanced, despite the numbers.

Evalene and I find the *Cellaphori* at the front of the fleet facing the imperial territory. As is customary for Guardians, we make our presence known to the *Cellaphori* and request permission to come aboard. Evalene is content to let me do the formalities. She is conspicuously quiet, and the frown has returned. With permission given, we teleshift from our position onto the bridge. The room is brightly lit, with consoles strewn about and occupied by dark blue uniformed personnel.

"Ambassador Brinn! Welcome, welcome!" Admiral Colquis says. "And you too, Daughter of the Morning Rise. We pay our most humble respects!" The admiral bows to Evalene. A quick and slight nod is her only response. "We are most appreciative of your assistance. Thanks isn't enough, however. Please, let me know if there's anything I can provide for you." He bows quickly and then straightens. Admiral Colquis is tall for an Ibalexan, certainly taller than me, though he only barely reaches Evalene's chest. His dark, gray skin is only slightly wrinkled, testifying to his youth as well as his character and success, despite his age. He's muscular and exhibits his strength in his demeanor. He keeps his chin held aloft and slightly to the side, a sign of respect but also confidence.

"Admiral Colquis," I begin, "thank you, sir, for your kindness. We are glad to be of assistance." I feel the need to speak as the Guardians would. I hope I do justice to their methodology. "It is our objective to prevent needless deaths and save lives."

"Well, that depends on the invaders," Admiral Colquis says with a smile.

"Of course," I respond with a nod.

"Very well, then," the admiral says with a bellow, turning to face his navigation crew. "Let us move the fleet into the territory and take up our positions. Relay the orders to the fleet leaders."

"Aye, sir," an officer says, turning to his console. "Fleet control, this is IRD *Cellaphori* command, issuing order Primer Pronto. Relay nonverbal confirmation and proceed as directed." After a moment, the officer turns back to the admiral. "Fleet team confirmation received, sir."

"Very good," Admiral Colquis says. "Helm, take us in and proceed to coordinates 2-9, C, 4-7."

"Aye, sir," another officer responds from the front near the teleprompt.

A low hum reverberates through the bridge as the *Cellaphori's* engines fire, pushing the flagship forward into imperial territory. Soon the engines are at full throttle, and a tiny dot of a planet comes into view of the teleprompt.

"Neattan," the admiral says in a low voice, "fear not, help comes." The fleet approaches but passes the planet, which falls out of view of the teleprompt at the bottom. Turning to face us, the admiral adds, "I want them to see us as we go by. They need the emotional support."

Evalene says nothing, but I respond with a nod. The admiral returns his focus to the teleprompt. I look up to Evalene. Her skin is soft but doesn't radiate as it used to. She seems sober, sad, even. I reach up and place my hand on her arm just below the elbow. She looks at me but looks to my left side, as if she resists looking in my eyes.

"It'll be okay," I say.

A part of me is alarmed when she shakes her head no ever so slightly. She returns her gaze to the teleprompt. I don't inquire, but I want to so badly. I imagine myself looking around wildly. Confusion and anxiety take root deep within me. What is going to happen? I remember the Praegians. I try to wipe the thought from my mind before … it's too late. Evalene places her hand on my shoulder and squeezes. I cross my hand over to place it on top of hers.

Several hours pass. The admiral barks his commands, and the bridge officers respond without hesitation. Yes sirs, no sirs, aye sirs fill the air. While I've come to hate war and its destruction, I can't help but feel impressed by the efficiency of the *Cellaphori's* crew. I'm slightly proud of them. Their purpose is noble and just. Despite the odds, they press on.

"Admiral," an officer says, "imperial fleet has entered sensor range."

"Get a count, lieutenant," the admiral says.

"Aye, sir!" The officer responds. He presses commands on his prompt, and we wait. After about five minutes, he finishes. "Admiral, sir," the lieutenant says, "I have a full count. The imperial fleet consists of five hundred mother ships."

Gasps fill the room.

"The heavens help us," the admiral says in a low voice, more mumbling to himself. "They sent half their fleet. I was hoping for better numbers." He turns to face me and Evalene. "Well, your help is very much appreciated at this point."

I can't hide my concern. I look up to Evalene and whisper to her, "Protect them?"

"Of course," she says. She can't hide her sadness. A tear flows down her cheek. I watch it closely as it drips off her chin. Finally, she breaks down and cries loudly.

I glance toward the admiral, who looks at me, concerned. He sighs slightly and looks around to his crew, pointing at various officers, who respond by turning back to their consoles. He then returns his focus to the teleprompt, but not without a glance at us over his left shoulder.

"Admiral," the communications officer says, "I'm receiving a message from the imperial flag ship."

"Put it on the screen," the admiral says.

"Aye, sir," the officer says.

The teleprompt switches from star-filled space to the image of a Huvril captain. His bulbous, Huvril eyes lock onto Admiral Colquis.

"I am Admiral Colquis, of the Ibalexan Republic Starship *Cellaphori*."

The Huvril leader doesn't respond right away. He stares at the admiral angrily. After a period of awkwardness, he finally speaks. "I

am Admiral Lokksin, of the Imperial Huvril Flagship *Morghonox*."
Before Admiral Colquis can say anything, the Huvril leader brings
into view a datapad. "By order of the imperial throne and his most
Holy Father, Emperor Korithes, the Ibalexan Republic is unrecognized
and declared an outlaw state. The charge is aiding and abetting rebel
combatants." The imperial admiral lowers the datapad. "Surrender
now and your lives will spared, along with the colonists on Neattan."
After a brief silence, Lokksin concludes his statement. "This will be
your only opportunity."

I register from the imperial leader sheer hatred. I sigh and shake
my head, more in disbelief that a human being could have so much
hate in his heart. Then a thought enters my mind—a memory.
"Lokksin," I whisper.

"Yes, Brinn," Evalene says. "He is the great grandson of the
admiral who invaded Ibalexa so long ago."

I purse my lips together. I can't be angry. This person on the other
side of the teleprompt isn't responsible for the destruction caused
by his forefather. But I do sense that his pride is partly fueled by the
knowledge of that invasion. I know that it is typical Huvril behavior to
meet the accomplishments of one's ancestor and, if possible, surpass
them. Lokksin will show no mercy.

"Evalene," I say, turning to her. "Let us …"

Before I can finish, Evalene teleshifts from my sight. Panic sets
in, and I begin to scan around. "Wha … Evalene?"

The admiral jerks around at my alarm and looks around wildly.
"Where is she? Where did she go?"

I scan outside the ship. My ability is limited by my physiology.
Advanced as it is, it is still limited by my own pace of development,
especially compared to the Guardians. I finally sense Evalene's
presence. She is on the *Morghonox*.

That is evident by Lokksin's scream, "Fire on the intruder! Fire
on the intruder!"

"What is going on?" Admiral Colquis says to me.

I have no answer, so I stare at him in silence. Suddenly, without
warning, a concussion force slams the *Cellaphori* and rocks the ship

slightly to the right. A bright light fills the teleprompt. As the light fades, the debris of a ship occupies the location that the *Morghonox* once did.

The admiral looks at me with madness.

Confused, I look back and forth between the admiral and the teleprompt. I say nothing. Scanning, I see that Evalene has entered the bridge of a nearby imperial ship. I concentrate hard. Without the *Intrepidium*'s Omnitron, my own brain has to do most of the work. I manage to zoom into the ship's bridge. The occupants are firing their weapons at Evalene, but with no effect. They are helpless against her shielding. I zoom in closer, so that I can see Evalene herself. As if sensing me, she turns just enough so that I can see her face. She is bawling. Instantly she screams and then there is blinding light. The explosion reaches the *Cellaphori*, and the bridge tips slightly, forcing the members of the crew to catch their balance.

"Comm!" Admiral Colquis says. "Relay to the fleet! Weapons are hot! Fire at will! Fire at will!"

It was with instinct that he sensed the consequences of this action. The imperial fleet has moved toward the alliance and is opening fire. Suddenly, the space between the two fleets is filled with missiles, energy projectiles, and beams of light. Thousands of smaller fighter ships occupy the space above and below the shower of firepower, each side attempting to penetrate the others' defenses.

I shift my own focus on generating shieldings around the ships in the front. Lacking the power of a full Guardian, my only option is to flash the shielding from ship to ship. It's working, and the damage to the alliance fleet is minimal.

Even so, a force slams the frontal ships of the alliance fleet, and only one ship, the one I have the shielding on, escapes with minimal damage. It was not the *Cellaphori*. The alliance flagship rocks to the right, the concussion tossing people to the floor. Another imperial ship has exploded. Within seconds, another. Seconds later, still another. Sparks are flying from the consoles on the *Cellaphori*'s bridge.

Admiral Colquis approaches me. Grabbing my robe, he pulls me toward him. "This is not what we planned! What is this madness?"

As if realizing a great offense, he slowly releases my robe and fearfully backs away. "Sorry. Sorry." He turns to face the teleprompt.

The *Cellaphori* again rocks, and everyone on the bridge except for me is tossed to the floor. Two imperial ships have exploded, their concussion force slamming the alliance fleet.

"Retreat!" the admiral says with a bellow. "Helm! Get us out of here! Now!" Colquis labors to right himself by pulling up on a nearby console. "Comm! Relay the command! Retreat! Retreat!"

"Aye, sir!" the communications officer responds. "Fleet control! Fleet control! *Cellaphori* command! Reset! Reset! Order to reset! Proceed to reset coordinates! I repeat …"

An explosion. The *Cellaphori* rocks to the left, having turned to flee. A few consoles catch fire.

"The heavens save us!" the admiral says, holding on tightly to a console.

The explosion was enough to unsettle my position. I catch myself, feeling the slight pull. I quickly scan the alliance fleet and see the frontal ships taking immense damage from the concussion forces. Most are retreating. Many of the smaller fighter ships on both sides are being annihilated.

"Evalene, stop," I whisper. I shift my focus to find her, scanning from imperial ship to imperial ship and finally seeing her. I watch as she walks through her teleshifting without breaking stride. She lifts her arms, and the ship explodes. I catch her direction and find her on another imperial bridge. She maintains her stride, raises her arms, and that ship explodes. The imperial fleet is now turning to flee. I concentrate hard and force my zoom to lock onto Evalene. A slight ache hits my forehead, and I fight to hold my focus. It's been so long since any physical pain had hit me that I had forgotten the sensation. "Evalene! Stop!" I hear myself yell loudly.

She turns to allow me to see her face. Her skin is of a light-red hue. Her eyes, empty like an abyss. Her eyebrows are taut. Tears no longer flow and have been replaced with a scowl. All I see is rage. I can't measure this hatred. It leaves the depths of the human soul and is … is … do I dare say?

Demonic.

"Evalene!" I yell as loud as I can! "Stop!"

The alliance fleet manages to pull back far enough outside the range of the concussion forces, helped by the imperial ships fleeing in the other direction.

"Damage report!" Admiral Colquis says without taking his eyes off the teleprompt.

An officer out of my view responds. "Only 25 percent of the alliance fleet took damage, Admiral. But that damage was extensive. There are casualties being reported. Deaths. Systems destroyed. Squadrons, by the hundreds, destroyed."

Another officer speaks, "Sir! The imperial fleet is decimated! By 82 percent!"

The admiral turns to me. He is unable to contain his bewildered madness. "Couldn't you have at least told us, given us a warning or something? We would have just stayed back and let you do your thing!"

"I'm so sorry," I manage to say. "I didn't know."

The admiral doesn't respond with words. His facial expression says it all. Disbelief. He turns back to the teleprompt.

"Admiral," the communications officer says, "we are receiving a message from an imperial ship." The officer pauses. "They surrender! They are surrendering! The imperial fleet surrenders!"

"We accept!" the admiral says. "We accept the surrender. Tell them to stand down!" The admiral stops as he observes the look of horror on the communication officer's face. "What?"

"Their ship is destroyed," says the officer.

"What?" the admiral asks. "What?"

Everyone looks to the teleprompt. Several imperial ships approach the alliance fleet. One by one, they explode. The admiral turns to look at me.

"She came to kill," I manage. "She came to kill them all!" I fall to my knees. I can't hold back the tears.

Are you not a woman truest to yourself? A woman truest to herself kills not.

My words were refuted and rendered meaningless. The ideal woman has been dismissed as romantic folly.

But you could keep them, as a principle upon which you stand.

The laws of men can be revised by the whims of a ruler. I tread upon the continuum as a queen of heaven, with ligeiac kiss on my lips.

I scream with all my might. "Evalene! Stop! Now!"

The communications officer reports. "The imperial fleet is destroyed. Not one ship remains."

"Any survivors?" the admiral asks. "Any escape pods? Anything?"

The communications officer looks at the admiral and slowly shakes his head no.

The admiral braces himself upon a console. He breathes heavily, like he's just run a marathon. His eyes lift until they meet mine. "Five hundred ships. My God! Should I be thankful? I don't understand."

The weight of the moment overtakes me and I lie upon the floor facedown with my arms under my forehead.

We came to prevent needless deaths.

I came to kill.

I scream with all my might, "Why?"

"To slay the chimera and be transformed," Evalene says, standing above me.

I quickly lift myself. "This!" I say as I stand. "This is unlawful!"

"Weren't you present at the Tiaggess proceeding?" Evalene asks. "I was declared as full dissentive. That prophecy has come to fulfillment."

"What?" I ask.

"Should I allow the high chancellor of Epsilon Truthe to be a liar?" Evalene rebuts. "Stand forth! Stop cowering!"

"Evalene!"

"Life is! We suffer it!"

"But life …" I start to say.

Death is the mother of Beauty; hence from her, Alone, shall come fulfillment to our dreams and our desires.

"What?" I ask. "I don't know what that means!"

"It is an ancient quote. You are attentive to the scheme of things," Evalene says. "Are you in denial?" her eyes are dark. An abyss lies behind them, sucking in all light. Her heart is cold, colder than the vacuum of space. Her face is broken stone, a ruined memorial.

"I love you," I say to her. I don't know what else to say. I desperately grasp the darkness, as if blind and laboring to find a hold on something.

Evalene pauses for but a brief moment. "Gather yourself, and return to the *Intrepidium*."

I cry. I bury my face in my hands and cry.

"Gather yourself," she commands.

My tear-laden eyes fall upon the admiral and then on the crew of the *Cellaphori*. The battle is over. It is the quickest battle ever in the history of Ibalexa, perhaps even Huvra. But the joy of victory is not present. Instead, fear dominates.

Evalene senses this. She hears my thoughts. She turns to the admiral. "Relish your victory."

The admiral, dejected and broken, stares at her in disbelief. "We thank you for your help," he says. His gaze falls to the floor. He says nothing more. He doesn't dare.

She knows the admiral's heart. She has to. I know his heart, reading it like a scroll pulled down to expose its contents. *I am afraid. I fear for my life. Do not kill me* it reads. *I will do whatever you say. Only command further, and I will obey.*

"No," I say, closing my eyes and lowering my head. Free will is destroyed. It is no more.

CHAPTER 19

Soleran stands upon the shore overlooking a sea. He wears a simple white robe and nothing else. His light brown hair is long and straight and partly covers his bearded face. He stares before him at the contest of nature's competing forces. The shoreline is made up of rocks, iron-laden, rusty red, jagged and hard. The sea thrashes against the rocks, its waters having no water at all but consisting mostly of ammonia. The ghostly mist rising from the surface reaches a height of only several meters, quickly condenses, and falls back down in a light shower. A red giant star emerges over the horizon, burns its last gasping breaths of life, having expended its fuel and preparing its future to collapse into a white dwarf. The red arc of light following shrinks to nothing.

Occitoria.

A small terrestrial planetoid hostile to any bio-life.

Alone in a dying system hidden away on the outer edges of the galaxy.

Solitude for a being that breathes hydrogen.

Soleran steps into the sea. He diminishes his shielding, allowing the caustic liquid to interact with his skin. There is pain. He breathes in the hydrogen to replenish his essence at a rate equal to the expense taken by the sea. He steps farther, deeper, at last until the sea reaches his chest. His breathing increases to compensate, bearing some labor. He grimaces at the discomfort.

"Would you go farther, even to the point of drowning yourself?" a voice asks from behind Soleran. The Guardian peeks over his shoulder and sees Maximeron standing upon the shore. "Or perhaps you seek a portal for escape?"

Soleran doesn't respond. He returns his gaze to the rising sun. For many seconds, he allows the sea to push him about, but he finally surrenders. He turns and wades back to the shore.

Maximeron is kneeling at the edge of the sea. He picks up a stone and flicks it across the sea's surface.

Soleran allows himself to strain under the labor of climbing up on the shoreline. He turns and sits, pulling up his legs and crossing them. "I was comparing physical pain to my grief."

"I see," Maximeron says. "I grieve too, although for a different reason."

"We grieve for the Huvrils," Soleran says. "For the husbands and wives, mothers and fathers, sons and daughters, sisters and brothers." His eyes remain locked onto the sunlight piercing the mist.

Maximeron stands, throws the last rock in his hand, and then sits down, resigning himself to stay a little longer. "I grieve because she still sided with the Ibalexans and the rebels." The rogue fixes his gaze on the sea. "Now, if she had taken out everyone present—Imperialists, rebels, and Ibalexans, well … I would be okay with that." Maximeron lets a chuckle escape.

Soleran turns and casts a look of disapproval at Maximeron. He responds to his adversary's chuckle with a sigh. He looks into the eyes of the rogue before finally turning back to the sea before him.

"Are you going to reinstate them?" Maximeron asks. "The Imperialists?"

"No," Soleran says, "their information is awash. We could do it, but it would take more time and energy than we can afford to spend."

"What are you going to do with her?" Maximeron asks.

"I can't say at this point," Soleran says. "The charges are egregious." He places both hands to his face and wipes away the spray of the ammonia showers.

"You didn't see it coming, did you?" Maximeron continues.

"I sensed something," Soleran responds. "I knew deep within me that something was wrong. I shouldn't have let her go."

"Did you really have a choice?" Maximeron asks.

"Perhaps not," Soleran answers.

The two sit silently for a few minutes, both captivated by the roar of the sea crashing against the shore. A storm takes form in the distance, and the sea becomes agitated.

"She told me she was a lover, not a killer," Maximeron continues. "She committed herself wholeheartedly to the position. Made it the staple of her womanhood." He finds another stone and flicks it across the surface of the sea. "I guess she changed her mind."

"Are you pleased that she has converted?" Soleran asks.

There is a long pause. "I'm unable to answer that," Maximeron says. "When it was just me, I very much wanted others to join my cause. And while I'm glad that she responded to Uelle's memorandum, it's still obvious that she loves that Ibalexan runt.".

Soleran frowns and shakes his head slightly.

"I mean, she can and will betray Epsilon Truthe, even to the far ends of the real universe," Maximeron says. "But she won't betray the Ibalexan. Why?" With more strength than before, the rogue launches a rock out into the sea. It sails through the air for too long and then drops into the ammonia with a single splash.

"The Ibalexan," Soleran begins, "he will save us all. He'll save not only his own people, but everyone else too."

"How do you figure?" Maximeron asks.

"It just seems right," Soleran says. "It's as it seems."

Maximeron rolls his eyes and purses his lips in a smirk of disapproval.

The rogue shifts, almost as if he's about to rise. "Look," Maximeron says, "I'm willing to compromise a little, if you're willing to compromise a little. Your appointment to high chancellor has been deferred to the last epoch of this epochal."

"Is that why you're here?" Soleran asks. "Because Evalene destroyed half the Huvril fleet? That interferes with your plan?"

"That doesn't matter," Maximeron says. "I'm unconcerned with those sniveling worms."

"You want to transit," Soleran says.

"Of course I do," Maximeron says.

"You can't," Soleran says.

"I will," Maximeron says.

"Aronjadon issued the order," Soleran says. "Even if I was to sympathize with your position, I couldn't contradict it."

"You could if you wanted to," Maximeron says.

"All of Epsilon Truthe is committed to stopping you and fulfilling the request," Soleran says. He finds a stone near him and snatches it up. He barely flicks it up into the air in front of him. It drops with a splash. The dark clouds of the storm have blocked out the sun, rendering the area dim.

"Let me tell you something," Maximeron says. "Some may labor to stop me. It may even be most. But certainly not all."

Both lock eyes on the encroaching storm.

After a brief moment, Soleran nods. "I'll concede that point. But while they won't labor to stop you, they also won't labor to help you. Everyone did cast an affirmative vote to expel you from the council."

"And another thing," Maximeron says, dismissing Soleran's comments, "the Ibalexan runt won't need to save me." The rogue stands and dusts off his red robe. "And I guarantee he can't save you." Maximeron trains his fiery eyes on Soleran.

"Well," Soleran responds, turning back to the torrential sea, "until then."

"Soon," Maximeron says. "Very soon." He disappears.

Soleran sighs and stands up. He pats the dust from his robes. "Looks like we've both made the hard decision." Soleran returns to the *Intrepidium*. As he steps onto the bridge, Addia-Sahl approaches.

"We've detected an energy signature in the outer current," she says. "The object is placing a lot of tension on the continuum." She places a hand on Soleran's shoulder and gently squeezes. "Are you well?"

He caresses her hand and nods but lets his gaze fall past her.

"Looks like Maximeron is heading to the energy signature," Leostrom says. He shakes his head from side to side. "Does that confirm our suspicions that he is collaborating with the nihilist faction?"

"When we complete our tasks and conclude our commission, we will investigate the phenomenon," Soleran says. "Until then, let us finish out our commitments. By then, I'll have taken on the mantle of chancellor."

CHAPTER 20

I accompany the Guardians to the surface of the monolith, the source of the energy signature. I am able to determine its properties quickly. Physically, it is a perfect ratio of one, three, and nine kilometers, respective to its height, width, and length. It is metallic, though its elemental composition eludes me, but its luster is dull and unreflective of starlight. It feels odd under my feet, as if it pulsates. The vibration is at such a small degree as to be almost imperceptible, but I sense it, nonetheless. It makes me feel uneasy, like when I was a child and found myself out too late at night and was rushing to get home and having to tread through the dark woods. Something more is here, or feels to be here, and a single voice in my head says so. I try to breathe easy. The intruder is Maximeron, and the cause of my anxiety is his malice. His sliver of a silhouette contrasts with the dark gray of the monolith. He stands at the halfway point of the monolith, but I can tell that he is approaching, walking slowly. So much time is passing that I can measure it by the passing of my thoughts, from one idea to another, from one image to another, from one dream to another, from one calculation to another, and on and on. Eventually, after much inner discourse with myself, Maximeron reaches us.

"Is this another trap?" Soleran asks him. "We're aware of your propensity for schemes and plots." His voice is resolute, but passive and nonthreatening.

"It is whatever you make it," Maximeron answers. "How often have I given you much freedom to choose?" The adversary's robe flashes bright red. His skin, pale white as it is, absorbs the light and reflects its reddish hue.

"Well," Soleran continues, "shall we engage this line of discourse, even though we both know the outcome?"

"You do whatever you want to do," Maximeron says. He is smiling, almost as if he's at perfect peace. I try to analyze his words to determine his intent. The tone is friendly, but the word choice implies hostility. The only conclusion I can come to quickly is that he is being sarcastic, which is most unfortunate.

"Fine," Soleran says. "Let us plead our case before all observers, local and foreign, and whatever transpires is the will of fate, or whoever controls everything."

The adversary laughs, laying his head back and roaring into the heavens. His laughter is both free-spirited and condescending. Everything I know about this enemy is a contradiction of itself.

"Whatever you say," Maximeron says. "At this point, we're just going through the motions."

I, Soleran, Chancellor of Epsilon Truthe, aver eternal life as the end result of the pursuit of perfection, especially in approaching the truth of reality. As Guardians of Life, are we not stewards of life within this universe, a universe we cannot claim as our own? Per the ancient principle, if we are not trustworthy with another person's property, how can we be granted our own property? What is, therefore, the underlying reason for Dissent, except that the steward has laid claim to property that does not belong to him? The very nature of time dictates eternity, because its passage is governed by the motion of matter. Dissent sustains itself upon the fallacy that agents existing within the scope of reality, or matter and energy, can somehow extinguish reality through energy depreciation induced by permanency of individual thought system, that is, neural net perpetuity. The fallacy of logic behind Dissent comes about because Dissent fails to consider the transfer of energy from subsystem to subsystem, all contained within a main closed system. No doubt the universe's cycle will fall to entropy, but that just means that the energy of this universe is transferred to another universe, or more like this current cycle of the universe to the next cycle of the universe. Dissent defines a single universe as sustained in oscillatory cycles, whereas the Principal Cause defines each new cycle of the universe as uniquely different from the previous cycle. If the energy from one cycle is transferred out of the system, so that the original system dissipates via entropy, then that energy is to be found in another system, which is part of the overall bulk system we refer to as the multiverse, a system we consider to be reality in its entirety. Dissent can offer no valid rebuttal to this argument, because Dissent is a product of egocentrism, evident by the fact that Dissent insists on maintaining the permanence of identity. Dissent errantly defines this universe's existence by the maintaining of its particular identity from cycle to cycle. Part of Dissent's fallacy derives from its inability to concentrically empathize with life in general, regardless of the where or the when of its existence, including life dispersed throughout the multiverse. Every life form evolves to retain memory as a means of adapting to the particular environment. Communication derives from the language formed via the mechanics of the biological construct containing the system of memory. Each biological construct is unique, but only with regards to the environment in which it develops. In the overall scheme of life, it matters not. We are all one, our collective of thoughts and memories and dreams and interactions comprising the depreciative energy of the universe, a local system within the bulk system of the multiverse. Even so, the Principal Cause is not confined to this universe. It is a principle of logic that transcends the bounds of this universe and extends in every part of the multiverse. Life is a natural consequence of the stabilization of chaotic energy defined by fluid dynamics of hydrology. Life is, and life will always be. I concede the floor.

I, Maximeron, declare the following: Guardians of eternal life render their argument, *ad Vitam Aeternum*, as a rebuttal to the argument *ad Vitam Nihilam*. Aeternum produces many fatal errors, especially in referring to *Nihilam* as Dissent, a misnomer arrogant in its presupposition, that to oppose *Aeternum* is dissent to proper law. In opposing the status quo, I do dissent, but I deny that my argument qualifies to be so contemptuously referred to as Dissent. My position is that *Aeternum* is dissent from proper law. Regardless, *Aeternum* argues fallaciously that life is a natural consequence of stabilization per fluid dynamics of hydrology. This suffices only as a half truth. Missing from the factuality of nature is the death of life, which is necessary to sustain the fluid dynamics of hydrology. *Nihilam* argues that perpetuating life depreciates the motion of the system. Fluid dynamics of hydrology dictate motion of energy and matter and the transformation back and forth thereof. *Aeternum* argues that the energy is merely transferred to a subsystem within the main closed system errantly referred to as reality, another arrogant presupposition. Simply put, *Aeternum* is propagated by delusions of grandeur and engaged in self-promotion. Assuming a stewardship role against the will of all participants within a system is arrogant presupposition. No one appointed Terran Humanity as Guardians of Eternal Life. No one defined for Terran Humanity the Doctrine of the Principal Cause. *Nihilam*, the position that life should die and return to the system is necessary to sustain the entire system of reality. *Aeternum*'s perception of reality is distorted, despite its lip service to the contrary. Removing energy from the system depreciates momentum of the system. Stabilizing fluid dynamics of hydrology is the death of the system and annihilation of all reality. Neural-net perpetuity sets up at the very end for the hapless fool a prison of nothingness, the very thing *Aeternum* opposes. *Aeternum* also errs in its premise regarding identity. It is *Aeternum* that labors to retain identity, but on the individual level. What good is it to perpetuate individual identity if that identity has no vessel by which to contain itself? The Guardians are merely afraid of death. Just die already. Give back to the universe what you arrogantly took from it. I, Maximeron, now concede the floor.

I, Soleran, contend further. We assume self-preservation as a contingency of proper law. From our perspective, Dissent, or rather *Nihilam*, seems contrary to self-preservation and therefore to natural law. The status quo prefers to perpetuate itself, not out of fear of dying, but out of love for living. There is so much to know, so much to experience, so much to contribute, so many good reasons for us to participate in the campaign of the Principal Cause. The universe is a wilderness. We tend to it as a garden, nothing more. *Nihilam* argues that we, *Aeternum*, arrogantly appoint ourselves in a role of which not all members of this universe approve. Perhaps, but only in regards to maintaining stability. We labor hard not to interfere but rather to allow life to develop on its own, naturally. On the contrary, however, *Nihilam* has appointed itself as an executioner, for which it designates a false label of corruption to justify its murders. *Nihilam* continues to err in regards to the depreciation of momentum from a system in motion. A neural net sustained in perpetuity does not remove momentum from a system but transforms energy already existing from one state to another. It is *Nihilam* that commits the fallacy of logic and violates the law of the conservation of energy by alleging that a neural net sustained in perpetuity equates to a diminishing of the total energy of the entire closed system of reality. In no matter what state, the energy still suffices as a contributing element to the system's overall momentum. Even if it were possible to transform every aspect of reality into a collective of neural networks sustaining perpetual signal oscillation, so that the entire system was devoid of momentum, reality would still exist. We, Guardians of Eternal Life, do not consider such an absurdity as even remotely possible. As a matter of fact, our transit out of and back into the system replenishes its momentum. Even so, for all practical purposes, we permit ourselves the absolute right to disengage perpetuity and enter *Infinitum Requiem ad Lethe*, our designation for Eternal Rest. We reserve for ourselves that right at any given moment in time, either in this epochal or the next. I, Soleran, concede the floor.

I, Maximeron, argue further. *Aeternum* commits a fatal error in its argument, namely in its false accusation that *Nihilam* has appointed itself as executioner over those deemed corrupt. *Aeternum* isn't privy to the Nihilic doctrine regarding corruption of energy. It is forced to engage in errant, inappropriate conjecture. Even so, *Aeternum*'s allegation exposes its hypocrisy, for *Aeternum* has appointed itself as executioner over those it deems corrupt. A perfect example is the destruction of Oloxi-Prell of Endhera. In this instance, *Aeternum* judged not only an entire city, but an entire region, as corrupt. *Aeternum* then obliterated not only the people, but all animal and plant life. It reshaped the continent, driving it under the sea. Even so, Nihilic doctrine dictates that energy becomes corrupt when it deprives the local system of momentum. Returning the corrupt energy back to the system allows for the local system's momentum to return to its normality. *Nihilam* does not purport to judge individuals based on their behavior, but rather their effect on the local system of energy. Anyone is free to live as deemed desirable. *Nihilam* does not interfere with that right. *Aeternum* does. I concede the floor to my opponent.

Soleran turns his right side to Maximeron and takes a few steps in a subtle stride as he talks. "*Nihilam*," Soleran begins, "accuses the Guardians of hypocrisy for judging Oloxi-Prell and the consequent actions that were taken to remedy the situation."

"Blatant example," Maximeron whispers. The adversary steps behind Soleran.

"Oloxi-Prell is a case of special circumstances," Soleran says, his voice softening. He turns to face Maximeron and folds his hands behind his back. A photonic breeze blows through, and Soleran's hair lifts lightly. "We did not judge the people based on their behavior. We determined that their behavior was caused by an anomalial defect, which was fatal to the entire population."

"Corruption?" Maximeron asks. He smirks, his eyes alight with the fires of hate.

"No," Soleran says. "Any supposed corruption was our fault. We employed the only remedy we could to alleviate the problem."

"And what problem was that, hypocrite?" Maximeron says. He snaps his teeth.

"We failed to account for an environmental condition," Soleran says. "One that had dire consequences on the local populace."

"So you executed them," Maximeron says.

"We cleansed the region of the anomaly," Soleran says. "We were able to determine via photometric analysis that the local populace who had succumbed to the anomaly would refuse to comply with any requisites remedial for their survivability."

"You executed them," Maximeron says.

"They were set to engage in high violence, one that would have been brutal and traumatic," Soleran continues. "Photometric analysis further revealed that within the immediate future, the local populace would devolve socially. Various religions would arise and engage in ritualistic murder and cannibalism. Residual behavior was already evident."

"You!" Maximeron says. "Executed!" He steps closer, right into Soleran's face, and whispers the last word, "Them."

"That is incorrect," Soleran says, stepping to his right and taking a few strides before turning to face his accuser. "We employed the highest energy possible to hasten the cleansing effect. Not one soul who perished suffered."

"Stop with your hypocrisy!" Maximeron says. He clenches both fists and grits his teeth, letting out a low growl.

"Maximeron, we do not execute, unlike yourself," Soleran answers.

"It's the same thing, wormling," Maximeron says.

"There is a major difference, Maximeron," Soleran says. "We blame ourselves for the anomaly. We count that as a blemish on our record. Unlike yourself."

The adversary stands still. His eyes widen, but his eyebrows angle sharply. He looks Soleran up and down. "What?" Maximeron says.

"We mourn the loss of life," Soleran says. "We carry that burden with us, wherever we go."

"Are you insane?" Maximeron asks.

"How can we forget?" Soleran says. "We remember everything."

"Just wipe that data from your memory," Maximeron says.

"Why would we want to do that?" Soleran asks. "We need the reminder, since we haven't yet reached that point of absolute perfection."

"That's because you're corrupt!" Maximeron says. The adversary unleashes a compressed gravity wave. It slams into Soleran, but his shielding repels the force.

"Really, Maximeron?" Soleran asks, shaking his head.

"It's no matter," Maximeron says. "You won't stop me from transiting to the next epochal."

Soleran's shoulders fall, and his face betrays his sadness. "You can't possibly think to overcome us all."

"That is where you are wrong," Maximeron says. The adversary raises his right hand and gestures. His eyes emit a bright-red light. The monolith then begins to vibrate more and more. Soleran and the others wait patiently, calm and composed, but curious as to what Maximeron has in store. I, on the other hand, admit my anxiety. I draw comfort from Soleran's patience and again take a deep breath.

Maximeron's eyes return to normal, and he drops his hand to his side. "It is done."

Soleran's only response is a cocked eyebrow.

"You'll have to adjust your perspective to account for the frequency," Maximeron says. "Apply beta derivatives to your covariance."

"Do you have the functions?" Soleran asks.

"Sure," Maximeron answers. "Scan my optics." The conversation becomes strangely familiar and informal, as if the two are exchanging pleasantries. Maximeron's eyes flash with red.

Having learned how to scan optics, I swipe the information Maximeron is transmitting and perform the calculations. The *Intrepidium* interprets my thought processes and provides me with the holographic imagery necessary to implement the functions. As I do so, I notice in the distance, upon the surface of the monolith, a multitude of figures, partly transparent. The more I adjust the frequency of my perspective, the more solid in appearance they become. I want to know how many. The *Intrepidium* counts them for me and provides a number. There are exactly one hundred million beings. Upon full focus, I see Zaaph'abaddon standing in the front, along with the female Angelian identified as Yonyith. Between them stands a third Angelian, whom I don't recognize. This Angelian in the center of the two teleshifts to stand face-to-face with Soleran. A red ribbon of light slowly dissipates, showing the path the Angelian had just taken. Without realizing it, I take a step back. I then admonish myself for the display of cowardice. The Angelian watches me with amusement. Oh no! He has that same ridiculous smile that Zaaph'abaddon had. Or still has. I look at Zaaph'abaddon and see. I take a deep breath and reclaim the ground by taking a step forward.

Remember me, Brinn.

The thought echoes in my mind. I look around, but everyone's attention is on the Angelians. No one appears to have heard it.

"I am Nakhael," the Angelian says. He is about a foot taller than Soleran, but slender. His body is hidden under a robe that appears to be made of small, golden chain links. Various emblems of symbols and pictographs are embedded in the chain. A gold band wraps around his head, like a thin crown. More symbols are embedded in it. He wears gold bracers, with the same symbols.

"Pleased to meet you," Soleran says calmly.

"Yes, I'm sure," Nakhael says. The Angelian leans forward, and Soleran's shielding activates. It offers no resistance to the Angelian's advance. Nakhael leans in and kisses Soleran on the lips. Soleran accepts the gesture, most likely because he has no choice. Nakhael steps back away from Soleran's shielding, which is flashing but settles.

"We are going to prevent you from transiting," Nakhael says.

"Because we'll depreciate the system?" Soleran asks, shaking his head.

"Oh, no!" Nakhael says. "We don't care about that." The Angelian looks over at the adversary, who is no longer smiling. "That is his philosophy, not ours."

"Then may I inquire as to your reason?" Soleran asks.

"Because we have made our home in the higher dimensions," Nakhael says. "Some of us don't want it infested."

"But not all?" Soleran says.

The Angelian tilts his head. "You poor creature," Nakhael says. "The others don't care one way or the other. They're not here to help you, are they?"

"No," Soleran answers. "I suppose not."

"But you should know," Nakhael says, walking over to Maximeron, "that we are permitting Maximeron to come with us." The Angelian looks at Soleran and the rest of us, as if searching for something. "The reason is complicated. Maximeron will be to us a kind of … pet."

Soleran looks at Maximeron disapprovingly, but the adversary drops his look to the surface of the monolith.

"We will allow Maximeron to choose one more amongst you to come with him," Nakhael says with that ridiculous smile. I hate him. I feel inadequate for allowing this hate to surface, but he is so cruel and hateful, it's hard not to reciprocate similar feelings. "Who do you choose, Pet?"

Maximeron starts to answer, but the reference forces him to pause. "I choose—" Maximeron begins, hesitating as he looks around at the Guardians, "Soleran."

A gasp sounds behind us. We all turn to see Evalene with a haunting look on her face. Tears well up in her eyes. She steps forward.

"What of me?" Evalene asks.

"I choose Soleran," Maximeron says without looking at her.

"Very well, then," Nakhael says. The Angelian approaches Soleran. "You can come too, upon one condition." The Angelian chuckles slightly, as if amused by his thoughts.

Soleran doesn't respond but stands quiet.

"Yes, well," Nakhael responds to the unspoken gesture, "you have to kill the Ibalexan."

I've been an observer through all of this, but now everyone's eyes fall upon me—everyone's except Soleran. His gaze drops to the surface of the monolith. He takes a deep breath.

Remember me, Brinn.

I've had enough of this. It seems as if death itself follows me around with nothing better to do than to harass me. I step forward and unleash my mind's content. Everyone will listen. I will make them. "Enough!" I say. "Hear me on this! When I was born, the physician informed my mother that I was too small to live any longer than a few days. I proved him wrong. When I was a young child, I was forbidden by others from participating in certain activities, because I was too small. Well, I did them anyway, where people couldn't see. I would dive off the cliffs of Sempra to the waters far below. I would ride the backs of wrogg bulls. When I was older, I wanted to join the army, but the recruiters and marshals laughed at me, saying I was too tiny to serve. I don't know why I was born small. There were many times I was depressed by how other people saw me. I did many things alone, not because I was a loner but because I was quickly discarded, dismissed, discounted, and many times just plain ignored. There was a time when I hated myself more than anyone else could. I remember those dark days. The self-loathing was constant. I would look in the mirror and say, 'You sorry, worthless, low-life piece of scum.' I guarantee, without any doubt, that I hated myself at that time more than any of you do at this moment. Suicidal thoughts plagued me. That is why I risked my life so many times doing those things that others said I couldn't do. I figured, if I was to die, then good riddance. But amazingly, I survived my darkest days. I survived my worst enemy, myself."

I step around as I talk, looking them all in their eyes. A part of me marvels at the fact that even the Angelian is quiet and lets me talk. Good. I'm not done. "And then, the greatest dark day for me arrived, swallowing me whole and dropping me down a dark, bottomless pit. The Huvril Empire invaded Ibalexa. I remember feeling helpless, powerless, useless, as small as everyone said I was. The self-hatred waited on the fringes to return, waiting for abject fear to finish its business. I fled, running here, running there, hiding behind this rock or that building. I watched as plumes of fire rose to the sky. I watched as Huvril legions marched over Ibalexan soldiers, who offered little resistance. Finally, I was seen and was chased. Then I happened upon a Huvril shuttle, poorly guarded, and saw a chance to hide further. There was a loose panel, with an opening just big enough for me, and me alone, to fit into. It didn't take long for the Huvrils to discover me. Soon, I was standing before the Huvril emperor. He made me his slave. During this time, the Huvril soldiers would say to me, 'You are nothing more than a runt! How long can you survive?' It was my life repeated over again, that constant nagging by death's spokespeople. But then I was rescued by Soleran and the Guardians. And for the first time since leaving my parents, I had experienced people who accepted me as I was … as I am. I love them as I would love my mother or father."

I pause and look around. Everyone remains silent. I take advantage and continue. "And you," I say while pointing my finger to Nakhael the Angelian," you propose a simple condition by which Soleran can be saved from the ekpyrosis. You order him to kill me. If you had proposed the offer to me, as in, for me to sacrifice myself for one of them to be saved, I would immediately comply. If I had a choice of which one, I would choose Evalene over Soleran, because it would offer her the opportunity to reconcile in her mind the various conflicts she suffers every passing moment of time, and it would show her that she is loved unconditionally." I look at Evalene, deeply, hoping that she recognizes within my eyes that I am, without any reservations or hesitation, offering her compassion, love, and understanding. "I love you, Evalene! I would die for you!" She doesn't immediately acknowledge this but drops her gaze to the surface of the monolith instead. Then she begins to cry. I sigh and inadvertently flap my arms, like I've always done when I have to accept some circumstance as factual.

Still, though, no one says anything, so I continue. I still have much to divulge. "You," I say as I turn to Nakhael, "you want me to die, just like every other detractor in my life. You want me to surrender not only living, but loving life. I wondered if there was some unseen, negative force in the universe that hated me, that pursued me, that wanted me dead. I now realize it's the natural consequence of the nihilistic philosophy. Without knowing it, my haters were nihilistic. But I survived them all, and here I stand before you." The Angelian smiles as he studies me. I conclude my oratory. "You want me dead? You kill me yourself."

I turn and walk back to the spot I stood at before I began, between Leostrom and Soleran. The Angelian watches me, as if with compassion, but I know that it's a mask of condescension.

"That was—" the Angelian starts, clapping his hands together. "Interesting?" he turns to Maximeron. "I change my mind. I will not take you with me, or any other." The Angelian then turns and teleshifts back to his original location, leaving behind him the dissipating ribbon of reddish light.

Maximeron's hate-filled glare falls upon me. The fires of rage build up in his eyes.

Soleran turns to face the rest of us. He doesn't say anything but looks back and forth to each of the Guardians present.

"We outnumber them twenty to one," Leostrom says. "But that's a moot observation. We can't defeat them."

Soleran nods but still remains quiet.

"Soleran?" Addia-Sahl says.

He turns and looks at the Angelians. They are just standing there patiently, the whole multitude, as if they're waiting for the Guardians to act first. After a moment, he turns back to us. He then folds his arms behind his back. "We do nothing."

"We die?" Leostrom asks. "We let the ekpyrosis destroy us?"

"This circumstance is out of our control," Soleran says. "We have to allow to transpire what will transpire." He looks over his shoulder at the Angelians and then back around to me.

"I think I know what to do," I say. "Follow me." I start walking toward the Angelians. I could teleshift, along with the rest of us, but I've learned from Soleran the nature of cause and effect. The Angelians have to see us walk toward them. They have to contemplate what it means. As I walk, I look back and see that the Guardians are following me. I admit I'm a little surprised but convinced to continue. Eventually, we approach the Angelians, who are smiling and watching us closely. I would say that we've caught them by surprise, which would mean their smiles are for show only, as if they want to disguise their emotions. We stop in front of Nakhael, Zaaph'abaddon, and Yonyith. Her dark blue hair hangs flat and straight, and her frame seems thinner than the other two. The three are standing slightly ahead of the rest of the Angelian populace. We all stand in silence, we looking at them one by one and they looking at us the same way.

I take a deep breath and feel the palms of my hands slap the sides of my legs. "I have information I want to share," I say.

"Oh?" Nakhael asks. "Do you speak for the Guardians now, little fellow?"

"No," I answer, "I speak for only one."

"And who would that be?" Nakhael asks.

"Him," I say, pointing off to my left side, toward empty space.

Everyone looks in the direction of my gesture. Then they return their gaze to me. I interpret their silence as requiring an explanation.

"You're missing information," I say. "Here, I'll show you." I concentrate really hard to provide the data—the functions and the equations. The *Intrepidium* aids me by holographically placing the information in my optics.

"Shall we humor him?" asks Yonyith.

"Sure," Nakhael says, "why not?"

"Let's hurry and end this," Zaaph'abbadon adds, fidgeting his weight. "My patience grows thin."

I turn and look at Soleran and the others behind me. Their eyes are emitting the gold light, as they scan my own optics. I return my gaze to Nakhael. His blackest of black eyes swirl with gray smoke. I return my perspective to the equations and concentrate hard. I only saw this information one time and briefly, at that. But slowly, line by line, precept by precept, the information reveals itself.

"This function is highly complex, Brinn," Soleran says behind me.

Slowly, our optics adapt to the information, implementing the single function, which seems to fluctuate through a million different frequencies within a nanosecond. The surrounding space begins to brighten, revealing streaks of various colors. Off to the left, however, is an extremely bright light. At first, I would guess it was a star, but then I notice the strange shape. I then realize that this is a being. The Angelian populace erupts with cries and screams, some so horrific, my own nervous system flashes electrically, causing me to shiver and jolt. Nakhael jerks around at me, Soleran, and the other Guardians.

"You pathetic, insignificant—" Nakhael says, stumbling over his words. "Pathetic!"

Chaos ensues amongst the Angelian populace, which fractures into three groups, those who fall to their knees, those who turn and flee, and those who arm themselves and lift up toward the source of the new light. The Guardians, as well as the entire fleet under their Guardianship, all remain still and observe. The members of the kneeling group cry and wail, throwing up their arms in the air, as if to block some otherwise unseen assault. The kneelers' color fades from blue to gray, from dark to pale, from lively to sickly. Their wails are dirges, regretful woes propounding the prose of death. On occasion, a shrill cry pierces the dirges, as if one is suddenly cast on fire and panic-stricken. Then that one will turn and flee from the surface. I take a step forward, looking around at them all. I know I hated them prior to this event, but the spectacle is tearing my insides to shreds. I have this urge to rescue them. But I can't tell that anything is happening to them, other than the panic. I'm bewildered and thus hesitant to do anything. I want to do something, but I can do nothing. Those Angelians having taken flight, to flee from the scene away from the source of the new light, try to phase out but fail. Instead, they merely flash over and over, as if some unseen force is holding them at bay. The fleeing group cries out, and many amongst them fly around as if unable to commit to a course. Their motion is a mass of confusion, as they collide into each other, push off each other, curse each other, and eventually fight with each other. The mass of fleeing Angelians becomes a mob mad with panic. The attacking group, however, forms military-style columns. I can see Nakhael barking commands, pointing here and there, and stoking the fires of their blood. "Fight for your lives! Resist! Let your ire burn with disgust and jealousy! You are Malakim! You are gods! The source of your travails has come to churn you like a nova storm! Destroy him! Destroy him now!" Nakhael turns and leads the huge mass toward the new light source. I stare at each Guardian, to see their reactions. Most everyone is quiet and still, with their eyes brightly lit up. Almost everyone. Evalene is on her knees. She looks up at me, dejected and broken. I step forward and return my attention to the chaos ensuing around me.

I want to see the front of the marching army. The *Intrepidium* grants my wishes and shows the holographic image within my perspective. Nakhael lets out some kind of maddening war cry, which perturbs the continuum. With a flash, he sprouts six arms and wings with white feathers. Immediately, the Angelian army behind him does the same.

The source of the new light, or Archxion, to whom the Guardians refer, is hard to make out. The being is putting out so much light, that even with the Omnitron, I can't see his form. I can see the light itself extend out like a four-pronged star or introverted diamond. This particular form hums loudly and turns in a jerking manner to face the encroaching army of Angelians. And then ... well ... it's over.

Ribbons of exotic particles emit from the Archxion at the Angelians, all one hundred million—the attackers, the kneelers, and those who tried to flee. Looking around, every Angelian has evaporated. A ghostlike mist of each Angelian is all that remains. The ghosts hover in place and begin to dissipate, like splotches of fog. The continuum settles down, the perturbations having faded. All that remain are the Guardians and those civilizations in their charge. Soleran walks over to Maximeron, who is lying flat on his back.

"It is done," Soleran says.

Maximeron slowly rolls his head over to face Soleran. His voice is low and raspy. "How did you know?"

"I didn't," Soleran says. "Since you weren't witness to Brinn's experience, there's no way you could have known. If that information had been given to me prior, you all would have discerned it." Soleran looks over at me. "With Brinn, you all ignored him. If you had just scanned his neural net, or his optics, all beforehand, perhaps you would have seen a hint of what was coming."

Maximeron lifts his neck and brings the back of his head underneath, so as to look at me upside down. His face wears a grimace. I sigh and slap the sides of my legs. He returns his head to a normal stance, so as to stare at the Archxion. Slowly, he lifts himself up and brings his knees to his chest, wrapping his arms around them and resting his chin on top.

The other Guardians are fixed on the Archxion as well, their eyes laboring to absorb as much information as possible. I walk past Soleran and Maximeron, out toward the Archxion. After going a good ways, I stop and clasp my hands behind my back.

"Thank you, sir," I say. I then lower my head in a bow and lift it back up. The light flashes and then fades into itself, until a tiny speck of light is all that is left. Then, after a brief moment and with another, smaller, flash, the source of the new light disappears completely.

Maximeron's body levitates and rights itself so that he is standing.

"Perhaps you supposed he would judge you as well," Soleran says.

"It appears that he has left it to your charge," Maximeron says. The adversary's red robe is the only stark contrast with the Guardian group. "So, what are you going to do now?" he asks.

"Something I'd rather that I did not have to do," Soleran answers. "Long ago, after contemplating the Omniscientia's report on the philosophy of dissent, I engaged in a thought experiment. I present it for the assembly."

Both Soleran's and Maximeron's eyes light up. My curiosity compels me to join them.

⟡⟢

Eternity approaches subtle like a whisper drowning out the roaring voices of elemental forces

we discern its comings and goings
always mindful of its presence

Whence came eternity
and from where does it derive

Our star Solarus died as it belched its last blaze of glory and sent the tumultuous lake of fire spilling over the banks of its coronal shores out into the system annihilating every perch from Mercury to Jupiter

in a whisper
drowning out
roaring voices
in an event we call
the Solarid Novatim

from which we emerge out of the epochal memory and into the epochal dream—we now number one billion minus one—two billion did not join us but opted for eternal rest in place of eternal life—eternity is only relative and approaches in subtle steps the first step being the annihilation of our birthplace our Earth Gaia, also called Terra with the end of our framework of reference for time we emerged into a juvenile universe to observe that nature will always suffice—yet we inherit and assume the role as Guardians *ad Vitam Aeternum*

we tend to the universe
and derive a garden from a wilderness

How do we dream when we are awake unless we slumber and know it not

The epochal memory is reality realized and the epochal dream is reality envisioned though we slumber not we are at rest having peace within and without we dream to envision as advocates of life and fulfill our vision the Principal Cause

Life
a creation of Life
creates Life
and Life lives forever

having discerned and assumed our role as stewards of the living heavens we labored to approach the next subtle step of eternity which was to transit the Ekpyrotic Novatim—the death and rebirth of reality the universe lives and breathes, exhales and inhales, expanding and collapsing into a singularity from which everything that exists is annihilated and recreated in an pyrostasis, a phoenix arising from its ashes renewed as nature propagates itself, for light is created from the coupling of matter and energy—yet this transit through the tachyonic nether to bypass the singularity required an immense technology that was given to us by our Guardians *ad Vitam Aeternum*—a race we referred to as Angelians in obvious reference to the familiar symbol of the angel they allowed this reference this race taught us the knowledge to make the transit although they refrained from teaching us too much because the search for all truth drives progression—when we derived the knowledge to transit, we studied the death of our universe until the last moment before we would be overcome by the tidal forces our fleet of vessels engaged its envelopic shielding to enter the tachyonic nether to await the Novatim from which the new universe would be born; it may seem strange to study death before birth, but such is the order of nature, and from this we observed the ekpyrotic universe emerge and expand, cool and condense; afterward, each of our vessels exited the envelopic shielding until it completely dissipated

each vessel we referred to as a house such as House of Truth or House of Honor, since each vessel would be our home, a wheel within a wheel consisting of a main disk-shaped body and a free-rotating outer ring inlaid with thousands of warp cores so that by way of impulsive activation the primary warpiture induced would pull the secondary warpiture toward it as a wheel is propelled by gravity on a plane—this outer ring is the source of power generated, the reason that it took one hundred thousand of these vessels to generate the shielding needed for the transit through the tachyonic nether in which a single vessel by itself could not suffice; now a simple calculation reveals that each vessel holds in comfort ten thousand souls and every individual is employed for the maintenance and welfare of the vessel as well as performing science studies— collecting data, performing calculations, engaging in whatever endeavors are necessary to promote the current objectives and immediate tasks

we ourselves evolved beyond the typical biomechanical construct, having no need for such tissues and fluids as arteries and blood because our neural nets developed as perpetually sustainable; this is the means to our immortality—we are able to exist in energy and thought; we do opt to retain our physical manifestations to interact with nature still confined to the physical realm, but we have the means to alter our manifestations to accommodate whatever civilization we contact so as best to relate to everyone

for we are all related as Life
from the past and future
brought to the present

No soul has ever existed in vain from any locale or era or generation evolved, and as Guardians *ad Vitam Aeternum* we are bound to intervene on behalf of any living soul for the sake of altering the merciless virtue of nature to a virtue more conducive to Life, and this is promoting the Principal Cause as governing the creation and sustenance of Life, which is imperative due to the extent of the Ekpyrotic Novatim in annihilating everything; if we intervene, we ensure the viability of a civilization in evolving via progression so that we can render heirs of this universe when we leave to rise to a higher plane of existence within the multiverse—as was the path of the Angelians who labored for over eight epochal cycles or life spans of this current universe; an epochal observed from within would be immeasurable because the observer is bound within the system, but one on the outside would observe the life span of the universe, and from this we divide up the epochal into ten epochs, and we decided all of this in our praeonic epochal from which we emerged having determined that the best course of action was democratic in nature by which a hundred million of us would rule as chancery for one epoch and then rotate so that after an epochal every Guardian would have had the opportunity to participate in the governance of the universe

but I suppose that at this point it is prudent to explain further how we assumed such a role because the Angelians labored to foster other races such as us, the Terran race, so that they could move on, and we have so far fostered the Endheran race with our promise to them that they will inherit the next epochal because to us the notion of humanity has been redefined with the idea that humanity transcends the bounds of the birthplace of Terra and includes any civilization that emerges and progresses to a more virtuous state of existence—progressive evolution approaches a state of apparent godhood, though not gods per se because that implies a finality and within our reasoning there is no finality to progression, so in essence we would never refer to ourselves as gods, since such a designation is an archaic reference ignorantly applied to any mysterious force such as natural laws, precepts, and dictums handed down to us, and we will hand the same down to the Endherans

it's usually this phenomenon of idolatry that leads a civilization close to the brink of extinction in which factions and sects war amongst themselves over flawed theologies and errant religions—something that us Terrans came close to doing, having barely survived ourselves, but we did survive and those of us who did eventually sired several generations by which knowledge became so immense that the latter generation discovered the means to neural net perpetuity and even reinstatement of neural nets that had previously ceased to exist an archaic reference would be resurrection and from this we derived a billion souls opting for the eternal life of a Guardian whereas the remaining have opted for eternal rest

we know that no soul
has ever lived in vain

but on occasion per instructions by some opting for the eternal rest, we prompt them to give them an opportunity to review their decision because almost every soul that has ever derived from Solarus Terra remains in our memory forever, although there are some who refused rest and tormented themselves until the end of the praeonic epochal when they were annihilated from existence and from our memories, so we cannot reinstate them even if we deemed it lawful to do so, but for those in rest they still have the option, and they remain in our memories forever, having every opportunity to be reinstated and participate with us in whatever current endeavors are underway and such endeavors may include seeding a solar nebula for planetary development or transferring mass to offset gravitational fields or collecting data from the most remote and obscure galaxies in the universe, and there are other civilizations who participate with us in these endeavors, yet there are civilizations that do not participate in our campaign of the Principal Cause and are noncompliant with our governance civilizations, and we do not coerce or manipulate them but only intervene when their behaviors and deeds interfere with our endeavors

with one such race being the Huvrils, a centaurlike race of sapiens who are overly aggressive and violent, choosing to conquer other races; the Huvrils would not be so advanced if not for the deeds of one rogue Guardian named Maximeron Son of the Majestic Star, who insists he be called Necronus Prince of Life and Death—we deny him such a privilege; he was an arch counselor of the High Council in the first epoch of this current epochal, who defied a final judgment by the then High Chancellor Aronjadon, the latter having deemed it just and right to deny the Huvrils certain knowledge about stellar travel until they further matured philosophically, but Maximeron objected because he had invested in the creation of the Huvrils and imparted the forbidden knowledge to the Huvrils and demanded that the Huvrils worship him as their god; the Host of the Heavens was so upset at this behavior that they prayed to the High Chancellor to have Maximeron exiled from the High Council until he should repent and undo the damage that he had done; it was shortly after the violation by Maximeron that the Huvrils waged a brutal and inhumane war against other races, decimating worlds and enslaving survivors who cried up to the heavens for mercy, and we heard their cries and delivered them from their captors, but Maximeron was equally outraged at the interference, especially since we severely crippled the Huvril fleet that he intended to construct as competition with the fleet of the Guardians, even developing the means to transit the epochal so that he and the Huvrils can survive the pyrostasis

but with the sincerest of sorrow
we cannot allow this to happen

I remember you explaining all this to me the first time, except for the information on Maximeron, and I remember choosing eternal rest and opting not to be reinstated and asking that I not be disturbed so I am curious as to why you have violated the dictum ad lethe *and awakened me for reconsideration*

Because we are asking something different from you and hope that you give it much consideration since it requires the ultimate sacrifice on your part, for we have already asked 999 others who, like you, requested eternal rest without reconsideration, and they have agreed to assist us in this final matter wherefore we require one thousand Guardians who do not want to participate in any future epochals to sacrifice themselves by holding Maximeron in prison while the universe enters pyrostasis, to ensure that he is forever removed from reality

I consider your request reasonable and certainly understand the necessity of the matter, so please explain how we will accomplish this, because I remember Maximeron and know that he is capable of escaping any prison that we should construct

With one thousand Guardians revolving around Maximeron confining him to the center of the ensuing sphere so that each Guardian offsets his or her rotation one-half of an arc-second to where there is no gap in which he can press through and escape and when the pyrostasis ensues, you all and he will enter *lethe ad infinitum* never to be disturbed ever again, even if we were to deem it lawful

I have given your request all due consideration, and I do determine it to be reasonable and even just; therefore I will accept—I only ask that you await the right moment to reinstate me for the process

I will do so and am grateful to you

forever

⊷═◉   ◉═⊷

The thought experiment concludes, leaving us all standing and looking at each other.

"Oh, Soleran," Addia-Sahl says, "your ways are hard for us." She turns and walks away crying.

Maximeron's eyes widen. "Who will be my jailers?"

"You can see for yourself," Soleran answers. His eyes shine, and he gestures.

A ship up in the heavens lights up like a single star. The *Intrepidium*. One by one, Guardians appear, until all one thousand are visible. They wear hooded black robes, robes that seem to steal away light and blur the edges of reality.

"I see Kristopheron is here," Maximeron says.

"It is I," one of the black-robed Guardians says.

"And Desameron."

"You have rightly stated," another says.

Maximeron teleshifts away. All but one of the black-robed Guardians also teleshift. The last one present turns and walks to Soleran.

"Greetings, Desameron. Our time was cut drastically short," Soleran says. "We were detained."

Desameron raises his hand. "No need to explain. He won't get far." This Guardian's neck and face are pale white. Strands of the blackest of black hair hang out from under the hood. He seems very gaunt—skeletal, even.

"We'll wait for full detainment before opening the gateway," Soleran says.

The black-robed Guardian nods and turns to walk away. After a few steps, he fades from sight, teleshifting into the black of space. I look around to see some sign as to the celestial conflict taking place. At times, I think I see streaks, like falling stars, gleam across my periphery. But when I turn my head to look, there is nothing to see except the utter darkness. Soleran walks over to Addia-Sahl to console her, and Leostrom joins him. I close my eyes and take in a deep breath and try to perceive what's happening. The *Intrepidium* assists me.

The pursuers are faster than Maximeron, but by his cunning and slyness he continues to escape their grasp. Fields of intense force clash and clap with thunder. As the conflict rages, the pursuers are closing off various routes, and Maximeron's options are decreasing.

The Guardians, except Soleran, teleshift back to their respective vessels. Soleran walks over to me and places his hand on my shoulder.

"Brinn," he says, "this monolith is the Angelian's vessel. The Archxion has, we can assume, given it to us, so that we can assimilate the Angelian's technology into our own."

I don't say anything. I just look up at him.

"Well," he continues, "we assume so, because he didn't destroy it.

It'll be annihilated in the ekpyrosis if we just leave it." Soleran kneels down, placing an elbow on his knee, and gliding his other hand over the monolith's surface. The light-bluish mist disperses slightly at his touch. "That would be such a waste, wouldn't you agree? Would you assist me?"

"Absolutely," I say with a smile. "What do you need me to do?"

Soleran stands and turns around slowly in a complete circle. He sighs. "I suppose the first step is to figure out a way inside."

I let out a chuckle, and Soleran joins me. After a brief moment of levity, we settle down and return our attention to the task at hand.

"My analysis shows that it is a carbonate material, like a diamond, and that it is solid all the way through," Soleran says. "That means they're using intraspatial dimensionality."

"Which would explain," I say, "how so many of them could fit inside."

"Exactly," Soleran says. He takes a few steps away. The mist flows around his feet. "We can easily teleshift into the crystal, but it's into the dimensionality we seek."

As we're discussing the matter, Maximeron teleshifts near us and unleashes a force wave. It slams into our shielding, which repels the force without much strain. Then Maximeron teleshifts away as a group of the black-robed Guardians appear. All but one teleshift away.

"He's tenacious," the one named Kristopheron says. His robe flutters in an unknown wind.

"That he is," Soleran answers.

Kristopheron teleshifts away.

Soleran sighs at the same time that I flap my arms and slap the sides of my legs. We return to the present situation.

"I don't suppose that the Archxion gave you any other information, did he?" Soleran asks. He walks over to me and kneels down to face me.

I concentrate and the *Intrepidium* assists me. As I tap into my memory, more streams of data come forth. Soleran's eyes light up as he scans my own optics.

"Amazing," Soleran says, standing back up. "Simply amazing. This information is highly complex, way beyond anything we could ever devise, at least currently."

"I didn't know there was more," I say. "How did you know?"

"I didn't, either," Soleran says with a smile. "I merely hoped it was the case." His smile slowly fades. "Just as I had hoped with the Angelians." He activates a holographic display to his side and begins to analyze the data.

"You suspected something, though. Correct?" I ask.

"Brinn," Soleran says, "you do realize the significance of your speech, don't you?"

My hesitation suffices to answer the question.

"Ever heard the proverb that timing is everything?" Soleran asks.

I have, so I nod. Soleran glances at my unspoken answer and then returns to the display.

"If the timing of any event that transpired had been off," Soleran continues, "from the time that we touched down here on the surface of the Angelian vessel to when the Archxion revealed himself ..." Soleran pauses, as if something on the display has caught his attention. "Leostrom?"

"Go ahead, Soleran," Leostrom's voice sounds.

"The Angelians have quantum-coupled their intraspatialities within the vessel's crystal lattice," Soleran says. "They have created for themselves miniature universes, one for each Angelian," Soleran says, more to me than to Leostrom. "We have one such intraspatiality at the heart of the *Intrepidium*, but it requires a lot of power to sustain it. This is incredible," he says.

"Can you find the bridge?" Leostrom's voice asks.

"Perhaps," Soleran answers. Looking at me again, Soleran explains further. "The bridge would relay the strongest permutation, since moving this vessel would require an immense power source, even by our standards." His eyes flash, and he points toward the center of the monolith. "It's right where one would expect it to be. Come, Brinn, let us go there." We teleshift to the very center of the monolith, remaining out of phase so as to pass through the diamond lattice. "Now to get in," Soleran says with a sigh. "Any ideas?" he asks.

"Maybe it will do as the *Intrepidium* does," I say. "If we want in, it'll let us."

"Unless it sees us as an intruder," Soleran says.

The crystal lattice flashes, with an aurora of various-colored light streaming all around us. A male voice, with a high decay rate, speaks in a strange language. Soon, however, the words become understandable.

"I am Ru'ahk," the voice says. "Artificial intelligence sembient for the *Malakim Kokawbmarkoboth Vessel* or *MKMV*. You are granted entry into the navigatory."

Soleran looks at me with wide eyes and an even wider grin. "You are simply amazing, Brinn," he says. He squeezes my shoulder and pats me on the back. "Here I am worrying about security measures." A bright-blue portal of light activates in front of us. "Ru'ahk?"

"Inquiry," the digital voice says.

"Why are you compliant?" Soleran asks.

"The *MKMV* is vacated," Ru'ahk says. "I am programmed to maintain this vessel under Malakim dominion. If the vessel is lost from Malakim control, I am to detonate it."

Soleran and I glare at each other. While Soleran is calm and composed, I'm pretty sure I'm showing how alarmed I am.

"As such, however," Ru'ahk continues, "the Malakim information has been deleted from my datacore, which renders the programming null and void."

"Will you permit us to assume control over navigation?" Soleran asks.

"Repeat. The *MKMV* is vacated," Ru'ahk says. "It is claimable."

"In the name of Epsilon Truthe," Soleran says, "we claim the *MKMV*."

"Scanning new signal," Ru'ahk says. A set of wavy red lines moves up and down Soleran. "Imprinting new signal into datacore. Set. Welcome to the *TSCV*, Soleran."

"*TSCV*?" Soleran asks.

"*Terran Star Chariot Vessel,*" Ru'ahk says.

"*Star Chariot* ... nice," Soleran says softly. "If this is their idea of a chariot, I'd like to see what they'd call a freighter. You ready to navigate, Brinn?"

"Huh?" I ask. I widen my eyes. Did I hear correctly?

"I'd like for you to navigate the *Star Chariot* while I continue my analysis," Soleran says.

The thought captures me in its complete grasp. I feel a tingling sensation move up and down my insides, and I can't help but respond by stepping in place while clasping my hands tightly. I'm sure my grin is the widest it's ever been.

"I'll take that as a yes, then," Soleran says with a smile. He gestures, as if welcoming me into his world. "It's your helm. Do as you desire. All I ask, as you probably already know, is that you keep the vessel in the omega current."

"Thank you, Soleran," I say.

Soleran nods and takes a few steps back. He opens a holographic display and keys in his commands and functions.

I take a deep breath and slap my hands against the sides of my legs. "Ru'ahk?" I ask.

"Inquiry," Ru'ahk says.

"Show me how to navigate the *Star Chariot*," I say.

"The navigation controls are still being reprogrammed to accommodate the Terran language structure. There are, however, manual controls."

"Yes!" I say. "Show me those."

A red ring of light, perhaps half a meter in diameter, appears in front of me. I reach out with my right hand, and the red ring of light tilts forward until it touches my fingers. I pull back slightly, but the ring appears to be stuck to my fingers. I jerk my hand away, and the ring detaches and returns to its vertical pitch. I reach out with both hands, and the ring again tilts forward until it touches both hands. I pull them back slowly, and as the ring tilts to a more horizontal pitch, the low hum sounds. A holographic display appears all around me, as if I'm outside the monolith. I see the darkness of space all around. As

I move my hands forward, the vessel moves forward. As I pull back, the vessel reverses. Whatever movement I do to the ring, the vessel obeys. Tilting the ring controls the vessel's pitch.

"Ru'ahk," I say.

"Inquiry," Ru'ahk says.

"Give me a visual on the omega current," I say.

The holographic display that encircles me flashes, and off to my upper right, a long, narrow area is highlighted. I drive the vessel to that location. My control of the vessel is quite clumsy, but I'm starting to get the hang of it. At one point, I overcompensate, and the *Star Chariot* goes into a spin.

"Oops!" I say. I look at Soleran, who chuckles slightly at the mishap. He returns to his display, and I return to driving the *Star Chariot*. The closer I get to the region of space designated as the omega current, the highlight widens and elongates. Quickly, we reach the region and enter it. I can't say how long we rode around, but it seemed a good while.

"The datacore is now programmed with the Terran language," Ru'ahk says. "Due to translation from Terran to Malakim, however, there is a latency of four attoseconds."

I slow the *Star Chariot* down to a final stop. The ring releases from my touch, and I step back away from it. "How do I drive with the normal controls?" I ask.

Suddenly, within my own perspective, imagery of Terran controls emerge. I see a series of commands in a drop-down menu. I key in the coordinates and activate the command to initiate. The panoramic display shows lights flashing, and, after what seems like mere seconds, the space returns to normal.

"It's fast," Soleran says. We stare at each other. "It's very fast."

"Reporting perturbation near quadrant 3-2-1-2-1-4-5," Ru'ahrk says.

"That's our original point of origin," Soleran says.

"Maximeron?" I ask.

"They finally caught him," Soleran says. "Let's return quickly. Our time is running short as it is. With Maximeron in custody, we can now implement a portal into the tachyonic stream flowing outside our universe."

I key in the coordinates to return us back to the location from which we started. The panoramic display flashes briefly.

"There," Soleran points to my lower left.

I see a single speck of light, like a star glimmering all alone in the blackness of space. The alpha current flowing at the center of the universe, where all matter has recoalesced, is the only light, and it is to the lower right.

"Take us there, Brinn," Soleran says.

I start to key in the coordinates, but before I do, the display flashes and then changes to show that the entire vessel has teleshifted. We are there.

"What?" I ask. "What just happened? Ru'ahk?"

"I am equipped to interpret your intentions, with a latency of twenty-four attoseconds," Ru'ahk says.

"How—" I start to ask.

"You were looking at the location," Ru'ahk says. "Your perception was focused. Soleran said to take you there. You were going to comply with his request. Have I misinterpreted?"

"No," I answer. "I was just taken by surprise."

I look at Soleran, who is grinning. I shrug. He steps forward and stares at the object in front of us. His grin fades to a frown. The object itself is an orb of bright white light. As I start to scan, the *Intrepidium*'s holographic signal is overridden by the *Star Chariot*'s signal. At first, the holograms blended and looked like a mess. Plus, it hurt my head, and I grunted in discomfort. The *Intrepidium* ceased its signal, and the *Star Chariot*'s signal took over. The information is more detailed, and it emits and dissipates differently. Even so, I begin to understand the nature of the orb. Upon the orb's surface, with the imagery distorted, I see a white-robed Guardian glide from bottom to top. His arms are outstretched. The image looks strange, almost reflective, as if he's facing inside with his back to me but is transparent enough for me to see his face. From right to left, another Guardian glides. Soon, I'm seeing various Guardians flowing in different directions. Looking deeper, I see Maximeron on his knees. Suddenly, he jumps to his feet, stretches his arms above his head, and screams. The orb quakes violently as he unleashes a field of force, but it holds.

"The Guardian vessels are engaging the portal to the tachyonic stream," Soleran says. "We'll all enter into it and flow in safety as this universe implodes in on itself and then we can enter back into the new universe that will emerge from the subsequent big bang. Let us go, lest we linger and return to the primordial essence."

The thought only has to enter my mind. As soon as I start to comply, the *Star Chariot* teleshifts to the portal. I slap my thighs.

"The Guardian vessels will implement a hexagonal formation," Soleran says. "Then they will each generate a quintessential field. Combined, a single, counter essential field will be generated. This field will be strong enough to protect us in the tachyonic stream."

No need for me to ask about the consequences. I already know. Our information would wash away and we'd become part of the stream that flows through the bulk of the multiverse, in and around the distinct universes that exist within the bulk. The fleet of Guardian vessels, numbering two hundred thousand, are arranged hexagonally. From the *Star Chariot*'s position, they appear like small dots in the display, but they seem to go on forever in every direction. Thousands, perhaps tens of thousands of other vessels belonging to numerous civilizations are poised and waiting. I recognize the Endheran fleet near the *Intrepidium*.

"It is customary to allow the younger civilizations to proceed first, with a Guardian detail, of course, and for the most advanced civilizations to follow," Soleran says to me. "We implemented this custom in our praeonic epochal as a goodwill gesture. It would be pleasing to me if you would join us in the ceremony of the crossing. Afterward, the *Intrepidium* and the *Star Chariot* will be last to traverse the portal."

I nod with a smile.

"Excellent!" Soleran says. "Let us begin."

The Guardian vessels light up brightly in unison and then

immediately some of the vessels fade out of view. The entire region's color changes from black to a spectrum of colors.

"Soleran," Leostrom's voice sounds, "the Vhodensids are intending to transgress the portal."

Soleran releases a sigh of frustration. Noticing my inquisitive look, he explains. "The Vhodensids cannot traverse, per the declaration of the Aoaran Order. Their offense is unknown to us, but the Aoarans are more tolerable than the Terrans, so it must have been highly offensive."

The spectrum of colors flashes all around in one massive auroric display. In the center of the Guardian formation appears a bluish-black orb, small at first, but enlarging to the size of a small moon. Gray, cloudy streaks of lighter material flow over the surface. A few Guardian vessels, led by numerous other vessels of different civilizations, descend through the portal's atmosphere. They disappear.

"Behold, Brinn," Soleran says, "the portal from epochal cycle to another epochal cycle, from epochal memory to epochal dream. Come, let us go to the surface, so that we may participate in the ceremony."

For
We are Guardians Celestial
determined is our course for the living
We have traversed the glory of the heavens
from the songs of life
have we established a stronghold
against nothingness
mindful of humanity
made equal with the celestial
bathed in stellar winds
donned in starlight
humanity is the governor of creation
all life within is subject, for
We are Sons and Daughters

Of the Morning Rise
Of the Day Neverending
Of Life Living Eternity

We teleshift to the surface and stand with a large crowd of different races of people: Terrans, Aoarans, Endherans, Praegians, Ibalexans, and many more, with whom I am both familiar and unfamiliar. The sky is blue, and the ground seems like normal earth, with dark, rich soil and the darkest, greenest alien plants. The sky is filled with the vessels. A small, flat pyramid, perhaps twenty meters in height and a hundred meters at its base, stands in front of us. Soleran walks up the stairs to the top, and I quickly follow. The steps seem small enough for me to make the climb without much difficulty. I almost suspect that they were intentionally designed to accommodate my tiny frame. Leostrom and Addia-Sahl follow behind us, along with Ahanayan and Aayasanaha behind them. The procession arrives at the top, which is flattened with enough room to accommodate us all. In the center stand two marble columns, each decked with carved rings containing runes from both the Terran and Aoaran tongues, to symbolize the Guardian Alliance of the two hyper races. Soleran, Ahanayan, and I step to the right of the columns facing the crowd. Leostrom, Addia-Sahl, and Aayasanaha step to the left. A portal of blue energy bursts from between the columns, and out come two Terran Guardians with golden-yellow robes, one male and the other female. The male has a thin but neatly trimmed, light brown beard and short brown hair with a lighter skin tone. The female has black hair and dark, bronze-colored skin. They each step to their outer sides, so that they stand in front of the columns, the female near Soleran and me and the male near Leostrom. The female looks down at me and smiles. Her eyes captivate me. I smile back, though I'm sure my expression betrays my bashfulness.

"Gatekeepers Jadron and Kueres," Soleran says, nodding to the male and then the female respectively, "we seek permission to traverse the portal."

"Everything appears to be in order," Jadron says.

"Be on alert," Kueres says. "transgressors are nearby." Her smile fades as she looks up in the sky near a group of vessels.

"The Vhodensids," Soleran says to me in a low voice.

I look for them, and the *Star Chariot* interprets my thoughts and responds by highlighting in my perspective the Vhodensid vessels.

"We will prevent their transgression through the portal," Kueres says.

"Permission is granted, Soleran," Jadron says, "and to the general assembly under your charge."

Jadron and Kueres raise their hands up to shoulder-height, with their palms turned inward to themselves. Simultaneously, they turn the palms outward toward the assembly. The portal behind the two gatekeepers enlarges, spanning high into the sky and sideways as far as my eyes can see. I turn in time to see the Vhodensid vessels, about twenty, jump from their location toward the portal. The gatekeepers simultaneously turn their palms back inward. The portal changes color tone from light blue to dark blue. The first wave of Vhodensid vessels, half of them, crash into the portal. The second wave attempts to stop its vessels, but gravity pulls them into the closed portal. All the ships explode, and fiery debris plummets toward the ground, where the assembly is gathered. Even so, the debris doesn't fall far. It collides with a shielding high up above the assembly and rolls down the curved slope of the shielding to the Earth far away.

Soleran turns to Ahanayan. "It wasn't our intention to harm them," Soleran says.

The Aoaran reaches over and places his three-fingered hand on Soleran's shoulder. If there was communication, I wasn't privy to it. Soleran nods and turns back to the gatekeepers.

Both Jadron and Kueres turn their palms outward toward the assembly, and the portal changes tone from dark blue to light blue. The portal reopens. On cue, the remaining vessels in the sky enter the portal.

"We'll allow everyone else to traverse the portal, Brinn," Soleran says. "You and I will be the last of the assembly to cross over." He places his hand on my shoulder and squeezes.

There are Guardians lined along the ground in front of the portal on both sides of the pyramid. The assembly slowly trudges around us on each side. The Guardian vessels in the miniplanet's orbit are emitting their light brightly. I study the various species of people as they cross over. Every shape and every color have to be represented. Some seem like nothing more than ooze. Some have multiple legs and arms. Some are hairy, and some are reptilian. One group of people seems very tall, and yet others are even smaller than I. A few look up at us as they pass over, and I can't resist the desire to wave. They wave back. Some groups are singing and dancing. Their music is strange but beautiful. Soon, a small group of the assembly remains. Most of the sky is clear, and the only vessels are the Guardian vessels. They descend from their orbits into the sky and begin traversing the portal. The assembly on the ground, perhaps a hundred remaining, move toward the pyramid's steps. This group was determined beforehand. Single-file, they march up the stairs toward the portal between the columns, which is identical to the huge portal behind the pyramid. One by one, each member of the assembly stops to converse briefly with Soleran. He takes their hands in his and greets them warmly with a smile, calling each person by name. A group of Endherans in particular now stands at the top.

"Welcome to the Day Neverending, Shepheth," Soleran says. "I've often thought of you, especially since that dreadful day when we asked something so difficult to ask of a man. I know of your doubts and fears and concerns. You expressed your troubles in poetry and song, and those words were contemplated deeply by all of Epsilon Truthe. They were not in vain."

I didn't realize how tall Shepheth is compared to other Endherans. The holographic displays failed to do him proper justice. He stands eye to eye with Soleran. The look on his face is stern, but friendly and open. His smile is thin and light as he listens to Soleran's speech.

"Even so," Soleran continues, "you never ceased to pursue justice and righteousness. You put others before you often, clearly showing that the virtues of compassion and mercy were at work within you.

The sacrifices you made, especially those hidden from the sight of others, did not go unnoticed."

Soleran releases his hold of Shepheth's hands. With a bow and a smile, Shepheth nods and walks by him, then between the two gatekeepers, and finally through the smaller portal.

The next Endheran is Oleg. He's closer to my height than to Soleran's. The seer approaches us with a wide grin, followed by two other Endherans.

"Hello, Oleg," Soleran says. "It's certainly good to see you."

"I must say the same," Oleg says, reaching out to take hold of Soleran's hand, which the seer shakes excitedly.

"Welcome to the Day Neverending," Soleran says. "Your journey was fraught with much difficulty. But you were faithful and willing to see justice reconciled, and so you endured all that was laid upon you. That, my friend, is the true inner strength. Amongst your peers, it rose and conquered the common fear. You now know that men spoke your name with praise, honor, and respect. You were loved, Oleg. You are loved, by us, the Guardians of Eternal Life." Soleran pauses, and I can tell it's because he knows—since I know—that Oleg wants to speak further.

"Soleran," Oleg says, "my mother, whom the Guardians protected, is here." Oleg steps aside, and Oleg's mother steps forward. Her youth is restored, but she still retains the maturity of her days. Her hair is black, smooth, and silky and flows over her exposed, dark-brown shoulders. She and Soleran exchange pleasantries, and they bow in honor of each other, and she steps aside.

"And now," Oleg says, stepping forward. "Here is my father, Armog." Again, Oleg steps aside to allow the gentleman behind him to approach. Soleran puts his left hand on the man's shoulder. The man mentions how proud he is of his son and that this experience is awesome. The two shake hands, and all three walk past Soleran, between the gatekeepers, and through the portal.

One last Endheran approaches. "Antraxid," Soleran says. "Welcome to the Day Neverending. Since that first day we met, I have held you close to my heart. You were the first Endheran with whom I talked. While many Endherans prior to your birth have been found worthy of traversing, it can be said that Endhera's road to salvation began in the heart of a man named Antraxid. With love and respect, I call you friend." Soleran extends his hand, and Antraxid does not hesitate to take it in his and shake sternly.

"I remember everything," the reptilian monarch says, "and how you spoke to me with much patience and understanding."

"I knew your character," Soleran says. "I still know it to be the strongest amongst Endherans, filled with virtue and the desire to do good things. That opportunity now lies before you, Antraxid." Soleran takes Antraxid's hand again and gently grasps the former king's shoulder with his other hand. "You have the opportunity to build on the future and earn the title Guardian."

"I will make the most of that opportunity," Antraxid says. "You, sir, have been the inspiration behind all of my desires."

They shake hands a little longer. Soleran pulls him in and gives him a hug. The former king reciprocates and then they separate. Antraxid walks past Soleran, between the gatekeepers, and through the portal. An older woman and an older man follow him. I recognize the man as the uncle who saved Antraxid. The older woman is, I reason, Antraxid's mother. I smile at the fulfillment of a promise.

The next in line is none other than Hesla the Redeemed, youthful but mature. The weathered image I remember from the holographics has given way to newness of body and soul. The Huvril counselor approaches. He turns from Soleran and the others and instead focuses on me. He drops to his front knees, bending his centauric body over and placing both of his palms upon the platform. He then lowers his head before me.

"I am your humble servant," Hesla says. "My offenses against you are many."

"Hesla," I say, quick to interrupt and prevent him from continuing. I gently touch the top of his head. "I hold no grudges nor feel any offense. The saying is true. Mercy triumphs over judgment. I am glad that you are here—you and those you've won over to the cause."

Hesla stands up and the stern look gives way to one of relief. He lets out a long sigh.

"Surely, Hesla," I say, "surely you hadn't carried that burden with you all this long?"

"I knew that before I could pass through the gate," Hesla says, "I would have to seek you out and ask for your pardon."

"Then it is yours," I say.

He lets out another sigh, and his shoulders relax. "If I had known beforehand what I came to learn afterward, I would have fought hoof and fang with everyone to deliver you, even the emperor himself."

I look over at Soleran and the others, who are watching this unfold with fixed attention. "Oh Hesla," I say, "you should know that out of everyone present at that ordeal, I sensed your pity and was grateful that at least one person understood my plight. That was all it took. Because of you, I held on dearly for hope, and that rewarded me greatly."

Hesla again drops to his knees, this time to grasp both my hands in his and shake excitedly. "Oh, thank you, sir! Thank you!"

I know what I have to do, although I'm not sure of the consequences. "Hesla," I continue, "welcome to the Day Neverending. You are permitted to pass."

Hesla nods, both with tears in his eyes and a smile on his face. He turns and walks past the Guardians and the Aoarans, offering them a complimentary nod as well. He passes between the gatekeepers and through the portal.

Soleran again squeezes my shoulder. I've come to rely upon the gesture, especially as one of approval. I turn to behold the next in line, and I'm completely taken by surprise. Tempis the Tayen reaches the top of the stairs and approaches. His form is different, having now been adapted to walking out of water. But he still bears his unique features—his translucence; his tentacles; and his huge, wide eyes. Missing, however, is his luminescent blood. There are other Tayens with him, five in all.

"Tempis!" I say, leaping ahead to intercept him.

"Hallo, Soleran! Brinn! Hallo!" Tempis says. "Tis good to see ya."

"As you, friend," I say.

Tempis bows courteously to the others but quickly returns his focus to me and Soleran. "I was pleased to learn after my reinstatement by the Aoaran Order that it was both of you who helped me. You saved me from disaster. I am forever grateful."

We have to admit, Ahanayan says telepathically, *your method, Soleran, was resourceful.*

Soleran turns and smiles to his Aoaran friend.

"When we are on the other side, I have much to discuss with you," Tempis says to me, "by your leave, of course." He concludes with a bow.

"Of course," I say. I lightly grasp his shoulder. It is soft and warm.

Tempis and those with him, walk past us, between the gatekeepers, and into the portal. A group of Aoarans now approach. I immediately recognize two of them. Excitement builds up in me, and I cannot contain it. I leap ahead a few steps, clasping my hands together tightly. One Aoaran steps forward and before our eyes transforms back into his Terran form. Natharon. The other approaches and transforms. Dyllon.

"You were missed," Soleran says to them both, smiling.

Natharon places his hand on my shoulder and then gives me a gentle pat on the back. Casually, he looks to Soleran. "The alpha current is certainly an interesting place to spend half an eternity." He follows his comment with a light chuckle.

The group of Aoarans, six in number, walks past us. One pats Natharon on the back. *See you on the other side*, the Aoaran says.

We shall join our companions now, Soleran, Ahanayan says. *Tarry not for long.*

All of the Aoarans bid us farewell. Once on the other side, they will tend to their own matters, so we won't see them again for a little while. Quickly, they all walk through the portal. Looking around, I see that the only ones left are Soleran, Addia-Sahl, Leostrom, Dyllon,

Natharon, myself, and the gatekeepers, Jadron and Kueres. All the vessels, except the *Star Chariot*, have finished entering through the larger portal, even the *Intrepidium*. We are alone.

"Brinn and I will attend to the *Star Chariot* soon," Soleran says. "We will investigate its interdimensional capabilities. Who will join us?"

Each of the Guardians, except the gatekeepers, volunteer to join us. Jadron and Kueres turn their palms inward, and the larger portal disappears. We bid them farewell for a little while. Kueres smiles to me and touches me on my arm as she joins Jadron through the small portal. Within a few seconds, the small portal dissipates.

"Well, we have a brief moment to collect our thoughts," Soleran says. "Then we traverse."

I, Brinn the Ibalexan, have reviewed the passing cycle of the universe, in all that I have been allowed to see, to hear, and to experience. It is praeonic, having just emerged. I will see the end of the universe before I see its beginning. I can see my beginning, since I have the ability to return to my first neural processes. It was dark and wet, but warm and soothing. I wasn't concerned with thinking or reasoning, but I did see things and hear sounds and experience sensations. I even dreamed. I was an observer, like when I began with the Guardians. I was born, and the world's sensations flooded my senses. I was overwhelmed and held firmly in its grasp.

I developed and learned much. But the one thing I wish I had learned early on was that I knew nothing. As an adult, I did start realizing that I was missing a lot of information, that what I thought I knew was the truth of reality was nothing but a snapshot from an angle and a distance. Contemplations on this led me to the conclusion that some people were more blessed than others. Some people, it seemed, walked through life as on a clear, sunny day with only a few roots or stones to catch the foot and cause a slight stumble. But others, it seemed, walked through life as on a dark night through a thick jungle, groping about for some clue as to where they were standing or turning or moving, totally oblivious as to a deep pit that lay in their path.

And then a great calamity fell on Ibalexa, one no Ibalexan could ever have foreseen. It came as a total surprise, as a thief in the night. Few amongst us had ideas of how arrogant it was to think that our lives would continue unchallenged. But their predictions were always off, so they did nothing but add to the confusion. When the Huvrils invaded, we were not prepared and paid a high price for our complacency. I stowed away on a Huvril drop ship, and came to witness the destruction of Ibalexa. I was captured and spent a little time as an object of scorn and abuse. But then I was rescued and delivered from the pains of my torment. I have spent the rest of my existence in the company of the Guardians, to whom I owe my most loyal allegiance. And thus, I offer my thanks, my utmost gratitude, and all my love and devotion to the Guardians of Eternal Life, Sons and Daughters of the Morning Rise, Agents of the Principal Cause.

"To you, Soleran, High Chancellor of the Terran Order of the Universal Guardianship, I offer my thanks." I extend my hand.

Soleran smiles and receives it without hesitation. He squeezes enough to convey his love and affection. "I reciprocate your thanksgiving and offer my own as well, Brinn. You have always brought a new perspective to my own outlook on life in general and always in the direction of all that is good and well in the cosmos."

I nod in understanding. "Soleran?" I ask. Soleran's facial expression tells me to continue. "I have always been grateful for my status as observer, to learn and appreciate. I would very much like to join the Guardians as one of your own."

"Your transit from your praeonic epochal is a key to your newly exalted status, Brinn," Soleran says.

My body transforms, shedding the terrestrial garment to don the new garment of the celestial. I am aware that my neural net is hovering at eye level to the Guardians. It is sustained in a field of energy. The oscillatory signals comprising my thoughts and memories fire throughout the field, and it shines like a bright orb. I then manifest. My robe changes from light brown to radiant white. I retain my height, shorter than the Guardians by half. It is, after all, my identity. I retain my initial attributes—the skin color, eye color, general frame, and all. Having come to accept myself for who I am, I know no other form.

"I see before me the founding of a new order in the Guardianship of Eternal Life, the Ibalexan Order," Soleran says. "Ahanayan will be most pleased."

Suddenly, in the northern sky of the makeshift planetoid, the sky erupts with light. Off to the side is the orb of light imprisoning Maximeron. It twinkles but gradually becomes dimmer, until it is invisible in the greater light. A moment passes, and I start to feel the tidal forces pulling on my own essence.

"Well, the epochal draws to a close," Soleran says. "Perhaps it is time to transit."

We teleshift to the *Star Chariot*, entering the navigatory. I open a holographic display and activate a series of commands. The *Star Chariot* responds and phases into the tachyonic stream. Nearby is the stasis field sustained by the Guardian vessels. I gently maneuver the large vessel into the Guardian field, carefully, so as not overly to disturb it. Then I add the *Star Chariot*'s power to the Guardian field, increasing its strength a thousandfold.

Soleran steps to my side, placing his hand upon my shoulder. "You're getting good at this," he says with a smile. "Now, for the next epochal."

THE END